VOICES

Anne Yarbu 2000

VOICES

ANNE GARBER

LEGACY PUBLISHING
Studio One, 201 Monroe Ave., Maitland, Florida   32751

This is a work of fiction. The characters, incidents, and dialogues are products of the author's imagination and are not to be construed as real. Any resemblance to actual people, living or dead, is entirely coincidental.

Published by:
LEGACY PUBLISHING
Studio One, 201 Monroe Avenue
Maitland, Florida 32751
www.legacy-publishing.com

Copyright © 2000 by Anne Garber
ISBN 0-9628733-8-1

Cover Design by Gabriel H. Vaughn
Cover Photograph by Jimm Roberts
Interior Photographs by John Marsh

Printed in U.S.A.

All rights reserved. Written permission must be secured from the publisher to use or reproduce any part of this book, except for brief critical reviews or articles.

Dedication

I dedicate this book to, Steve, for his love and support. Special thanks are in order for Swanee Ballman, my editor and dear friend; Kathy Riggs and Mimi Pacifico for their expertise and belief in my work; Gabriel Vaughn, my publisher, for his artistry; my children and father, for their encouragement; and most importantly, I thank God, for bringing me to this point in my life.

CHAPTER 1

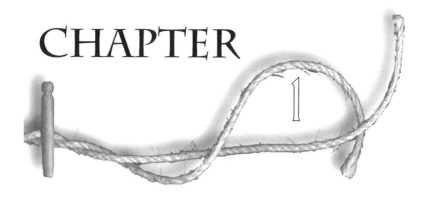

August 8, 1999, Orlando, Florida

At 10:00 a.m. the mercury rocketed past 95 degrees and humidity-burdened air rose in sluggish eddies from the blacktop. The stench of death hung like an ominous cloud.

Three white cruisers with light bars flashing blocked the street. An ambulance, a fire truck, and three unmarked police units accompanied them. Early arriving reporters interviewed the Chief of Police, who answered their questions with measured words. The back end of a crime lab van faced a narrow alley where agents busily accumulated evidence.

Neighbors gathered on the opposite side of the road. Some watched in silence, while others mumbled among themselves. An elderly woman, in a cotton bathrobe, screeched her complaints against the police department, blaming them for the moral decay of her neighborhood. She and the other long time residents had witnessed the steady decline of South Orange Blossom Trail. Prostitutes, strip joints, and drugs had taken over their once respectable neighborhood.

Oblivious to the uncomfortable weather and the disconcerted crowd, Lieutenant Tom Lindsey, formerly of the NYCPD, stared down at the body. He'd seen prostitutes murdered in alleyways before, but this case immediately smacked him with a high sense of foreboding. Two cases with similar M.O.'s occurred over the last two months in neighboring Osceola County. He knew exactly what he faced. He wished he hadn't been called.

The victim, in her early teens, had tangled dark hair that hung below her shoulders. She wore a beige tube top, short shorts and dangling ear rings. Her frail torso lay on the roach infested ground; her head and upper back carefully propped against a trashcan. Large X's cut across both eyes and a small slit marked the upper corner of her mouth. Her black mascara, smeared down around her cheekbones. Her hands were tied behind her back. A rope wound tightly around her neck was held in place with a wooden clothespin. She carried nothing but a money belt containing thirty-five dollars, several packages of condoms, and a photograph of herself and an older woman. No I.D. was present.

Lindsey and the Chief of Police, Lawrence Henry had taken a careful walk-through of the area when they'd first arrived. Now Lindsey stood alone on the outer edge of the scene. He watched the forensic specialist and his crime scene agents video tape the entire area, outline the body with chalk, take photographs, and collect evidence.

With meticulous care to maintain the integrity of the scene, they documented and labeled everything even remotely useful. Lindsey reviewed the crime scene log started by the first arriving officers. One of the agents, kneeling near him, carefully ran a razor-sharp penknife under each of the victim's fingernails and placed the residue in evidence envelopes.

Detective Richard Patterson got out of his car and strutted over to Lindsey. He glanced at the corpse and winced slightly. "And you thought New York was screwed up." Patterson looked around. "Henry here?"

"Yeah," Lindsey gestured toward the street. "Talking with the reporters."

Patterson spied Chief Henry wiping his brow with his sleeve, exposing a sweaty half moon beneath his armpit. "Look at him. He's sweating like a pig. It's coming right through his jacket." He turned back to the crime scene and leaned over the tape for a better view. "Aren't you glad he talked you into staying in the department for another two months? Look what you would've missed."

"Yeah, right. Like Henry gave me a choice. It was either I do my two months time or get kicked out on my butt. How could I say no?" He grinned. "Plus there's the fear factor...even when Henry's happy, he scares the hell out of me."

Patterson snickered. "Tell me about it."

Lindsey's gray eyes scanned the alleyway as he smoothed back his brown, silver flecked hair. "Looks like a repeat of what's happening in Osceola." He unbuttoned his suit jacket and loosened his tie. His brawny V-shaped form towered over his partner.

Patterson nodded. "Ain't no doubt about it."

"We're going by the book on this one. No screw ups." Lindsey's lips thinned into a straight line.

"Doesn't sound like much fun."

"There isn't going to be anything fun about this case."

Patterson scowled as he scrutinized Lindsey's face. "Hey, did ya hear the one about the pig with one leg?"

Lindsey rolled his eyes. "About a million times."

"Lighten up, man. What's wrong with you."

"Time and a place for everything."

"What? Since when?"

Lindsey watched Patterson tilt his neck to the right, then left...scrunch his shoulders up near his ears for several seconds, and then let them fall back down into place. Patterson said this was a good relaxation technique, but Lindsey considered it just another one of his partner's numerous idiosyncrasies...sometimes amusing, more often annoying and one he repeated, (in Lindsey's estimation), at least three hundred times a day.

Patterson paced up and down the tapeline like a banty rooster. Lindsey shook his head. He often wished his partner's rampant enthusiasm were contagious, because his own fire had long since faded to an ember. Fifteen years as a NYC homicide detective had left him jaded, disillusioned and angry. His partner was only on his second year in the Criminal Investigations Division, loving every minute of it.

Lindsey lit a cigarette and drew, thoughtfully looking down at the body again. He assumed she and his daughter were probably around the same age. If this had been Jennifer, he'd never rest until he personally blew the killer's brains out. He imagined himself poised, Glock aimed between the murderer's eyes, watching with satisfaction, as the man's body shook and blood drained from his face with the crumbling sensation of certain death. He'd plead to be spared, but Lindsey would shake his head, smiling cruelly as his finger tightened, then pulled the trigger again and again. He could almost see the blood fly, feel the sharp kickback from the gun and smell the sulfuric aftermath of released ammunition, followed by the exquisite exhilaration of revenge.

A familiar wave of nausea roused him from his fantasy. He glanced around to see if anyone had been watching. As the queasiness traveled from his stomach into his esophagus, he swallowed hard. His face tightened as he fought to regain composure. Only two more months and he'd be sitting behind a desk and all this would be behind him. He had to keep it together. This would be his last big case, and he was determined not to blow it this time. He had to leave the department with his reputation intact and the bad guy sentenced to a blind date with "Old Sparky".

At least this was happening in Orlando. The murder of a prostitute in the "Big Apple" didn't exactly round up the troops. There were just too many crimes per officers in the field, and prostitutes were low on the priority list. Few cared enough to push for justice on their behalf. Without pressure placed on the precinct, cases like these were often swept under the carpet. Despite Orlando's increasing size, the gangs, drive-by shootings, drugs, assorted murders and random tourist hits, he believed he would be able to give this case the attention it deserved. The media alone would serve as a catalyst.

But despite that assurance, he couldn't shake the feeling of dread that had invaded him like a parasite. He was dealing with another serial killer. What irony! What were the chances of this happening again? Especially since he was so close to being transferred. He gazed down at his cigarette, focused on the long ash that had accumulated, then flicked it and watched it fall to the ground.

There was only one way he was going to get through it. Patterson was right. He had to stay detached. Lighten up and treat this case like all the rest he'd handled since he'd arrived in Orlando. As much as he hated to admit it, he needed Patterson and all the stupid jokes and gestures that came along with him.

He returned his attention back to the alley, to rethink and confirm his earlier impressions. He'd already deduced how the murder had gone down. He didn't think the killer lurked in an alley, waiting for a woman to walk by at random. There were no signs of struggle in the entrance of the alley. Therefore, he believed their meeting was pre-arranged.

The alley was dark and about sixty feet deep. The ground was a mixture of compacted sand and shell, with a few scattered patches of broken black top...telltale remnants of either a time gone by or merely a dumping spot for left over asphalt. Approximately half-way back, the murder occurred. There were no windows on the sides of the buildings facing the alley.

At the very end a six-foot chain link fence, laced with ivy and an assortment of high growing weeds and underbrush, camouflaged the small lot on the other side. Trampled foliage was observed, along with several undisturbed footprints. Casts would be made of the prints. They would pay particular attention to this area, as it appeared that the murderer had climbed over the fence either coming, going, or both. A large commercial dumpster partially obstructed the view from the street. Several residential trashcans sat in a zigzag fashion along the first twenty feet, obviously positioned to secure added cover. The top third of the victim's body was carefully propped and painstakingly centered against the last can.

"What's your take on this?" Patterson asked when he

returned.

Lindsey explained his theory. "What have you come up with?"

"About the same as you...plus, we're dealing with a real sick puppy." He wiped the sweat off his brow with the back of his hand and adjusted his sunglasses, which kept sliding down his nose. He nodded toward the forensic agents. "What's the story on them? I ask them a question and they cop an attitude. Who the hell do they think they're dealing with?" His voice rose with intensity. "They're acting like their stinking boss." He stepped away, then quickly returned. "What's taking them so long anyway? I wish they'd hurry the hell up and get out of here."

"Give 'em a break."

Patterson did that thing with his shoulders again. "Maybe you don't mind standing around looking like a chump, but we little guys like to look like we're in charge of something." He gave his belt-line a tug and puffed out his chest.

"I guess I'm just too secure to relate," Lindsey quipped. "Meanwhile, there's no sense in us all waiting around." He spotted the rookie on his team, who was doing a good job of avoiding the corpse by studying his shoes. Lindsey motioned him to join them. "Steve, we'll be tied up here for hours." He handed him the photo they found on the victim. "Get copies made at the photo lab and bring a few back here to me. Then hit the streets with the rest of them. Go to every little dive this end of Orange Blossom Trail and every side street connecting to it. Try to get her name, and her pimp's. Also, get a list of her johns...who saw her last...where she lived. Dig up as much information as you can." He glanced at his watch. "I probably won't be back at the office until three or four to write my report. Stop in then."

Steve nodded. "Okay. I'll get right on it."

Patterson nudged Lindsey and jerked his thumb toward the street. Lindsey turned and gave a quick nod to Maxwell Thompson, the Chief Medical Examiner as he approached. Lindsey watched him cross under the yellow tape and into the crime scene to make the pronouncement. Without moving the body from it's original position, he made a quick examination, then turned to Lindsey. "Cut marks on the eyes were post-mortem. Death, by asphyxiation due to ligature strangulation." He pointed to the cord wrapped around her neck.

"Duh," Patterson muttered.

"Your assistant M.E. told us that much." Lindsey pointed to his watch. "Kind of late, aren't you? Decided to sleep in?"

Max snarled. "I completed two autopsies before you even got out of bed this morning."

"Yeah, I'm sure." Lindsey gestured toward the victim. "This case look familiar?"

Max's voice was low. "Third one. The F.D.L.E will be all over this thing."

Lindsey nodded.

Patterson's eye twitched as he looked at the corpse. "Clothespin kind of adds a nice touch, don't you think?"

The examiner shook his head. "You're a sick S.O.B. Sometimes it's hard to know who's worse, the killers or the police." He put his hands on his wide hips and rocked several times from his heels to his toes and back again. "Ever since you Yankees started taking over this town, we got sick freaks coming out the walls."

"You're a funny guy, Max." Lindsey dropped his cigarette and crushed it with his foot.

"Yeah...that's what they tell me back at the morgue. A regular barrel of laughs."

"Why are you southerners still fighting the war?" Patterson chided.

Max crossed back under the tape to join them. He pulled out a cigar and lit it. "Y'all's bitching and complaining for one thing. We're slow, we're stupid, we can't drive and we don't know how to dress." He stepped closer to Patterson. "We also don't know how to make good rolls, subs or pizzas and we can't make a decent cheese steak to save our souls." He puffed smoke into Patterson's face. "What I can't figure out is, why the hell y'all keep moving down to this sorry place? Why don't you friggin' move back to where you came from?" He pointed to his temple.

"Or at the very least, get it into your heads once and for all, that we don't give a damn how you do it up north."

"Gee...that would make a great bumper sticker." Lindsey shook his head. "You really need to start coming up with some original material, if you want to keep up with me and Patterson."

"Okay, how's this? Go choke on a Jersey tomato and leave me the hell alone. I've got work to do." He clamped down on his cigar, in an effort to suppress a grin. "I'll call you when it's time to do the autopsy. I doubt it'll be today. We're swamped."

"That ain't gonna get it, Max. You know what we're dealing with here."

"No, I'm a southerner. Maybe you should spell it out for me," he grumbled, "I'll see what I can do."

Lindsey sat down at his desk. He pushed aside piles of folders and several half-read newspapers to accommodate a small area for his cup of coffee. He popped a cigarette into his mouth and lit it quickly, then noticed his ashtray was missing, buried among the piles of papers he'd just shuffled. Rather than searching for it, he flicked the ashes on the floor and then with a tap of the mouse, snapped the computer screen to attention. He had to document all the information he had gathered about the murder, including his impressions while it was fresh in his mind. Time was precious. He planned to work well into the night.

He was half way through his report when Patterson walked in with Steve Brown. "Got something for me?" Tom asked as he typed.

"Jane Doe has a first name, it's Amy," Brown said.

Patterson chimed in, "General consensus is she'd only been on the streets for about four or five weeks. No one seems to know where she came from, but they all said she didn't have a pimp. Hung out on Orange Blossom Trail by herself, on the block where we found her. She rented a small room above a hobby store a few blocks north."

Lindsey turned from the keyboard, giving them his

full attention.

Patterson continued, "I checked the room...didn't find anything there except two dresses and a pair of shoes and some underwear and," he pulled out a picture, "this." He handed it to Lindsey.

"Cute baby." He turned the picture over. " It says (baby Kayla, born June 26, 1999). There wasn't any sign of a baby in her apartment?"

Patterson shook his head. "Nada."

Lindsey picked up the phone. "Forensics, please. This is Tom Lindsey. Let me talk to Max." He waited several minutes. "Max, I need a favor."

"What the hell is it now? I'm in the middle of an autopsy." He shouted above the winding down of a Stryker saw.

"Look, you know we're dealing with a serial killer, Max. I need as much information as fast as I can get. I was wondering if you'd take a quick look and see if our girl might have had a baby recently."

Max groaned, "You're a pain in the ass, you know it?" He reluctantly set the saw aside, threw his gloves in a trashcan, and entered the refrigerator room. He pulled on a new pair of gloves, a cell phone stuck under the rolls of his chin. "Hold on a second, let me find her gurney."

"By the way, just when is her autopsy scheduled?" Lindsey asked.

"Soon. I told you I'd call. 'Course if you keep interrupting like this I might not get to it until a week from tomorrow!"

"Last interruption. I promise you that, buddy."

"Don't call me *buddy*, I hate that."

"Oh that's right. You southerners prefer Bubba. I'll try to keep that in mind."

Max pulled her gurney away from several others and unzipped the body bag. "I forgot my damn jacket and it's friggin' cold in here." Max checked her stomach. "Recent stretch marks on the abdomen." He lifted each leg up from the bag and separated them to take a quick look at her vagina. "Perineum shows a semi-healed episiotomy.

I think it's safe to assume she'd given birth within the last five or six weeks." He stuffed the legs back into the bag and zipped it up. "At a glance, I'd say she wasn't sexually assaulted either, at least not the day she died."

"Thanks, Max. I owe you one."

Max snapped, "You owe me more than one, you sorry son-of-a-gun." His teeth chattered. "I want to know when you're going to pay up."

"I'll take you out to dinner sometime, how's that?"

"Okay. But we're talking steak, man and lots of it."

Lindsey hung up and shook his head. "You gotta love him."

Patterson asked, "Is that an order?"

Lindsey quickly explained what he'd just learned, then said, "Okay, this'll give us something to work on. Steve, I want you to check with the maternity ward of every hospital in Central Florida for a girl delivering around June twenty-sixth matching Amy's description."

Steve frowned. "Man, that could take awhile."

"I hope you're not complaining. You'll be sitting in air-conditioning while everybody else is out pounding the sidewalks. Actually, I think you should be kissing my feet instead of whining."

Patterson groaned. "I hate a whiner."

"Okay, okay." Color tinged Steve's neck and cheeks. In an attempt to change the subject, he asked, "So you really think these murders are tied together? That we're dealing with a serial killer?"

Lindsey opened a file and pulled out two crime scene pictures. "What do you think?" He held the photographs up for inspection.

Steve flinched. Patterson did the neck thing.

"Three young girls, strangled. Clothespin found in all three cases," Lindsey said. "They have X marks over their eyes and mouths." He slid Amy's picture next to the others. "See that tiny slit on her upper lip? I'm sure the bastard was starting another X right there, but was interrupted before finishing."

Steve studied the photo. "Where were the other bodies found?"

"One in St. Cloud on June twenty-ninth, the other in Kissimmee on July fifteenth. All appeared to be prostitutes."

"Ever handle a serial killer case before?" Steve asked Lindsey.

Lindsey turned back to his computer without answering.

Patterson examined his cuticles for awhile. When he looked up, a grin filled his face. "Henry must have given you this assignment as a going away present."

"Yeah, remind me to thank him." Lindsey kept his eyes on the screen. "Now you two get out of here. I've got to finish my report."

An hour later, Chief Henry trudged into Lindsey's office. A woman followed him. A simple gold clip held her auburn hair in a tight knot against the back of her head. Her cold green eyes looked capable of quick appraisals and Lindsey felt like he'd just received one. She had the kind of build Lindsey's mother would have called *sturdy*. Lindsey called it "being in better shape" than he was. She also looked like she worked as hard to look plain as she did to look fit. She wore no make-up and her expression was stern. But, there was a small gold pin on the lapel of her teal jacket that appeared delicate and feminine. Lindsey found it curiously contradictory. Then realizing Henry and the woman were both aware of his preoccupation, he quickly tore his eyes away.

"Tom Lindsey, this is Special Agent, Sharon Cross." Henry's hound-dog face didn't know how to smile and today was no exception. "Agent Cross is with F.D.L.E.. She assisted Kissimmee and St. Cloud over the past few days, so she's had a head start. She should be a big help to you."

Lindsey pushed back his chair. He frowned. "In what capacity?"

"Agent Cross studied criminology at Quantico. Her specialty is profiling. You'll be working as equal partners on this thing," Henry barked.

Lindsey's eyes drilled into Henry's. "What the hell are you talking about? I thought I was in charge of this case."

Henry ignored him, then pointed to an empty chair. "Have a seat, Agent Cross. You two need to get your crap together before the briefing."

Sharon glanced down at Lindsey's cluttered desk. "Is this where we'll be working?"

Henry grunted. "Never mind. Grab up your stuff and we'll use the conference room."

Lindsey paused, rubbed the back of his neck, weighing his options. Two more months...two more months. He carelessly stuffed papers in his files as Sharon watched with one eyebrow skeptically raised. When he was finished, Tom observed her expression, then said, "Photographic memory. Everything I hear and see gets stored right here." He pointed to his head, hoping for a grin.

She raised an eyebrow. "How handy." She turned and followed Henry. They crossed the squad room, and Lindsey's face reflected his anger. A small group of officers nudged each other as the trio passed by.

One large table and at least a dozen chairs filled the conference room. Sharon quickly set her files down in chronological order, while Lindsey fumbled with the mess in his arms.

"I'd like to see the crime scene photos first. I want to get a feel for the murder scene," Sharon said.

Lindsey dug through the pile then slapped the manila folder down on the table. It was marked *Amy, August 8, 1999*. Sharon removed the contents and moved down a few feet to spread out the pictures. She removed a magnifying glass from her brief case and examined the photographs. Her face lacked emotion. "I'll need some of these blown up for the briefing."

"Already took care of that," Lindsey muttered.

"Hmmm," she said, as she took another look. "There's a cut mark above the corner of her upper lip."

"Yup." Lindsey leaned against the wall, his arms crossed at his chest.

"I trust you're aware that the other victims had the X's, too. Obviously, the killer was interrupted before he had time to finish the X on her mouth."

Lindsey took a deep breath and released it sharply.

"It's a little premature to speculate the significance of this man's signature," she said.

"Well, it doesn't take a rocket scientist to know we're dealing with one strange bastard."

"You're right about that...but then all serial killers are strange, Detective Lindsey. And if we don't get to this one soon, he'll keep getting stranger."

Lindsey looked away. Like this was news? "Well, maybe he'll blow his brains out and save us the bother."

"Possible, but not likely. We see that more with mass murderers and spree killers. Serial killers tend to think of killing as their occupation or mission. They usually feel very justified in what they're doing." She picked up another photo. "Like they're performing a service. It's their passion, so suicide usually isn't considered until after they're caught."

Lindsey studied the ceiling.

"Autopsy report?" She held out her hand without looking up.

"I have the CME-1 report," Lindsey growled. "And the verbal information I collected from Max." He tossed several more papers across the table.

Henry's eyebrows knit into a deep frown. Lindsey shrugged in response.

Sharon looked at Lindsey. "When is the autopsy scheduled?"

He cleared his throat. "Max promised me he'd get to it soon."

"Soon, as in within the next couple hours or soon, as in a day or two?" She turned her attention to Henry. "These people are going to have to realize time is of the essence when dealing with a serial killer. This should take precedence over every other case." She pointed to a phone sitting at the far end of the table. "May I?"

Henry grumbled, "Be my guest."

Lindsey rolled his eyes back to the ceiling.

She spoke with Max in a quiet yet firm manner. When she was finished, she walked back. "We can expect a more extensive report in about forty-five minutes. Meanwhile, may I see the rest of your findings, Detective Lindsey?"

While locating the papers, Lindsey imagined himself wringing Max's neck. She paged through the grisly account, background investigation, and numerous interviews. "I see several footprints were cast. It will be interesting to see if they match the set of prints we lifted from the other two crime scenes. If so, it'll confirm what we already suspect. All three murders were committed by the same person." She continued reading, then commented. "It says she recently had a baby."

"We're checking with all Central Florida hospitals," Lindsey's voice droned.

"If that doesn't get you anywhere, include mid-wives to your list. Either way, I want to know the minute you come up with something."

Lindsey saluted and Henry caught it out of the side of his eye. Lindsey thought Henry might have given him a dirty look. But with the Chief's permanent frown lines, it was sometimes hard to tell.

Cross saw the gesture too. Without missing a beat, she turned to Lindsey and said, "I appreciate your respect, detective, but a salute really isn't necessary." She picked up the documentation again. "We've identified the St. Cloud victim. After the briefing, I'm going to speak with her parents. The police have already interviewed them, but I'd like to see the Miller family myself. It would be a good idea for you to go with me."

"Well, gee thanks, but I'm going to be swamped after the briefing, Agent Cross." Mockery sparkled in his eyes. "I'll visit them myself when I'm finished."

"Bull crap!" Henry huffed. "The two of you go together. I'll take care of everything here."

As he tried to create another excuse, Lindsey's eyes darted around the room. None immediately came to mind. "Then I guess I'm going. It's such a privilege to have the opportunity of watching a real live profiler at work. I'm sure it will be a true learning experience."

Ignoring him, Sharon continued reviewing the pictures.

Thirty minutes later the awaited report arrived. They leaned against each other, trying to read it at the same time.

After several pages, Sharon pointed to a paragraph. "He's escalating."

Lindsey's brow furrowed as he searched the sentences.

"The underside of the eyelids revealed unusually severe petechial hemorrhages, which are ruptures of the capillaries. They look like fine pinpoint hemorrhages and they're caused by extreme pressure on the vascular supply, preventing the venous return to the neck."

Exasperated, Lindsey shook his head. "I wasn't born yesterday, Agent Cross. I know what a petechial hemorrhage is, for God's sake. And I would expect to see it in a strangulation victim anyway."

"Not to this degree. There are three deeply gouged rings around the victim's neck where the ligature was applied, released, then reapplied. Which means the killer intermittently tightened, and loosened the ligature, utilizing the clothespin in this case, over a period of forty-five minutes or even up to an hour."

Lindsey nodded reluctantly.

Henry glanced at his watch. "Look, the guys will be waiting to meet with you at six. So park your egos at the door and get down to business. Don't keep them or me waiting." Henry left the room.

"Pain in the ass," Lindsey muttered.

"That makes two of you," Sharon said, as she continued leafing through the information.

CHAPTER 2

John was breathless when he caught up with his friends. He tried telling them about what he'd seen, but they weren't interested. They were wrestling their own demons. After many attempts and rejections, he gave up. At least he wasn't alone. In silence, he followed them in their nightly quest for food, which usually took them behind restaurants, searching from trashcan to trashcan. With the enthusiasm of entering an abundant pantry, they opened the lids. They scrambled for the food on top, which was the most recently discarded and less apt to be spoiled. However, just a few minutes in the can tainted the freshest morsels with the putrid smell of the food below, which had sat stewing and decaying all day in the oppressive heat. Quick, bare hands weeded out the desirable garbage from the slop. They filled their plastic bags and held them protectively against their bodies, as if they were sacks of gold.

The group migrated to an abandoned shack behind a Chinese grocery store. Rotted siding and holes in the walls offered poor refuge, but the roof didn't leak and the police seldom checked it.

John sat on the floor. With his back against the wall, he had clear view of the door. If the devil started coming in, he wanted to be prepared. He removed a knife from his pocket and set it under his leg, then opened his bag of treats. He ate two greasy chicken wings first and then scooped clumps of mashed potatoes into his palms, and smeared them into his mouth. Afterwards, he licked away the potatoes that had oozed between his fingers. Reaching back into the bag, he held up a stringy green vegetable, and let it dangle for a moment in mid-air as he tried to identify it. Shrugging his shoulders, he tilted his head back, opened his mouth, and dropped it in. After he finished his meal, he wiped his mouth and beard with his hands. He licked each finger individually, until he consumed most of the residue.

He rested his head against the wall and yawned sleepily. His body and mind craved sleep, but he refused to succumb. He had to stand guard against the enemy. For three hours his eyes strained to stay open. His friends' snoring and mutterings beat with hypnotic rhythms, lulling him closer and closer to the edge of slumber. Sometime around dawn, he surrendered and slept until mid-afternoon.

He awoke to the sound of a growl. His eyes snapped open and a scream filled his throat. A wolf leered down at him, just inches from his face, it's yellow irises gleaming with evil anticipation and its' long teeth bared. He squeezed his eyes shut and froze. Somewhere in his clouded past, he'd heard that was the best tactic to use when trapped by a wild animal. But with the wolf's hot breath bathing his face, it didn't seem practical.

His pulse beat so hard he thought he was going to have a heart attack. Finally, fear superceded composure as the drip drop of the animal's saliva trickled down his neck. Without looking, he knew its' incisors were coming closer and closer. He had to get away before it was too late. With a scream like a battle call, he thrashed his arms and legs wildly through the air. But he made contact with nothing. When he opened his eyes, the wolf was gone. Where was he? And how could he have gotten through the closed door? His heart hammered as he braced himself against the wall.

He looked around. All of his friends had left, but he wasn't alone. Seemingly unruffled, an elderly man with a gray stubble beard stared at him from across the room. John blinked his eyes, expecting the man to disappear as the wolf had. But he didn't. John breathed deeply, attempting to clear the fog from his brain. He reached under his leg and felt for the security of his knife, but it had slid a couple feet from him during his rampage with the wolf. He reached over and tucked it under his thigh again, then concentrated on the stranger.

The man sat with legs crossed, his hands resting on his lap, his palms facing the ceiling. He appeared too emaciated to be a threat, so John began to relax.

Gradually, John's pulse returned to normal. His eyes felt heavy and gritty, so he closed them. Just before falling back to sleep, he heard a voice shout, "You can't point your finger at me!"

John's eyes popped open and locked on the stranger. "You can't point your finger at me!" It sounded again but it wasn't coming from the old man. John sat straight up. So where was it coming from? And why did it sound so familiar? Where had he heard it before? He trembled as he willed it to stop.

However, it continued. "You can't point your finger at me!" Raspy, cruel, and heartless. Suddenly he recognized it. He heard it last night. It came from the evil one that reprimanded the dead and carved like a sculptor. John held his hands over his ears, but it didn't help.

"You can't point your finger at me! You can't point your finger at me!" Louder and louder, over and over. Dropping his hands, John grabbed his switchblade and held it in front of him, twisting it from side to side in a threatening manner. His demented eyes circled the room. His pulse raced furiously as the voice resounded to an unbearable pitch. Then, as suddenly as it began, it ended. His heart pounded and sweat dripped off his face and ran down his arms. Still clutching the knife, John took his free hand and rubbed his wet scalp with vehemence. Clarity...clarity was what he needed! He had an important task ahead of him and he couldn't do it with a dysfunctional mind. Nevertheless, his efforts were in vain. His thoughts short-circuited, scattering in every direction.

He needed help. He knew he had to do something, but he was too confused to plan his strategy. He needed someone more stable than himself to advise him. Somewhere behind the clutter in his frontal lobe, he vaguely recalled the comfort of counsel. If only he could tap that source now. He shook his head. He wouldn't know where to begin to look. He just couldn't remember much of anything these days.

He studied the old man carefully. He realized the man had not been afraid of the wolf or the voice. In fact, he stayed perfectly calm. Like a man of great inner strength and wisdom. There almost seemed to be something mystical in his demeanor.

John scooted across the floor and sat close to him. He folded his knife and put it back into his pocket, then timidly asked permission to confer. The man didn't refuse. Encouraged, John related his story...every detail. He was thankful that at last someone was listening.

John marveled at the stranger's attentiveness. He actually looked captivated. After awhile, the man's jaw slackened, his mouth swung open, and his faded eyes stared straight ahead. John told him every detail. His one-man audience never interrupted. John knew when he was finished, he'd receive his much-needed advice.

When he stopped talking, the stranger remained silent. John thought the man was taking time to contemplate, so he waited patiently. However, after an hour, he grew impatient and fidgeted. Too much time had elapsed already. The evil one was still out there.

He lightly tapped the man's shoulder. "Excuse me." He received no response. "Look, I really need to know what to do. Time's running out." Still no reaction.

"Hey! What's wrong with you?" John moved close to his face. "Are you in a trance?" He put his hands on the man's cold shoulders. "Snap out of it. You've got to help me." John shook him hard. Offering no resistance, the stranger flip-flopped from side to side and nearly fell over. John glanced at his watch. It was five o'clock.

"You've had plenty of time to think. Come on, you've got to talk to me." Red fury colored John's face.

He gave the man a hard push. The man keeled over. John bent down, laying his cheek on the floor, parallel to the stranger's pale-blue face. Why wasn't he moving or talking? John concentrated on the old man's eyes. They seemed unnatural. Why hadn't he noticed before? What exactly was it? The faded color? The blank expression? Yes...yes...that was all part of it. But, there was something else. What could it be? His mind struggled for meaning, as he continued scrutinizing him.

He waved his fingers past the man's unblinking eyes. A deep chill reverberated throughout his body as the answer took form. The stranger's eyes had a reptilian appearance. A primitive stare. Now he knew the truth. The man was part snake! He knew the devil took on many forms and a snake was his original disguise. Had he spent the whole day talking to Satan? Yes! That was it. The devil tricked him. His fear soared to panic.

John scrambled to his feet and ran out of the shack, and bolted into the middle of the road and wove in and out of heavy traffic. Occasionally he looked over his shoulder to make sure he wasn't being followed. His blue eyes bulged with fear as his arms flailed in an attempt to flag someone down. It was rush hour. Horns honked and brakes slammed, and a man in an old mustang nudged the back of John's legs. John was oblivious to it all. Blocking traffic, he searched passing faces, hoping to find someone who would listen and understand the mission. Why didn't they stop? Couldn't they see this was an emergency?

As one driver slowed to maneuver around him, John bent down and screamed, "Stop the devil! Stop him from making axes." The driver shook his head and laughed. John pounded his fist on the windshield. The driver just missed John's feet as he drove away.

Men waited in the squad room. Some cracked jokes while others paired up, discussing cases. Henry barged through the door. "All right!" He roared. "Get in your seats and shut up." All conversations ceased.

"This might be the most important case any of you will ever handle. We'll be working hard...around the clock, if need be. We won't stop until this man is put away.

"This case requires the concerted effort of both counties. You'll be reporting to Detective Tom Lindsey but, we'll all be sharing information...passing it freely among jurisdictions. The goal is to catch the killer, not to be a hometown hero. Mavericks will be penalized."

"A profiler, from F.D.L.E will be working with us. I expect you to give her your full cooperation." He visually toured the room. "Another thing. This case is already making the national news." He pressed his lips together. "I don't want anyone talking to the press. The D.A. and I will handle the reporters. Understood?" His voice carried a stern warning as he looked out over his reading glasses at each of their faces. "If information does leak out of here, I'm going to personally track down the person responsible and kick 'em out on his ass." Henry's hard eyes scanned the room again. "Anyone doubt my sincerity?"

Henry watched Lindsey and Agent Cross walk into the room. Lindsey's face looked hard and tight as he opened the investigation file. Sharon appeared calm and confident as she placed several large charts on the table.

Chief Henry gestured toward the new arrivals. "Detective Lindsey and Agent Cross will give you the details." Henry sat down, his heavy body overlapping the sides of the chair.

Lindsey started the meeting at a chalkboard where he wrote the causes of death and the M.O. He pointed out the characteristics of the victims...all three apparently prostitutes, all sixteen and under, all had long dark hair and two had heavily made up faces. None had been sexually assaulted. Tom also described the killer's signature and gave his theory on how the recent murder took place.

When finished, he hesitated, then mumbled through Sharon's introduction. With reluctance, he asked her to explain the nature of her job and the psychological profile of a serial killer.

When she stood, feet shuffled and men shifted in their seats. She ignored it and walked between the aisle of chairs. "Profilers are trained in psychological criminology, specializing in the minds of killers. Compiling information about serial killers from all over the world has enabled us to recognize their commonalities. Interviews with Ted Bundy and interviews Bundy himself conducted with other serial killers while on death row have also been enlightening. Some specialists feel they've been more helpful than all the others put together. Having so many profiles to draw from sheds light on the significance of genetics and environment. It shows how each mind twists in its own peculiar and unique way. But as valuable as this information is, we realize there are still exceptions to every rule." She added, "There's still room for good old street smarts and intuition."

She looked around, meeting their eyes boldly. "The murderer expresses anger through certain rituals and these rituals are set off by a motivation that is not readily clear to a normal person. Once we understand his motivation, we have a better chance of catching him." She scanned the room to make sure she had their attention, then picked up three blown up crime-scene pictures and placed them side by side on the chalk board ledge. "For example, this killer seems to have singled out prostitutes." She pointed to the clothes the girls were wearing, then left the board, and moved toward the officers.

Patterson sat up in his chair, trying to see over the head of the cop in front of him. Lindsey looked out the window.

"Is it because he doesn't respect prostitutes?" Sharon asked. "Of course not. That would be simplistic. This individual has a deeper reason behind his madness, so we need to discover what that driving force is so we can narrow down the search.

"Serial killers continue to kill until forced to stop. There may be cooling down periods in between where they take a break for awhile...sometimes for a month...sometimes even as long as a year. But sooner or later, they will be back at it and their fervor will escalate steadily."

"Most serial killers are males, between the ages of twenty-five and thirty-five. They're usually white and their victims are, too." Sharon walked back to the chalkboard. "The victims are strangers to the killer, but often resemble someone who has hurt him."

She paused, then took down the photos and replaced them with four large charts. "There are four different types of serial killers. One is the "thrill-oriented type". She pointed to the first exhibit. "He does it for the fun of it. He's sadistic and gets a high from killing. The second type is the "lust-killer". She tapped her fingers on the top of the poster. "There is a direct correlation between the extent of torture and the level of arousal." She picked up the next chart and carried it closer to the men. "The third is the "visionary", which is one of the four I am considering in this case. This group is insane...psychotic. They often hear imaginary voices telling them to kill." She returned the chart to the board.

She picked up the remaining one and held it up like the last. "This is the other category that I am considering. It's called the "missionary-oriented" type. This man is your next door neighbor, a seemingly normal guy who has no apparent psychosis. But, on the inside, he has an insatiable need to rid the world of what he considers unworthy or immoral people. He will select groups of individuals to murder...like prostitutes."

She glanced around. "In all four cases, a tremendous sense of relief and pleasure is derived when the killer has acted out. However, that gratification is temporary. In some cases, fleeting. Before long, his needs skyrocket again and the cycle repeats itself." She paused, then asked, "Are there any questions?"

"Yeah." Patterson spoke up, "You said number three, the visionary. He's supposed to be insane. What the hell are the rest of them? Choir boys?" His comment brought a few snickers.

"Criteria must be met to medically and legally diagnose insanity. In a court of law, it comes down to whether the killer knows the difference between right and wrong."

She approached a chart displaying a drawing of one of the victims and pointed to the marks on the face. "These X's are highly significant. Sometimes a calling card is merely the killer's way of leaving his autograph, or it's executed simply for shock value. But I have a feeling this particular signature has more meaning than that or the desire to mutilate a prostitute's face."

"Come on, there's nothing mystical about it. The guy's just a class A freak." Patterson's right eye twitched.

Sharon looked around the room. "Are there any other comments or questions?"

Steve Brown spoke up, "You say all three had the signature. The one body was so badly decomposed, how could you tell if it had the X's?"

Sharon reached down and retrieved the close-up photo of that victim's face. She pointed to it. "Our killer is unusually strong. When this man cuts, he goes right down to the bone. Any more questions?" No one responded.

Lindsey stood, his face expressionless. "Henry is going to hand out your assignments. Let's meet back here tomorrow morning at ten."

With clenched teeth, Lindsey hurried into his office, his stomach gnawing.

"Well, la dee dah." Patterson laughed, as he walked in after him. "This is going to be real interesting."

Lindsey frowned. "What?"

"You and that profiler working side by side."

"What's wrong? You jealous?" Lindsey sat behind his desk.

Patterson thought for a moment. "Hey! This better not mean I'm getting cut out of the loop."

"Hell no! You'll be there for all the blood and guts, I promise." Lindsey leaned back, then set his heels on his desk.

"I better be." Patterson tilted his neck.

"There'll be plenty of work for all of us."

"Well," he said, "if nothing else, this should be good for a few laughs. Wait 'til she starts bossing you around. I can see it all now," he laughed. "Not only that, you'll also have to put up with "feelings" and "mental imagery" and all that bullshit. Tom Lindsey and his partner, Agent Hocus-Pocus."

Lindsey's smile stretched into a Cheshire cat grin. "Well, I for one, plan to be completely cooperative. Of course, if she asks to read my palm, I'll have to draw the line. Other than that, I'll be a real gentleman."

"We'll see how long that lasts. She's a control freak and she's already got her eyes set on the helm."

Lindsey clasped his hands behind his neck. "She can look at it all she wants, but she's never going to take it."

Lindsey and Cross didn't speak during their ride to St. Cloud. By the time they arrived at the Miller's oak shaded home, they were relieved to get out of the car. The house overlooking east Lake Tohopokaliga reflected the architecture of northeastern neighborhoods in the late nineteen fifties. Long lush St. Augustine grass needed mowing. Azalea and lagustrum hedges took advantage of the neglect and competed in their rush to display their new growth; tall, spindly, over-achievers blatantly disrupted the straight manicured lines of the past. Mounds of Indian hawthorn had lost their snowball shapes, and abundantly blooming hibiscus bore early stages of defiance. Even so, every growing thing appeared well nourished and disease free, a sure indication that a once diligent caretaker had recently undergone a dramatic change of pattern.

They rang the bell. The door opened, and the aroma of roast beef flooded the doorway. They apologized for being early. Donna Miller wiped her hands on her apron as she reassured them that they had just finished eating. Sharon observed dull hopelessness in the woman's eyes.

"Please." She motioned to the couch. "Have a seat. My husband will be right in. He's cleaning up the kitchen." She sat on an upholstered chair to the left of them. "I don't know why he bothered making supper. Neither one of us ate very much. My husband's been so helpful since Monica disappeared." She ran trembling fingers across her pale brow. "I don't know what I would have done without him. I just don't seem to have much energy anymore. The doctor gave me these anti-depressants, and all I want to do is sleep. To tell you the truth, I think I feel worse now than I did before." She smiled feebly.

"I'm sure this has been a devastating ordeal. We're

truly sorry for your loss," Sharon said.

She nodded, then removed a handkerchief from a pocket in her apron. "Thank you. Everyone has been so kind...our neighbors, the people from our church. A person never knows just how good others really are until a time like this." She wiped a tear from her eye.

Lindsey cleared his throat. "Mrs. Miller, we know it's not easy having to answer questions at a time like this. I wish it could be avoided."

"That's okay. I understand." She wrung her hands in her lap. "Larry? Will you be done soon?"

Water stopped running in the kitchen and Mr. Miller entered the room. "Well, I guess you're the detectives who called."

Lindsey stood up and made introductions. The two men shook hands and Larry nodded to Sharon. "Pleased to meet you both." He had a strong square chin and deep set eyes that seemed as angry as they did sad. "How can we help?"

"By telling us everything you possibly can about your daughter."

Mr. Miller stood silent for several awkward moments. His lower lip quivered slightly while he fought for control. Finally, he took a deep breath. "My daughter was sixteen years old. This is her last school picture." He walked over to the fireplace and picked up a beautifully framed photograph of a pretty girl with long, dark, brown hair and bright, kind eyes. He handed it to Sharon. "She was our world. She was a good girl, never gave us a single problem. She was an "A" student, class president, and assistant music director for the youth choir at our church. She could sing like an angel. You couldn't ask for a better daughter." Larry paused to clear his throat.

"When the officers came and told me she was dead, I knew in my heart they were right and that I'd have to learn to accept it. But when they insinuated that she'd been prostituting, I told them there was nothing they could ever say that would convince me of that. I don't care how she was dressed when they found her... my little girl would not have resorted to such a thing. She just didn't have it in her."

Sharon looked down again at the picture in her hands. "I can see why you feel that way."

Mr. Miller blinked his eyes hard, then took the picture, and carefully returned it to the mantle. With his back to them, he said, "Now you just go ahead, detectives. You ask us anything and we'll answer you truthfully. I want this man caught more than you do. I don't want anyone else to lose their child to this evil monster. We'll do anything to help you out."

"Thank you." Sharon smiled warmly. "Then let's get started." She set a tape recorder on the coffee table in front of them. "You mind?"

He turned around, looked at the recorder and then at his wife. "Not at all."

"Okay." She pressed the record button. "How long have you lived here in St. Cloud?"

"My wife and I moved here from Indiana about twenty years ago. Monica was born and raised in St. Cloud."

"What kind of work do you do, Larry?"

"My wife and I are florists. Our shop is downtown. We started our business when we moved here, and we've done well."

"That's wonderful." Sharon's smile concealed her surprise. She'd have guessed he was a retired rancher or farmer. His face appeared defeated by the elements, rough and heavily lined. He was dressed in old-fashioned work jeans and a light shirt that was paper thin from countless washings. His white hair lacked style and his unruly eyebrows begged for a trimming. Somehow, she just couldn't imagine him arranging flowers with any sort of finesse. "Did Monica ever work at your shop?" She asked, after breaking from her appraisal.

"Mostly on holidays when we got swamped."

"Did she ever make deliveries?" Lindsey interjected.

"Sure did."

"We'll need those records."

"No problem. The information is in our computer at the shop. I'll fax them to you tomorrow."

"Now, I'd like to know about Monica's hobbies."

"Hobbies?" Larry smiled through his sorrow. "The girl was crazy about horses. We bought her one when she turned five years old. You should have seen her. She was ecstatic...named him 'Stormy'. She loved that horse. And ride? That girl was barrel-racing by the time she was seven and winning, too. Her room is still filled with blue ribbons and trophies." His eyes glistened.

"Was she still interested in horses by the time she disappeared?" Sharon asked.

"Well, it was kind of strange." Mr. Miller collected himself. "Just about three weeks before she left, she stopped going out to the barn. You see, we stabled her horse just outside of town at the Baker's ranch. They're a good family, two children around Monica's age. Shelley is fourteen, and I think her brother Chris is around seventeen. They're both well-mannered kids. Anyway, one day she comes home with her riding gear. I asked her what was wrong and she said she wanted to find another place to keep Stormy." Larry scratched the back of his neck. "I tried to find out what the problem was, but she told me not to worry about it and so I didn't. I figured she and the kids probably had a little spat or something, and that it would all blow over in a few days. But when she wouldn't even go down there to feed the horse, I started getting worried. So finally, I talked to the Bakers. They said they didn't know why she was upset either.

"Right before she left, I hauled the horse to another stable, and two days later Monica was gone. Never did go back to see Stormy or say good-bye to us." Mr. Miller's eyes drifted. "I swear I think that horse senses something happened to her. Seems almost as beat up as we do."

"Girls Monica's age often lose interest in their horses because boys suddenly become more interesting," Sharon said. "Did she have a boyfriend?"

"Not that we know of," Larry replied. "Certainly never talked about any special boy."

"We'll need directions to the Baker's ranch before we leave," Tom said. "Had you noticed any other changes in Monica's behavior during those three weeks before she left?"

Mrs. Miller wiped her nose. "It seemed like she was

trying to work out a solution to a very serious problem. I kept encouraging her to talk to me, but she just wouldn't open up. Monica and I had always discussed everything freely."

"Did she have many friends?"

"Oh yes." Larry removed a paper from his shirt pocket. "I knew you'd want a list of them because the St Cloud police did, too. I got their names, addresses and phone numbers."

"Thanks." Sharon took the list and put it in a file. "I'm very impressed with your efficiency."

Larry pursed his lips and nodded.

"Who is the last person that saw Monica alive?" Lindsey asked.

"Police tracked it down to one of the girls in our neighborhood, Tracy Applegate. Monica stopped by her house which is just two doors up the road." He gestured to the right. "When you're on their upstairs balcony, they've got almost as good a view of the lake as we do. Anyway, that's where the girls were sitting and talking right before Monica left. Tracy said Monica told her she was going out of town for a week, because she had to take care of something important. The girl insists Monica didn't go into any details about the problem, but Monica asked to borrow some money. Tracy had saved up fifty dollars to buy her parents an anniversary present, but she felt Monica was desperate, so she handed it over. Apparently, Monica made her promise not to tell anyone, especially us. I just don't understand it."

"Is her name on this list you gave me?"

"Absolutely." Larry's grave eyes glowed with determination.

"So we know for sure that Monica was not kidnapped, that she left here on her own accord and she planned on returning in a week. That's a big help." Sharon tapped her pen against her chin. "Now we have to find out where she went and why."

Mr. Miller's voice was thick with his plea. "When you find that out, you make sure I'm the first person you tell."

CHAPTER 3

Carol Randolph, a middle-aged blonde with weary eyes and trembling hands, talked into a cell phone, while signing papers on a clipboard.

"Allen, I know it's early, but I wanted to let you and Debbie know John's back. He was brought here to MHC an hour ago."

Allen yawned on the other end of the phone. "So where did they find him this time?" His voice was hoarse from sleep.

"Orlando. He'd been living on the streets." She paused to collect her thoughts. "At least he's getting the help he needs now." She winced as one side of her head pounded. "The police had a difficult time getting him to cooperate. He actually punched a couple of them."

"Oh, that's just great. I hope the incident doesn't make the newspapers."

"I'm sure you have nothing to worry about." Her toned cooled.

He sat up in bed. "When is he ever going to stop this nonsense?"

"It's the disease, Allen. Why is it so hard for you to understand that?"

"Whatever."

"Allen, for the life of me I'll never be able to..." She looked up and saw John's doctor walking toward her. "Look, I've got to go, I'll call Debbie to let her know how John's doing. I know she cares about him." She hung up, greeted Dr. Walters, and handed the signed papers to a nurse.

As they walked down the hall, she touched the

doctor's arm and stopped. "Could we talk for a minute before we go to his room?"

"Of course." He smiled and motioned to a door a few feet away. A distinguished looking man in his fifties, Dr. Walters' gray hair and hazel eyes complimented his tanned face. In his perfectly pressed Armani suit, he walked with the kind of confidence that reeked of success.

They sat across from each other in a small plain room, normally used for brief, first time emergency evaluations. She pressed the palm of her hand against her temple.

"Are you getting another migraine?" The doctor asked.

She nodded. "Yeah. Great timing, isn't it?"

"Well, you've been through a terrible ordeal." He glanced at his watch. "It's five o'clock. You need to go home and get some sleep."

"That's exactly what I'm planning to do. But first, I want to see him."

"Okay, but he's messy and he's hallucinating again."

She nodded. "It's nothing I haven't seen before."

"I know, I just wanted to prepare you. Just keep in mind, the important thing is, we have him here where we can make sure he stays on his medications."

"I'm grateful, believe me." She sighed. "I'm so glad they found him. I can't believe he was in Orlando all this time. Practically under our noses. But I wish I hadn't had to get the police involved." Carol fought back tears. "He must hate me."

Dr. Walters shook his head. "Nonsense. When he's feeling better, he'll thank you for intervening." His smile offered encouragement. "Besides, the police would have gone after him anyway, even if you hadn't requested an APB. They were receiving complaints about a man matching his description causing havoc on OBT around quitting time yesterday evening. When they got there, he was gone, but they suspected it was John. Then around two a.m. he showed up right outside of the police department, screaming for help. They said he kept ranting about the devil. He was in bad shape at that point...even violent."

"I know, I talked to one of the officers when I first got here. I've never known him to hit anyone."

"Well, he was completely psychotic and still is, I'm afraid." Dr. Walters shook his head. "That's why it's not a good idea for you to see him right now. Besides, he won't even remember you were here."

"Maybe not, but it'll make me feel better." A distant glaze transformed her eyes. "If only I'd prevented him from taking off, things wouldn't have deteriorated to this point." She traced an enlarged vein on the right side of her temple with her forefinger.

"You're not a mind reader, Carol. You had no idea he was going to run."

"I should have known he'd gone off his medicine. He wasn't making much sense that whole week before he left. I just assumed he was going through a temporary phase."

"From now on, you're going to have to watch him take his medication, because it could easily happen again, he said. "Schizophrenics often stop meds once they start feeling better. Keep that in mind."

Carol nodded. "I will."

Dr. Walters stood up. "Come on, let's get this over with before that migraine gets any worse." He placed his arm across her shoulders and led her down the hallway. He stopped before heavy double doors. He punched several numbers on a keyboard panel and the doors swung open. The sound of moaning and hysterical laughter assaulted her ears. When a sudden scream rose above all the other noises, her stomach lurched. She instinctively covered her mouth with her hand and tears welled in her eyes. She fought for control. As she approached John's room, she took a deep breath and brushed the tears from her cheeks. The screaming grew louder as the door opened. Inside, a male nurse struggled to adjust the straps of a straight jacket.

Above the uproar, Dr. Walters looked apologetic as he turned to her and shouted, "Hopefully he won't need that by tomorrow."

Carol bit her lower lip. She stepped into the room

slowly. John's face and body were so much thinner than they were two months ago. His blood shot eyes darted around the room, searching the shadows. He reminded her of a trapped animal.

As she neared his bed, he groaned, unaware of her presence.

Dr. Walters said. "John, your mother is here to see you."

He showed no reaction to the doctor's voice.

"Hi, John." Carol continued moving closer. "Are you okay?"

He shook his head very slowly. "Axes...axes."

"What?" She glanced at Dr. Walters. He shrugged. She kneeled at his side and reached for his shaking hand. "There, there...everything is going to be all right, I love you. Do you hear me?"

He suddenly squeezed her hand like a vise. "Somebody has got to stop the devil, before he makes more axes."

"John, please! You're hurting me." She struggled to pull her hand free. "You're going to be okay. There is no devil."

"Yes, there is!" He screamed, his eyes wandering in her direction.

Dr. Walters stepped forward and attempted to pry John's fingers from her hand, but his hold was powerful. He turned to the nurse, and nodded toward the syringe on the tray stand beside the bed.

"Why doesn't anyone believe me?" He strained against the straps as he jerked her hand, throwing her off balance, and then pulled her closer to his face. He spoke directly into her ear. "I saw him turn a girl into a jack-o-lantern. I was there...he was dressed in black...I saw him...I really did."

Carol pushed against his shoulder with her free hand. Desperate, she yelled, "John! Let go!" She used her fingernails against his grip. The nurse quickly injected the sedative into the heplock on John's wrist.

Dr. Walters held on to Carol's shoulders. "He'll let go any second now."

"Hurry up! Stop him...please...make him stop!" Carol screamed.

John released his hold and began breathing deeply. Carol pulled her hand away, then flopped down on the floor sobbing. She gingerly rubbed her injured hand.

Dr. Walters examined her by gently bending her fingers and checking the joints. "You're lucky. No fractures. But you're going to have to put some ice on it. You'll have quite a bit of bruising."

"I've never seen him like this. It's the first time he's ever hurt me." She shook her head, as tears flowed in continuous rows along her cheeks.

"I shouldn't have let you come back here. I'm sorry," Dr. Walters said. "We'll have to keep him on a strong sedative until the anti-psychotics kick in." He helped her to her feet, then escorted her to the door. "I'll call you tomorrow after I make my rounds and let you know how he's doing. I don't want you visiting him until he's under control. Do you want me to arrange to have someone drive you home?"

She shook her head. "I'll be fine."

"Okay then. Get some rest."

Carol nodded. "I'll try."

He looked over his shoulder as he headed down the hall. "A month from now he'll be back to his old self."

Carol nodded. She had to believe that.

When his mother had hung up, Allen rolled his eyes, then slammed down the phone.

His wife, Debbie, rolled over in bed. "What's wrong?"

"John's back in the psych ward."

"Oh, thank God they found him," she whispered.

Allen threw the blankets aside and sat on the edge of the bed. Debbie crawled over, kneeled behind him and massaged his shoulders. He brushed her hands aside and stood up.

"I got to get ready for work." He went into the bathroom and stepped into the shower. He gradually increased the heat of the water until it was as hot as he could stand it. Thoughts of his childhood flashed through his mind. He remembered how John was always there for him, especially when he got into trouble. No matter how rotten Allen treated him, John was kind and forgiving. Allen felt a twinge of guilt when he thought how frequently he'd mocked his brother. He was embarrassed because of him and could never quite understand why he acted so strangely. Allen recalled the event that finally gave John's strangeness a name; a diagnosis he couldn't understand and even today had trouble accepting.

He, John and his mother sat down for supper one night. John threw his plate onto the floor and pointed at him. "It's in the food!" John screamed. "You've been putting it in there." John turned to his mother. "I've got to get my blood analyzed."

"John! What are you saying?" His mother pushed back from the table.

"Allen's trying to get rid of me." John's his eyes drilled into Allen's.

Allen scoffed. "Look, freak, I don't even know what you're talking about." He'd felt shocked...had never experienced his brother's wrath.

"Stop calling him a freak!" his mother shouted.

"I have all the symptoms of poisoning. I'm not imagining it." John pointed to Allen. "You above anyone should know what I'm talking about," he screamed.

"He thinks I'm poisoning him!" Allen had turned to his mother for back up. "Mom, he's getting crazier every day. You're going to have to face it. He's really nuts."

"Shut up, Allen! Don't you ever say that again. If anyone is nuts around here, it's you." He could still remember his mother's pale face and glaring eyes penetrating his. She grabbed John by the hand and took him into the living room. Allen tiptoed behind them and stopped at the doorway.

"Now, tell me why you think Allen is poisoning you." Allen watched as his mother smoothed John's hair back off his forehead.

"They told me," his brother mumbled.

"They?" His mother's brow dipped into a slight frown.

"The voices." He lowered his eyes to the floor. "I hear voices sometimes. They told me what Allen was doing."

Allen recalled the fear that washed over his mother. "How long has this been going on?"

"Ever since he started poisoning me," John said. "I see things, too." John shook his head. "I thought I was turning into a cockroach last night. My arms looked like tentacles and my back felt like a shell. I thought of spraying myself with Raid, but then I knew that wouldn't be good, since I already have so much poison in my body."

John's mother wrapped him up into her arms and rocked him back and forth like a child. "My God, why didn't you tell me before? I've got to get you to a doctor." She cried. For a long time, Allen watched them rocking; love and neediness molding them into an impenetrable unit. A bond he'd sensed for as long as he could remember had finally solidified before his eyes.

He shook his head and raised his face toward the showerhead. He had enough on his mind without having to deal with his brother and mother's problems. He had to worry about his own life.

Like his marriage. He and Debbie had been married for seven years. They had been crazy about each other throughout high school. She was a cheerleader and he was a football hero. Allen had a personality that matched his exceptional good looks, so he had no trouble winning her over. He knew from the beginning that she was the girl he wanted to marry and their life together had been good despite his many flaws, until their two-week-old baby girl died. That had been the turning point.

After soaping up, he let the steaming water hit hard against his tight neck and shoulder muscles. There were other problems too. His job. He constantly feared exposure of his inadequacies. He always knew he wasn't an intellectual. He barely graduated from business school. However, he had charisma and was a masterful manipulator. Those two gifts had taken him a long way. He could uplift people's moods and convince them that he cared for their well beings. At work, nearly everyone thought his business knowledge bordered on genius. Actually, his success was due to his ruthlessness and ability to manipulate other people's minds and skills.

Using ruthless tactics, he climbed the ladder by maiming, then replacing, his superiors one by one. Eventually, he became State Director of Marketing for the Hoebel Hotel chains. His rise to the top was thrilling, but he lived in fear it would all catch up with him someday.

Then there was Heather, his secretary. What the hell was he going to do about her?

The alarm clock shook Lindsey from a nightmare that desperately screamed for closure. He pounded the button, then collapsed back on his bed, his heart racing. At first, he dreamed about the day his daughter was born. His ex-wife, Sara, cradled their baby against her chest and smiled down at her with adoration. They remarked about how beautiful she was and how miraculous the whole experience had been. He believed it was the most wonderful moment in their lives.

Suddenly, Sara looked up. Her eyes seemed to exude more love than he'd ever seen before. Tears of joy and appreciation flowed. But as he bent to kiss her, he noticed she was looking up over his shoulder. Without hesitation, she pushed him aside and handed their newborn to this intruder, who caressed the child in his arms. Lindsey flamed with rage and lifted his fist in retaliation. Just before he could land the punch, he'd been catapulted into consciousness by the alarm and left with an overdose of adrenaline surging through his body. The smoldering resentment that had consumed him ever since that man had taken his wife and child away was set ablaze. Again he'd been forced to refrain from acting out and the anger turned inward and his stomach suffered the consequences. He kicked the blankets aside, sat up and reached for his pack of cigarettes lying next to his bed.

Women. He shook his head. He had sworn off them. Hadn't dated since the divorce and didn't plan to ever get involved again. He'd never again subject himself to the kind of hurt he'd been through. The sense of loss had peeled down to his core, leaving it raw and festering.

He drew hungrily on his cigarette and held the smoke in his lungs a little longer than usual. He'd have to get his mind on something else, or he'd be facing a worse day than he had already anticipated. Having to work with Sharon Cross was bad enough without starting the morning off like this.

He never liked outside interference. The fact that Agent Cross was a cold, humorless robot only made matters worse. His team could handle the case better on its own...he was sure of it. The disdain he and Cross shared kept them from conferring about the interviews last night and that was not the way to do business. Freely comparing notes and ideas was crucial to a case. He and Patterson always fed off each other in that way.

He inhaled more smoke, then coughed with annoyance. He hated to admit it, but he knew he was not doing himself or anyone else any good by harboring negative feelings.

He thought about Monica. He owed it to her and her parents to somehow get along with Cross, but he hated to make the first move. He glanced at the clock, then crushed his cigarette out in an ashtray. He believed Monica was most likely just as sweet and innocent as his own daughter. They even shared interest in horses. They were probably alike in many ways. That poor family. How could they find the strength to go on? They loved their daughter just as much as he loved his.

Suddenly his eyes widened with realization. He snatched up the phone and stabbed out numbers.

"Sara." Just saying her name brought back a flood of conflicting memories.

"Yes. Hi Tom, how are you?" Her voice was warm and whispery.

"Where is Jen?" His tone was intense, his face hard.

She paused slightly. "In the kitchen...eating breakfast."

"What's she doing today?"

"She's planning on going to the mall with her friends a little later, why?"

"Unsupervised?"

"Of course, Tom. She's fourteen years old. What's the big deal?"

"Look, I'm working on this case. There's a serial-killer..."

"I know, I read about it in the papers. Weren't they all prostitutes? What does it have to do with Jennifer?"

"They weren't all prostitutes, like we first thought. So that means any girl could be in danger."

She lowered her voice. "You're scaring me, Tom."

"Good. Maybe you'll start keeping a better eye on her."

"I resent that. You know I'm not a negligent mother."

"I know that. It's just..." He paused. "Sara, if you saw this guy's handiwork, you'd understand."

"Well, what should I do? Keep her home? Not let her go out at all? How much do I need to protect her, Tom? I can't be with her every second."

Tom rubbed the back of his neck. "I know but you're going to have to be cautious until we get him behind bars."

"Okay. I'll do my best. I promise. But it won't be easy. You know how independent she is. She'll want to know what's wrong, and I don't really want to tell her. She could be traumatized."

"Look, suffering a little anxiety would be nothing compared to suffering at the hands of this lunatic. Just tell her the truth."

Sara heard the certainty in his voice. "I'll have to think about that. Meanwhile, I'll do everything I can. You have my word."

"Thank you." He hesitated. "Are you doing all right? I mean, is he treating you good?"

"Yes, Tom." She paused. They'd been down this road so many times before. "I'm sorry, Tom...for everything."

He nodded, his thoughts drifted to a far away place. "Yeah...me too. I'll talk to you later," he said quietly, then hung up.

Allen got out of the shower and dried off quickly. Debbie had laid out his clothes on the bed and was downstairs cooking his breakfast.

When he sat down at the dining room table, he looked into the kitchen and watched her at the stove. Her once long, flowing auburn hair was short now. He wondered why women always seemed to cut their hair when they got married. Her bathrobe didn't do much to excite him, either. It was thick terry cloth and accentuated her wide waist. Sensing him staring, she turned suddenly and smiled self-consciously as she brought food to the table."

He forced a brief smile in return, then began piling his plate with pancakes and bacon. She sat across from him and took a sip of her orange juice.

"Is there anything I can do to help?" Before taking a bite of her pancake, she said, "I thought about visiting your mother. She's been through so much."

Allen shrugged. "Suit yourself. I don't care."

Debbie lowered her eyes to her glass. She never could understand why he was so cold toward his mother and brother. They were the only family he had besides her. It just didn't make sense. "I'll wait until five or so. She was probably up most of the night."

Allen nodded indifferently, as he wolfed down his food. He avoided Debbie's eyes, as usual. When he finished, he hurriedly wiped his mouth with a napkin. Without looking up, he pushed back his chair and headed for the door. "See you around eleven."

"Another late meeting?"

"Yeah," He mumbled as he left.

Debbie sighed, as she stared down at the remaining pancakes on the table. She grabbed her fork and stabbed it through the pile. Plopping the pancakes onto her plate, she lathered them with butter and poured on the syrup. It had been this way ever since their baby died. A week after the funeral, Allen told her she'd grieved long enough. So she stopped and then she ate. The rest was history.

Each time the sedative wore off, John felt the restraints and awoke panic-stricken. He thrashed like a man with his head held under water. Consequently, his wrists became bruised and swollen. Red welts formed on his chest. This time, as he bridged the gap from sleep to consciousness, he immediately struggled to maintain control. His mind was clearer now, capable of understanding cause and effect. He realized if he had another panic attack, he would inflict more injury upon himself. Without looking down at the straight jacket, he opened his eyes to assess his surroundings. The room had a familiar feel. He told himself that he was reasonably safe. He would survive this, as long as he remained calm.

The door opened and Dr. Walters entered. "Good morning, John."

"What time is it?"

"Nine-thirty."

"How long have I been here?" The dryness in his throat accentuated the weakness in his voice.

Dr. Walters hesitated. "About twenty-eight hours."

"Why am I here and why am I tied down to this bed?"

"We'll get to all of that in a minute. First I need to find out how you are feeling."

"I'm strapped down and can't move. How do you think I'm feeling?" John spoke in monotones.

"Do you know who I am?"

John's eyes narrowed in confusion. "Of course, you're Dr. Walters. And this room seems familiar. But I don't remember being tied down like this before. It's inhumane."

"I didn't have any other choice, John. You were in very bad shape last night."

"And this medieval contraption is suppose to improve my state of mind? This thing is enough to make a normal person crazy."

The doctor slipped a pill into John's mouth, then held a cup of water to his lips. John swallowed obediently. "Let's give the medicine a few minutes to take effect. I'd like to talk with you for awhile. Then if I feel you're stable, we'll be able to remove it."

"All right. What do you want to know?"

"When you arrived last night, you were very upset. You'd been hallucinating and you were very frightened. Do you remember?"

John's forehead wrinkled. "I remember being afraid of someone."

"It was a hallucination."

"No, it wasn't. I experienced something very real."

"How much do you remember?" Dr. Walters asked.

John closed his eyes, hoping for recollection. Bits and pieces of past events flashed before him like black and white photographs. Each picture slowly interlocked like a puzzle. He viewed the scant information with benign objectivity, until a series of new pictures appeared. His body tensed against the straps as fright overtook him.

"John?" Dr. Walters leaned forward. "What's wrong?"

"Please...please get me out of this thing. I have to be able to defend myself. I'm vulnerable. Can't you see that?"

"John, I'm right here. I won't let anything happen to you."

"I don't believe you." John studied his doctor's eyes. "You might be part of the plan. You might be working for him."

"Him? I'm not following you."

In silence, John stared straight ahead, not answering. He had to compose himself, or he'd never be free.

"John, don't shut me out."

"I'm sorry. It's this straight jacket; I just can't take it anymore. You have no idea how much it hurts. It's hard for me to trust you since you're the person who has the power to remove it and you're not doing it."

Dr. Walters rubbed his chin. "I don't think we've settled anything."

"Look," John's eyes moved slowly to meet the doctor's. "What are you afraid of? Are you afraid I might escape? Even if I wanted to run out of here, I wouldn't be able to do it. I'm exhausted...can't you tell?"

Dr. Walters hesitated. "All right, we'll give it a try. But if you get too excited, we'll have to put it back on."

"Don't worry, I'll be okay."

Dr. Walters stepped out into the hallway, and motioned for an orderly.

John stayed still while the straight jacket was unlatched. He sighed. "Thank you."

"You're welcome. But I need your word, John, that you won't try to leave. Will you promise me that?"

John nodded. "I promise."

He sat up in bed, gently touching his bruised skin and studying the taped heplock on his wrists. He didn't like seeing the traces of blood in the little tube that led to the needle which was embedded in his vein. "Can you take this out?" He held up his wrist. "It hurts too."

Walters shook his head. "Not now. Maybe in a few days."

John stretched his aching muscles and stepped to the window. "I know he's out there. He's trying to find me. He wants to kill me, too."

Dr. Walters walked behind him and placed his hand on John's shoulder. "Who is this person you keep referring to?

"The devil." He glanced at Dr. Walter's face. "Never mind. Either you don't want to believe me, or you're part of it. Whatever the reason, I think it's best I don't say anymore." John staggered away from him.

"John, you're right, I don't believe you saw the devil. But that doesn't mean I'm plotting against you or part of some devious plan. You've known me long enough to realize that."

"Have I?" He stood quiet for a moment, then changed the subject. "I'm drugged to the hilt. I'd much rather be insane than feel like this."

"John, you were living on the streets, eating out of garbage cans. Before you went off your meds, you were functioning normally."

"The side-effects of these anti-psychotics are horrendous. You don't know what it's like. My muscles spasm and my heart races. I feel dizzy and half the time I can't think straight. I hate them."

"I do know it can be unpleasant at times. That's why I've decided to take you off your regular medicine and see how you respond to Risperdal. You should experience fewer side effects, plus you won't have to have blood tests. Unfortunately, I've had to start you out on a high dosage, so I know you must be feeling lousy right now. We'll be able to cut back on it as you improve. Another reason you feel so bad is you've also been receiving sedatives. Hopefully, we can stop them in a day or two."

John shook his head. "You have no idea at all what these drugs are actually doing to my brain and what the long-term effects will be. And yet you prescribe them and consider them scientifically proven medicines."

"They are the best we have so far."

"Well, you're best is not good enough for me."

"John, without the drugs, you see devils and block traffic in the middle of Orlando during rush hour! Doesn't that tell you something? Is that how you want to spend your life?"

"Of course not." John's voice droned with flatness. He walked back to the window and stared out at the street. After several minutes passed, his senses dulled dramatically. When he turned around, his eyes were beginning to droop. John yawned again. "That sedative is going to knock me out, isn't it?" He said more to himself than his doctor.

He was still very dirty and his oily hair hung in matted ropes. No one attempted to clean him the night before. He sat down on the bed and mumbled, "I feel like I need to take a nap. I hope I don't have anymore nightmares. My mother was in a dream I had last night. She was working for the police."

He gingerly touched a light bruise over his eye. "Will you look at this? Is there an axe on my eye? Do I need stitches?"

Dr. Walters stepped forward and shook his head. "There's nothing there but a little bruise." It never ceased to amaze him how a person with mental illness could be completely rational one minute and then delusional the next. He watched as John sat down on the bed. John's eyes narrowed to thin slits.

John felt the bruise again, then mumbled, "I love my

mother, but sometimes she spies on me. Sends people out to watch me. I can hear them telling her I'm out there. People say, *there he is...he's got dog crap on his shoes again.* Doesn't bother me...dog crap that is. But my mother gets upset when I'm dirty."

"Yes, well." Dr. Walters hesitated. "Why don't you try sleeping for awhile, John? When you wake up, I'll send someone in to get you cleaned up and looking presentable so when your mother visits, she won't be upset. How's that sound?"

John lay down and muttered something incoherent. He was still worried about what he thought he'd seen, but there was no point in trying to talk about it. No one would believe him anyway, so he decided to forget about it.

CHAPTER 4

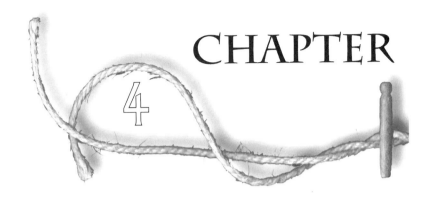

Twenty-three year old Heather Martin carried a cup of coffee into Allen's office. Her tightly tailored jacket accentuated her tiny waist and her short skirt barely covered her buttocks. Allen feasted on every attribute, including her intriguing full lips. "Good morning, sir." She closed the door behind her and tossed long, raven hair over her shoulder. Her dark blue eyes teased.

"Sir?" Allen chuckled.

"That was for the benefit of everybody out there." She winked and set the cup on his desk. "You thought you were a tough guy last night, didn't you."

"I didn't hear you complaining."

"True. As long as it just stays a game."

"Hey. You know I'm an angel at heart." His smug smile pulled harder on one side of his mouth than the other.

"Yeah, right." She pushed up her sleeve. "Look, I've got a bruise on my wrist. How am I going to explain that?"

"You're clumsy." He smiled.

"You're so bad." She shook her finger at him. "Are we still on for tonight?"

"You bet, baby." Allen looked her over leisurely.

Heather leaned over and kissed him slowly on his lips, then stood up. "Now!" She turned and grabbed a file from his desk. "We've got work to do."

Allen fell back in his chair, faking collapse. "You have no mercy." He flashed his famous smile.

"Yeah, the shoe's on the other foot for once." She stuck her tongue out at him. "The meeting is in thirty minutes. I thought I'd better get you up to speed."

Allen got serious. "Sounds like a plan." He slapped his hands on the surface of the desk. "Let's get started."

She briefed him quickly. Heather was a lifesaver. She kept up with everything that was going on in the company. She attended all the meetings and seemed to understand planning and strategies better than Allen. They were the perfect team inside and outside the office. There was only one problem. Lately, she was pressuring him to get a divorce and marry her. Even if he did leave Debbie, Heather would be the last woman he'd want to marry. Besides, there were rules against dating employees and his boss, Phillip Towers, was a stickler about such things.

"Remember, baby, we've got to be discreet. Okay?"

"How many times a day do you think you need to remind me of that? Do you think I'm an idiot?" Heather's eyes flashed with anger.

"Of course not. I don't think you would intentionally let anything slip. But sometimes people pick up on attitudes."

"Don't worry. No one suspects anything." She planted her hands firmly on her hips. "Have you thought about how we'll explain it when you finally get divorced and we get married?'

Allen shrugged his shoulders. "We'll cross that bridge when we come to it."

"Well, we better be crossing that bridge soon, or I'll be making it to the other side without you."

"Hey, don't be like that. You know I love you."

"You better." Heather pouted wantonly and walked toward the door.

Allen rushed past her and blocked her way. "Hey, come here." He grabbed her hand and yanked her towards him. Heather's eyes half closed, suddenly turning dreamy. He squeezed her hand tighter, and with a jerk, bent her arm up behind her back. She smiled provocatively and pressed closer.

With a turn of the knob, the door swung open and Paul Shield, one of Allen's employees, faced them, eyes wide with surprise.

Allen's stomach flip-flopped and a wave of heat spread from his neck to his face. Heather pushed away, adjusting her jacket, as she rushed past Paul on her way out the door.

Paul scratched the back of his head. He stretched out his arm to hand Allen a stack of papers without making eye contact. "I brought you the figures you needed."

Allen's eyes flamed. "What the hell do you think you're doing barging in like that?" He snatched the papers. "Next time, knock. You understand?"

"Sure. No problem." Paul's face was red as he turned to leave. "I'm sorry."

Allen slammed the door behind him. "Damn it!" He threw the papers across the room and watched them float to the floor. He paced for a moment, then sat down and rubbed his forehead. He trembled. He had to control himself. He couldn't let anyone see him like this.

"That little faggot could screw up everything," he whispered. He closed his eyes for a minute and took a few deep breaths. He'd made a big mistake. He shouldn't have taken it out on Paul, of all people. He needed him on his side. His job depended on it. The man was a genius. He had to rectify things quickly.

Allen walked to the door and caught Paul's eye as he looked up from his desk. Motioning for him, he opened the door wider and waited for him to come back. Allen smiled sheepishly as he shut the door behind them. "Paul, I apologize. The truth is, I was embarrassed and mad at myself and I took it out on you. Heather has been flirtatious lately and today she finally got to me. I'm only human. I just weakened for a second and that's when you walked in. Nothing like this has ever happened between Heather and me before. Actually, I'm glad you came in when you did. I don't know what in the world I was thinking. I would never want to do anything to hurt my wife. She means everything to me."

Paul put his hand up to stop him. "I understand. Besides, it's none of my business anyway. In fact, it's already forgotten as far as I'm concerned." Shield's reassuring words didn't match the stoniness in his eyes.

"Thanks, buddy." Allen reached out and they shook hands. When he left, Allen pressed his back to the door, the blood drained from his face and the room suddenly felt chilly.

Lindsey and Cross entered the squad room with files and briefcases bulging with new information. Sergeant Henry came out of his office when he saw them.

"Let's go!" Henry barked. "Got another meeting in a half hour."

Lindsey's men took their seats. The room was louder than usual, and Henry was getting irritated. "Hey! Shut up over there."

Lindsey distributed a file to each of them. "Okay, guys, let's start with what you've come up with so far?"

Patterson bolted through the door, waving a paper in his hand. "I've got a positive I.D. on Amy. Missing Persons in San Francisco called and notified us of a girl that's been missing for six weeks. They faxed me this photograph. It resembles the picture we found in the victim's purse...the one with her and the older lady. The old lady is her mother." He handed the fax to Lindsey. "The missing girl's name is Amy Rockwell and the baby's name is Kayla. Same name we found on the baby picture in her apartment. The mother said Amy didn't want to take care of the child. She left two days after she was born. The mother gave the baby to Children's Services."

Lindsey gave him a thumb's up. "Good work."

Patterson nodded smugly and leaned back in his chair.

"So far none of the fingerprints are consistent with the other crime scenes," Steve Brown said. "But the footprints we cast were a size eleven Nike sneaker. Had quite of bit of wear on the outside portion of the heel. Forensics said that it matched the other ones."

"Great. Sounds like we're off to a fairly good start," Lindsey said. He held up a paper. "A prostitute, originally from Gainesville, moved here several months ago and no one had seen or heard from her since. Forensics compared dental records and they matched the Kissimmee victim. Name, Susan James, seventeen years old. She recently gave her baby up for adoption. I want you two to gather as much information as you can on her." He handed the paper to Young and Brown.

"Okay." Lindsey rubbed his palms together. "This is what we came up with yesterday. The St. Cloud victim's name was Monica Miller. She'd left home three weeks before she was killed. From all accounts, she was a decent girl. Nice family, too. The father gave us a convincing argument against his daughter being a prostitute. It's very possible that the killer dressed her up to look the part. We're basing that on the fact that her clothes were several sizes too large for her, including the shoes. And the general consensus of her friends and the rest of her family strongly support the father's assessment of her."

He looked at Steve Brown. "I want you to track down the stores in the area that sell the type of dress and shoes found on the body. I'm sure the guy was smart enough to pay with cash, but maybe someone would remember something out of the ordinary. Someone making a purchase who seemed unusually intense or in any way out of the ordinary. It's worth a shot."

Steve nodded.

"We talked with Monica's friend, Tracy Applegate, who revealed some new information. Monica was pregnant and had an abortion in Orlando. The medical report verified this. The father of the baby was a teen-age boy named Christopher Baker, whose father owns a ranch outside of town where Monica boarded her horse. The Baker kid said he gave Monica money for the procedure. The girl rented a room for a couple of days. A few days after the abortion, Monica called and said she'd developed a bad infection and had to stay another week longer for follow up health checks and she needed more money." Lindsey thumbed through several pages. "The autopsy backed up the infection. She didn't want to return to St Cloud and go to a local doctor because her parents knew everyone in town and she was afraid the word would get out.

"The Baker boy borrowed money from everyone he knew and mailed her fifteen hundred dollars. We don't consider the boy a suspect, as of yet. He seemed to be leveling with us. We checked with the people he borrowed money from, and they confirmed his story. Plus, the address where he claimed he mailed the money checked out and the landlord verified that Monica was staying there. She also said the girl seemed respectable and stayed in her room without visitors and barely left. The Baker kid seemed genuine. Plus, he wears size nine shoes, not eleven." Lindsey looked down at his notes. "Black wool fibers were found on the bodies of all three victims. They were the type you would expect from a knit hat. Also, other black fibers were found, most likely from a lightweight sweat suit or jacket. In addition, a fine white powder, consistent with the type used inside surgical gloves, was present at all three scenes. Therefore, we probably will never get a fingerprint on this guy. An assortment of hairs have been collected, but are inconsequential at the moment."

Lindsey eyed Sharon. "Agent Cross. Do you have anything to add?"

Sharon remained sitting this time. Her expression was hard as she met each of their eyes. "I believe the man we are looking for was abandoned by his mother. We know Amy abandoned her baby, Susan James gave hers up for adoption, and Monica had an abortion. In this man's eyes, these are all forms of abandonment and therefore, these women remind him of his mother. Every step he takes during the murder is evidence of this.

"Killers often choose alleys because they are secluded. But I believe in this man's case, an alley is symbolic. He chooses it because it sub-consciously represents a birth canal." She noticed a few snickers, especially, from Patterson. She quickly continued before it got out of hand. "Think about it. An alley is a dark, private passage. Each time he kills a mother, he chooses this location to rewrite history. As a child, he was left helpless and vulnerable. But now, as a strong grown man, he is in control."

They still didn't look convinced. Lindsey seemed more interested in the tiled floor than what she was saying.

"He not only hates his mother because she abandoned him. He hates her because he thinks she was a prostitute. We can be sure his mother had long dark hair, wore heavy eye make-up and revealing clothes. This is evident by the appearance of all three of his victims.

"Then there is another dimension to his ritual. He props the corpse up against a trashcan in a very precise manner. Centered. Almost framed by the can. Like a bizarre work of art. He exposes her guilt to the world and abstractly reveals his painful story at the same time...a story he has possibly never verbalized." She paused.

"In addition to this, I think there is another component that pushed him over the edge. When his mother left him, I believe he suffered extreme abuse by whoever became his guardian. He went through torture and he blames all of it on his mother.

"Despite his abnormal thinking, there is a side of him that is highly intelligent and organized. He does considerable research. He starts with the victim's history. He uses a computer adeptly, a hacker of sorts. He knows how to access sites like abortion clinics and adoption centers. This is where he finds his victims. Then he stalks them. If they don't fit the physical description, he eliminates them from his list. If they meet both background requirements and physical characteristics, but fail the personality traits, he will not exclude them if his ideal isn't readily available. Instead, he will improvise. Alter their appearances as he did with Monica."

She glanced again at Lindsey who now stared at her. "If this man is married, his wife will be the complete opposite of his victims. Perhaps a blonde or redhead, whose character is beyond reproach. He will treat her with tremendous respect, even during times when his obsession is building. Now, on the other hand, he might have a girlfriend who actually fits the description of the victim. He may alternate between being civil and violent without much warning. He'll often refer to her as a whore...or more likely in this case, as trash. Also, he knows that some day when the timing is right, he will kill her, too." She turned to Lindsey and nodded slightly, indicating she was finished.

Lindsey scanned the room. Some of the men kept their eyes down at the papers in their hands, to conceal their grins. Others were watching for his reaction. He decided to appear neutral. "When you are interviewing suspects, find out as much as you can regarding their past and keep these theories in mind." He turned to his female assistant. "Anything else, Agent Cross?"

"No. That should be enough for everyone to digest. At least for now."

CHAPTER 5

Unable to ignore the incessant knocking, Carol reluctantly opened her door and found Debbie on her doorstep. Carol tried in vain to transform her frown to a smile. Disheveled hair plastered her face and framed her swollen, white-circled eyes. Pillowcase creases etched her cheek.

Debbie clasped her hand over her mouth. "Oh gosh, you're having a migraine. I wish I'd have known. I wouldn't have come over. Go back to bed and I'll stop by to see you tomorrow."

"No, you've come all this way. Besides, the worse is over." She wobbled on her way to the sofa. "We can visit for a few minutes." She sat down carefully. "I've been in bed all day. What time is it?"

Debbie glanced at her watch. "Six-thirty. Are you sure you don't want me to leave?"

"No. I'll tell you when I need to go back to bed." Carol gestured toward the sofa.

"Okay." Debbie sat down. "I wanted to make sure you were all right and if you wanted me to go with you when you visit John?"

"That's not necessary, but it's very kind of you to offer." She laid her head back against the sofa. "I wish Allen had your compassion."

Debbie hesitated. "Allen doesn't handle things like this very well. I don't know why. Sometimes he just seems...." She lowered her eyes to her hands. "I'm sorry. I don't want to talk badly about him."

"Don't worry about it. I know how he is." Carol reached back and massaged a muscle spasm at the base of her skull. "I feel terrible not offering you anything. Feel free to make a cup of coffee. I've got cookies in the jar on the counter, if you'd like something to go with it."

"No, I'm wired. I've been drinking coffee all day. And I sure don't need the cookies."

Carol sighed. "I hope Allen isn't pressuring you to diet again. That just makes matters worse."

Debbie's eyes glistened with tears. "Actually, he doesn't even mention it anymore." She stood up. "Excuse me." She rushed to the bathroom.

Carol sighed. She remembered the bubbly girl she'd met on the night of Allen's prom; eyes sparkled, hopeful of the future; her conversation was witty and animated. But time and circumstance had changed her. The loss of the baby had been bad enough, but Allen's lack of support and subsequent rejection destroyed her spirit. Though Debbie went through the motions of her former self, her eyes betrayed her. Carol was ashamed of Allen. What a cruel irony to have two inflicted sons: One, kind and sensitive, who could have been a wonderful husband, had it not been for his devastating illness; the other, mean and self-centered, but capable of charming everyone in his path.

Debbie returned. "You look like you're in deep thought."

Carol opened weary eyes. "Guess I was." She studied her for a moment. "If you ever need to talk about anything...even Allen, please don't hesitate. I just want you to know I'm here for you. You're like a daughter to me. I can tell you're unhappy. You shouldn't keep things bottled up."

Debbie's eyes filled again.

"Is Allen still coming home late every night?" She asked.

Debbie nodded. "And sometimes he takes off in the middle of the night when he thinks I'm sleeping."

"Don't you ever ask for an explanation?"

"Not anymore." She wiped her eyes with the back of her hand and stood up. "Listen, I've taken up enough of your time. You don't need to be worrying about me at a time like this," she said. "You better get back to bed. I'm going to get out of your hair. Let me know if there's anything I can do to help."

"Thanks, honey, I appreciate it." Carol walked her to the door and gave her a hug.

Behind the teller station the next day, Carol's hands shook as she counted, then recounted the money several times before stuffing it into an envelope. Just before handing it to the customer, she saw the transaction slip still sitting on the counter. She clumsily reopened the envelope and slipped it in with the cash. Apologizing to the customer, she felt like a newly hired employee, awkward and uncertain of procedures.

She felt ten years older; she could almost feel the unhealthy pallor on her face and the look of defeat in her heavy-lidded eyes. She watched the clock all morning. When lunch break finally came, she hurried out the door with her co-worker and friend, Linda.

Seated in a booth at Robin's Gourmet Restaurant, both women ordered fancy omelets with sourdough toast. While Carol took small bites, Linda ate with gusto. Linda approached everything in life the way she ate. Short and thin, she moved as if faced with a life or death deadline. She had the metabolism of a hummingbird. Her sun-streaked hair and pixie face, along with her vivacious and contagious personality, attracted men like a magnet.

"I'm glad you're back." She dabbed the corners of her mouth with a napkin. "I hate eating alone. Everybody else had the early lunch break last week so here I sat...all by myself, looking like a total loser." She stuffed a piece of bread in her mouth and chewed hastily. "I'm so glad John is back. I know how worried you were."

Carol nodded. Each time she swallowed, she felt the food plunk in her empty stomach. "John was in rough shape, but I talked to his doctor this morning. He told me he's improving, but he asked me not to visit. John was overexcited when I was there and it only made matters worse."

Linda studied her for a moment. "You shouldn't have come to work today. You look terrible."

"Yeah I know. I hate being seen in public, but I have to make money. By the time I start looking like my old self again, I'll be due for the next headache."

"Don't even say that. It's bad juju." She looked down at Carol's bruised hand. "What in the world happened there?"

Carol shrugged her shoulders. "I don't remember. Must have happened while I was having the migraine. Probably hit it against the wall or something." Carol averted her eyes.

Linda shook her head. "You've got so much to deal with."

"I can handle it," Carol snapped. "What do you say we talk about something a little more cheerful."

"Okay." Linda glanced toward the foyer. Her eyes suddenly sparkled. "Well now, there's a cheerful subject! See that guy who just walked in?"

Carol turned to look.

"He's been coming in every day this week. Is he gorgeous or what? I haven't been able to keep my eyes off him." She took another bite of her food then said, "I'm sorry for getting off track. We started talking about John. Maybe this time it won't take as long for him to recuperate. Will he be staying with you again?"

"Yes. And while I'm at work, he'll be at the day-center."

"I don't know how you do it. It's a wonder you've managed to keep your sanity. I'd have lost mine a long time ago." She poured sugar into her iced-tea and stirred so vigorously, a liquid tornado formed in her glass.

"He'd do the same for me." Carol looked down at her plate, and picked at her food with a fork.

"I don't doubt that one bit. He's a super kid." Linda chuckled. "Listen to me calling John a kid! He's my age, isn't he?"

"Yes, thirty-five."

Linda rose a bit from her chair, trying to see over the counter. It presently blocked her view from the good-looking man who sat in the foyer, waiting for a table. "That hostess is going to keep him over there as long as she can. Look at her. Could she possibly be any more obvious?" Linda rolled her eyes. "Anyway, back to your situation. I wish you had a little more freedom. It'd be nice if we could go out together. Catch some movies. Maybe even hit some clubs. Wouldn't that be great?" Her eyes were as effervescent as her chatter. She paused to guzzle her drink. "I'm going to talk to Allen one of these days and set him straight. He needs to start lending you a hand." She smiled. "Then we can par'tee."

Carol frowned. "Linda, in the first place, I am too old to par'tee, as you put it. And, in the second place, you'd be wasting your time trying to talk Allen into helping."

"What's wrong with him anyway?" Linda's eyes drifted from Carol to the foyer and back again.

Carol shrugged. "He's a paradox." She looked off to the side. "Don't turn around, but Mr. Gorgeous is being led to the booth right across from ours and he's looking your way."

Linda leaned toward Carol, her eyes wide. "Are you serious? Does my hair look okay? I mean it was windy outside. It didn't get messed up, did it?" She quickly scrunched the bouncy curls at the back of her head. "What about my lipstick? Did it come off while I was eating?"

"You look fine. Besides, he wouldn't be looking at you like that if you didn't." Carol snickered. "I think I'll go over and tell him to ask you out and get it over with." Carol pushed her chair away from the table.

Linda grabbed Carol's wrist. "Don't you dare!" Linda's eyes maximized to full enlargement. "Maybe you have lost your mind, after all!"

Carol grinned, "Relax, I was just kidding."

"That's a relief." Linda casually glanced his way. The man gave her an immediate smile and she returned it. She whispered through gritted teeth. "See, I don't need your help. I know the procedure. I ought to. I've played this game enough to be a pro. By next week, he and I will have already slept together and broken up. No sense in bothering with all the preliminaries. It all ends up the same way, no matter what. Might as well enjoy the moment, right?"

Carol shook her head and smiled.

"What? You know I'm telling the truth. If you don't have big expectations, you're never disappointed." Linda returned to her food.

Carol barely moved her lips. "He's coming to the table. Do you want me to leave?"

Linda swallowed quickly and dabbed her lips with the napkin. "Of course not. Stick around, you might learn something."

"Hello, ladies." He looked even better close up. He turned to Linda. "I hope I'm not intruding. I saw you eating alone this week and was beginning to think we had something in common. I'm new to the area and haven't had a chance to make friends."

"Oh no, I've lived here all my life." She nodded toward Carol. "My best friend took a few days off, that's all. We usually dine together."

"I'm sure you're glad to have her back." Perfect dimples followed a magnificent smile. Pure white teeth flashed, contrasting against his tanned complexion. "Why don't you sit down and join us?" Linda pointed to the chair next to her.

"If you're sure you don't mind."

"Not at all," both said, almost in unison.

"Well, thank you." He pulled out a chair. "I hate eating alone, so I'd already decided to ask you to join me, before coming in here today."

"You must have been disappointed when I showed up," Carol said.

His eyes twinkled. "Quite the contrary. What more could a man ask for than the company of two lovely ladies?" He turned and motioned the waiter to bring his food to their table. "My name is Anthony Pinto."

"Nice to meet you." Linda flashed a flirtatious smile. "I'm Linda and this is Carol."

"It's nice to meet you both."

Linda did the fluttery thing with her eyes that she

reserved for handsome men. Carol had seen it often.

"How long have you worked at the bank?"

"How did you know I worked there?" Linda pressed her palm against her upper chest, with practiced flair.

He sat back in his chair, grinning fabulously. "I'm a stalker."

She laughed.

"Actually, I was waiting at the red light a couple days ago when I saw you get in your car. Something about the way you whizzed out of the parking lot told me you weren't just a customer."

Linda forgot about the food on her plate. "Carol works there, too. I guess we're both going to be at that bank until the day we die or get fired. Whichever comes first."

Carol picked at her omelet. "What do you do for a living, Anthony?"

He smiled. "I'm in real estate. My family bought up cow pastures right before Disney announced their intentions. They purchased the land for peanuts and we're selling it now at a tidy profit."

"Lucky you." Linda's eyes devoured every inch of his face.

Carol glanced at her watch, then set her napkin on the table. "I hate to rush off, but I'm really not feeling very well."

Linda reached over and placed her fingertips on Anthony's forearm. "She's just getting over a migraine."

"I've got about a half hour left before I have to get back to work, so I'm going to make the most of that time resting in my car," Carol said. "It was nice meeting you, Anthony. Hope to see you again."

He stood up and shook her hand gently. "I'm counting on it." His dark eyes were intense. "I hope you feel better soon."

"Thank you." Carol felt awkward, and as ugly as the bride of Frankenstein. She slid her hand from his and told them to enjoy their lunch, then turned to leave. She felt heat in her face as she walked away.

With Paul's report and Heather's notes and suggestions, Allen performed well at the meeting. However, he was far from feeling comfortable. Making eye contact with Paul Shield had become a Herculean task. Allen saw him as a broken link in the chain of his admirers. Normally, when Allen knew someone was wise to him, he'd distance himself immediately. But, Paul was too valuable to cast aside.

It didn't matter that Heather had seen glimpses of his true self. Allen learned early in their relationship that she liked his ruthless and deceitful nature. The worse he acted around her, the more she seemed to want him.

However, the rest of his business acquaintances were different. Being forced to resume a normal relationship with someone, who'd made this sort of discovery, was almost beyond his scope. He contemplated his coping skills, when Heather peeked through his office door at quitting time and winked. "See ya tomorrow, Mr. Randolph."

He motioned her to enter.

She shut the door, and walked closer to his desk.

"Hey, I know you expected me to stop over tonight, but I've got a bad headache coming on." He lied.

"Oh great." She placed her hands on her hips. "So you're standing me up."

"Look, I don't like it anymore than you do. I was looking forward to it too. But I'd be lousy company, believe me." His eyes twinkled. "Forgive me?"

"I'll think about it." She pouted. "You know I don't like being disappointed."

"Hey, it's only one night. I promise I'll make up for it tomorrow. You've got my word."

"Oh yeah, like your word should mean something to me. Actions, speak volumes. Words just tickle my ears."

"By tomorrow night, you'll see more action than you can handle. That is if you stop giving me a hard time." He smirked.

As she walked toward him, he stopped her with his hand. "No, there aren't going to be any more incidents like what happened this morning."

She shrugged her shoulders. "Well, Paul seemed fine earlier, like nothing ever happened."

His brows knit into a frown. "I don't know. I'm still concerned. We need to watch it."

After work, he stopped by the gym, worked out for an hour and then headed home. When he arrived, Debbie was not in sight. He removed his jacket, loosened his tie, and poured himself a tall glass of scotch.

The look in Paul Shield's eyes followed him home. He hated it. How was he going to work with this man?

He gulped his drink. Before long he relaxed, and his situation gradually seemed less troublesome. He quickly refilled his glass.

He heard Debbie turn on the shower. The sound curiously comforted him. After pondering his reaction, he realized the cause. Debbie was a refuge, dependable, never making demands and loyal beyond expectations. Despite the way he'd treated her, he'd never come home to an empty house. During the early years, he looked forward to returning home from work. The smell of dinner in the oven and the sound of Debbie's cheerful conversation provided an oasis from life's pressures. He ached for those days when she considered him perfect and he thought she was beautiful.

Their marriage had meant everything to him. He wished things hadn't changed and that her eyes hadn't replaced adoration with disenchantment. He sighed deeply, drained the glass and refilled it.

Debbie would be surprised that he was home earlier than usual. It had been a long time. He reminisced about school days, when he and Debbie longed to be together. He had thought she was everything he ever wanted. As he rested his head on the back of the chair, he recalled the first time he held her in his arms. He smiled as he sipped his drink and remembered that night. The fragrance of her perfume. How it lingered on his clothes for days afterwards. Just the thought of it resurrected old feelings.

Most of their dreams had come true. As he scanned

the living room with nostalgic eyes, he continued to drink. Good memories abounded in this place now. A desire to recapture the past nudged his heart. It was as if he'd awakened from a long sleep and found his marriage whole and intact.

He slowly swirled the small amount of scotch in his glass. In it, he pictured his wife's pretty face. Suddenly, her weight problem was no longer a barrier and his former aversion was incomprehensible. When his thoughts drifted upstairs to visions of Debbie spraying her neck and wrists with that wonderful perfume, he stood up.

He unbuttoned his shirt as he staggered up the staircase. When she came out of the bathroom, he was laying in bed, calling her to his side. She hesitated for just a moment, then sat down next to him. As his arms encircled her, she forgot former hurts and all misgivings.

The next morning, Allen's head pounded. His dry mouth made swallowing difficult. He hadn't been that drunk since he was a kid. As he slowly remembered what occurred the night before, he felt sick. He glanced over at Debbie who slept peacefully beside him. He couldn't believe he'd made love to her. Alcohol definitely altered his judgment. He couldn't let it happen again. In order to have a normal marriage, he'd have to get drunk every night. It wasn't worth it.

He quietly slipped out of bed and headed for the bathroom. He swallowed a couple of aspirins, dressed, and then left without having to face her. By the time he got to the office, he'd put it behind him and was feeling better. He drifted through one appointment after another; by lunchtime, he was eager to get away. As he rose to leave, someone knocked on his door.

"Hi, how you doing, Don?" A big smile masked Allen's impatience.

Don smiled self-consciously. "Oh, pretty good."

"What can I do for you?"

Don lowered his eyes to the floor.

"Sit down." Allen pointed to a chair. "Would you like a cup of coffee? Got some fresh doughnuts too."

Don shook his head. He took a seat. "Thanks, but I just had lunch."

Allen checked his watch. "Oh yeah, it is about that time." He leaned back in his chair, raised his arms, and stretched. "So what can I do for you, buddy?"

"Well." Don blushed slightly. "I'm not very good at this."

"Hey, you can tell me anything, Don. We're all family here. What is it?"

Don's mouth twitched inside a smile. "Janice and I have had a lot of medical bills since she came down with Lupus. Of course, the insurance covers a good deal of it, but the co-pay alone is still killing us...and the prescriptions..."

"I heard she was sick. I'm really sorry." Allen got up from his chair. "I'll meet with Mr. Towers and see what I can do about getting you a raise. You're very important to me and this company."

Don sighed with relief. "Thanks, Allen. That means a lot to me."

"No problem." Allen extended his hand. "I'll get back to you as soon as I have an answer."

As Don left, Allen smiled with satisfaction. He felt good about himself. He was sure his boss wouldn't mind giving the guy a token raise. He'd request just enough to show Don he was trying.

Another quick knock at the door and Heather sauntered in. "Hey, you." She smiled as she stepped closer.

Allen waved off her advance again. "We've got to chill, remember?"

Heather performed her famous pout. "You're no fun." She studied him for a moment. "Headache go away?"

"Huh?" His eyes squinted. "Oh yeah, still had it this morning, but it's okay now." He glanced at his watch, then turned his attention back to her. "So what's up?"

"I heard something interesting a few minutes ago." She grinned mischievously.

"Yeah, so?"

"Your mom was having lunch with a man yesterday." His eyebrows cramped together.

"Shelly told me. She didn't notice them until your mother got up to leave and he stood up with her and held her hand. Shelly said your mom was blushing."

"Get out of here." Allen laughed uncomfortably.

"I'm serious." Heather put her hands on her hips. "She said the guy was drop-dead gorgeous, too, and young. Early thirties, slicked- back black hair, smoldering dark eyes, and built like there's no tomorrow. She said he gave her the look. You know the kind you're always giving me?"

Allen shook his head and snickered. "You're nuts."

"I'm only repeating what she told me."

"Well, I don't believe it. My mother hasn't been out with anyone since she and my father got divorced."

"You're kidding!"

"It's true. Besides, my mom is in her fifties. Why would she suddenly want to start dating?"

Heather blew him a sexy kiss, then turned to leave. "You think I'm going to stop having boyfriends when I'm in my fifties? I don't think so." She shook her head. "Anyway, believe what you want, but I think your mother's got something going on."

"No way." Allen dismissed her comment with a chuckle.

"Go to Robin's for lunch sometime and see for yourself."

Allen flopped back in his chair and tried to laugh, but nothing came out. He looked at his watch again. One-thirty. His mother's lunch break was over. Maybe tomorrow.

Carol returned home with an Italian sub. When she removed the wrapper, the smell of salami, provolone cheese and raw onions permeated the air. Her stomach growled with hunger. No sooner did she set the sub on a plate and was about to take her first bite, when the phone rang.

Linda's voice rang staccato. "Anthony called! I just got off the phone with him."

Carol slipped out of her shoes, and sat down on the sofa. "So what did he have to say?"

"He asked me out. He's taking me to Wolfgang Puck's for dinner." She giggled. "I've got to admit, I'm a little nervous about the date. I've never been out with a guy who's prettier than I am. He is so good looking, it's scary. I just can't figure out what in the world he's doing wasting time in St. Cloud. He should be in Hollywood making movies."

"He's definitely not hard to look at, that's for sure. But aren't you rushing things? You don't even know this guy."

"Yeah, yeah, thank you Mom."

Reminded of the age difference between them, Carol said, "Ouch!"

"I'm sorry." Linda laughed. "If anyone is guilty of playing "Mom" in our relationship, it's me."

"True." Carol smiled. "So what are you wearing?"

"Something black and silky of course. I bought a great dress two weeks ago for just such an occasion and I've been exercising and lifting weights so I'm fit and ready to go."

Carol groaned. "You're hopeless."

Hoping to keep his mother from spotting him, Allen asked for a back-cornered booth in Robin's. According to his watch, she was five minutes late. He ate slowly, observing every man that walked through the door. So far, none seemed to meet Heather's description.

Finally Carol walked in and sat at a booth towards the front, with her back to Allen. After a few minutes passed without a trace of the mystery man, Allen wondered if Heather had lied.

Just before he asked for his check, a man walked in whose presence seemed to fill the room. Several waitresses and female customers turned to watch him. Allen resented the attention the man received. He wasn't used to sharing.

The man ignored the commotion he'd started and headed toward Carol. Allen couldn't see her expression, but he figured it was reciprocal, since the man seemed very much at ease when they exchanged greetings. Allen watched, in disbelief, wishing he could hear their conversation.

Anthony looked down at Carol, his dimples already at work. "Well, you look like you're feeling better."

"I'm getting there." She ran her fingers through her hair.

"Where's your beautiful friend today?"

"She's sick. She called this morning and told me to say hello if I saw you."

"Sorry to hear she's not feeling well." He grinned. "I hope I didn't keep her out too late."

"No. She came down with a bad cold."

He raised his eye brows, "That's a shame." He motioned for the waiter. "Have you ordered yet?"

Carol nodded.

Without hesitation, he sat down across from her. After placing his order, he leaned back against the cushioned booth. "So, tell me. How long have you known Linda?"

"Ever since she started working at the bank. I guess it's been at least twelve years."

"She's a fascinating woman. Very attractive...and she has a great sense of humor. I was surprised she'd never been married. I'd have thought someone would have grabbed her up years ago."

"Linda's a free spirit."

"She said as much last night. She seems very honest. I like that. I really enjoyed our date."

"I have reason to believe she did, too."

Anthony's face lit up. "Well, that's good news." He hesitated while the waiter placed a napkin and silverware on the table before him. "Linda told me all about you. I'm very impressed."

Carol blushed. "What in the world did she say?"

"Relax. Everything was very complimentary."

"Such as?"

"She told me about your dedication and loyalty toward your family, for one thing. I admire that trait so much." He paused. "How is John? Is he doing better?"

Carol frowned, puzzled. "Yes, he's improving. I saw him a few minutes ago."

"Good. I'm glad to hear it." He paused. "Linda said you've sacrificed your whole life for him. Do you ever feel resentful?"

Carol's mouth dropped suddenly. "Of course not!" Her voice blurted. She looked around to see if anyone had noticed. Lowering the volume, she leaned forward. "No offense, Anthony, but I don't make a practice of discussing my personal life with people I hardly know. And I'm a little aggravated that Linda told you so much about me."

"Forgive me." He apologized. "I didn't mean to offend you. I liked you right off the bat. And when I like someone, I have a tendency to want to know all about them. Please don't blame Linda, I pried it out of her. She wasn't gossiping, if that's what you think. She's just proud of you."

Carol blushed. She wasn't good at this.

"Linda thinks the world of you. That's all."

She shook her head. "Well, I don't know why."

"I think you underestimate yourself."

As the redness on her cheeks deepened, she averted his eyes.

"I can see I've made you uncomfortable." He waved his hands to dismiss the subject.

They sat quietly for a few minutes. Anthony casually looked around the room. Carol rummaged through her purse. Soon, the waiter returned with their plates. They ate for awhile until the silence between them grew blatantly awkward. Carol broke the standoff. "I guess I've been ungracious. I'm sorry."

"Then, you're not angry with me?" One dimple showed a second before the other.

Carol smiled shyly. "Well, no. I'm just a little confused. I'm not used to this sort of attention."

"That's unfortunate." Anthony's warm eyes sparkled. He reached for her hand and gently squeezed it.

Carol withdrew slowly, her embarrassment reheating her cheeks.

"Are you mad?"

"No. Just uncomfortable."

He held his hand up to silence her. "I've got to stop being so nosey and demonstrative."

"And I've got to stop being so touchy."

As his mother and her companion talked, Allen sat at his table, his eyes fixed in a cold blue stare. He couldn't believe what was going on. They were obviously having a very intense conversation. Thoughts raced across his mind. What was wrong with her? Couldn't she see he was a con man? Allen recognized all the signals loud and clear. But what he couldn't figure out was what the guy was after. It wasn't sex. A guy like that could have any woman he wanted. Besides, this man was young enough to be her son. So what was he after? It couldn't be money or advancement. Maybe he was a bank robber and thought she could give him some inside information about where she worked. But his mother was just a teller. How could she possibly know anything that would be useful to him?

As he ruled out that possibility, he thought of a worse scenario. What if he actually preferred older women and genuinely wanted a legitimate relationship with her? The thought of that sickened him. The more he watched, the angrier he became. His lips pressed into a fine line. This was all he needed. One more problem to add to his list.

When they finished eating, Anthony and Carol walked to her car. Allen cringed when the man placed his hand on his mother's back just before she got in. As soon as Carol backed out of her parking place, Allen got in his Lincoln Continental. He followed Anthony, who headed down the highway in a gleaming new Lexus. Anthony stopped at an apartment complex, he walked up a flight of stairs, removed his keys, and unlocked the door to his suite. After the door closed, Allen sat in the parking lot for several minutes. A mailman stuffed envelopes in the boxes on the first floor. After he turned the corner, Allen got out, walked over to Anthony's mailbox, and pulled out some letters. A smug expression covered his face. He knew the man's name and where he lived.

CHAPTER 6

Lindsey spied his partner as soon as he entered the bar. On the stool to Patterson's right sat a huge man wearing a sweaty tank top. His arms were as large as thighs and the rolls around his middle looked like truck tires. Two men stood around the stool to his left. They bumped and shoved as they reached for drinks and sparred with each other whenever a pretty woman walked past. Patterson had just taken an elbow to the ear, when Lindsey walked up.

"Man, this just ain't gonna get it." Patterson held the palm of his hand over the top of his beer glass. "If I get pushed one more time, I'm gonna dump my drink on somebody's head."

Lindsey nodded toward the big man on his friend's right. "Including the Suma wrestler's?"

Patterson stood, and tugged up his pants. "Especially his."

"Come on." Lindsey nodded toward the back of the room. "Let's take that spot before you get hurt."

They maneuvered around the crowd and squeezed into their seats at a lopsided table. Patterson checked out a blonde who stood next to him, her hip only inches from his face. "I got to admit, the ambiance is much better on this side of the room."

"I'm glad you approve. Maybe you'll stop complaining."

"Yeah, yeah, yeah." He nodded in time to the music. "So what's up? How'd it go in San Francisco?"

Lindsey frowned. "Met with Amy Rockwell's mother. The girl had a pattern of prostitution. Other than that, we didn't turn up anything significant. A waste of time. I don't want to talk about it"

Patterson's eyes lit up. "I think I know what's wrong with you. Your anger represents the birth canal, which in turn represents the person responsible for your...shall we say, cranky, mood."

"Shut up." Lindsey lit a cigarette.

"I take it Agent Hocus Pocus is driving you up the proverbial wall. As I predicted, I might add."

Lindsey fanned out the match. "You got that right. And this case is going nowhere because of it."

"Then get me back in the loop. I've been feeling like a messenger boy." He scrunched his shoulders. "We'll get this thing wrapped up in no time." His eyes followed the blonde as she walked away, then returned to Lindsey. "You know what I mean?"

"You're right," Lindsey said. "I can't stop her interference, but I sure as hell can ignore her. It's time you and I get down to business."

"Now you are talking, my man!" Patterson tapped his fingers on the table. "This calls for a celebration. In a minute, I'm gonna ask some lucky lady to dance."

"You dance?" Lindsey laughed.

"Hell, yeah. Women like that crap. Where you been all your life?"

Lindsey shook his head. "How about that one?" He pointed to a red head in a two piece black spandex outfit that showed her perfect six-pack abdominal muscles.

"Too butch."

"Okay, how about her?" He gestured toward a girl in a short skirt, whose eyes seemed mesmerized as she gyrated to the beat.

"Too home-spun."

"Home–spun?" Lindsey shook his head. "For a little guy, you sure are picky."

"Little guy?" He retaliated with the neck thing. "I ain't had no complaints lately."

"That's because you ain't had no dates."

"No, no, my man. That ain't true." He smirked. "I went out with Tess from Central Communications last week."

Lindsey grinned. "You've been seeing her?"

"You better believe it." He winked. "I can hook you up with her girlfriend, too. Just say the word."

"Forget it." Lindsey scowled.

"What are ya, on an abstinence marathon or what?"

"Don't worry about it," he snapped.

"Don't worry about it, he says." Patterson shook his head. "I think her girlfriend would be just what the doctor ordered. You know what I mean?"

Lindsey stood up and threw a five-dollar bill on the table. "What I need is some sleep."

After a month passed, John went home. Carol took the day off from work to get him settled. He regained some weight, was clean and neatly dressed. However, his medication dosage was very high and the side effects were painfully apparent. John's eyes were wide and vacant. He stared at her passively, answering her questions but lending little effort at making a conversation.

"Come on, John, it's lunch time." She motioned him to join her at the table.

He walked very slowly. As he approached, his arms were stiff and bounced in unison, rather than swinging in the normal fashion.

"It's tuna," she said.

He nodded, took a bite, then chewed with his mouth open. Carol turned her eyes away. She swallowed with difficulty. "Dr. Walters thinks we'll be able to decrease your dosages soon. You'll feel a lot better then."

As he chewed, mayonnaise accumulated at the corners of his mouth.

"Linda is dating a new man. She thinks he's wonderful. And it's lasted for a month now, which is longer than I gave it at the beginning." She picked at her food. "Anyway, I'm so glad to have you back. I really missed you."

"I missed you too." He glanced at her for a moment, then retreated to the empty place from which he'd come.

Carol fought back tears. "Listen, after you're feeling better, let's go away for a weekend. Maybe up north to Allen and Debbie's cabin. The leaves will be changing and it'll be beautiful."

"Okay." Every few minutes his tongue protruded from his mouth, another side effect of the medicine. He lifted his sandwich up in a mechanical manner and took a bite. The mayonnaise dripped from his chin.

Carol handed him a napkin.

John ignored it. "Is she sleeping with him?"

"What?" She frowned. "Oh, you mean Linda? Well, I don't know. She hasn't really said. But you know, even if she is, times have changed, John. It's become acceptable." She took a bite of her sandwich and wondered how to change the subject.

"Acceptable to who? The world maybe, but not to God."

"Oh I agree, honey." She hoped he wasn't going to step up on his soapbox again. The psychiatrist told her long ago that his obsession with religion was indicative of his disease and she felt uncomfortable whenever the subject emerged. Besides, she'd stopped believing in God years ago.

She patted his hand. "Well, don't worry about it. It's her problem."

"She's your friend." His voice was flat.

"True, but she has a mind and will of her own." Carol set her napkin on the table, and pushed back her chair. "Everyone has been asking for you. Mrs. Murray wants you to come downstairs to see her dog's new litter of puppies. They're only four weeks old and they're so cute."

He nodded slightly. "Has Pastor Davis asked about me?"

Carol shrugged. "I haven't seen him." Her voice turned cool.

"I know you don't like him anymore, but I can't remember why."

"I was afraid he was doing you more harm than good."

"Oh." He looked like he was observing her through a clouded glass.

Carol stood and gathered up their dishes. She didn't want to get on this again. At the peak of her frustration, she blamed the pastor for making things worse. She'd known the man for years, attended his church and admired him. Actually, he was the one person she could always count on. After she and her husband divorced, it was the pastor and the congregation who helped financially.

When John got sick, she became furious with God and at the pastor. Since Dr. Walters advised her to keep John's religious interests within bounds, she finally cut ties with the pastor. To this day, Pastor Davis still waved and smiled whenever he saw her. She went out of her way to avoid him as much as possible. She wished she could forget about how much he had helped all of them.

John didn't get up. He seemed satisfied just watching his mother in the kitchen.

Carol glanced over her shoulder. They locked eyes for a second. She searched, hoping to find something that reflected human emotion inside those once bright, eyes. She was disappointed.

Debbie knocked on the door.

Carol smiled when she saw her. "Well, hi, come on in."

Debbie smoothed down her hair. "Looks like it's going to storm. The wind is really kicking up." She looked over at John. "Hi! Welcome home. I baked you an apple pie. I know it's your favorite."

"Hello, Debbie." He sat on the couch, his eyes cast downward. "Thanks."

"Are you feeling any better? I've been praying for you."

John nodded. "I guess I'm feeling better. I don't remember much, so I can't really make a comparison," he said. "But thanks for your prayers."

"You're welcome." Compassion warmed her smile. "So, do you want a slice?"

"Maybe later, I'm kind of tired. I think I'm going to lie down for awhile." He stood up.

"Oh really? I was hoping we could visit for awhile. But if you're tired, go on. I understand. We can do it some other time."

Carol shrugged as John walked into his room. She pointed toward the kitchen table. "Come on, let's sit down and have some coffee with that pie."

"No coffee for me. Do you have any milk?"

"Milk? I can't believe you're refusing a cup of coffee. What's the deal?" Carol asked as she opened the refrigerator.

"Well..." Debbie hesitated. "Pregnant women are suppose to stay away from caffeine."

Carol's mouth dropped as she spun around.

"I know, I know." Her face grew taut with tension.

"Are you absolutely sure?" She handed her the glass.

"I'm two weeks late, and every pregnancy test I've taken turned out positive."

Carol sat down at the kitchen table and motioned her to do the same. "Have you told Allen?"

She shook her head. "I haven't been able to muster up the courage." She sipped her milk. "I know he's going to explode."

Carol sighed. "Well, he's just going to have to accept it, that's all. I mean an abortion is out of the question."

"Absolutely," Debbie said firmly. Her trembling lip gave way to a mournful cry.

Carol reached over and hugged her. "Come on. Try to get hold of yourself. It's not good for you or the baby. I know you dread having to tell him. Do you want me to do it?"

"Oh no!" She pulled back. "If he ever found out I told you first, he'd be furious. Please don't tell him or anyone else."

"Okay, I promise I won't."

Debbie wiped her tears with her napkin and blew her nose. "I'm sorry, I know I shouldn't be laying this on you. I'm putting you in an awkward position. Plus, you have enough on your hands right now. It's just that I don't have anyone else to talk to."

"I told you to talk to me any time and I meant it. I feel more like a mother to you than I do to Allen. He's practically cut me out of his life."

"He's just all caught up with his career. He's in a world of his own."

"Yes, and his family isn't part of it." Carol shook her head. "I know things have been very difficult for you."

"Worse than you can imagine."

"I am so sorry. Sometimes I don't even know who he is. He's not like me or John. He's getting more and more like his father every day."

"It's been awful. He's had nothing to do with me. Then one night last month, he got drunk and one thing lead to another. I was so shocked, I didn't think to tell him to use protection. I'd gone off the pill months before, because I didn't think I'd never need them again. Also, I hoped I'd lose some weight once I stopped taking them. As it turned out, I didn't lose a pound and now I'm pregnant." Debbie blew her nose. "And I'm sure he has a mistress. With all his late hours, I'd have to be an idiot to think otherwise. What else could he be doing?"

Carol shook her head. "Have you ever considered leaving him?"

Debbie dabbed her eyes. "Yes. In fact, I've been trying to work up the nerve to do it."

"Why have you waited so long?"

Debbie shrugged. "I don't know."

"Do you mind if I'm candid?"

"Of course not."

"I think Allen has made you insecure."

Debbie stared straight ahead. "That's putting it mildly."

"Do you still love him?

Debbie lowered her eyes. "I don't know how I feel anymore...other than desperate and stupid."

"You can change things. Being alone isn't all that bad. I've managed just fine."

Debbie wiped her eyes. "But you're a strong person."

"Well, you're going to have to learn to be strong, too. Not just for your sake, but for the baby's as well."

"I know that. And I want to be happy and I know as long as I stay in this marriage, I'm going to be miserable. I want to be happy about this pregnancy, too. I'm not going to let him spoil things."

"You and your baby could start a whole new life together."

Debbie wiped her eyes again. "Yes. And we can do it

without Allen. Even if he is happy about me being pregnant, it still won't change the way he feels about me. So why should I stay with him?"

"That's right," Carol said. "You deserve a husband who loves you."

As he stood at the window, it started again. Adrenaline released and pumped, then traveled to and invigorated that secret portion of his brain. In an attempt to ignore it, he watched the torrential rain strike the road below and turn puddles into creeks of whitewater. The wind undulated and lifted the mist from the road in erratic patterns. Pedestrians wrestled their useless umbrellas as they ran for cover. Thunderclouds rushed in from the west and formed high, black peaks. The atmosphere took on an eerie shade of greenish-yellow. Lightning drew nearer. A gust hit a small trashcan, setting its contents into flight. Papers twirled in a circular fashion almost as high as his second floor window, then abruptly dispersed and spiraled toward the ground, blocks away.

The storm didn't take his mind off the urge. It reminded him of it. It too, started low, spun out of control, and wouldn't stop until it peaked and detonated.

It had been over a month now and it was definitely building again. In the first stages, he was able to keep it under control. But as it grew, it took on a life of its own. His power would ultimately yield to this force within. The urge was always victorious.

He hurried to his desk and tapped his fingers as he waited to get on line. It was time to begin the process in an intelligent manner. Before the urge became irrational and reckless in its judgement, or lack thereof. He liked good planning and that required thorough research. He had several sights he used religiously. Adoption agencies, the HRS and Women's Family Planning Centers. He accessed their private files without difficulty. He'd compile information and spend the next few days tracking his potential marks. He would choose at least three women who met the requirements. Then he'd follow and record each victim's daily habits, patterns of behavior, who they associated with and when. With this information obtained, he would plan his strategy.

As Allen stared at his computer monitor, the lights flickered from lightning, but he was deep in thought and didn't notice. A quick knock at the door got his attention. Paul Shield walked in. "Sorry for the interruption, but I really need to talk to you." Paul looked down at him.

"Sure, no problem." Allen slid his chair from his desk. "Some storm we're having, huh?"

"Yeah, we're under a tornado warning."

"I'm not surprised." Allen glanced toward the window, then turned back to Paul. "So what's up?"

"I'm having money problems, Allen. I don't want to get into the particulars, but the bottom line is, I need a raise." Paul sat down.

Allen's smile turned into a thin line. "Reviews are coming up in two months, I'm sure I'll be able to take good care of you then."

"I can't wait that long." Paul eyed Allen with uncharacteristic confidence. "I'm sure you could work something out. I heard you did it for Don."

Allen exhaled deeply. Paul's boldness shocked him. He shook his head and attempted a grin. "This is why it's bad policy to make an exception for anyone. Word gets out and before you know it, everybody wants a raise. It's not as easy to arrange as you think. Towers made an exception in Don's case. As I'm sure you know, Don's wife has been sick and they're up to their eyeballs in medical debt. That's why I went out on the limb for him."

"I'd like you to make an exception for me, too. I won't tell anyone. I can be good at keeping my mouth shut...if I want to be." Paul removed a soft piece of cloth from his jacket pocket, then took off his glasses. He slowly polished the lenses.

"What's that suppose to mean?"

Paul looked him in the eye without answering.

Allen studied him. No doubt about it, he thought.

Paul Shield was blackmailing him.

Paul stood up. "When can I expect an answer?"

Allen studied him for several seconds. He considered taking a hard line, then thought better of it. "I'll get back with you tomorrow."

"Okay, I'll be waiting to hear from you." He put on his glasses and left the room.

Allen fumed. "This is just the beginning. That little faggot isn't going to stop with just a raise." Allen knew he had to get Paul under control or there would be no stopping him. There was no way he'd let his affair with Heather become public knowledge. He'd come too far in his career. He'd have to deal with Paul Shield.

Allen returned home, and found Debbie at the kitchen table. Her eyes had acquired an odd expression. He immediately wondered if Paul Shield told her about his involvement with Heather. "What's wrong?" He casually walked over to the sink to get a glass of water.

"You'd better sit down."

"Why?" His heart beat faster and he could feel himself starting to sweat. But his face showed no signs of anxiety.

"I'm pregnant."

Within a second, his mind went from relief to fury and his eyes assaulted her. He slammed the glass on the counter. Water spilled everywhere. "This is all the hell I need right now. As if things weren't bad enough, now this! How could you have let this happen? I thought you were on the pill?"

"I went off the pill a long time ago because there wasn't any reason to stay on it. You do remember the night it happened, don't you? Or were you too drunk?"

His face flushed as he paced. She watched him quietly.

"Why didn't you tell me to use protection?" He pointed his finger at her. "Oh, I know. This was deliberate, wasn't it? You wanted to replace the first baby, so you let yourself get pregnant without even consulting me."

"That's ridiculous."

"Is it?" He stopped in front of her. "I don't think so." He paused. "Did you think this would improve our marriage?"

"No. I've known for years that our marriage is beyond hope. It's a disaster."

He looked her up and down. "And I wonder why."

She turned away and took in a deep breath. "You got turned off with my body and I got turned off with your mind. The important thing is, I've finally fallen out of love with you."

Allen's mouth dropped open slightly. "Where's this coming from?"

"I'm going to take care of myself and the baby. You don't have to be a part of our lives." Her voice was firm. "In fact, I'd prefer it that way."

"Oh really? And how do you plan to support yourself? You haven't worked since I got out of business school."

She snickered. "Because you didn't think it would be good for your precious image. Remember?" She paused. "Besides, you'll be paying child support. And until I finish school and get a decent job, the judge will have you pay alimony too."

Allen wanted to hit her, but refrained. What was he going to do? How was he going to explain this to people? He didn't know how to handle the situation. He needed time to come up with a plan. "I'm going out for a drive to clear my head. You better do something to clear yours, too, while I'm gone."

"My mind has never been clearer."

Allen stared at her in disbelief, then stormed out the door.

Allen headed straight for Heather's apartment. She was dressed in a short red silk bathrobe when she let him in.

"Hey, I thought you said you weren't coming over tonight." She purred.

Allen pushed past her. "Yeah, well I changed my mind," he snapped. "Why are you dressed like that? Expecting someone else?"

"Insecurity is a turn off."

"So is a tramp."

"What?" She hissed. "If that's what you think of me, you can get the hell out of here."

"Shut up." He glanced around the room.

She studied him for a moment. "What's gotten into you?"

"Nothing." Allen headed for the bar. "Don't tell me you're out of scotch?" He rummaged recklessly, knocking bottles together.

"Take it easy, you'll break something. The scotch is down below. For crying out loud, what's going on?"

His hands shook as he poured himself a shot and guzzled it down. "Nothing I can't handle."

"You could have fooled me." Heather walked cat-like to the couch, sat down, and crossed her long legs. "Are you going to tell me about it or what?"

"Paul Shield." He refilled his glass and carried it with him as he paced.

"What about him?"

He stopped in front of her. "He's blackmailing me."

"Are you serious?" She gestured him to sit next to her.

Allen refused. He paced back and forth in front of the sofa. He tipped his glass and swallowed quickly. "If he thinks he's going to manipulate me, he has another thought coming"

"What can you do? It seems to me he has you over the barrel."

"Maybe for the time being, but he's not going to have the upper hand for long."

"What are you thinking about doing?"

"Never mind. I'll handle it."

"Well, then sit down and relax a little?"

He glanced at her, then flopped on the couch.

She put her hand on his thigh. "Why don't we just forget about all that for now. Let's have some fun."

He drained his glass. "I'm not up to it."

She pressed her lips against his ear. "Sure you are."

He pulled away from her. "No! Leave me alone. I'm

not in the mood. There's too much going down."

"Is there something you're not telling me? I mean besides this Shield thing?"

"I'm having problems with Debbie too." He paused. He couldn't let her know his wife was pregnant. She'd freak. "I don't really want to get into the details, but I can tell you this. She's driving me nuts."

"So what's holding up the divorce? I've been waiting for over a year now."

His mouth tightened. "I told you I filed. These things take time."

"How do I know you're telling me the truth? Who is your lawyer?"

"Oh, so now you want to check up on me. You think I'm a liar."

"Think it? I know you're a liar and a damn good one." She laughed. "Look, I'm getting tired of waiting. You're going to have to make a move very soon, or I'm walking." She stood up.

"Nothing like kicking a person when they're down."

"You haven't seen anything yet. I better not find out you've been leading me on."

Allen sprang off the couch. "You women are all alike." He threw his glass against the wall. It splintered into tiny bits.

She jumped up and faced him head on. "You've crossed the line now. Get out of here and stay out!"

He grabbed her arms and squeezed until she gasped. "Don't ever talk to me like that again. Do you hear me?" His mouth turned ugly and his eyes overpowered hers. He could feel her shudder slightly, but her eyes didn't shy away from his. Fighting for composure, he shook his head almost imperceptibly and changed slowly back to himself. "I've got to get out of here." He let go and walked out.

She drew in a deep breath and exhaled loudly. She wobbled to the wet bar. With trembling hands, she poured herself a drink. "I've turned him into a monster. I've got to stop it. No more games," she whispered. "Or history might repeat itself."

CHAPTER

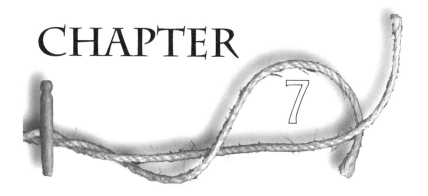

Lindsey drove to the quaint town of Windermere. On the outskirts of town, upscale developments dominated the landscape. The most exclusive, a gated community surrounded by high brick walls, blocked the view of non-residents. Only by air or boat could an outsider get a glimpse of the mansions within. Many athletic stars, including members of the Orlando Magic basketball team, made this their home. Keenly successful entrepreneurs, company CEO's, rock stars, actors, and other famous people also dwelt within these walls. Most residents displayed their wealth through multi-million dollar lakeside houses, complete with giant pools, covered with grand screen enclosures, sometimes spanning entire back yards. Private docks with floating piers dotted the shoreline. Covered boathouses protected made-to-order vessels.

Sara and Lindsey's daughter lived closer to town where the narrow roads remained unpaved in order to maintain the rustic charm of the area. Roads twisted and turned along the edge of the highly prized, scenic Butler Chain-of-Lakes. Small vacant lots in this area toted above two hundred, fifty thousand-dollar price tags. Moderate sized, fix-me-upper houses often went for a half million or more. A small price to pay, in the homeowners' minds, for close proximity and access to one of Florida's most treasured locations.

Fifty per cent of Sara's property consisted of water. The main section of the house was on land, but the family room and screened-in porch, were perched on pillars above the lake. In the middle of a large pond to the right, was a small island. Connected to the house by a floating walkway, it displayed a charming white gazebo. Giving access to the entrance, a wooden bridge crossed over a long pond running parallel with the front of the house. Below, large yellow and orange and white Koi swam in the shade of a weeping willow tree. On the opposite side, the enclosed swimming pool, made private by a jungle of sub-tropical plants, added more length to the sprawling water world estate.

Tom observed from the top of the hill. The knot in his stomach tightened with anger and envy. Joe, his daughter's stepfather, was a successful financial advisor, well invested in the stock market. He was able to sit back and let his money work for him. Lindsey worked sometimes around the clock, often risking his life, for a yearly salary that equaled what Joe earned in a month.

Lindsey was glad his daughter could live so well, but he hated the man who made it possible. Lindsey would have decked him every time they met if it were not for one revelation: He had seen Joe in a bathing suit. He was doughy and he jiggled when he walked. Besides that, Joe's hands were pale and soft. He often swished them through the air in exaggerated gestures, making the average man a little uncomfortable.

Tom's heavily muscled body, and his large weathered hands had no trouble moving within the bounds of masculinity.

Tom had made the obligatory call to make sure it was okay to visit Jennifer. He resented having to ask permission to schedule time with his own flesh and blood. He took a deep breath, then drove down the remainder of the driveway.

Joe walked out of the house, and headed for his black Mercedes, parked near the front door. He looked the part of an executive. Well-dressed, even in casual attire, wearing a white Ralph Lauren knitted shirt and crisply creased tan cotton pants. His meticulously styled hair framed his smoothly shaven face.

When Joe saw Lindsey pull up, he turned from his car and walked in his direction. "How ya doing?" he asked,

cheerfully.
   Tom got out of his car without acknowledging him.
   "Keeping busy?" Joe asked.
   Did this guy ever stop smiling? "Yeah...keeping busy. Jen ready?"
   "She just got out of the pool. Come on in. She won't be long."
   Lindsey mumbled profanities under his breath as he followed him.
   "Sara told me you're working on the murders we've been hearing so much about."
   Lindsey didn't answer. He was aggravated that everything he told Sara automatically went to Joe's ears.
   "We've been looking out for Jen. We'll do everything we can to protect her." He glanced back at Lindsey. "It must be hell doing your job. I wouldn't trade places with you for all the money in the world."
   Tom scowled. *That's because you already have all the money in the world.*
   Joe reached for the doorknob. "Are you any closer to solving the crimes?"
   "We're working on it," he muttered.
   When they walked into the three-story foyer, Joe called for Jennifer. "Your father's here. Hurry up. He's waiting."
   Lindsey winced. This jerk had no business giving his daughter orders. It might take more than the memory of Joe in a bathing suit to keep Lindsey from decking him this time.
   "Oh good!" She answered, sweetly. "I'll be there in a second."
   His daughter's voice calmed him.
   They entered the expansive living room. Enclosed from floor to ceiling in glass, it provided a full view of the sparkling lake, swimming pool, and fountains. A white grand piano sat off in one corner. Lindsey remembered how much Sara had wanted to learn to play. He couldn't even afford the lessons, much less purchase a piano.
   Sara walked in from the pool, toweling her long, damp, spiraled curls. Her bathing suit was miniscule and her

wet tanned body was as perfect as he remembered. She smelled fresh with a hint of chlorine. Her face glowed. He had a tough time prying his eyes off her.

"Tom! Good to see you." She walked over and kissed his cheek. "Did Joe tell you about Jen making honor roll again?"

"No." Lindsey cleared his throat.

"She's doing great this year."

"I'm glad to hear that."

"So what are you two going to do today?" She asked.

"I don't know. Play it by ear."

"Why doesn't that surprise me? You always were the spontaneous type."

"Whatever," Lindsey said. He glanced at his watch, then looked down at his feet.

"Is everything all right? You seem a little down in the dumps."

He wondered how she expected him to feel. *Like a damn jerk*, he felt like saying. "Just got a lot on my mind, that's all."

"We've been keeping tabs on Jen, but I haven't told her why," she whispered, "I really don't want to worry her. You know how much she loves you and how concerned she'd be about you. She's getting a little aggravated with the limitations we've set and its getting increasingly hard evading her questions."

Lindsey nodded. "You think she's about ready?"

"Daddy!" Jennifer ran down the steps and flew into Lindsey's arms. The sting of tears threatened his eyes. He blinked several times to get rid of them.

"Hi sweetheart. You look wonderful."

"Thanks, Daddy." Jennifer beamed. "Come on! Let's go." She dragged him by his hand. "What time do I have to be back, Mom?"

Sara hesitated. "No set time. You and your dad have fun."

"Thanks, Mom." Jen blew her a kiss and they headed for the door. "See ya later."

Sara's eyes misted slightly as she watched them leave. Joe walked outside with them. When they reached

Lindsey's car, he patted him on his shoulder. "Good to see you again. Good luck on the job."

"Yeah," Tom said, impatient to leave.

Sara watched from the window. As Tom opened the car door, her eyes stayed fixed on him. She brushed away tears, then bit her lower lip, and backed away from the window.

When they drove off, Tom turned to Jen. "I need to tell you something. You're mother's not going to like this, but I know you're mature enough to handle it."

Her face turned, concerned. "What is it, Dad?"

"I'm sure you've noticed how your mom and what's his name have been overly protective lately."

"Oh, that. You just wouldn't believe it. They're treating me like a baby! Maybe you could talk to them."

"Actually, it's my fault."

She frowned. "You? Why?"

"Have you heard about the serial killer?"

"Of course, everyone has. The kids at school are talking about it."

"I'm working on that case, Jen. That's why I'm concerned when you go out."

"I thought he only went after prostitutes."

"We thought that at first, too. I can't go into details. I just need you to trust me, okay? No young girl is safe from this guy. I don't want you to be scared, but I do want you to keep it in mind and use common sense. Make sure you don't go out alone."

She nodded. "Okay. I'm glad you told me."

"I'm going to get this guy, Sweetheart. But it might take a little while, so hang in there."

"Now that I know what's up, it won't be a problem. But please be careful, Daddy, I couldn't stand it if something happened to you." She leaned over and kissed his cheek. "I really admire you, Dad. You're the bravest person I know."

Lindsey's chest swelled, nearly exploding with pride. "Thanks, Baby." He turned the corner, heading back to his own territory. "So where would you like to go?"

"Let's go to downtown Disney. They're having an art

show today."

"An art show?" He rolled his eyes. "Okay, if you insist."

Traffic was bad. By the time they arrived, there was a long line of cars waiting to get in the parking lot.

"Hey, are you coming to my horse show next month?" Jennifer's face beamed. "Sebastian's in show condition now and he's riding great. He looks gorgeous, Dad. My trainer is pleased. Wait 'til you see his hip."

"The trainer or the horse's?"

"Oh, Daddy. Sebastian's of course."

"I didn't even know horses had hips."

"Oh please." Jennifer giggled. "Anyway, can you come?"

"I'll try, sweetheart...I promise."

"Please...please...make sure you're there."

"I suppose Joe will be there." He scratched his chin.

"Who cares. You're the one that counts."

"Well, that gives me even more incentive." He reached over and tweaked her nose. "I'll be there...one way or another. I wouldn't miss it for the world."

"Oh thank you, Daddy, I love you." She kissed his cheek again.

They pulled into a grassy area, temporarily used for parking. "It'll take us half the day to get there. By then, I'll be worn out." They got out of the car.

"I think you can make it." She poked his belly. "You look like you're in good shape to me."

"You got that right. I put what's-his-name to shame, don't I?"

"You sure do. I bought him a gift certificate for the gym last Christmas. I think he used it twice. Mom calls him the Pillsbury dough boy."

Lindsey snickered. "To his face?"

"Well, no, behind his back. It's funny how she talks about him sometimes," Jennifer lied. "I know she doesn't think he's as handsome as you."

"Really?"

"Absolutely. Don't ever tell her I told you."

Lindsey felt the tension drain from his shoulders.

"He's still treating her okay, right?"

"Oh sure. He's nice enough, but he'll never replace you. You're the best, Daddy."

Lindsey suddenly felt life was good again.

Later, that evening, Tom went back to the station. He stopped short before entering his office. Through his window, he spied Agent Cross working at his desk. With her face pale and drawn, she flipped through pages in a file and scrolled down statistics on the computer screen. After several minutes passed, she rubbed her eyes, then laid her head on her outstretched arm. Her hand balled into a fist.

Tom could almost feel her frustration. For the first time, he realized that this case was as important to her as it was to him and that they were equally committed and qualified, with one mutual goal. He knocked lightly and walked in.

Cross bolted upright. "I'm sorry." She gathered sheets of paper and jammed them into a folder. "I hope you don't mind. The conference room was locked and since I don't have an office of my own, I didn't know where else to work."

"Oh, and I thought you'd just suddenly become fond of sloppy desks." Lindsey noticed a shadow of a smile flicker across the ice maiden's face.

A trace of crimson stained her cheeks. "So, what are you doing here?"

"I thought I'd take some files home with me."

"Homework? Don't you have another life besides this one?" Sharon smoothed back her hair.

"A great looking guy like me? You bet I do." He leaned against the wall.

"Well, good. A lot of law enforcement officers forfeit their personal lives."

"Yourself, included?"

She shrugged. "Perhaps."

Lindsey studied her for a moment. Was she just punchy from pressure or was a different person breaking through that hard façade? "I've been thinking about the profile you came up with. It seemed a little left field at first, but I have to admit some of it seems plausible. Have you come up with any other ideas about the killer?"

She shook her head. "Not really. That's what I hoped to achieve tonight, but to be honest with you, I'm drawing blanks."

"Me too. I hoped we would have come up with something concrete by now."

She nodded. "I've been doing some thinking about that." She hesitated briefly. "I'm afraid a lot of it has to do with the fact that we don't talk enough. Actually, I think this is the most we've talked since the case began."

He was amazed that she'd come to the same revelation as he had.

"We need to be working together like a team. I'm willing to meet you half way. That is if you're willing to do the same."

Lindsey nodded. "No problem here."

She arched her eyebrows. "So we have an understanding?"

"Absolutely." He paused. "But I'd like to bring Richard Patterson into the loop. He's a pain in the butt, but he's a good detective."

She straightened the pile of papers. "That's fine with me."

During this last month, an increased hollowness beneath Lindsey's cheekbones had appeared...along with a deeper furrow across his brow and a look in his eyes that said he'd seen too much. Sharon seemed to be taking this in. "You know what?" Her tone was more upbeat. "I'm tired and I know you must be, too. Why don't we stop thinking about this case for awhile? It might do us both some good."

"That's a capitol idea." Lindsey hesitated, then pointed to his desk. "I've got a bottle of bourbon in the bottom right hand drawer. Would you like some?"

Sharon didn't take too long to mull it over. "Sure, why not? We're both off duty. A drink sounds great." She placed the bottle on his desk.

He walked over to a file cabinet and removed two glasses. When he handed them to her, she asked, "Do you do this often, Detective Lindsey?"

"I'm not about to give out trade secrets to the FBI."

She filled both glasses, then handed one to Lindsey.

Lindsey grabbed a chair and sat down. He stretched his long legs out in front of him and then crossed them at the ankles. "So what do we talk about?"

Sharon shrugged. "Anything, as long as it doesn't have to do with the case." She kicked off her shoes beneath the desk and removed her conservative jacket, exposing an emerald satin blouse that complimented her light green eyes. Lindsey wondered if her irises could glow in the dark. After she removed the gold barrette, she shook her head, and her hair cascaded below her shoulders.

When she turned to Lindsey, she asked, "Why is your mouth hanging open like that?"

Lindsey shrugged. "I guess I'm getting weird in my old age."

"You don't look so old to me."

Lindsey raised an eyebrow. "Have I stepped into the twilight zone or did you actually pay me a compliment?"

"Yes, I suppose, but don't get a big head about it. I didn't say you weren't weird."

Lindsey's eyes opened with mock surprise. "You have a sense of humor."

"Of course I do."

"Then why have you been hiding it?"

"I was more concerned with good investigative work than doing stand up." Her eyes turned serious. "One thing I learned a long time ago, was I had to earn respect before people would accept me."

Lindsey looked down at the floor. "It never entered my mind that..." He paused, then looked up. "Look, I didn't want to admit it, even to myself, but I've respected you all along. You handle yourself professionally. I've been impressed."

"Thank you. That means a lot, especially coming from you."

"And I also like this side of you. You're like a different woman."

"Really?" She grinned. "I have to say, I prefer the new you as well. It sure beats your old macho, cocky, I ain't-gonna-let-no-woman-interfere-with-my-case attitude."

Lindsey laughed. "You mean I was that obvious?"

"Like you were wearing a sign."

Lindsey drank heartily, enjoying the unexpected banter.

Sharon sighed. "I feel so much better now. I needed a break more than I realized." She stretched her arms over her head. "What do you do for relaxation, Tom?"

"Hang out with my daughter."

She straightened up slightly in her chair. "I didn't realize you had a family."

"She's the only family I have. I'm divorced." He thought he saw a hint of relief cross her face.

"I'm sorry to hear that." She lowered her eyes to the desk.

After a silent, awkward moment, she asked, "Do you want to talk about it?"

"Talk about it? What do you think this is, the Oprah show?"

"Oh please!" She groaned. "I thought you were going to drop that machismo crap."

He scrutinized her carefully. "Why are you interested?"

"Inquisitive minds want to know. Actually, I think it would be good to reveal a little about our personal lives."

"Okay, but I don't have any dramatic story to tell. It's really pretty common. I worked too many hours away from home, doing a job few people appreciate. It wasn't fair to my wife or my daughter. I should have quit and become a used car salesman or an accountant."

"Don't blame yourself for doing something you believe in."

"Well, that's how I used to justify it. But in retrospect, I realize my family should have been more important than my cause. Instead, while I left my wife alone, someone else filled in for me." He returned to his drink.

"It's funny how smart you get after it's too late."

"It's never too late."

"Yes it is. She married him a couple years ago. The guy's good to both of them and he's rolling in money. They're much better off now."

"Let's go beat him up."

"Don't tempt me." He handed her his glass. "Would you mind pouring me another?"

"Not at all." She reached for the bottle. "I think I'll have a little more too." As she poured the bourbon, she asked, "So is that why you moved down here? You're from New York originally, aren't you?"

"How'd you know that?"

"Your accent. It's obvious." Sharon handed him a filled glass.

"I came down here to be near my daughter and to have a change of scenery." Lindsey hesitated. "Hell, the truth is, I got burnt out. It was a gradual process. I screwed up my last major case. After that, something had to give. Vigilantism was becoming more and more appealing every day."

"You're not the only cop who has had that thought flash through their minds."

"This was more than a flash. I'd tracked a serial killer for months. One night I spotted him coming out of a bar. I didn't have any back up. I got on my radio, but no one was near my location. I had to move then, or he'd get away, so I decided to go for it. He resisted, bigtime. I nearly beat his brains out before he finally submitted to handcuffs. When we got to the station, he confessed and a conviction looked guaranteed.

"But later, he said his confession was a lie. He felt pressured to confess because he was intimidated by me and afraid that if he didn't, I'd beat him up again. To make matters worse, his attorney had pictures showing his battered face and bruised body. He got the jury's sympathy. We had an incredible amount of circumstantial evidence, but nothing tangible. Without the confession, the jury exonerated him. He walked. Two days later, he killed three kids under twelve years old and raped their mother before killing her, too."

Lindsey shook his head. "It was my fault. If I'd have handled things differently, he wouldn't have had the opportunity to take four more lives."

"You're talking about the Bentley case," she said, surprised. "I remember it well. I just didn't realize you were the arresting officer." Her voice softened. "As far as I'm concerned, you did what any cop would have done. That man had been evading the police for a long time. You had to move in and do whatever it took to keep him from getting away."

Lindsey shook his head, wearily. "Other people didn't see it like that. I was reassigned. The Chief didn't want me anywhere near the case. But I had a personal vendetta. I made plans to kill him. Fortunately, I got drunk one night and ran my mouth to a couple of my buddies. They talked some sense into me before it was too late. I knew I had to straighten up. I'd been way too close to crossing the line." Lindsey shrugged. "Law enforcement was all I knew and I had been damn good at it. I decided to transfer to Central Florida so I could be near my daughter. I also figured I wouldn't be dealing with another case like this."

"Unfortunately, no town is exempt." She paused. "So what are your plans?"

He shrugged. "I'm resigning as Lieutenant and becoming a Crime Consultant. The Chief Henry essentially created a new position for me. At least I'm getting off the playing field."

"You actually want to leave all this fun?" She grinned, then turned thoughtful. "You don't seem like you've lost your drive. I can't believe you're really ready to stop chasing the bad guys. And you probably have more restraint than you realize. I get the feeling Chief Henry is a good judge of character. Despite the incident that took place in New York, he put you in charge of this assignment. He wouldn't have done that if he didn't think you were the best person for the job."

Lindsey shook his head. "I'm holding it together because when this case is over I know I'm home free. I don't want to do anything to screw that up. But if I were to stay longer than that, I'm afraid it would only be a matter of time before I make a lethal decision. These killers are plain evil. There's no excuse for what they do. I've grown to hate them so much that..." He closed his eyes and tucked his chin to his chest. It seemed like a convenient time to change the subject. "Enough about me. Now it's your turn. What's your story?"

"Well..." She set her glass on the desk and studied it for a moment. "Ever since I was in my teens, I knew I wanted to be involved in homicide investigations. I wanted to know what made people tick." She licked her bottom lip.

"Why were you so curious about homicides?"

She looked at him thoughtfully. "When I was a kid, my Dad came home from work and I ran to the front door to greet him. I'd normally jump right up into his arms. But this time I never made it. A car drove up. A guy spotted my father in the doorway, rolled down the car window, and blew my family's life to bits. My Dad's blood was all over me. One second he was alive, the next, he was dead."

Lindsey scrunched his eyes and shook his head. "My God. How did you ever maintain your sanity after witnessing something like that?"

"I didn't manage very well at all. My mother wouldn't let me go to the trial. She thought she was protecting me. All I knew was the killer pleaded guilty in court and that my dad was the fourth man he had killed that day. When they asked the killer why he did it, he said it was just for thrills." Her voice broke slightly. "Well, that just wasn't enough of an explanation for me. I couldn't rest. I hated him and I was making myself sick inside.

"My mother arranged for me to talk with our family minister. He gave me a lecture on forgiveness. I thought he was out of his mind.

"After a year went by without resolution, I decided to take action. I got my hands on the court records. I found out the killer had been severely abused by his own father throughout his childhood. I mean, his history was pathetic. Then one day, he got his hands on a rifle and ran back to his house to kill his old man. When he got there, his father had left a note saying he'd taken off with a woman and didn't plan on coming back. Right after that was when he started his killing spree. It didn't take me long to understand why he was going around killing other people's fathers. I still wanted justice served and considered what he had done indefensible. But somehow, knowing his motivation, helped me to do what that minister had suggested a year before. I forgave him."

"Forgave him?" Lindsey sat up in his chair. "You've got to be kidding me! You're not one of those left wingers who believes every sob story that comes down the pike, are you?"

"Far from it. Like I said, I believe in justice and-if-need-be, the death penalty. Forgiveness doesn't have as much to do with the person you're forgiving as it has to do with freeing yourself. The hatred was hurting me, not him." She paused. "You'd be surprised how liberating forgiveness really is."

Lindsey shook his head. "I don't have a forgiving bone in my body."

"Maybe that's what's wrong with you."

He didn't answer.

"You're a good cop, Lindsey. Don't waste your talents."

Lindsey hadn't blushed in years. The heat that spread across his face felt foreign. He stood up and walked to the file cabinet. He kept his back to her. "I'm sorry I was such a jerk before. I guess you've had to put up with a lot of men like me."

"True, but that's okay, I wasn't exactly warm and cuddly, either."

A cup of coffee and an opened book set on the table at the front window. His back was to the crowd as they browsed through the shelves behind him. His attention focused on the barroom across the street. With his head tilted downward, he appeared to be reading. The urge was powerful and restless. It was difficult to sit still.

His mark waited tables at Bennigan's during the day and worked the six to midnight shift at the bar. She was nineteen years old, and had given her infant son up for adoption three months ago.

He was disappointed when he first saw her at the restaurant earlier in the day. Her dark hair was pulled back into a ponytail, she wore little make up and her uniform was respectable. However, he sensed potential.

Sitting at a table where she would be his server, he said everything she wanted to hear, listened intently when she spoke and smiled at all her stupid jokes. Each time she refilled his glass of tea, she lingered, stressed her availability, and flirted shamelessly. He gazed into her eyes, as if everything about her fascinated him.

She'd definitely remember him in the evening as she headed home from work. She'd stop him on the sidewalk, excitedly. He'd say he had to run an errand, but would like to meet with her later. She wouldn't refuse. He'd tell her to wait in front of a store at two o'clock, next to a suitable alley. She'd be too thrilled to question it.

He'd approach from the rear of the alley, dressed in his jogging suit. From the shadows, he'd call her name. She'd peek into the alley from the entrance, and see him bent over with his hands on his knees, like he couldn't catch his breath. Concerned, she'd step into his web without hesitation, and the spider would get to work.

He held out hope that she would look differently tonight and she did. He'd watched her walk to work. Her hips swayed in tiny shorts, revealing wicked legs in black stockings. Breasts bulged, and spilled over a low neckline. Her blackened eyes seemed to suck up the corruption of the night, like a black hole. Receiving whistles and vulgar comments with a smile, she swayed down the street, leading men into the bar like a pied piper. He couldn't have been more pleased. She turned out to be a perfect selection.

When the bookstore owner announced the store's closing, the killer walked to the cash register on the other side of the store. He hoped she wouldn't leave the bar until he had her in view. Receipt crumpled and jammed in his pocket, he hurried out the door, and scanned the area anxiously. He didn't see her. He walked slowly, stopping from time to time to gaze into storefronts with faked interest. If he lingered too long, he could arouse suspicion. If he moved too fast, he could miss a great opportunity.

He reached into his pocket to withdraw some coins, then let them fall to the ground. He crouched down to retrieve them, and kept his eyes on the bar. There was still no sign of her. He took time to gather the money. Several people stepped around him, and he felt conspicuous. Frustrated, he stood up and walked further down the road to a bus stop. There, he stood poised like a future passenger, which gave him an excuse for looking in the direction of the bar.

The urge turned cartwheels inside his head. Concentration proved difficult. He looked at his watch. Twelve-ten. He hadn't anticipated it would take this long. A man walked up to the bus stop and stood behind him. The killer grew apprehensive. Being identified was his biggest concern, unlike the monster from within who had a different priority. He left nonchalantly and walked further down the block toward her apartment. He bent and re-tied his shoelaces several times, which gave him a few more minutes.

As the monster grew more forceful, his hands shook. The fiend demanded satisfaction, and authority. It was becoming more difficult to contain. But the logical part of him had to consider how long the preliminary work had taken and how many people had seen him.

He was about to tear himself away and forfeit his plans, when he spotted her. She walked with a blonde girl of about the same caliber, who didn't interest him in the least. He crossed to their side of the street and ducked into a store alcove where he watched them talk outside a building. When the blonde went inside, the brunette continued in his direction. He glanced at his watch. He'd been on the street for twenty-five minutes. If it hadn't been so long since his last hit, he'd postpone the plan for another night. He debated if it was worth the risk. Common sense battled against need and finally, need was victorious.

He stepped from the shadows and walked briskly toward her. His heart beat wildly as they drew nearer. The liberation of restraint finally lifted. He and the power were one. Increased strength surged through his muscles. Determination welled in his depths. Until the unexpected happened.

A white police car pulled up to the intersection at the end of the block, made a left turn, and slowly headed his way. The killer slowed his gate while the mark maintained hers, still decreasing the gap between them. He kept his eyes straight ahead, but as the patrol car crept past, he could sense the cop's appraisal.

His senses fought for perspective, while the creature refused defeat. He dragged himself off course and crossed the street before she had a chance to recognize him. He walked back to the bus stop and waited until she entered her apartment building. Then he returned, but on the opposite side of the street. When he was about to pass her building, an upstairs window lit up and he saw her. His hands turned to fists, and his knuckles blanched. It took all the strength he could muster to keep on going.

CHAPTER 8

Linda and Anthony engaged in an animated conversation at an Italian restaurant on New York Avenue. When Carol walked in, they smiled.

"Why are you so late?" Linda asked.

"I checked in with the day center to make sure John was doing okay."

"And is he?"

Carol nodded. "Yeah, he doesn't seem to mind being there, and he's improved more than I ever thought possible. His doctor lowered his dosage and his personality is coming back. He won't have to stay there much longer."

"That's wonderful." Anthony smiled warmly. "I know how much that means to you. I'm sure your TLC has had a lot to do with his recovery. John is a lucky young man."

Carol blushed. She was always blushing around him. "So, how are you two doing today?"

"Fabulous." Linda winked at Anthony. "Guess where we went last night for a Cajun dinner."

Carol shook her head. "I don't have the slightest idea."

"New Orleans." Linda's eyes sparked.

Carol turned to Anthony. "Just for dinner?"

"Why not?" He laughed.

"He has his own jet!" Linda grinned. "Can you believe it?"

"My goodness," Carol said. "You two are certainly having a good time together."

The waiter brought their plates to the table.

"We ordered for you. I knew you liked lasagna and it was the special of the day." Linda bit her bottom lip. "Is that okay?"

"Sure. It looks great."

Linda smiled. "Carol, we were wondering if you'd do us a favor."

"What is it?"

"A client of Anthony's is coming into town and we were wondering if we could all go out to dinner together. We're not trying to fix you up or anything. I mean, he lives up north and you'll probably never see him again. But we just thought it might be good for you to get out of the house for awhile. What do you think?"

"Sounds like a blind date to me. No thank you. You should have known my answer before you even asked."

"It's not really a date. You'd be more like a companion. What harm would it do? Even if you didn't like him, you'd at least be getting out and going to the best restaurant in town. Plus you'd really be helping us out."

"You know I can't leave John alone yet."

"You just said he was doing better."

"Well, yes. But Dr. Walters said it'll be awhile before he can be by himself."

"Well, maybe Debbie could come over."

"No, I talked to her earlier. She's not feeling good today. And I wouldn't even think of asking Allen."

"That's so unfair." She sighed. "Would you go if we could find someone else?"

Carol hesitated. "I wouldn't feel right leaving him with a stranger. John wouldn't feel comfortable either."

"Oh, I can understand that." Linda tapped her lip with her forefinger. "If we come up with someone you'd approve of, would you go then?"

"If it really means that much to you, yes, but I can't imagine who it could be."

Linda shrugged as the waiter served their food.

The squad room had been a storm of activity all month. The detectives scurried in and out, following leads that seemed to be going nowhere. Most of the men worked on the streets interviewing people who frequented OBT and the areas in St. Cloud and Kissimmee where the other crime scenes had occurred. Those who stayed behind worked constantly at their computers to gather information from all over the country. At break time, they often huddled together comparing notes, their weariness showing in their slumped postures.

Lindsey, Cross and Patterson worked nearly around the clock. Lindsey dropped at least six or seven pounds and Cross resorted to foundation to help conceal the dark circles below her eyes.

Patterson still plowed full steam ahead. He ran on nervous energy and used the shrug to the hilt now as he paced the floor. He was waiting for Lindsey to return from his meeting with Chief Henry and the District Attorney. Cross sat at the desk, leafing through files.

Lindsey burst through the door and stormed over to the window.

"Looks like it went real well." Patterson readjusted his pants.

Lindsey lit a cigarette.

Patterson shook his head. "So? What they say?"

Lindsey ignored him.

"Look," Patterson said, "maybe this guy skipped town. He could be halfway across the world. I mean, he hasn't killed anyone here in over a month."

Lindsey drew on his cigarette.

"Hey! You forget how to talk?"

Lindsey fought back the impulse to hit his partner. He leaned against the file cabinet exhaling smoke.

"I'm going back to the trail," Patterson said, "I can't hang around here doing nothing." He stared at Lindsey, "You coming, or what?"

"Will you just shut up!" He coughed. "I just need a minute to...man, I am sick of this damn case!" He spun around and punched the wall, then looked down at his throbbing fist. "Damn it, what the hell did I do that for?"

Patterson laughed. "Hell if I know."

Lindsey's knuckles were swelling fast. As he held his hand, he kicked a dent in the file cabinet.

Sharon looked up. "Getting a tad testy, are we, detective?"

"You're damn right I am," he snapped. "I know any

day now, we're going to get a call and we'll find out he did it again. We don't have a single suspect. No DNA. Only a few footprints. What the hell is wrong with us? We've got to be missing something." He positioned his foot on the seat of his chair and shoved it half way across the room.

Sharon continued thumbing through the file. "We've compiled a lot of useful information and eventually we're going to get this guy. We can't afford to get discouraged now."

As Patterson's eyes darted back and forth between them, they looked eager for an explosion.

"I'm sick of your damn optimism too." Lindsey glared down at her. "Just once I'd like to see you start pulling out your hair and stomping your feet or something. Maybe even, throw in a few cuss words. Anything, to break up the monotony."

"Monotony?" She set her file on his desk and stood up.

Patterson rubbed his hands together, grinning.

"Look, I'm sorry if my optimism bores you." She planted her hands on her hips. "But at least I'm still thinking straight and not taking my frustration out on inanimate objects."

Lindsey growled. "It's easy for you to be calm. You don't have Henry and the D.A. breathing down your neck and every newspaper in town calling you a screw up. If I don't catch the killer soon, I'll probably lose my job."

"I'm surprised that would upset you." Sharon smiled ever so slightly.

Lindsey stared at her angrily. After a moment, his eyes sparkled with mischief. "You think you're slick, don't you?"

Sharon nodded.

Patterson shook his head. "I'm out of here." He slammed the door behind him.

The telephone rang, and Lindsey snatched it up. "Lindsey," he mumbled.

"This is Max." He paused. "Got something here."

"What?" Lindsey glanced at Sharon.

"You know the clothespins this idiot keeps leaving as souvenirs?"

"Yeah? What about 'em?" Lindsey asked, impatiently.

"They've been tracked down to a small clothespin factory in Pennsylvania. Went out of business fifteen years ago. The lab thinks these particular clothespins are older than that and they were well used."

"And?" Lindsey opened the palms of his hands.

"We found bits of soil in the crotch of each pin. Didn't match with any of the dirt we got down here. The experts are telling me it came from somewhere around your neck of the woods."

"Interesting. Thanks, Max."

Lindsey hung up, then turned to Sharon. "Clothespins are old and were used in the New York area." He squinted. "When we did our national search, we didn't come up with any strangulation cases from that region with the same MO."

Sharon thought for a moment. "We need to go over all the possibilities again. Remember, if the killer has been at this for a long period of time, we're seeing the results of escalation. He might have started off less dramatically."

Lindsey scratched the back of his head. "True. Come on. We've got work to do."

After they worked steadily for several hours, Sharon moved closer to her monitor. "I might have something."

Lindsey leaned over to look down at the screen.

"Two unsolved strangulation cases. One in ninety-eight. The other in ninety-seven." She clicked her mouse and the first picture appeared. "Check out these crime scene pictures. Long dark hair. No sexual assault. Wearing revealing clothes. Heavy eye make-up. Location? An alley."

Lindsey nodded. "Let me see the other one."

"This one is a year later. Same victimology and it, too, took place in an alley."

"How did we miss this before?"

Sharon shook her head. "Police thought they were isolated murders and we were too busy looking for our serial killer's pattern."

"Any suspects on either case?"

"No."

"So what have we got?" Lindsey sighed. "We got two murders, spaced a year apart, with a few similarities."

"It's hard to tell at this point whether they have anything to do with our case. But at least we received intriguing information about those clothespin today." Sharon shoved away from the computer and spun her chair to face Lindsey. "Our murderer has saved these old clothespins and used them for a more significant reason than a handy way of winding a tight ligature. He's probably had them in his possession for over fifteen years. There's a deep meaning here somewhere."

Lindsey nodded. "So it looks like our killer is from the north."

"Most likely. However, he could have just visited the area at some time or lived there temporarily. Too early to know what we really have."

"Then what good is it?" Lindsey yawned. "I'm sorry. I don't know about you, but I've got to get some sleep." He stretched. "What day is this?"

"Friday."

"Oh man!" He snapped his fingers, then walked to the calendar on the wall. "My daughter has a horse show tomorrow morning. I almost forgot about it."

"Really?" Sharon smiled. "I like horses. Can I come?"

Lindsey grinned. "Are you serious?"

"Is your ex-wife going to be there?" Sharon's eyes twinkled.

"Of course."

"Then I'm very serious. You and I can have some fun."

The next morning, Lindsey and Cross pulled into the Lakeland fairgrounds, parked their car, and scanned the grounds. Low-lying fog transformed riders and cantering horses into ghostly figures in far-off exercise rings. Closer to the stables, horses were hosed, their tails braided and legs wrapped. The smell of horses and manure mixed with fresh sawdust and filled the air, forming the heavenly aroma of a horse lover's paradise.

"She said she'd be at stable A," Tom said.

Sharon pointed. "Right over there."

As they headed toward the stable, Tom eagerly watched for a glimpse of his daughter. "There's my baby." The pride in his voice quickly melted into disgust. "With her mother and that jack-ass."

"Be good," Sharon whispered. Her hair draped over her shoulders. She was dressed in shorts that revealed well-toned tanned legs. For the first time, she wore eye-make up and lipstick.

Sara looked up when they approached. Her mouth dropped and her brows knitted together. She flashed a smile that was unlike any Lindsey had ever seen before... kind of tight and saccharine around the edges.

Jennifer's eyes widened as she looked from Sharon to her father, then back again.

After introductions Sharon said, "Tom has told me so much about all of you."

"Really?" One of Sara's eyebrows lifted slightly above the other. "He's never mentioned you."

"Didn't think you'd be interested." Lindsey put his arm around Sharon's shoulders. "You mind if I talk with Jen for a minute?"

"Of course not, sweetheart, go right ahead," Sharon said, gazing up into his eyes.

Lindsey pressed his lips to suppress a grin. He was going to make this up to Cross someday. She was really coming through for him.

He took his daughter by the hand, and walked to the end of the barn. "Hey, I hope you don't mind that I brought Sharon."

"I just wish you had prepared me. I always kind of figured I'd be your best girl forever." She faked a pout.

"You always will be, sweetheart."

"Good. Then I guess I don't mind sharing you a little." She poked him in the belly.

"Come on. Show me this horse you been bragging about." Lindsey tousled the top of her hair with his hand.

She led him back to where the others stood; Sara

faced another direction, Joe and Sharon talked politely. Jennifer opened the stall and brought the horse out into the aisle, backed him a few feet, then squared him up.

"He's beautiful, Jen," Lindsey said.

"He sure is." Sharon walked in front of the horse, noted his straight legs and muscular forearms, then went to his side and stood back as far as possible. "Nice short pasterns and what a hip! And that flat croup and low tail set. He looks like he can halter as well as pleasure." She tapped a finger on her chin. "What is he, about sixteen hands?

"Exactly." Jennifer smiled. "You must know something about quarter horses."

Sharon stepped forward and ran her hand across the horse's shiny back. "Used to own one. As a matter-of-fact, I showed him right here during a quarter horse futurity. We placed in the top three in western pleasure all three days. It was the most wonderful time of my life."

"Really?" Jen beamed. "Would you like to ride with me sometime?"

"I'd love it," Sharon said. "But I've got to warn you, it's been a long time." Lindsey slipped his arm around her waist and she moved closer, eliminating the small gap between them.

"No problem. A friend of mine has a thirty year old gelding that wouldn't shy if a bomb exploded right next to him." Jen grinned.

"Sounds like my kind of horse." Sharon winked at Lindsey. "At least until I'm back into the swing of things."

Sara started coughing. "Sorry, must be the hay, I'm going to go get some fresh air," she said, as she hurried out of the barn.

Linda avoided Carol at break time. She rushed to an unoccupied office in the back of the bank to make a call. When she and Allen talked, he tried to sound friendly, despite her request.

Thinking fast, he said, "I wish I could, but I have a late meeting tonight."

"Can't you cancel it?"

He laughed slightly. "Sorry. This is too important."

"And your mother isn't?"

Allen tried to control himself. "I didn't say that. I'm just very busy."

"Maybe you need to check your priorities, Allen. I know your job is important to you, but your family should come first. Your mother needs to get out once in awhile and we have something special planned for tonight."

"I know but..."

"I don't want to hear any excuses. You should be ashamed of yourself for not helping. I bet you haven't even called her. Or your brother, for that matter. Don't you know how much that would mean to both of them?"

Allen's face seared with anger.

"Couldn't you at least try to reschedule that meeting?"

"I wish I could. Really. Hey, I'm sure my wife wouldn't mind doing it. I'll call her right now."

"No. Your mother told me Debbie wasn't feeling good today."

"Oh." He gritted his teeth. "Well, let me call you back, I'll see what I can do."

Allen slowly set the receiver in the cradle. He leaned back in his chair, his eyes like slits. Where did this woman get off? He couldn't believe her nerve! What in the world was happening? It was one thing after another. Then to top it off, his mother was dating a young stud. The whole idea made him angry and the thought of him enabling her to do it made him sick. He'd have to come up with a good excuse. There had to be some way to get around it, without making himself look bad to Linda. He pegged her for a big mouth the first time they met.

He rubbed his finger across his bottom lip. He knew if John seemed upset when his mother got back from the date, she'd never go out again. She'd sacrifice anything to keep John from decompensating, including giving up that playboy. Allen smirked. He hadn't had a heart-to-heart talk with his brother for a long time. He picked up the phone, dialed the bank and asked for Linda.

Carol was surprised to see Allen smiling when he walked through the door. "Hi! Come on in," she said. "I was afraid you'd be upset. I'm sorry if Linda pressured you into doing this."

"No problem. I planned to stop by soon anyway." He glanced around the room. Nothing had changed.

"You look real good." Carol observed him. "You must be working out a lot."

"Every day," Allen said.

"John is too. He looks wonderful." She smiled. "He was so happy when I told him you were coming over."

Allen looked over her shoulder. "How is he doing?"

"Much better. I'm optimistic."

How many times had he heard that before? "Great, glad to hear it." He looked at her. "Great dress. You look nice."

"You think so?" She smiled shyly, and patted the back of her hair. "I'm kind of nervous."

"Really?"

"I don't get out much, as you know. Barely know how to act."

Who did she think she was kidding? She'd been dating this guy for a couple months now. Maybe even longer. "So where are you going?"

"I'm not sure, but they said it would be some place really nice."

"Good. I hope you have a good time."

"Oh thank you, sweetheart." She looked toward the hallway. "Oh, here comes John now."

Allen walked over, reached out, and shook John's hand. "Good to see you, man. You're looking good."

"You, too. It's been a long time. I've missed you."

"Same here, buddy." Allen patted him on the back.

Carol glanced at her watch. "I better get going. I don't want to keep anyone waiting."

Of course not, Allen thought.

When she was gone, they sat down and looked at each other awkwardly for a moment. "Mom told me what happened. It must have been pretty rough, huh?" Allen asked.

John shrugged, "To tell you the truth, I don't remember that much about it. I've decided to stay on my medication, though. I realize how stupid it was to go off of it again."

Allen nodded. "So, what have you been doing with yourself?"

"I've been trying to finish my pastoral degree by taking classes right here at home on the computer."

"Really?" Allen raised an eyebrow. He thought John had given up on that idea long ago. "What's your shrink say about that?"

"Actually, he's had a change of heart. Over the years we've debated Christianity so much, I think he's finally leaning my way."

"No kidding."

John nodded. "Yeah, it's amazing." His eyes sparkled. "Anyway, I'm almost finished with the courses."

"So you plan on being a pastor?" Allen scratched his chin.

"I plan on doing whatever God asks of me. I know the Lord has called me to serve him. It's just a matter of time and I'll be doing it. It might mean just standing on a street corner somewhere passing out tracts. I don't know yet what He has in store, I just know as unlikely as it might seem, He's going to use me."

Allen nodded. "Well, what do you think about Mom dating this guy?"

John frowned. "What are you talking about? I thought she was going out with friends."

Allen leaned towards him. "No way! She's been seeing him for awhile. Don't tell her I told you, but I even know who he is. I saw them having lunch together." He shook his head. "Bad news, man. Don't get a good feeling about him at all."

John blinked hard several times. "Are you sure about this? Mom never mentioned him to me."

He shrugged, "Guess she wants to keep it a secret."

"What's his name?"

"Anthony Pinto. Lives at a big apartment complex on

John Young. He's a lot younger than her." Allen paused, allowing his words to sink in. "He's up to something, but I don't know what yet."

"I don't want Mom getting hurt." John frowned. "Do you think he's dangerous?"

Allen hesitated. "Could be. But I'm keeping an eye on him, so don't worry about it."

"How can I not worry about it?" John crossed his arms. "I'm going to have to talk to her."

"Look, I told you this in confidence. Understand? I'm handling it. Trust me." Allen pressed his hand on John's shoulder. "If I need your help, I'll let you know," he said. "Now promise me you won't say anything."

John shook his head. "I don't like this sort of thing, Allen. But, I guess I do have to honor your wishes. As long as you watch out for her."

Allen smiled, "That's my bro." He leaned his head against the sofa. "Now, what else is new?"

"Nothing really." John's hand shook slightly. "Tell me what's going on in your life. It's been so long since we've talked."

"Ah, man. You don't even want to know. Everything is screwed up."

"Why? What's wrong?" John's face grew more tense.

"Well...oh, never mind, I better not talk about it. It could get you upset. I'll get through it on my own. Don't worry."

"I've been doing much better. I won't have a setback, if that's what you're worried about. Besides, I'm your brother. I'm suppose to be there for you. Maybe I can help in some way."

Allen sighed. "Are you sure? I mean the last thing I want to do is mess you up."

"Please, tell me what's wrong."

"Well, Debbie and I haven't been getting along. I got involved with my secretary, Heather Martin. Now she's putting on the pressure. Wants me to divorce Debbie and marry her...which I have no intention of doing. Meanwhile, Debbie is thinking about leaving me. It's one big screwed up mess. If either one of them turns on me, they could mess me up at Hoebel. I don't know what I'm going to do." Allen checked John's facial expression, then continued. "Then to make matters worse, one of the guys at the office, Paul Shield, walked in and caught me with Heather, and now he's blackmailing me. Can you believe the mess I've gotten myself into this time? It never seems to end, does it?"

John studied him for a moment, his brow heavy and stern. "I don't approve of what you've done, you know that. But I feel bad you've gotten yourself into this situation. I'd like to help. Would you like me to talk to any of them?"

Allen panicked. "Oh no. That wouldn't be a good idea, but thanks anyway. It's a help just being able to talk to someone. I appreciate it."

John nodded. "What are you going to do?"

"I don't know yet. The pressure's on. I've got to take some kind of action soon."

"Well, Debbie should be your first priority."

"I know, but I screwed up royally where she's concerned. What will people think of me? They'll figure I must have done something pretty bad for her to leave me."

John glared at him. "Well, you have."

Allen sighed deeply. "I know. But what's done is done."

"Have you prayed about this?"

"No." Allen chuckled. "I haven't prayed since I was a kid."

"Well, that explains things." John's voice grew firm and commanding. "You need to get your act together. You don't have any excuse not to. You had it all. God blessed you and you've abused it."

Allen clenched his teeth as if he was chewing gum. "I know. I know. But in the meantime, I've got to come up with a way to keep these three people quiet, or I'll be ruined."

John thought about this. "Don't worry. That's not going to happen."

Allen laughed half-heartedly. "That's easy for you to

say."

"Haven't I always gotten you out of trouble?"

Allen nodded. "Yeah, but I can't see how you could help me this time."

"I know what I have to do, since you probably won't do it yourself."

Allen squinted slightly. "What are you talking about?"

"You'll see. Just remember, everything's going to be okay."

Anthony noticed the strain on Carol's face as soon as she walked up to their table. "Are you all right?"

"Yeah, what's wrong?" Linda frowned. "I was worried when you didn't come into work this morning."

"John was upset. I didn't feel comfortable leaving him until we had a chance to talk things out."

"Why, what happened?"

Carol slammed her purse on the empty seat beside her. "Allen!" She set her elbow on the table and supported her cheek with her fist. Her eyes filled with angry tears. "I could break his neck!"

"What in the world did he do?" Linda's eyes were big.

Carol shook her head. "He unloaded on John," she sighed. "He knows better than to do something like that."

"What did he tell him?" Anthony put his hand on her shoulder.

Carol took a deep breath. "Basically, he told him that his life was in shambles. His marriage is falling apart, he's' having an affair with his secretary, Heather, and he's being blackmailed by one of his employees named Paul Shield." Carol rolled her eyes. "He thinks they're all going to talk about him and get him fired."

As Anthony processed this information, his eyes turned somber.

Linda patted Carol's hand. "Sound's like he really messed things up this time." She shook her head. "I'm sorry I talked him into staying with John. I should have kept my nose out of it."

"It's not your fault," Carol said. "Allen used very bad judgment. I don't get it. Allen hasn't opened up to either of us for years. Why now? And to John, of all people? I'll never understand him."

"That makes two of us," Linda said.

Anthony shook his head slightly. He knew Carol was angry, but he also realized that she loved her sons. Whatever hurt them would ultimately hurt her, too. "I'm so sorry. Maybe I can talk to them."

"I don't think that would be a good idea, but thank you for offering." Carol brushed away tears. "You're both wonderful friends."

Debbie was packing her bags when Allen came home. He didn't go upstairs immediately, but went straight to the kitchen where she heard the icemaker working. She assumed he'd fix a scotch and soda. He made a habit of that lately. But that didn't matter now. The only thing she cared about was her baby and herself.

She was in touch with her feelings for the first time in years and felt strengthened. Once she made her decision, she felt like a blindfold fell from her eyes. She called a lawyer who had been a friend of her parents and made an appointment to meet with him in his St. Augustine office to file divorce papers. She was so glad she'd confided in her mother-in-law, because Carol's advice triggered her decision. She knew she was doing the right thing.

She glanced at her watch. It was after twelve. No more fretting over where he spent his nights. All of his late meetings at the office and walks in the middle of the night to soothe his nerves no longer mattered. She no longer blamed herself for their problems. She knew what destroyed their marriage now. She had married a jerk. She couldn't believe it had taken her so long to realize it. She was sick of him and his selfishness.

She heard his footsteps on the stairs. She casually sat on the bed folding a blue cardigan, her suitcase open, and nearly filled. She was ready for him.

He stopped short in the doorway. "What do you think you're doing?"

"What's it look like? I'm packing. I'm getting out of

here."

"Oh really?"

"Yes really." She liked the sound of her own voice. "Do you have a problem with that?"

Allen was suddenly quiet. After a moment, he asked, "What's gotten into you?"

"Did you forget what I told you the other night? Nothing has changed."

Allen looked confused."

"I meant what I said. I want out of this marriage."

He glanced around the room. "But you're pregnant."

"What difference does that make?"

"It just doesn't seem like a good time to be doing this."

"It seems like the best time to me."

"So, you're leaving. Just like that."

Debbie nodded. "Yep. Just like that."

"So where do you think you're going?"

"I'll be in St. Augustine for a few days, then I'll come back and take care of loose ends. After that, I don't know. I haven't planned that far ahead. What I do know, is I don't want to be with you." She watched his mouth twitch and his eyes blink more rapidly than usual. "Actually, I would think you'd be relieved. You and your girlfriend won't have to sneak around anymore."

Allen walked over to the window. He waited for the heat to leave his cheeks before he turned to face her. "I don't know what you're talking about."

"Oh, please. Do you think I'm an idiot? Give me credit for having some intelligence."

"Intelligence? It's more like a wild imagination!"

She raised her eyes to the ceiling. "Look, I don't even care at this point. So there's no need to discuss the subject any further." She closed her suitcase to punctuate her statement.

He rubbed his forehead with his thumb and forefinger. "Have you told anyone else you're pregnant?"

"What difference does that make?"

"I just want to know."

"Who would I talk to? I don't have a family of my

own."

Allen shrugged. "I guess you've seen a doctor."

"No, not yet."

"All right, look. If you want to leave, I won't stop you."

"Well, that's big of you."

He ignored her sarcasm. "I just ask one thing." He paused. "Let's just keep all this to ourselves. I don't want anyone else to know about our problems. It's none of their business. Okay?"

Debbie clicked her tongue. "You're pathetic. Absolutely pathetic. Even at a time like this, your image is still all you're worried about. It's all that has ever mattered to you." She locked eyes with him. "What's wrong? You afraid someone might wonder why a nice girl like me would leave a terrific guy like you? Especially when she's pregnant? There might be embarrassing questions. People might find out the truth!" She paused. "Poor Allen."

"Yeah? Well, that image you're talking about has been feeding you all these years. I never heard you complaining about the things my money could buy."

She briefly scanned his face. "I don't know whether to pity you or hate you. It's hard to decide."

Allen was speechless. He recovered, to say, "Maybe I am screwed up. I don't know. But I don't deserve your betrayal."

"You don't deserve betrayal?" Debbie's mouth fell open. "You're hilarious."

His eyes narrowed. "I'm warning you, Debbie. You're making me mad. You better stop before this gets out of hand."

She stretched her arms above her head and faked a yawn. "You don't scare me, Allen. In fact, you make me want to laugh.

"Don't mess with me." His face was hard.

She pointed her finger directly at his face. "And don't you mess with me!"

He lunged toward her and grabbed her shoulders. "If you talk to anyone about me, if you say one word, so help me God, I'll kill you."

Toxicity danced in his eyes, but she refused to back down. "Your threats don't scare me, Allen. Your days of ruling over me are finished. Do you understand?" Debbie's eyes met his boldly.

He punched her on the cheek. Her body flew backwards, and the back of her head slammed against the headboard. She groaned, then rolled to her side, and shielded her face with her hands. Allen hovered over her, wild-eyed.

Allen stood outside the door of *Missing Person's*, drying the palms of his hands on his pant legs. He knocked twice.

"In," called a man's voice.

Allen opened the door and watched the man behind the desk whose eyes never left the reports in his hands. "Detective Morris?"

"You got 'em." He held up his forefinger and read for another minute.

Allen shifted his weight several times and then removed a folded paper from his suit jacket.

Finally, the man jerked his thumb toward the nearest chair and asked. "What can I do for you?" He reached out for the paper.

Allen breathed deeply. "I guess I want to file a missing person's report."

He glanced at the form. "This says she's your wife? Missing how long?" He squinted as he tried to read. "You're handwriting is worse than mine." He closed the old file and opened a new one.

"Debbie's been missing..." Allen wet his dry lips with his tongue. "She's been gone about two weeks now."

Morris eyed him skeptically. "Your wife disappeared two weeks ago?"

"Well, not exactly. She went to St. Augustine. Things have been too hectic at work for me to take the time off. But I wanted her to have a vacation."

"How long was she planning on staying?" Morris asked.

"We left that open. One or two weeks."

"When did you talk to her last?"

"Well, that's just it." Allen swallowed hard. "I haven't heard from her since the night she left."

"She left at night? What time?"

"Oh, around twelve-thirty."

"Didn't it seem a little odd to you that she'd leave that late? Why didn't she wait until morning?" His eyes turned hard as granite.

Allen thought quickly. "Debbie's like that. Once she makes up her mind to do something, she doesn't like to wait around."

The detective stared at him a little too long to suit Allen. "Do you at least know where she was going to stay?"

"Well, no. I assumed she'd stay at one of the beachfront hotels if there were any vacancies."

"So, obviously she didn't plan this out very well. I mean, she didn't make reservations. That's a little unusual, don't you think?" He tapped his fingers on the desk. "Or even weirder, she made reservations, but didn't bother telling you where she'd be."

Allen forced a smile. "Debbie is spontaneous."

"You're her husband. Weren't you concerned she wouldn't be able to get a decent room?"

Allen shrugged. "Women are independent today."

"Independent. I see." He jotted down some notes. "Now let me get this straight. Your wife decides to go on a vacation, doesn't prepare for it. She never calls to tell you how to get in touch with her. And, after two weeks of not hearing from her, you're just now filing a missing person's report?"

Allen's face dropped. "Well, it's not like I haven't been concerned. I've been worried as hell."

"Really? Did you drive up there to look for her?"

"Well, like I said, things have been hectic at work." Allen lowered his eyes to the desk.

"So what do you want us to do at this point, Mr. Randolph?"

"Well, I don't know. What do you usually do when someone is missing?"

"If foul play is suspected, we do an all out investigation." His eyes seemed to appraise Allen carefully. "Is that what you think has happened? Do you think your wife has run into trouble?"

"I don't know what to think." His words rushed. "I guess I just wanted to touch base with your department. I mean, I doubt an all out investigation is necessary at this point. Maybe she's just having so much fun, she hasn't thought to call."

"Let me ask you something." He leaned back in his chair. "What kind of a relationship do you have with your wife?"

He swallowed hard again. "We have a good relationship. We get along great. Why?"

"Just wondering, Mr. Randolph. Just wondering." He locked eyes with him. "If you haven't heard from her in a couple more days, you get on in here." He stood up. "If not, we'll be calling on you."

Allen nodded.

No one had found the body of his last victim. When he strangled her two weeks ago, he felt nothing except a sense of necessity. It had been purely perfunctory. Since she didn't meet any of the prerequisites, the urge had not been sated. So a few hours ago, when what he considered a perfect mark didn't show up as expected, he forfeited his well-laid plans and decided to kill whoever was available. He slipped into another bar further down the strip and ordered a drink. Casually, he scanned for prey. The urge didn't care if he'd spent hours researching or not. It just wanted to pick out a reasonable facsimile, an adequate mark, and hit it, quick and fast. Before long, he spotted a potential target and moved in its direction.

He sat at a table across from three girls and listened to their conversation. They looked cheap in their short skirts and low cut tops. Two of them smoked cigarettes and asked for refills about every fifteen minutes. The more they drank the louder their voices became. Trash...all three of them.

The blonde bragged about her boyfriend's muscles and virility. The other two were apparently not dating now and were jealous.

"I bet he ain't all that." The brunette giggled. "You're just trying to make me and Donna feel bad."

"Hey, at least you've been married." The blonde said to the brunette.

"What good does that do me now? My old man kicked me out a year ago."

"Well, whose fault was that? He caught you with his own brother!" The redhead laughed.

"Oh, shut up. His brother is good lookin'." The brunette smiled. "You'd have done the same thing if you were me."

"No doubt." The redhead giggled.

The blonde suddenly saw him. She nudged the other two. "Would you look at that?" They waved and made kissing noises.

He unfolded his newspaper and pretended to be reading.

"Stuck up." The blonde rolled her eyes. "Anyway, I've been wondering how things are going between you and your mother-in-law since she got custody of your kids, Tina. You haven't said anything about it lately."

"It's okay." The brunette answered. "We're gettin' along better, and she's good to 'em. I miss 'em sometimes but...hey...if they were living with me, I wouldn't be able to be out partying with y'all tonight, right?"

"That's right!" They clicked their glasses together.

The brunette looked his way and waved again. "Sure wouldn't mind taking him home with me."

The blonde shook her head as she watched him peruse the newspaper. "He ain't your type. He can read."

"Shut up." The brunette giggled. "Hey, good-lookin'!" She tried again. "What's so interesting about that paper?"

He shifted in his seat, turning his back to them.

"Oooh. You been told, girl," the blonde jeered. "Pretty boy ain't interested."

"Hey, I'm goin' to the bathroom. Anybody else got to

go?" The third girl asked.

"Yeah, I'll come with ya." The blonde stood up. Together, they walked to the back of the bar and entered the rest room.

The brunette stayed at the table and cleared her throat loudly. "Hey! Why you got to be so stuck up?"

This time he looked over his shoulder and flashed an incredible smile.

"Well, it's about time." She teased.

"Hi, beautiful." His light eyes danced with anticipation. This one was perfect. "I had my mind on other things. I didn't mean to ignore you."

"That's okay. Let's make up for lost time."

His eyes returned to the paper and he barely moved his lips as he talked. "Sounds good to me. I'm bored with this place. Would you like to go somewhere else?"

"Your place or mine?" She asked, barely able to contain herself.

"Yours." He felt like a snake, ready to strike.

She gathered up her purse and started to rise from her seat. He caught the movement from the side of his eye. He gestured for her to wait.

"Listen, we can't walk out of here together." He looked around to see if anyone was watching. "I'm married. You know how it is."

"Sure, I know where you're coming from."

Looking straight ahead, he asked, "How about if we meet in that alley down the block just past the hardware store?"

She frowned. "Why the alley?"

"It's private. You can give me directions on how to get to your place there without anyone seeing us."

"Oh." She smiled coyly. "Okay, I get ya. Let's see, you mean the alley down there on the right?"

"Yeah." He glanced around the room. "Wait a about five minutes after I leave, then go on in there." He laid a ten-dollar bill on the table to cover his drink. "I'll stall around for awhile, then meet you a few minutes later."

"Okay, but don't take too long. That alley is pretty dark and creepy." She watched him walk out, then removed a mirror from her purse and touched up her make up.

He walked down several blocks, turned the corner, and then entered an empty lot. Bending over, he picked up a knapsack that had been lying under a bush. He stripped down to his jogging suit. Reaching into the bag, he removed a light jacket. Then he retrieved his rope, clothespin, knife, and gloves and stuffed them into the pockets. He hid the clothes he just removed under the bush with the knapsack.

He felt sparks arcing in his brain as the urge took complete charge of his body. It's presence took over his eyes, and he viewed everything through an evil lens. As he left the lot, he rechecked his pockets to be sure his equipment was still there. Heading toward their meeting place, he entered the alley from the rear.

When the girl left the bar, she wore a smile so wide, it lifted her ears.

CHAPTER

Two sanitation workers emptied trashcans at the front of the alley. The air smelled exceptionally bad. Some of the cans were pushed back in the alley where the odor seemed to be the strongest.

"What the hell they doin' back that far?" The biggest man complained. "When I quit this job, I ain't never gonna have nothin' to do with garbage again." He held his nose as they walked toward the center of the alley. "I ain't even gonna touch my own garbage. My wife gonna have to get her butt out on trash day, whether she likes it or not."

His partner laughed. "You ain't ever gonna get another job and you know it, fool." He shook his head as he grabbed a can and dragged it toward the entrance.

"Man, you don't know what you're talking about," the bigger man said as he grabbed the handle of the last can. When he gave it a jerk, the corpse flopped back towards him, face up. The sightless eyes were quartered and crawling with maggots, as they stared blankly at the narrow strip of sky above the alley. The big man spun around, knocking over his partner and the other trashcan as he bolted for the street. Before reaching the sidewalk, he staggered, fell to his knees, and vomited. His partner scrambled past him, jumped in the truck, and called the police.

When Allen returned to the Missing Person's Department, he shook Morris' hand and sighed.

"Still haven't heard from her?" The detective asked.
Allen bit his lower lip. "No. Nothing."

Morris searched for the Randolph folder, then opened it on his desk.

"I made some calls to St. Augustine," Allen said. "Her parents lived there for awhile. We visited them occasionally and got to know some of their neighbors. A few years ago, Debbie's parents died in a car crash. After that, we didn't keep in touch with their friends, but they remembered me when I called. They haven't heard from her."

"What about friends or family around here? Maybe they'd know something."

"Tell you the truth, Debbie used to have friends, but she changed a lot after our baby died a few years back and she seemed to lose interest in them. She has no other family but me, my mother and brother."

Morris rubbed his cheek with his knuckles. "And you're positive she was going?' You couldn't have misunderstood her?"

"No way." Allen brought his hand up to cover his mouth. "We talked about it. The places she wanted to visit, the time she was going to spend on the beach and all."

"You said the two of you got along great. You didn't have an argument before she left?"

"Absolutely not. Everything was fine."

"There was nothing unusual about her manner? I mean you believed she was telling you the truth."

Allen's heart raced. "Well, yeah. I never knew Debbie to lie." He hesitated. "But now, I'm not so sure."

"Why is that?" Morris studied Allen's face as if measuring its sincerity.

"I went through her drawers, her personal things and didn't find anything unusual. Then I looked inside her closet and noticed her red winter coat was gone. The only time she ever wore it was when we'd go to our cabin in the Poconos. At first, I thought maybe she'd taken it to the cleaners, so I called them this morning. They said she'd dropped off a few items several weeks ago, but no coat." Allen sighed. "Then I wondered if she went to the cabin instead. So, I called our closest neighbor in the mountains and asked them to use the key we gave them to see if Debbie was there. Not a trace of her."

"Maybe she took the coat to a different dry cleaner."

"No. She's been using the same place for the last seven years. She never went anywhere else."

"So, what are you thinking?"

"Part of me doesn't even want to consider this, because Debbie is the last person in the world anyone would ever expect to do something wrong."

The detective shrugged indifferently. "Go on."

"Well, I started thinking about the phone calls we were getting lately. If I picked up the phone, I'd get a hang up. It never seemed to happen when Debbie answered. In fact, she seemed to be on the phone quite a bit lately. A lot of times she'd walk off into the other room where I couldn't hear her conversation. I didn't think much about it then, but like I told you, she'd lost her friends. Didn't socialize much.

He took in a deep breath, then exhaled slowly. "Another thing. There were several times when I got home earlier than she'd expected and she wasn't there. We're talking ten...sometimes eleven o'clock at night. She told me she'd been out running an errand or something and I never thought much of that, either. But now, I can't help but wonder if..." He looked serious, then smiled sadly, "No, this is crazy. I can't imagine her doing anything like...I mean Debbie is a decent person."

"Decent people make mistakes, too."

"I know but..." He got out of his chair and walked to the other side of the room. "I trusted her. I thought everything was fine with us. I can't imagine her having an affair. We've been together since we were in high school."

The detective set his pen on the desk and rolled it back and forth with the palm of his hand. "If you consider the length of time she's been gone and what you just told me, I'd be willing to bet you've hit the nail on the head and she's probably living somewhere up north with another man."

Allen nodded and made his lip quiver just enough to draw sympathy.

"I'm sorry, buddy, I see cases like this all the time." He picked up his pen. "Of course, foul play is still on the table. Let's see if she's left a trail with her credit cards, ATM withdrawals, and so on. That's the best way to start. If that works, it'll eliminate time and money spent on an all out investigation, and it will make it easier on you. Nobody wants their personal life made public if it's not necessary."

"Thanks." Allen sighed. "I really appreciate that." Mission accomplished.

After eight hours at the new crime scene, Lindsey, Patterson and Cross, came back to the station to meet with the squad. Patterson hiked up his pants as he walked into the room full of his peers.

"The killer's going down." He winked at the cop next to him. "Trust me." He sat down cockily, his tongue poked against the inside of his cheek.

Lindsey stood at the front, his back to his men, still reeling from it all. The reporters followed him everywhere now and questioned his abilities. They showed up at the alley before he even got there; the rookie who first arrived hadn't been able to maintain a totally protected crime scene. A tabloid reporter managed to step into the restricted area, and took a photograph of the corpse. When Lindsey met up with the reporter, he threatened him with prosecution if he didn't hand over the film. Fortunately, for both of them, the man complied. He had the rookie take the man down to the station to talk to Chief Henry. Lindsey knew Henry could put the fear of God into a man like no one else.

Lindsey's stomach was on fire. He'd run out of antacids earlier in the day and he felt miserable. He kept asking himself two questions: Who in the hell was this guy? And, how was he going to stop him?

Sharon took a seat at the table. Her eyes lowered slightly as Lindsey turned to face his men. "For those of you who weren't at the scene, I'll briefly summarize what we know. The latest victim, Tina Styer, was found early this morning in an alley like the others. We're sure it's the same killer. Same MO, signature and victimology. She'd moved recently and hadn't changed the address on her license. We're in the process of tracking her family down." He handed them their assignments. "Now, has anyone come up with anything significant since the last time we met?" He glanced around and saw a lot of head-shaking. He paused for just a moment, then stormed out of the room.

When he entered his office, he slammed the door behind him, then noticed Chief Henry sitting at his desk. Henry appraised Lindsey's face, pushed back the chair, and slowly rose to his feet. "Get me something. Something I can tell the press, or this whole town is gonna come unglued." On his way to the door, he stopped and turned to Lindsey. He looked him in the eye and started to open his mouth, then subtly shook his head. He left without saying another word.

After a couple minutes of self-flagellation, Lindsey got in his car. Since the victim had been drinking, he headed for the bar closest to the crime scene. He walked in and the smell of stale beer and vomit hit his nose. His nausea hit new heights. The owner was behind the bar, cleaning scum out of the ice bin. He eyed Lindsey suspiciously. Men in suits rarely frequented his establishment.

"What can I do for ya?" He wiped his hands on a soiled towel tucked in at his waist.

Lindsey flashed his badge.

"This about the murder down the street?"

Lindsey nodded. "Were you here three nights ago?"

"Sure was. I'm here, twenty-four/seven."

"The victim was a white female, had long dark hair, built." He showed him the picture on the license. "Name was Tina Styer.

He shook his head and laughed. "Half the girls that come in here look like that and I don't know many of them by their names."

"Surely you have regulars."

"Yeah. But after awhile, you see one you've seen them all."

"This girl was wearing a red tank top, cut low. Showed a lot of cleavage. She had on a matching skirt and big dangling gold colored earrings. She had her eyes made up real heavy, she smoked, and apparently drank a lot."

The owner laughed again. "Yeah, well that still doesn't narrow it down much for me." He wiped the bar next to Lindsey with the same dirty towel. Lindsey got another whiff of vomit as the towel passed by him. He stood up, swallowed hard, then handed him his card. "Look, we're trying to contact next of kin. Ask around and if you find out anything, give me a call."

The owner shrugged. "No problem."

Lindsey hurried out. He squinted as he reached into his jacket pocket to remove his sunglasses. Then his heart pounded as he glanced at the alley. Reporters invaded the street with tape-recorders and camera crews. Several stood just yards from each other, trying to outdo the competition with their slant on what had transpired. One young female reporter with stiffly sprayed blonde hair separated from her peers and rushed towards Lindsey. Tom slipped on his sunglasses and headed for his car.

She caught up to him and her cameraman zoomed in on Lindsey's face. "Can you give us any information on last night's murder, detective?"

Lindsey ignored her as he kept walking.

"Any leads? Do you have a suspect yet? If you catch up with him, Detective Lindsey, will you handle it differently than the fiasco you caused with the Bentley case?"

Lindsey climbed into his car, cranked the engine, and took off with a squeal.

Heather avoided Allen whenever possible, talking to him only when she had to discuss business. She had a paper that needed his signature, so she laid it on his desk and turned to leave.

He sat in his chair, his back to her, as he looked out the window. "You really don't care, do you?" He decided it was time to get her back into his corner.

"Why should I?"

"I'm going through hell." He spoke just slightly above a whisper.

"Yeah, well, that's still no excuse. You were totally out of line the other night."

"I know I was. I'm sorry. You didn't deserve that."

She put her hand on the doorknob, then turned back. "Is anything happening that I should know about?" She asked casually.

He suppressed a smile. He knew she'd come around. "Things look pretty bad."

She sat down.

He turned around. "I'm not sure I want to talk about it."

Her eyes focused on his handsome face. "Sounds serious. Tell me."

He threw up his hands in surrender. "Debbie's missing. I haven't seen her for almost three weeks."

"And this is bad news?"

His jaw clenched. "I knew I shouldn't have confided in you."

"I don't get it. What's going on?"

Allen shook his head. "She told me she was going away for a few days and then she never came back. I have no idea where she is."

"So what?"

"Don't you see the ramifications?" Allen walked toward her. "I had to file a missing person's report, and now the police might start asking personal questions."

Heather looked puzzled. "Why did you file the report to begin with?"

"First of all, I really don't know where she is. I thought she'd be back by now. If I didn't file and she turned up dead, they'd wonder why I hadn't been concerned."

"Dead? Don't be ridiculous. You should have just told them the truth. That the two of you were getting a divorce and that's why she left. Everything could have finally been out in the open."

He looked past her to the door. "Will you please keep your voice down? Heather, I can't let them know the truth. Don't you see? If something has happened to her and they find out our marriage was in trouble, they'll think I had something to do with it."

Heather digested this for a moment. "Did you?"

"Did I what?" Allen frowned.

"Did you have something to do with it?"

Allen slapped his forehead with the palm of his hand. "I don't believe this. You of all people? You're not serious."

"Well, you do have a violent temper and you are desperate. A desperate person is capable of doing almost anything."

"Desperate! Is that what you think I am?" Allen's eyes were wide.

Heather thought for a moment. "I know you wanted out."

"That's right. That's why I hired a lawyer."

Heather picked at her nails. "Are the police going to be nosing around? Asking a bunch of questions?"

"For the time being, they think she left me for another man."

"You've got to be kidding."

He nodded. "It's possible. Who could blame her?"

Heather laughed. "Debbie? That's ridiculous. Virtue oozes out of the woman's pores."

"Well, that's what I always thought, too, but who knows?" Allen shrugged. "My bet is she's just staying away long enough to try to make me worry. At least I hope that's all it is, because if something bad has happened to her, an investigation will take place." He lowered his voice slightly. "I hope you don't tell them about the divorce or our relationship. I don't want them to have any ammunition against me."

"Don't worry. I won't say a word, that is, as long as we still have an agreement. No matter what happens, we are going to get married. You promised and I'm going to make sure you keep it."

Allen swallowed his rage. "That's the plan, baby. You know that. Nothing has changed. But we do need to be discreet. Especially now."

"What about Paul Shield? What if he tells them about

what he saw?"

Allen rolled his eyes. "We'll deny it. Our word against his. We'll say he's lying. Don't worry about it."

"The way I look at it, I'm not the one who needs to worry, sweetheart."

He wondered why he had ever found her so attractive. She was a witch. Just like every other woman he'd ever known. They start out thinking you're wonderful, they treat you great and then they change. Everything changes. He rubbed his eyes. "I'm sure she'll turn up. We had a bad argument before she left so now she's trying to shake me up. Get even with me."

Heather raised an eyebrow. "So you and Debbie had a big argument before she disappeared. You're digging yourself deeper and deeper, big boy. I sure would hate to see information like that get out. Let's just hope no one ever has to tell."

His face turned cold. He pushed her backwards and pressed her against the wall. "You don't know who you're fooling with. If you know what's good for you, you'll keep your mouth shut."

"Ooooooh.... I'm shaking." Heather slid away from him and walked out the door.

Lindsey and Patterson met with Tina Styer's mother. They obtained the names of her daughter's best friends. They also discovered the bar Lindsey had visited earlier was where she'd last been seen.

The detectives arranged to meet the two girls at the bar for questioning. Patterson sat in a chair. His thumb pressed one corner of his lip, his forefinger tapped the other. "You say the three of you were sitting at this table. You two went to the rest room and when you came back, she was gone?"

They nodded in unison. "Yep." The blonde wound a strand of hair around her forefinger. "We didn't think a whole lot about it because Tina, well, she really liked the guys, you know? It wasn't unusual for her to take off with somebody. Even somebody she'd just met. Tina was like that."

Patterson cracked his knuckles. "She ever take off without letting you know who she was going with?"

"Oh yeah, plenty of times. It ain't like we had to report to each other or nothing."

Lindsey asked, "Did anyone show interest in her that night?"

"No," the blonde answered again. "She must have been having a bad hair day or something. She was trying hard, though, especially with this great looking guy who was sitting at the table next to us."

"She was flirting with him?" Patterson leaned back, and the two front legs of the chair lifted off the floor.

"Oh yeah, I guess we all were a little bit. But Tina was pouring it on thick," she laughed, "I couldn't blame her. He looked like a movie star. Wasn't the usual type of guy that comes in here."

"How did he react towards her?" Lindsey asked.

"Didn't give her the time of day. All he did was read a newspaper. Never even looked at her."

"Are you sure?"

"Positive."

"Think real hard." Lindsey was intense. "Are you sure there weren't any other men watching her, maybe someone smiling once in awhile?"

"Nope, least I didn't notice anyone. But then we were busy laughing and acting crazy. I wasn't really paying a whole lot of attention."

"What about old boyfriends?" Patterson's asked.

The blonde looked at her friend. "Was Bobby in here that night?"

The redhead squinted. "Yeah, he was here. He was standing over in the corner drinking like a fish, as usual."

"What's the story with him?"

"After Tina's husband kicked her out, Bobby and her had something going on for awhile." The redhead lit a cigarette. "But that was over months ago. He wasn't paying attention to Tina as far as I could see. In fact he was with some other chick."

"How can we get in touch with him?" Patterson asked.

"That's easy," the blonde nodded toward the door.

"He just walked in."

Patterson turned to look at the door, lost balance and his chair nearly flipped over backwards. When his chair was back on all fours, he gave himself a shrug.

Bobby wore a torn tee shirt, so badly stained that the country singer on the front was unidentifiable. Lindsey gestured for Patterson to stay with the girls while he went over to talk to the redneck.

The man planted himself on a barstool and ordered a drink. Lindsey sat next to him and immediately regretted it. The man's sweat smelled like recycled beer.

"Bobby, I'm Detective Lindsey from the Orlando Police Department. I'd like to ask you a few questions."

The man frowned through hazy eyes. "What about?"

"I was just talking to the two girls over there. They told me you used to date a friend of theirs, Tina Styer."

"Yeah, so?" He snatched up the beer bottle as soon as the bartender set it down.

"When was the last time you saw Tina?"

"I don't remember. Why? What's it to you, anyway?"

"I'm sure you've heard she was murdered."

"Yeah, but I don't know nothing about that." He popped a cigarette in his mouth and patted himself down for matches.

"Her two friends said you were here three nights ago. That was the last night anyone saw her."

"I'm here pretty much every night, but I don't know nothing that's gonna help you." The cigarette wagged in his mouth as he started to get up.

Lindsey placed his hand on Bobby's shoulder and pressed down firmly. "Maybe you don't. But just in case, I need to ask some questions. And you need to give me some answers."

"Dang." He turned his last pocket inside out. "You got a light?"

Lindsey removed his lighter and lit the man's cigarette. "Now, how long were you here and were you with anyone?"

He inhaled, then talked with smoke billowing between his words. "Hell, I always stay until closing. Ask anybody. They all know me. And yeah I was with somebody. My girlfriend, Sheila. She'll tell ya."

"Did you ever leave during the course of the night?"

"Nope." His lopsided smile displayed several missing teeth. "When I come in, I'm here for the long haul."

"I wouldn't doubt that one bit. What did you do after the bar closed?"

"Went home with Sheila. Stayed there until the next afternoon."

"Good. You see? You have an alibi already." Lindsey tried to look a little friendlier. "If it checks out, you'll have nothing to worry about. What I'd like to find out from you is, what you observed that night regarding Tina. Did you see her with another guy? Did you see her leave?"

He hesitated for a moment. "Yeah, I remember seeing her leave. She was smiling like she just won the daggone lottery or something."

"Was she with anyone?"

"Nope," he burped. "She walked out of here by herself."

"Had she been talking to anybody?"

"She spent the night laughing and acting stupid with those two bimbo friends of hers." He pointed to the blonde and red head. "When those idiots took off for the back, some dude started talking to Tina. He was sittin' over yonder." He nodded toward the table next to where the girls were sitting. "He got up and left and then she left a little while later."

Lindsey's eyes narrowed slightly. "What did this guy look like?"

"Looked like one of those faggot model types, if you ask me. Hair styled fancy and dressed neat. Nobody comes to this bar looking like that." He looked Lindsey over quickly. "No offense."

"None taken, I assure you." Lindsey lit a cigarette for himself. "Tell me more about this guy. Describe him."

"Man, I was talking to my girl at the time. I didn't pay that much attention. Me and Tina were history." He tapped the bottom of the bottle against the counter. "His hair was dark. That's all I can tell you."

"What about his face? His nose. Was it big or small? What about his eyes?"

"I told you I didn't notice that stuff. The only thing I remember thinking was, there goes another one of them there pansies."

"I'm going to need you to come down to the station with me and give a statement."

"What the hell for? I ain't done nothing but get drunk."

"It's standard procedure."

He shrugged his shoulders. "Do I have to? I don't feel like going nowhere."

"Yes, you have to."

"Dang." He guzzled down the rest of his beer.

Lindsey walked back to the girls who were laughing with Patterson at the table. "Listen, give me a description of the guy that sat over there. The one you said was good looking."

"He was to die for, mister." The blonde giggled. "He had these gorgeous blue eyes. I ain't never seen eyes that blue before. He had dark hair. Kind of a rich man's hair-cut...short and gelled. He had high cheek bones and a straight nose, thin mustache and a real sexy mouth." She nudged her friend. "Did you notice his mouth?"

"Oh yeah. Great mouth, but it looked like it could be mean, too. You know?"

"Yeah...that's right. Great eyes and a dangerous mouth. Looked like he could kick butt if he wanted to and enjoy the hell out of doing it. He kind of reminded me of Antonio Banderas."

"How tall?" Lindsey asked.

"He was sitting down when I noticed him, but he looked like he could be tall. Maybe six one or so. He had broad shoulders. Real muscular, kind of like you." She winked at Lindsey.

Patterson straightened himself up in his chair. Lindsey said, "I'd like you both to come down town with us and work with our forensic artist. He'll draw up a composite from your descriptions."

The blonde's eyes widened with excitement. "Do you

think that guy killed Tina?"

One composite resembled Banderas, the other, Steven Segall. Each girl admitted their pictures resembled their favorite actors. The redneck's composite looked like Pee Wee Herman. After a good laugh, Lindsey passed all three renditions out to his men. "At least we know one thing men, the guy we are now calling suspect #1 has dark hair, blue eyes, a mustache and is probably over six feet tall. He's either of Italian or Latino decent and, in the words of my female witness, "to die for". He smiled. "At least we got something." He filled them in on the details of the interviews and dismissed them.

Chief Henry stood in his doorway listening. When Lindsey looked his way, the Chief gave him a nod, then returned to his office.

Lindsey hadn't seen Sharon since morning and she wasn't responding to her pager. He was aggravated at first, and then it dawned on him that something might be wrong. Patterson followed him as he headed for his office. Lindsey turned and scratched the back of his head and said, "Hey, I got to make a personal call, I'll catch up with you in a few minutes."

Patterson grinned. "So you finally took my advice. Got a little something going on the side, huh? Who is she?" Lindsey shook his head, stepped into his office, and closed the door in Patterson's face.

He picked up the phone and jabbed the numbers. She mumbled when she answered.

"Hey! What's going on? Where've you been?"

"Lindsey?"

"Yeah. You don't sound too good."

"I've been puking my guts out." She groaned. "Aren't you glad you asked?"

"Sounds bad," he hesitated. "Can I do something to help?"

"Other than maybe trading places with me, I can't think of a thing." He heard the phone drop, followed by distant retching sounds. He swallowed with difficulty.

His own stomach was still rebelling.
After several minutes of what sounded like pure agony, she returned to the phone.
"Have you called a doctor?"
"Yeah. He said it's a twenty-four hour bug that's going around. He told me to drink plenty of fluids and take Tylenol for the fever. Yeah, right, easier said than done."
"Want me to come over?"
"So you can catch this thing? What are you, a masochist, or something? Of course I don't want you to come over"
Lindsey sighed. "That's a relief."
"Very funny. So what's up? Anything new?"
"Got a description of a possible suspect, that's all."
"Are you serious?"
"Yeah, I'll fill you in when you're up to it. Meanwhile, I'll let you go."
"Sounds good. I'd like to get some sleep before the next wave hits me, if you know what I mean."
"I definitely do. Take care."
"You, too."

Red digital numbers flashed two o'clock into the darkness. John couldn't sleep. He'd tossed and turned for hours. He couldn't get Allen off his mind. How did his brother ever end up with so many problems? Sometimes God chooses to put his children through the fire in order to change and perfect them. Maybe that's what was happening. Regardless, John would be there to support him.
He turned over. His body was uncomfortable in every position. As much as he needed sleep, he was certain it would elude him tonight. The medicine made his legs restless. He hated to go out again. He knew his mother was bound to catch him coming back from one of his excursions. He flipped over to his other side, then heard something. At first, he thought it might be the radio. Maybe his mother couldn't sleep, either, and was listening to the news in the kitchen. Then he heard it again. It was a man's voice, and it sounded like it was in his room.

He jumped up and switched on his bedside lamp. No one. He shook his head and whispered. "No more hallucinations. Don't let it be happening again." His heart pounded.

"You can't point your finger at me!" The raspy voice was loud and clear. It sent shivers down his back.

John covered his ears and ran to the door, then stopped short. If his mother knew he was hallucinating again, she'd tell the doctor and his dosage would be increased. He'd have to be quiet. He stood with his back pressed against the door, hyperventilating.

"You can't point your finger at me!" It screamed. John clasped his ears again. The voice was so loud it hurt. His whole body shook and his mind reeled. He knew he'd heard that voice before. The sense of familiarity alarmed him more than the sound.

He looked down on the floor and saw his clothes and tennis shoes in a pile next to him. He dressed quickly.

John walked down Pennsylvania Avenue. In front of an antique store that dated back to the thirties, he stopped. Paul Shield and his roommate shared an apartment above the store.

John stood at the bottom of the stairs that led to Paul's apartment and wondered if the man was sleeping. Was he at peace? Did he know the Lord? John walked up the steps, stood outside the door, and listened.

Lindsey and Patterson arrived at the new crime scene at 7:45 a.m. They were about to go upstairs when a car honked and Sharon rushed out of her car to catch up to them.

"Ah, man." Patterson frowned as he looked over his shoulder. "I thought you said she was sick."

Lindsey turned in her direction. "What are you doing here? I thought you'd still be in bed."

"I stopped throwing up about an hour ago, so leave it alone." Her face was ashen, and she wore wrinkled jeans and a sweatshirt.

Patterson looked at Lindsey. "Why did Henry say he thought it was the same perp? After all, our killer is an alley man. Gets his jollies by pretending it's a birth canal and all that mumbo jumbo, remember?"

Sharon ignored him and started up the stairs.

"Perp? Did you just call him a perp?" Lindsey shook his head. "Do you have any idea how stupid that sounds?"

Patterson tilted his neck and started the routine.

"Ah, geez. Can't you lay off that shoulder thing at least until noon?"

"What the hell are you talking about?" Patterson looked around like he didn't have a clue.

"Ah, forget it." Lindsey followed Sharon.

When they reached the living room of the apartment, Sharon removed a small tape-recorder and talked into it. "Curious," Sharon said, after a quick observation. "A different motive. No real hatred involved. Nothing out of place, no sign of a struggle. Fascinating."

Her eyes scanned the immaculate living room again. Overlooking the street, a bay window held four large plants on its wide marble sill. All well cared for, leaves clean and shiny and not a withered one in the bunch. Several well-executed large paintings by unfamiliar artists graced the walls. On the handsome end tables at both sides of the couch sat small framed photographs. One, apparently taken at Daytona, as there were vehicles parked behind two men who stood with their backs to the sea. Both men were balding. One was taller and huskier than the other. The smaller man wore glasses. Another photo revealed a mountainous region, she guessed Canada, with the same two men paddling a canoe in mild whitewater.

The victim lay crumpled on his side, next to the end table. He was still wearing his glasses. Blood spotted the light taupe carpet beside his head. In the midst of the cleanliness and order of the room, it was an assault to the senses.

Patterson nudged Lindsey. "I'm telling you right now, ain't no way our killer did this one."

Lindsey took a drag from his cigarette, then exhaled thoughtfully. He approached Sharon. "Do you think it was the same freak? Male victim, no clothespin this time."

Hands aren't even tied. We withheld all that information from the public. Could be a poor attempt by a copy-cat."

"We also withheld the X's and there they are." She pointed to the victim's face."

"Could have been a leak."

"No. Look at those X's. Very precise. No one else would have taken the time. It's definitely him." She walked into the bright kitchen: Counters, appliances, and white tiled floor sparkled like sun on a creek. No food or even crumbs anywhere. A vase of assorted fresh cut flowers reflected crisply on the highly polished cherry table where it stood. "It's hard to believe anyone actually lives here, let alone believe a struggle took place."

Patterson glanced around. "If you ask me, it's hard to believe any man lives here, if you get my drift." He fluttered his eyes at Lindsey, who agreed with a grin.

"Henry said the roommate would be available for an interview," Lindsey said.

Sharon nodded her head toward the bedroom. "He must be in there. I can hear someone crying."

"This ought to be fun." Patterson's right eye twitched as he strutted up to the door and knocked hard.

A cop let them in. A man lying on the bed dabbed at his nose.

"I just can't believe this," he cried. "Paul never hurt a soul."

"You're going to have to pull it together, Mr. Benson." Patterson barked like a Drill Sergeant, "We need to ask you some questions."

"Yes. Yes of course." He sat up. "I'll give you my full cooperation." He wiped his eyes with a handkerchief.

"We appreciate that," Lindsey said. "Were you at work all night?"

"Yes. You can check it out. We all work in the same room. My fellow employees will confirm it."

"Okay, we will," Lindsey said. "How long did you know Mr. Shield?

"Almost five years." He looked uncomfortable. "We had a very special relationship."

"You mean you were lovers?" Sharon asked matter-of-factly.

Mr. Benson nodded. "He meant everything to me. He was a wonderful man."

"I'm sure." Lindsey glanced quickly at Patterson who rolled his eyes, then returned his attention to Benson. "Can you think of anyone he didn't get along with? Anyone who might have given him a problem recently?"

Benson hesitated. "The only person I can think of is our landlord. He told us he was going to raise our rent." He looked at each one of them. "You see, he raised it last year around fifty dollars a month. It really made us mad because Paul had just spent a couple thousand dollars making improvements on this apartment. It just seemed so unfair. I mean, we didn't have to put our own money out like that. Fixing up a place that doesn't even belong to us. Anyway, that was bad enough, but then this year he decided to raise the rent again. This time he wanted two hundred more a month. It was outlandish!" He brushed fresh tears from his cheeks.

"Paul hit the roof, and I didn't blame him one bit. We felt he was just trying to get rid of us because of our...well, you know, our lifestyle. They got into a big argument several weeks ago. I was worried Paul might get hurt."

"Is the landlord a violent man?"

"Well, I don't know about that. He's certainly mean and ruthless."

Sharon stepped forward. "We'll want his name and address." She paused. "Did you and Mr. Shield have an exclusive relationship? Could someone else have been here with him while you were gone?"

"We were committed to one another." Benson was indignant. "We had casual friends, of course, but I don't think anyone was here because it didn't look like he'd been entertaining. Paul always was an excellent host. Could put out a full buffet with only a half hour's notice."

Patterson had to turn away.

Sharon continued her investigation. "Is there anyone else you can think of that Paul didn't get along with?"

Benson rubbed his forehead. "I can't think of a single soul. Everyone liked Paul. He had a wonderful personality." He started crying again.

Patterson shook his head and walked over to the window.

After regaining control, Mr. Benson wiped his eyes. "Of course, you know it could have been a 'hate crime'. Some homophobic person. Other than that I can't think...well now, wait a minute. There was an incident with his boss, Allen Randolph."

"Could you elaborate?" Sharon urged.

"Yes. Paul walked in on him and his secretary once at an inopportune time, if you get my drift. At first, Mr. Randolph was furious, like it was Paul's fault or something. Anyway, after he calmed down he was nice to Paul and everything more or less got back to normal until...well this might tend to put Paul in a bad light. I mean, normally, Paul wouldn't have resorted to such tactics." He shook his head. "Oh I'm getting ahead of myself. You see, Paul was feeling a little desperate for extra money to meet the increase in the rent, so he asked Mr. Randolph for a raise and apparently he was a tad firm about it."

"Firm?" Lindsey asked.

"Well...you know."

Lindsey shoved his hand into his pant pocket. "You mean he was blackmailing Randolph."

"The way Paul described it, he conducted himself in such a way as to make Randolph wonder if that's what he was doing." Benson was a little embarrassed. "He wouldn't have really caused a problem for the man."

"Did he get the raise?"

He nodded. "The next day. Five hundred dollars more a month," Benson said. "It was not only enough to cover the raise in rent, but it would have given us three hundred extra dollars to do with as we pleased. We were so excited."

"Did he ever express any fear toward Mr. Randolph after that?" Lindsey asked

"Well, no, not really. Actually, he didn't talk much about it. He was just happy to have the raise."

Sharon pushed. "He didn't say whether Randolph's

attitude had changed any?"

"No, and I didn't press. I knew he felt a little guilty about the way he went about getting the raise. So I just never brought it up again and neither did he."

"Did he tell you what kind of guy Randolph was to work for?" Lindsey asked.

"He often said the man was very nice to everyone, but Paul didn't respect his abilities or lack thereof. He acted like he was everybody's friend and like he had a handle on everything. But Paul knew better. He said if it weren't for him and Randolph's secretary and the rest of the staff making him look good, Randolph would have lost his job long ago."

"Well, a good manager does know how to delegate. He's suppose to motivate his employees so the job gets done," Sharon stated.

"Oh, I know. That's absolutely true, but apparently this went way beyond that. They had to prop him up so he wouldn't fall flat on his face." Benson's voice grew defensive. "It's true. Paul was his right hand man. No one else would have been more in a position to know than him."

"You've been very helpful. We know this is a difficult time, but you're going to have to come with us to make a statement. Plus, the crime scene specialists need to do their work and seal this place off." She nodded toward the cop standing in the corner. "Officer Scott will escort you." Sharon picked up her brief case.

Outside, Lindsey spoke to Sharon and Patterson. "I had lunch with Fred Morris, in charge of Missing Persons yesterday. We were shooting the bull about our cases and he happened to mention this Randolph character. Apparently, he's handling a missing person's investigation for him. It seems his wife has been missing for several weeks."

"Really?" Sharon raised an eyebrow. "Imagine our excitement if Allen Randolph turns out to look like Steven Segall."

"Or Pee Wee Herman," Patterson added.

As Allen walked down the long corridor, Mr. Towers motioned him into his large office.

Towers' face was grave. "You better sit down." His hands rested on his desk and his fingers clamped together.

Allen sat in a chair across from his boss. Allen's heart and mind raced. "What's wrong?"

"I hate to tell you this. I know how much you liked the guy, but I figured I'd better break the news to you before you heard it from someone else." He took in a deep breath. "Paul Shield is dead. His roommate found him in his apartment this morning. He was murdered."

"Oh my God!" Allen's eyes widened. "I can't believe this! Paul Shield? Who in the world would want to hurt him?"

Towers shook his head. "I can't imagine. The detective said he would probably be in here today to talk to everyone. So, meet with your staff and ask for their complete cooperation. Tell them to try very hard to recall anything Paul might have said or done lately that was unusual. No matter how trivial it might seem. You never know what information might help to find the killer."

"Of course. Of course." Allen's stomach churned. "Did they say how he died?"

He nodded, his face pinched with pain. "He was strangled."

"Strangled." Allen touched his neck. "What a horrible way to go."

"I know. I hate to even think about it."

Allen took a deep breath, then exhaled heavily. "I'll talk to my people right now. Thanks for letting me know first."

His staff was deeply shocked. The rest of the morning was unproductive. They speculated about who could have done it and finally decided it had to be the roommate.

Allen stared out the window of his office. Nothing seemed real. He felt numb. He left work early and wondered what would happen next.

Heather spent the day at her desk. She didn't talk or

speculate with the rest of them.

Later in the afternoon, the detectives arrived at Hoebel. They were told Paul Shield was well liked and a hard worker. Allen Randolph was also highly praised. They were disappointed that Randolph had left early and wasn't available for an interview. Their disappointment multiplied when they saw his picture in the hallway outside his office.

"Blonde hair and no mustache," Lindsey said.

Sharon nodded. "But he has pale blue eyes and an unusually dark complexion for a blonde. Also, he has the high cheek bones, the straight nose, and look at that mouth. I'd say he has American Indian or Italian ancestry."

"Looks like he's doing an Elvis Presley impersonation," Patterson said, pulling his lip up on one side.

"So the hair isn't a problem with you?" Lindsey looked back at Sharon.

"There's quite a few temporary rinses on the market. Wash it in and wash it out. Also, the mustache could be fake."

"Let's kick butt and take names!" Patterson nodded toward the door."

CHAPTER 10

When they didn't find Allen at home, the investigators stopped at Carol's apartment. She was reading a book when they knocked at her door. The detectives displayed their badges. She invited them in and told them to have a seat.

"We wanted to ask you a few questions about your daughter-in-law's disappearance. Your son has been to Missing Person's and is worried about her. We hoped you might be able to help us," Lindsey said.

Carol's voice rang loud. "Oh my goodness! Allen thinks Debbie is missing? I can't believe he's been to the police department about this." Carol covered her mouth, then continued. "We're going to have to be quiet." She gestured toward John's bedroom. "My other son, John, just went in his room to take a nap. He's on medication and it usually catches up to him around this time of day."

"No problem." Lindsey spoke softly. He removed a pad and pen from his pocket while Patterson walked around the room. "When was the last time you spoke to Debbie?"

"The day she left. She told me she needed to get away for awhile to do some thinking."

"About what?" Sharon asked.

"Well, Allen doesn't know this, but Debbie told me weeks ago that she was pregnant. She didn't want me to tell Allen that I knew."

"Why is that?"

"She needed someone to talk to. Allen's a private person. He wouldn't have liked her telling me about their problems. Debbie didn't think he was going to be real happy that she was pregnant."

"Did she say how he reacted?" Sharon asked.

Carol lowered her eyes to her lap. "Yes. Debbie said they quarreled about it. Allen accused her of purposely getting pregnant. Things quieted down between them for a couple days, but Debbie knew in her heart that their relationship was over. She called to let me know she was going to talk to Allen again and tell him she definitely wanted out of the marriage. I felt she was doing the right thing. In fact, I actually encouraged her to do it."

"Why is that?" Sharon asked.

"Don't get me wrong. Allen's not a bad person or abusive, or anything like that. He's just a workaholic and self-absorbed. He's been a fantastic provider, but a wife needs more than that. He's not the first husband who has fallen into that trap."

"True," Lindsey said wistfully. "Did she tell you where she was going?"

"Yes. St. Augustine. She knew a lawyer there who had been a family friend. She wanted him to represent her during the divorce proceeding."

"Did you ask his name?"

"No, I'm afraid not."

"Did she say how long she would be gone?"

Carol shook her head. "No. I got the impression she wouldn't be in a hurry to get back, since she didn't feel she had much to come back to."

"So their marriage had fallen apart," Lindsey said.

"I think Allen thought he didn't love her anymore. But if he was worried enough to go to the police, I can't help but wonder if he cares a lot more than he thought he did. Maybe this will be a wake-up call for him."

"The way it sounds, Allen didn't talk to you about his wife's disappearance. Don't you find that a little strange?" Lindsey asked.

"Not really. He rarely ever talks to me about

anything."

"So you really think she'll be back...that nothing bad has happened to her?"

"Of course. She'll be back after she's taken care of everything. I'm sorry you people have had to waste your time on this. Too bad you didn't come to me right away."

Patterson returned from his tour of the living room. "Allen told the detective that his marriage was good. Do you have any idea why he lied?"

Carol shrugged. "He doesn't want anyone to think he's a failure. He's always been overly concerned about what other people think of him." Carol looked suddenly thoughtful. "Early in life my two sons got along great. John, my oldest, looked after him. Allen couldn't stay out of trouble and John constantly had to rescue him. It seemed like I was always angry with Allen. John was much more patient than I was. When John got sick, Allen turned on him. He was embarrassed. Didn't want his friends to see him." She shook her head. "I had to pay a lot of attention to John, and Allen must have felt like he was being pushed aside. Being a single mother is difficult, especially when one of your children has a major illness. It's hard to find time for the normal one. I guess I failed miserably. Allen has overcompensated ever since. He's desperate to make people like him." Carol's eyes misted.

"Mrs. Randolph, have you and your boys lived here all your lives?" Patterson asked.

"Yes," she replied.

"Ever visit New York?"

"Oh yes, when my parents were still alive. They lived just outside the city. The boys and I visited most holidays."

They all exchanged glances.

Sharon spoke. "When Allen came back to Missing Person's a few days later, he suggested that Debbie might have taken off with another man."

"What?" Carol's mouth dropped open. "You can't be serious! Not in a million years. Debbie was not that kind of person." She shook her head. "Allen must have been very upset and confused to even think of such a thing."

"That's possible." Sharon added, "You mentioned that your other son isn't well, what's the nature of his illness?"

"Schizophrenia."

Sharon kept a poker face, despite the red flag that had immediately gone up. "I know that can be a devastating disease. How long has he had it?"

"It started in his early teens."

"We'd like to talk to John when he wakes up. Any bit of information could be useful."

"I'd really rather you didn't. Stress can exacerbate his disease. He's just recovering from a very bad episode."

"Oh really? What happened?"

Lindsey looked impressed with Sharon's nonchalant façade.

"Occasionally he takes off and doesn't take his medicine. This time he was gone for a couple of months. We found him living in the streets in Orlando. He just got out of the hospital. He'd been in there for a month."

"That must have been hard on you. When was he found?"

"Well, I guess it was around August the eleventh or twelfth." Carol shook her head.

Lindsey clicked his pen. "And you said he'd disappeared two months before? That would mean he'd been missing since June?"

Carol nodded. Lindsey jotted the information in his notepad.

Sharon prodded further. "Does your husband have contact with your sons?"

"Not anymore." She looked upset. "He was mentally ill also, and violent." Carol chewed on a fingernail. "I had to divorce him. He was just too dangerous. He saw the children off and on for several years. The court wouldn't let me take away his visitation rights. But, after awhile he just stopped coming over. It was a relief. We haven't seen him since."

"Do you have any idea where he might be?"

She shook her head. "No."

"What's his full name?"

"Robert John Randolph."

"What about your son? Has he ever been violent?"

"John?" She glanced at the hand John hurt. "Oh no. He's always been very passive...very sweet. A devout Christian. He wouldn't hurt anyone."

"What about when he's off his medication? From what I understand, that increases the possibility, especially if the person is drinking or taking drugs at the same time."

Carol nodded. "That's true, but I've never known him to drink or take drugs. His blood tests at the hospital never indicated anything like that."

"Who is his doctor?"

"Dr. Walters. He's with MHC. An excellent psychiatrist. He has an office in Kissimmee and Orlando."

Carol looked into Sharon's face. "Why all the questions about John? What does he have to do with Debbie going to St. Augustine?"

"Oh I'm sorry, Mrs. Randolph." Sharon lied. "I have a nephew that was just recently diagnosed with the same disease and my sister and I are trying to learn as much as we can about it."

"Oh, my goodness. If I can be of any help, let me know. How's she handling it?"

"Not well at all. She's devastated."

"I know exactly how she feels. But tell her that many people with schizophrenia return to being normal once they are on medication. Some are never quite the same but are still able to hold jobs and be productive. John was working for a convention services company, in the drafting department, just before he left this last time." Carol's shoulders relaxed a bit. "Of course, there are those with the disease who just seem to deteriorate and aren't capable of much at all. It's very sad. Hopefully, your nephew won't be in that category."

"Is John able to be left alone?"

"Not at this point. He stays at a day-center while I work and then I'm here with him every night and on weekends. I don't want to take a chance that he'll take off again. The doctor says as he continues to improve, I'll gradually be able to give him more independence."

"My sister is always worried her son will sneak out at night. How do you prevent that?"

"At night?" Carol hesitated for a moment. "That's never worried me. John gets very sleepy after he takes his evening medication. I'm sure he sleeps soundly."

"Oh well that's good." Sharon smiled. "My nephew hears voices. Has John had that problem?"

"Oh yes. That was one of the first symptoms that surfaced."

"My nephew was a little odd when he was a child. No one thought that much of it at the time but the doctor said his symptoms back then were significant."

"Oh? Like what?"

"He was mean to animals and other children."

"Oh, not John."

"My nephew also wet the bed until he was around six or seven and daydreamed a lot."

"Come to think of it, John did, too."

"He also lied, set fires and stole...."

Carol shook her head. "John never did anything like that. Actually, that sounds more like how Allen was as a child."

"What about temper tantrums or sleep problems or aggressiveness towards adults?"

Carol shook her head again. "Like I told you, he was a sweet child. The main thing with him was he had a lot of fears...phobias, nightmares and he isolated himself as he got a little older."

"He never hurt himself?"

"Not intentionally."

Sharon paused for a moment. "You said your husband was violent toward the end. Did he ever abuse John?"

"Once. I came home from shopping and found out he had locked John in a dark closet with his hands tied behind his back. The poor kid was in there for hours, terrified. That was the last time I ever left them alone together."

"Are you sure he never hurt him before that?"

"Well." Carol thought carefully, "I never thought so. At least I never saw him. And John never mentioned anything."

"You've been very helpful. I hope I can talk to you again. I'll let my sister know what you've told me. She might have more questions."

"I'd be glad to help."

"Well, I guess we've gotten a little off track," Sharon said. "We are also investigating another case besides Debbie's. I don't know if you've been told or not, one of Allen's employees, Paul Shield, was murdered."

"Oh gosh, that's terrible."

"Unfortunately, his roommate thinks Allen could have been involved. Apparently Allen and Paul Shield had a run-in not long before the murder took place."

"Allen? Involved in a murder?" Carol fidgeted. "That's impossible."

"I'm sure it is, too. But we have to explore every possible lead. When someone is murdered, everyone who had contact with the victim is considered a potential suspect. Statistics show that 80% of the murders committed are by friends, family members, or co-workers. So, please don't take offense to our questions. They're just standard procedure."

Carol nodded. "Oh, I see. I understand."

"Good." Sharon smiled warmly. "Did Allen ever talk to you about Mr. Shield?"

Carol looked embarrassed. "No." She remembered what John had told her about Paul Shield. He was the man who was blackmailing Allen. She didn't know what to do. She didn't want to lie, but she was already concerned she'd said too much. She decided to keep quiet. "I don't know anything about him."

"Well, thank you so much for your help." They gave her their cards. As they left, they looked at each other and smiled.

Patterson gave Lindsey a thumb's up. "It's Allen Randolph, for sure. He's our man, you can take that to the bank."

Lindsey shook his head as they walked toward the car. "Could just as easily be his brother. Let's do some research on both Randolph brothers and the father. As far as I'm concerned, they're all suspects at this point."

Once at the office, they immediately got to work. Within fifteen minutes, they learned the father committed suicide four years ago. That left the two sons. John had no police record, other than the recent APB Carol had requested. Allen had a juvenile rap sheet, shoplifting, arson, disturbing the peace, disorderly conduct.

Lindsey went to bed early, hoping to catch up on some sleep. He tossed and turned, and his mind raced with the information he'd received earlier. It was twelve-thirty. He decided to get up and have a shot of bourbon. When he reached his kitchen and saw his brief case on the table, he headed for the coffee maker instead. He needed answers more than he needed sleep.

Lindsey sipped his brew while he analyzed the brothers' profiles. Allen Randolph had motive. Blackmail could drive a person to drastic measures. Plus, he exhibited sociopathic symptoms as a child according to his mother's comment and his police record. However, as an adult, he had stayed clean and managed to become a successful businessman. In addition, why would he have killed the prostitutes? So far, that didn't make sense.

At this point, Lindsey leaned more toward John as the most likely candidate. John was schizophrenic and had possibly suffered some abuse at his father's hands. He also had some of the milder symptoms of a sociopath...late aged bed-wetting, phobias, excessive nightmares, daydreaming, and isolation. He also heard voices. In Sharon's profile, she mentioned an insane person could think he was being told to kill certain individuals. Most incriminating of all was the time line. The first three murders occurred while he was missing, living in Orlando, without medication. Then, during his hospitalization, the killings stopped and then started again after his release.

But why would John kill the prostitutes and an employee of his brother? Lindsey gave it some more thought, then smiled triumphantly. John Randolph was a Christian. Maybe, in his demented mind, he thought God was telling him to kill them. Killing sinful women and a man who was homosexual might have seemed justified. He probably didn't even know Paul Shield worked for his brother. His mother stressed the fact that Allen didn't communicate with either one of them. He might have seen Shield coming out of a gay bar or observed the roommate and Shield together.

As Tom poured himself another cup of coffee, his thoughts flowed. He considered the difference between the way the women and the man died. Paul Shield's murder lacked passion. Why was that? Lindsey knew this had to be significant. Did the killer think he was less a sinner than the women? Was that it? If the killer was John, could he possibly have homosexual tendencies, too? Lindsey was sure he'd read somewhere that homosexuality was higher in schizophrenics than in the normal population. If so, that would explain it.

Lindsey pondered this for a few minutes, then remembered how the redneck at the bar had insinuated the suspect was gay. Lindsey nodded his head. He was sure John Randolph was their man. He felt wired. He knew he'd never be able to sleep. He wondered if Sharon was having the same problem. He wanted to run his ideas past her.

Suddenly the phone rang. Coffee splashed out of his cup and spotted the carpet as he rushed to pick up the receiver. He hoped it was Sharon.

His face dropped and heart raced as soon as he heard Chief Henry's voice.

Just before dawn, the doorbell awakened Allen. He peeked out the side window before unlocking the latch. Two men and a woman stood on his doorstep, the tallest man holding up a badge. His heart sank.

"I'm Detective Lindsey." The man motioned to the others. "This is Agent Sharon Cross, and Detective Richard Patterson."

Allen tucked his shirt in his pants as he let them in.

He glanced at their somber faces. "Do you have news about Debbie?"

"Yes, I'm afraid so," Detective Lindsey answered.

"Oh God. It's bad, isn't it?" Allen staggered to the living room and flopped on the nearest chair.

"I'm sorry. I wish there were an easier way to tell you this." Lindsey paused. "She was found about an hour ago."

"Is she...?"

Lindsey nodded. "She's dead, Mr. Randolph"

Allen buried his face in his hands. The detectives glanced at each other uncomfortably. After several minutes, Allen looked up, his face and eyes red with grief. "Are you sure it's her?"

Lindsey nodded. "Her body was found inside her car, in a wooded area just outside of town. Her ID was on her. She also matched the description you gave missing persons, including the clothes you said she had been wearing the night she left. But we need you to come to the morgue and make a positive identification."

Allen was weak. "Do I have to? I don't think I can handle it."

Patterson glared at him. "It's your responsibility, man, let's get on with it."

"All right," Allen whispered, "just give me a minute, will you?"

"Would you like a drink?" Sharon asked.

Allen nodded. "There's a bottle of scotch under the bar."

Lindsey motioned Patterson to get it.

"I still can't believe it." His mouth trembled. "You didn't say how she died."

"She was murdered, Mr. Randolph," Lindsey said.

"Murdered?" He cried. "God, I hope she didn't suffer." He leaned forward in his chair, and covered his eyes again.

Patterson returned and nudged Allen's shoulder, then handed him the glass of scotch. They gave Allen a few minutes to be alone and stepped into the kitchen.

"Do you believe the show this guy's putting on?"

Patterson smirked.

"He's a hard read," Lindsey talked quietly.

"What do you mean?" Patterson's eye twitched.

"So far, his reaction seems genuine. But I admit, all roads do seem to point his way."

"You better believe it. First the person that was blackmailing him got it and now his wife who was about to divorce him." Patterson pressed his lips smugly. "Signed, sealed and delivered, if you ask me."

Lindsey shrugged, "Anything is possible at this point. I'm still not ruling anyone out."

Patterson shifted his weight from one foot to the other. "Hey, are you going to warn him about the decomposition?"

Lindsey shrugged.

"What about the cuts on her face?"

"The average person doesn't know what to expect when they see a corpse that's been rotting for weeks. If he mentions the X's, it'll be another red flag as far as I'm concerned. They're barely distinguishable."

"You're a calculating, mean S.O.B." Patterson smiled.

Lindsey grinned. "You must be rubbing off on me."

The morgue was colder than Allen anticipated as he followed the detectives down a harshly lit corridor. They stopped before a door on the right. "Her body is on the table." Lindsey's voice offered a last minute caution. "Prepare yourself, she's been dead quite awhile. She's messed up pretty bad. Here," he handed him a mask, "you're going to need this."

As the door swung open, the mask did little to disguise the fetid smell that struck his nostrils. They walked in and pulled down the sheet. Light auburn hair was stiff and caked with crusty blood, her face was badly rotted, and the tissue that remained was swollen to the point where the skin had detached from the muscle. Allen gasped in horror. He held his hand across his nose and mouth. The smell was overbearing and he felt faint. He stepped back and staggered toward the door. Before he reached the hallway, the blood drained from his face and the room suddenly went dark.

When he regained consciousness, he was in an upstairs office with a jacket thrown over him. He spotted Patterson first and then Lindsey. He sat up. "What happened?"

Sharon stood in the background, a quiet observer.

"You fainted, Mr. Randolph. Are you okay now?" Lindsey asked.

He shook his head, then took a deep breath.

"Was it your wife or not?" Patterson asked.

He sat silently for a moment, staring into space. "You said you found her I.D. and she was in her car. It has to be Debbie. Of course it's Debbie." He whispered almost to himself. "How does a person go on living after seeing something like that?"

Lindsey shook his head. "It's not easy." He handed him a cup of coffee. Allen's hands shook as he sipped.

"Her eyes and mouth. What was that?" Allen's eyes were growing wide and vacant. His facial muscles were slack, his mouth hung slightly open.

"What did it look like to you?" Lindsey asked.

Allen shook his head. "Almost like her eyes had been cut. Her mouth too." Allen shivered.

Sharon spoke up, "I know this is lousy timing, but I really need to ask you a few questions. It might help catch the person who did this."

"Now? Can't it wait?"

"I'm afraid not."

"I don't know what I could tell you. Nothing is making sense right now."

"There was another murder that took place recently. We believe the same person committed that murder. The same marks were on that victim. He was someone else you knew."

"Someone I knew? Who?"

"Paul Shield."

Allen's lips turned pale. "Paul's face was cut up like that, too?"

"There have been several other victims found the same way."

Allen's eyes glazed over.

"Well, I realize what you've just been through, but we're going to have to take you to the station to get your statement. We need your help."

"I'll do whatever I can." Allen's mouth quivered.

"By the way," Patterson asked, looking down at Randolph's feet, "what size shoes do you wear?"

"Eleven, why?"

Patterson gave him a cold stare while he put his neck and shoulders into gear.

In the interrogation room, Sharon sat off to one side to observe. Lindsey and Patterson sat directly across from him.

"Just make yourself comfortable. Would you like another cup of coffee? A coke? Something to eat?" Lindsey played the good cop.

Allen shook his head. "Please, don't mention food."

"All right." Patterson leaned forward aggressively. "Nitty gritty time. It's dark-stinking-thirty in the morning and I'm tired. I want to go home and get some rest. I'm going to ask you, very nicely, to be perfectly honest with us. You do that and we'll be able to wrap this up. If not, we'll all be here for hours and I'll get cranky as hell. And trust me, you don't want to see me when I'm in a bad mood."

Allen blinked hard, trying to make sense of Patterson's demeanor. "I have no reason to lie."

"Then why did you lie to Morris in Missing Persons?"

"What do you mean?"

"You told him you and your wife got along real well. You know that's a bald face lie. She was going away to hire a lawyer to divorce you."

"Who told you that?"

"Let's just say we have our sources."

"Well, your sources are wrong."

"Hey, Patterson, let's go easy on the guy. He's been through enough." Lindsey faked concern.

"Why didn't you tell Morris that you and your wife had an argument about her pregnancy."

"Debbie was pregnant?" Allen's face gained color.

"Oh, man." Patterson got up and walked to the door. "You just lit my short fuse, buddy. I got to get out of here for a minute to cool down." He stormed out of the room.

"Listen," Lindsey leaned toward Allen, speaking quietly. "Things don't look real good for you at this point. First, the spouse is always the prime suspect in a murder case. So you're going to be on the hot seat just on that principal alone. Second, you lied, which means you're covering up something and that only adds to our suspicion. Do you understand what I'm saying?"

"I'm not lying. I don't know who gave you that information, but it isn't true."

Lindsey sighed. "I'm just going to sit here for a few minutes. Give you time to think this over." He leaned back in his chair. "If you admit the truth, we can go from there. But if you continue to lie, there isn't a thing I can do for you."

Allen's forehead beaded with perspiration. His mind raced. He couldn't imagine with whom they'd been talking, unless it was Heather. He considered this, then dismissed it quickly. It couldn't have been her. She didn't know Debbie was pregnant. John! Did he tell him about the pregnancy? He couldn't remember. But if he did, maybe they got to him. If so, he could always blame John's illness for the misinformation. But he couldn't mention him unless they did. He decided to keep his mouth shut.

Patterson strutted back into the room, holding something behind his back. "So? What's the deal?"

Lindsey shook his head. "Zilch."

Patterson slammed a plastic evidence bag on the table. It contained a clothespin. "You left this somewhere. Thought you might like to have it back."

Allen looked at the bag, then looked up at Patterson, frowning. "Is this suppose to mean something to me?"

Patterson shook his head. "It should. It's yours."

"Mine! What are you talking about? I don't even use clothespins. I have a dryer." He turned to Lindsey. "What the hell is wrong with this guy?"

Lindsey didn't answer.

"I've got to hand it to you. You're pretty smooth. But I can see right through you." Patterson leered. "You better start telling the truth."

"I have." Allen crossed his arms.

"So in other words, that's your story and you're sticking to it, right?" Patterson snarled.

Allen nodded.

"You've just made a major mistake, my friend." Patterson nodded sternly. "You know what we heard? You're obsessed with trying to protect your good reputation. That's what started this whole thing, isn't it. You didn't want anyone to know you were having problems with your wife. Everybody at works thinks you wear a halo, don't they?"

Allen stared straight ahead.

Patterson slammed his hands on the table again, then sat down, keeping his eyes directly on Randolph's.

"That's it!" Allen rose from his seat. "If you want to question me anymore, you'll have to do it through my lawyer. I'm not saying another word."

"Fine," Patterson said, "but hire him fast. You got twenty-four hours." He held up a search warrant. "Meanwhile, don't go back to your house. We're going to be searching it for evidence. We'll let you know when we're done. You understand?"

Allen was furious. "I just found out my wife is dead. Now you people are making crazy accusations and tearing up my house as we speak. You guys are unbelievable. I ought to sue all of you."

Patterson snickered. "Be our guest."

The team turned the house upside down collecting anything that could potentially be evidentiary, including hair samples. There were no Nike tennis shoes. But they confiscated other shoes to make comparisons. Patterson supervised the operation. He loved it. He knew they had found their man.

The air was fresh and the sun appeared cheerful as its morning rays shimmered through the open window in Carol's living room. When Allen walked in, he didn't notice. Darkness engulfed him. His face harbored listless eyes. The skin around his mouth sagged slightly.

Carol walked out from the kitchen and took two steps in his direction, then stopped. "What's wrong? You look terrible!"

He glanced around, then sat on a chair. Ignoring her question, he asked. "John's not here?"

"Still asleep." Her eyes searched his face, then glanced at her watch. "Aren't you usually at work by now?"

He nodded. "Something terrible has happened."

"Oh, you mean about that man who worked for you? Yes, I heard. It's just awful."

"No. Not him."

"What is it? Have you lost your job?" She wiped her hands on a dishtowel.

"No, nothing like that," he answered in an irritable tone.

"Then tell me. What is it?"

He rubbed the bridge of his nose. "Its Debbie, Mom." He shook his head. "She's dead."

Confusion spread across her face. "No, there has to be some mistake. Debbie's in St. Augustine. She'll be back soon."

"No. It's true. The police found her body this morning. She was murdered."

Carol grasped the back of a chair for support.

Allen relayed the information, then watched his mother as she cried. Curiosity reflected in his expression.

"All this time, I thought she was okay," Carol said, "I knew she was meeting with her attorney and that she wasn't in a hurry to get back, so I wasn't worried. I never dreamed anything like this could have happened to her."

"How do you know these things?" His eyes were narrow. "And why didn't you tell me?"

Carol took a deep breath. "I'm sorry, son, but she made me promise not to."

His face turned taut. "What else are you keeping

from me, Mother?"

A long pause revealed her reluctance to speak.

"This is important." One side of his face twitched slightly. "What else did she say?"

"Well, she told me you two were having problems for a long time and that you were angry about the pregnancy. She said the two of you argued about it." Her hands shook. "Debbie had no one else to talk to. That's why she confided in me. Certainly you're not angry with her now...after what's happened." She dabbed her eyes with the towel.

Allen got up, walked into the kitchen and peeked out the window. "You told them, didn't you?"

"Told who?"

"The police."

"Well, they did stop over and I answered their questions truthfully, if that's what you mean."

Allen's face twisted with rage. "Why couldn't you have just kept your damn mouth shut?"

Carol eyes teetered between hurt and anger. "Is there more to this than I know?"

"You tell me! It seems like you know more than I do."

"I didn't know I was doing anything wrong. I thought Debbie was fine. I'd never do anything to intentionally hurt you." She stood and walked toward him. "Are you afraid they're going to think you did it? Is that what this is all about?"

"They already do, Mother, thanks to you. Can't you see how bad this looks?"

Carol considered this for a moment. "I really think you're overreacting. All you have to do is be honest with them and you'll be fine."

"That's a laugh," Allen smirked. "Do you have any idea how many innocent people go to jail?" He shook his head. "And even if I'm exonerated, the details of this thing will be in all the papers. Everyone will know the whole story. The people at work. My boss. Look what this will do to my image."

Carol shook her head incredulously. "How can you even think about yourself at a time like this. Doesn't worrying about your image seem just a wee bit trivial right now?"

"You don't get it, do you, Mother? You've never understood." He looked at her in disbelief. "My image is everything to me. It's all I've ever really had." His eyes filled with tears just before he stormed out of the apartment, slamming the door behind him.

Carol stared in silence at the spot where he had been standing.

"Are you okay, Mom?" John was suddenly behind her.

"Oh, John!" She searched his face. "Did you hear what happened?"

John nodded. "I feel so bad, I loved Debbie." He patted Carol on the back. "Don't take Allen's reaction too personally. He's upset. Maybe even in shock. He didn't mean to be so hard on you." John's eyes brimmed with tears. "I've got to find a way to help him."

Carol shook her head. "Most of what Allen is going through is what he's brought on himself. I don't think anyone can help him get out of this mess."

"He's my brother, I have to try."

John went back to his room and lay down on his bed to pray. He had to get direction. Had to get an answer. He'd been praying relentlessly, for over an hour, when he heard the voice. It was similar to the one that had haunted him for months. However, this time, it wasn't frightening or loud and he finally realized it wasn't the devil or a hallucination. It was part of an emerging memory.

As he stared at the ceiling, a feeling of familiarity swept over him. He'd forgotten so much of what occurred during his time on the streets. Somehow, he knew he'd heard this voice during that time and that it had something to do with the murderer. He believed if he prayed hard enough, God would help him remember everything and then the killings would stop. He prayed throughout the remainder of the morning and would have continued throughout the rest of the day, but around noon, the doorbell rang and distracted him.

CHAPTER 11

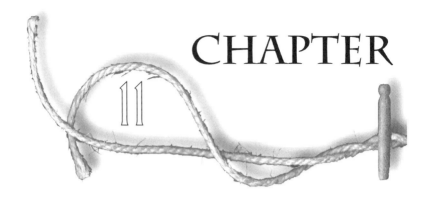

Linda and Anthony stood at Carol's door. "We know food is probably the last thing on your mind, but we brought lunch anyway. You should try to eat." Linda held up several bags from McDonald's.

"That's really nice of you." Carol's eyes were red and swollen. "Please, come on in."

Linda said, "I just can't believe what happened. I know how much Debbie meant to you. I'm so sorry."

"Me, too." Anthony reached for her hand. "Linda told me this morning how much you loved your daughter-in-law. I didn't realize how close the two of you were. You must be devastated."

Carol turned away, and wiped her eyes. "She was the sweetest person...she deserved so much more from life than she got."

Linda patted her shoulder. "How is Allen taking it?"

"He's in bad shape. He's not only grieving for Debbie, I think he's also feeling very guilty for the way he'd treated her these last few years. He's also afraid the police think he's the killer."

Anthony frowned. "Well, surely he has an alibi. Where was he when it happened?"

"I have no idea. He didn't stay very long. He was too upset."

Linda gave Anthony a meaningful look. "Well, I'm sure his name will be cleared as soon as all the facts are in."

Carol sighed. "I just don't understand why things like this happen."

Linda shook her head. "I know, it's hard to make sense of it. But they say everything happens for a reason. We don't always understand what God has planned, but..."

"Don't even mention God to me," Carol snapped.

"I'm sorry. But at times like these..."

Carol's eyes narrowed. "At times like these, I realize how right I was to turn my back on Him. How could He let this happen to someone as sweet as Debbie and that innocent baby inside of her?"

"Baby?" Anthony's mouth dropped open as he turned to Linda. "You didn't tell me she was pregnant."

"I didn't know," Linda said.

"Debbie didn't want me to tell anyone," Carol explained.

Anthony closed his eyes and rubbed his forehead. Tears slid down his cheeks. Both women looked surprised at the depth of his reaction. "I should have talked to both of them, helped them iron out their differences. Then she wouldn't have left and this wouldn't have happened."

"Anthony, there's nothing you could have done," Carol said.

Anthony got up, walked to the other side of the room, and kneaded the back of his neck with his hand. He took deep breaths in what appeared to be an effort to calm himself.

Linda pulled Carol aside. "He's really taking this hard."

Carol nodded. "I know and he didn't even know Debbie."

"But he knows you. I think that's what's bothering him so much. He hates knowing you are hurting like this." Her eyes misted. "He's a very sensitive man. He amazes me more and more every day."

Several minutes later, John came out of his bedroom and stopped short when he spotted Anthony.

Linda smiled. "John, come and join us."

John ignored her, then went

into the kitchen, and got a glass of water.

"Why don't you get started? Maybe if we see you enjoying lunch, we might get motivated."

"Okay." Linda removed a wrapper from a cheeseburger. "Come on over and sit down, Anthony. The food's getting cold."

With his back to them, he quickly wiped his face, then walked over to Carol. He placed his hands on her shoulders. "Listen, sweetheart," his dark eyes seemed to penetrate hers, "if there's anything you need...anyway I can help, I'm here for you."

"I know, Anthony. I appreciate it very much. Thank you."

John watched from the archway, then walked into the dining room, and addressed Anthony. "You must be the man Allen told me about."

Carol's forehead crinkled, as she turned and moved toward John. "How does Allen know Anthony?"

John shrugged, "That's not important." He returned his attention to Anthony. "How long have you known my mother?"

Carol felt blood rise to her face.

"A couple months now." He wiped away the remainder of his tears, with the heel of each hand. "She's a wonderful person."

"Yes, she is. She means everything to me."

"I'm sure she does. And you mean everything to her." Anthony turned halfway around from the table to wipe his nose with a napkin.

"You have an accent. Where are you from?"

Carol's cheeks were hot. "John! Why all the questions?"

Anthony smiled patiently as he turned back to face Carol. "It's no problem. He's just checking me out. That's a son's job." He winked at Carol, then looked at John. "Maybe if I tell you a little about myself it will relieve your apprehension. "I was raised in Virginia and moved here a few months ago to sell family real estate. I'm also a pilot and own a jet. In fact, I'd love to take you and your mother up sometime, if you're interested."

John shook his head.

"Well, maybe you'll change your mind once you get to know me better." Anthony smiled. "Anyway, John, I've never been arrested, I make a decent salary, I give to charities and my worst vice is being a little too inquisitive at times. Your mother could attest to that." He glanced at Carol again. "I've taken an interest in her because I think she's a very special person."

John considered this for a moment. "Have you ever been married? Have any children?"

"No." He sat back in his chair.

The doorbell rang. Carol looked relieved as she jumped up to answer it.

It was Lindsey and Cross. "Hi, Mrs. Randolph." Sharon looked past her at the people in the dining room. "We're very sorry about your daughter-in-law. Please accept our condolences. We were hoping we could talk to you, but I can see you're busy."

"Yes I am." Her tone was aloof.

"I understand." Sharon glanced toward the table. "Is that your son, John?"

Carol nodded.

"He looks so much like Allen. They could pass for twins."

"I know. Everyone says that," Carol replied.

"I'd really like to meet him," Sharon said. "But, I guess this isn't the best time."

"Maybe another day."

John called out, "Mother, are they from the police department?"

Carol's mouth turned downward. "Yes, dear, it's the detectives that are working on the case."

"Well, let them in," he said. "Maybe we can help them."

Carol shrugged and opened the door wider.

"Are you sure it's okay?" Sharon asked.

"Yes. I'm sorry, John's manners are much better than mine. Come on in."

"Well, thank you. It would mean a lot." Sharon moved toward the table.

After introductions, and an invitation to sit, Linda handed them sandwiches and fries. "Here. Dig in, we brought plenty."

"I feel terrible barging in like this. We didn't come here to eat," Sharon said.

Lindsey ate without the obligatory apology.

"Don't worry about it." Carol's voice warmed slightly. "Actually, it's probably good we have company. Maybe it'll help keep my mind off what happened." Carol waved to her son, "Come on, John. Sit down. You need to eat too."

John took a seat and scattered french-fries on his plate.

Carol walked toward the kitchen. "I'm going to get some coffee," she announced over her shoulder.

Anthony turned to Sharon. "How long have you been a detective?"

"About fifteen years altogether."

"You don't look old enough to have been working that long. What made you decide to get into it?"

She removed the wrapper from a quarter-pounder. "Curiosity."

"Really." Anthony studied her for a moment. "So, murder must intrigue you. That's interesting. It seems like an unlikely field for a woman."

"Not really," Sharon replied.

Anthony's dark eyes seemed thoughtful. "What does your husband think of your line of work?"

Lindsey looked up suddenly, taking a break from his sandwich.

"I'm not married."

"Anthony, for crying out loud." Linda turned to Sharon. "Don't mind him. He's nosey."

As Carol walked back in with a tray of coffee mugs, Linda nodded in her direction. "Ask Carol. He wouldn't leave her alone until he knew every aspect of her life."

"Oh?" Sharon smiled at Carol.

"Yes that's true. Frankly, I don't know why he finds me so interesting." She set the tray on the table.

"It's because you're a remarkable woman. Isn't that right, John?" Anthony winked.

John nodded, with obvious reluctance.

Carol sighed. "Please, let's change the subject, I've never been comfortable with compliments."

Anthony grinned. "She's also very humble."

John looked at Sharon. "I hope you find the murderer, Detective Cross. Debbie was a good person. Just like my mother. She'd never hurt anyone. I'll be praying for your success." Honesty and sincerity covered his face.

Lindsey peered at John over his whopper.

Sharon's eyes showed warmth. "Thank you, I appreciate that."

"I'm also praying for the murderer. It's not easy to do, but the Lord says we must love our neighbor as ourselves and to hate the sin, not the sinner. So I'm praying for his salvation and deliverance. Only God can change a man's heart."

"Do you really believe a person like this killer could actually change?" Sharon asked.

"With God, all things are possible."

"Not very many people have your kind of faith, John," Sharon said.

"That's because not very many people have a personal relationship with the Lord. Especially today. Most people are embarrassed to express their beliefs aloud. They've become complacent and satisfied in their comfort zones. They fear ridicule." John's eyes reflected sadness. "And let's face it, in today's world, if someone is fervent about God, he's rejected by society. He becomes a laughing stock. But what they're not remembering, is that Jesus said, 'if you are lukewarm about me, I will spew you out of my mouth'. I'd rather be called a zealot for God and face the ridicule of man, than be accepted by man and face the wrath of God." He sighed, "The Lord must look down at this country of ours, after blessing it so abundantly, and shake his head in disgust."

Carol shifted nervously in her chair.

Sharon smiled at John. "I'm sure He does." She paused. "I'd really like to talk to you about your beliefs sometime."

"I'd like that." John smiled. "The Lord is my favorite

subject.

"Sharon looked at Carol. "He's inspiring."

"I know," Carol answered. "I can't imagine my life without him."

Anthony gestured with his hands, palms turned upward. "You see what I'm talking about? Isn't she fantastic?"

Lindsey rolled his eyes.

Carol sighed. "Please, Anthony. Focus on Detective Cross for awhile. I'm really not up to this."

"Okay, I'm sorry." Anthony turned to Sharon. "Tell me, Agent Cross, what makes a serial-killer tick?"

"Funny. I don't recall mentioning a serial-killer." She said, her face emotionless.

"You didn't need to. It's pretty obvious. The news is full of information. First those prostitutes and now this. It seems likely they're tied together somehow."

"We're not sure yet who or what we're dealing with." Sharon frowned. "It's very complicated."

"Well, let's talk in generalities then. I've always wondered how this kind of murderer is created. Is it genetic or environmental?"

"Each case is different," she explained. "Sometimes it's a mixture of both."

"There's also another realm at work," John interjected. "The powers of good and evil. When a person chooses to open the door to good, he possesses the ability to overcome the worst of obstacles. But if the door to evil is chosen, those obstacles overtake him. Then, a monster emerges and lives amongst us."

They all stopped eating for a moment.

Anthony studied John, as he digested his comment. "So you believe a killer makes a conscious choice to take the wrong path. And that despite genetic predisposition or life experiences, he could have chosen the other direction and turned out normal."

"Maybe not normal, by society's standards. But he could have at least kept himself from hurting other people."

"There are professionals in my line of work that share

your theory," Sharon said. "Ted Bundy is a good example. It's obvious he had problems as far back as early childhood, but he openly admitted it wasn't until he delved into pornography and sadomasochistic material that he started killing. He chose to open that door."

Anthony turned to Sharon. "A person this evil could put you in jeopardy. Aren't you ever the least bit concerned that he might try to get rid of you since you're trying to stop him?"

"I don't waste time thinking about such things." She looked at Carol. "And under the circumstances, I'd prefer changing the subject. It just doesn't seem appropriate."

Anthony shook his head, smiling uncomfortably. "Of course. I'm afraid I'm not being very sensitive." His eyes turned to Carol. "I apologize. But I did have a reason for asking these questions. Something happened to me last night that might have to do with this case. Do you mind if I just take a few minutes more to discuss it?"

Carol shook her head. Her eyes looked weary.

"I was attacked after I got back to my apartment. It happened just as I got out of my car." He looked at Sharon.

"What? And you didn't tell me?" Linda was shocked.

Anthony stopped her with the palm of his hand. "Relax. It wasn't that big of a deal." He turned to Sharon. "But I thought I'd better mention it."

Lindsey's eyes shouted skepticism.

"You didn't report this to the police?" Sharon asked.

"No, I guess I should have."

"Yes you should. Did he have a weapon?"

Anthony nodded. "He came up from behind, grabbed me and held a knife to my throat." He shook his head. "I was more mad than scared. So I jabbed him with my elbow and he took off running." He smiled at Lindsey with a sense of comradery.

Lindsey rejected his gesture with a deadpan stare.

"What time did this happen?" Sharon asked.

"Well, let's see." He looked at Linda. "What time did I leave your place?"

"Around twelve."

"Then it must have been twenty after or so. Doesn't take me long to get back to my apartment."

"Could you give us a description of the attacker?" Sharon asked.

"About my height, maybe a little taller. I couldn't see his face. He was wearing a ski mask and was dressed in dark clothing."

"I can't believe you kept this to yourself. Your machismo could get you killed someday."

"Like I said, it wasn't a big deal." Anthony smiled proudly, his brown eyes sparkling. "I handled it, didn't I?"

Lindsey shook his head and chuckled under his breath.

Sharon pointed her forefinger at Anthony. "You definitely need to come to the station and file a report. He could very well have been the man we're looking for."

Anthony raised his eyebrows. "But that's all I know. There's nothing more to add."

"I'd still like to have the attack documented," Sharon insisted.

Anthony shrugged his shoulders. "Okay. If you really think it's important, I'll stop by later."

"Good." Sharon crumpled her napkin and placed it on the table. She turned to Carol. "Could I see you in the living room for a minute?"

Carol followed Sharon into the other room. "What's wrong?"

"Do you have power of attorney over John?"

"Yes, why?"

"We'd like to take a pair of John's tennis shoes into the lab for testing."

Her eyes narrowed with creeping anger. "What in the world for?"

"To help eliminate him as a possible suspect. Matched sets of footprints were found at each crime scene, so we're collecting shoes from as many people as possible. We don't believe John has done anything wrong. It's just routine."

"I hope you mean that, because there is no way in

this world John would hurt anyone. I'd bet my life on it."
"I'm sure you're right, Mrs. Randolph. He seems like a wonderful person."
"Do I have to give them to you?"
"Not without a warrant," Sharon explained. "But since you're convinced John had nothing to do with the murders, I don't understand why you'd refuse."
Carol tugged on her earlobe. "Well, I guess it won't hurt anything, John has nothing to hide."

When they were back in the car, Lindsey spoke first. "Okay, what's your take?"
"John seems genuine to me," Sharon said. "It's hard to imagine him killing anyone. Despite his illness, he seems to be a moral person and I didn't detect any apparent signs of delusional thinking at this point."
Lindsey slipped his key into the ignition. "Seems a little too wrapped up in religion, if you ask me."
"I don't think so. There's nothing wrong with having a firm belief in one's faith. If there were, every pastor, priest and rabbi would be hauled off to the funny farm. Besides, everything he said made good sense to me."
"I wouldn't know. The only time I set foot in a church was when I got married, and you know how that turned out." Lindsey shrugged. "What was that idiot's last name?"
Sharon's brows knitted together. "What idiot? Who are you talking about?"
"That jerk. You know, Anthony."
"I believe they said, *Pinto*." Her eyebrows crammed together. "Why are you calling him a jerk?"
"I don't believe his story, for one thing."
"You mean about being attacked?"
Lindsey nodded. "He could have made the whole thing up to impress everyone." Lindsey looked in the rearview mirror and smoothed back his hair. "The man's an idiot."
Sharon shook her head smiling slightly.
"I got the impression Pinto and Linda were a couple, so why was he gushing all over Carol Randolph? What's that all about anyway?" Lindsey rubbed his chin. "She's old enough to be his mother."

"I don't know. I guess he admires her."

"Yeah, to the point of being ridiculous. I'm surprised his girlfriend doesn't punch his lights out."

"She probably doesn't feel threatened. She most likely knows he doesn't think of Mrs. Randolph in a romantic way." She sat quietly for a moment. "But I have to admit, John didn't look real happy about the attention Anthony was showing his mother. Maybe he's not convinced that their relationship is platonic."

"I think you're right." Lindsey turned a corner and they were silent for a few minutes. He glanced at Sharon. "What are you thinking?"

"Well, if Anthony was attacked, like he claims and John strongly resents Anthony's intrusion, that would give John motive to kill him." She frowned. "I mean, he really hasn't had to share his mother with anyone for years."

"You just got done saying you couldn't imagine John killing anyone."

"I know. I'm just saying it's a possibility. I've got to stay open minded."

Lindsey cleared his throat. "Regardless, when Pinto shows up at the station, I'm going to run a background check on him."

"A background check?" Sharon laughed. "Any particular reason?"

"Yeah." Lindsey crossed into the passing lane. "He was just a little too curious about serial-killers, if you ask me."

"Everyone is curious about the serial-killer. You can't pick up a newspaper or listen to the news without hearing speculation about the murders."

"Yeah, well, I'm still going to check him out."

"Okay," Sharon grinned. "But I can't help wondering if maybe the real reason you don't like Anthony is because you're just a little bit jealous."

"Of what?" Lindsey asked, indignantly.

"Oh, I don't know. Maybe his disgustingly good looks, for starters."

"He was good looking?" Lindsey acted surprised. "I

didn't even notice. But even if I had, his looks wouldn't threaten me. After all, I'm not exactly chipped beef, you know." Lindsey straightened his tie. "In fact, when I get cleaned up I can give Tom Cruise a run for his money."

"In that case, I'm really looking forward to seeing you cleaned up."

Lindsey laughed.

Allen drove around aimlessly for hours. He couldn't go back home yet and he didn't want to go to work. Under the circumstances, he knew it wouldn't seem appropriate.

His mind rambled. At first, knowing his enemies were finally incapable of running their mouths gave him fleeting moments of relief. Now, reality set in. He realized they were more dangerous to him dead than alive. He determined to stick with his story, especially the part about Heather. All he had to do was make sure she didn't talk. He stopped at a strip mall and stepped into a phone booth, then called the office.

"It's me." His voice was husky.

"Allen?"

"Yeah, babe. I need to talk to you."

"I'm sure." She inspected her nails. "Heard about your wife. It was on the local news this morning. Everyone is talking about it. First Paul. Now Debbie. Who's going to get it next?"

"Heather, for God's sake, can anyone hear you talking? Things look bad enough."

"You can say that again."

"As I said, I need to talk to you. I'll meet you at your apartment at six o'clock tonight."

"Are you sure you want to do that? What if you're being followed."

"Will you cut it out? I don't think I'm being followed. At least, not yet."

"I'm not so sure. Anyway, I'm still mad at you for the way you spoke to me the other day."

"Look, I'm sorry, baby. I've been going through hell and I took it out on you. I know I shouldn't have done that."

"You got that right."

"Look, I don't want to get into this over the phone. I'll see you tonight."

An hour later, Detective Lindsey and Patterson interviewed Allen's staff again. This time their focus was on Allen. Everyone sang his praises and seemed sincere. Even their interview with his boss, Mr. Towers, seemed to confirm the consensus. He mentioned that Allen had arranged a raise recently for Shield. When asked if this was out of character, Towers said no. He explained how Allen had done the same thing for another employee just a week before. Patterson's shoulders tightened as they walked toward Heather Martin's desk.

When Heather turned her swivel chair to face them, her tight skirt shimmied up near the top of her firm thighs. Patterson made a feeble attempt to keep his eyes on her face. "I guess you know why we're here."

Heather nodded. "Yes, of course." She shook her head. "What a terrible tragedy." She wet her lips with her tongue. "I sure hope you find out who did it. We all loved Paul and Mrs. Randolph. Mr. Randolph must be devastated."

"Have you talked to him?" Lindsey asked.

Heather hesitated. "Yes, he called earlier to let me know he wouldn't be in. He sounded terrible."

"Did he say anything about the murder?" Lindsey asked.

"No."

Lindsey motioned toward an empty chair. "You mind?"

"Go ahead. There's another chair over there, if your partner would like to have a seat, too."

Lindsey removed his notepad from his jacket pocket while Patterson sat down. "What time do you think he called?"

"Oh gosh, I don't know. Maybe around one o'clock."

"Did Mr. Randolph ever talk about his wife?"

"In a general way, yes. I got the impression he cared

about her very much. But Mr. Randolph's a private person. He never discussed their relationship in depth with any of us."

"So he was secretive," Patterson said.

"I didn't say that." Heather's eyes narrowed. "Why all the questions?"

"Just routine." Patterson glanced at her legs again, which from his new vantage point, seemed to grow longer as they spoke. He caught himself. "How did Randolph and Shield get along?"

"They had an excellent relationship. Mr. Randolph got along with everyone, and so did Mr. Shield." She frowned. "I hope you don't think Mr. Randolph had anything to do with these murders. There's just no way."

Patterson studied her soberly.

"Well, I wish I could help you further. But like I said, Mr. Randolph never confided in me." Heather pushed back from her desk.

"That's a little hard to believe." Smugness slid across Patterson's face. "We heard you two were together all the time. Inseparable, in fact. We also heard that Mr. Shield caught you and Randolph in a compromising situation."

"Who told you that?"

"Paul Shield's room mate." One corner of Patterson's lip turned up slightly.

"That is not true. He's probably the one that killed Paul. He's trying to divert your attention." Her cheeks turned darker than the red blusher she was wearing.

"Impossible. He has an airtight alibi. Besides, it's common knowledge around here that you and Randolph were having an affair." Patterson's eyes twinkled.

"That's nonsense." Heather's eyes countered his twinkle with a glare.

Lindsey spoke up. "Are you willing to deny that rumor under oath? We could get you to take a deposition."

"I'm not doing anything I don't have to do."

"You might not have a choice."

Heather picked up a stack of papers, tapped them hastily together on her desk, then stood up, and began to walk away.

Lindsey's eyes opened wide. "At the risk of sounding overly sensitive, it seems like you're dismissing us."

Heather's eyes looked cold as she smiled. "How perceptive."

"We'll be back." Patterson hit her with his best "Arnold" accent.

Heather turned, shaking her head. "You guys have seen too many movies."

Patterson watched her walk out of the room. He sighed. "Lucky Allen."

"I'm not so sure." Lindsey nudged him with his elbow. "Come on, we've got work to do.

When they returned to the station, Sharon met them in the hall. "Just got word from forensics. John Randolph's tennis shoe matched a print that was found on the outside hallway of Paul Shield's apartment."

Lindsey raised his eyebrows. "I can't believe it!"

"Well, don't get too excited. The print was a one of a kind. It didn't match the prints found at any of the other crime scenes and the wear pattern on the heel was completely different. Plus, we found footprints inside the apartment that did match the other scenes."

Lindsey scratched the side of his head. "But we know John was there at some point."

"Yes. At least outside of the apartment. The print was undisturbed. So he had to have been there recently."

Patterson frowned. "I still say it was Allen. He probably wore John's shoes just to frame him." Patterson shrugged. "I wouldn't put anything past that bastard."

"If that's true, why would he wear the other shoes on the inside of the apartment? It doesn't make sense."

Patterson's eye twitched. "Maybe both brothers were involved. Allen talked John into staying outside to guard the place, while he went in and did the dirty work."

Lindsey stroked his chin. "That's possible."

Sharon gently placed her hand on Lindsey's arm. "I've got an appointment. I'll meet up with you later."

"Okay." His eyes lingered on her as she walked away.

Patterson waited until she was out of earshot. "What's up with that?"

"With what?"

"Come on man, I wasn't born yesterday. Something's going on between you and Agent Hocus-Pocus. Admit it."

"Not like you think. I've just come to realize she's a damn good investigator."

"Ain't buying." Patterson shook his head. "I'm a damn good investigator, too, but you don't look at me like that."

Lindsey waved him off with his hand. "You ought to be glad I don't."

Patterson nodded. "You got that right." He studied Lindsey for a moment. "I just don't know what you see in her. Of all the beautiful women around to choose from, you pick one that looks like Olive Oil on steroids." He shook his head. "Strange taste, if you ask me."

"I didn't ask you," Lindsey snapped.

"Detective Lindsey!" One of his men approached him. "We got Anthony Pinto's statement and the background check you wanted just came in." He handed Lindsey a folder.

"Good." Lindsey rifled through the report on the way to his office. Once inside, he propped his feet up on his desk, and leaned back in his chair, then continued to scan the pages. Patterson tapped his forefinger on his lower lip, while he waited. Finally, he asked, "Well?"

"Well, nothing. Not a damn thing. Not even a speeding ticket." Lindsey slammed the folder down on his desk. He grabbed his pack of cigarettes from the desk. "Pinto is disgustingly clean. In fact, if he ran for office he'd be one of the few politicians in this country the press couldn't pick apart." He lit a cigarette with a quick flash of his lighter.

"Why'd you suspect him to begin with?"

"I don't know. He got on my nerves. I guess I was just hoping it'd be somebody like him."

"You mean Allen Randolph isn't despicable enough to get you riled up?"

"Sure, but there was something about this other guy that got under my skin."

"Well, maybe we could at least rattle him a little...you

know, just for good measure." Patterson winked.

Lindsey nodded. "Yeah. Sometimes pretty boys like that need to be brought down a peg or two. We'd probably be doing him a favor in the long run. Help make him a little less shallow." He grinned slyly. "Besides, I've got to take my frustrations out on somebody or I'm going to lose it."

Patterson nodded. "Absolutely. You earned it. You're entitled."

"And I'm out of here." Lindsey jumped to his feet.

"Wait up! This sounds like fun."

They parked outside Anthony's apartment and stared at the upstairs window.

"Hold on," Lindsey said as Patterson started to open the door. "I think I saw his curtains move. He's probably checking us out. I want to stay put for awhile and let him sweat it."

Patterson strained his neck. "There ain't a back door, is there?"

"No. I checked before we turned the corner. He isn't going anywhere. Besides, he really doesn't have any reason to bolt, remember?"

"What are you going to say to him?"

"I don't know. I'll improvise." Lindsey gestured toward the window and laughed. "Look, there he is again. I just saw his face. He knows its us."

"Come on, man, I hate sitting around. Let's rock and roll."

"Man, you are so impatient. Got to have that instant gratification, don't you? You're worse than a kid." Lindsey shook his head. "All right, come on, for crying out loud."

When Patterson slammed his door, he gave himself a little shrug, puffed out his chest, and sucked in his gut. They climbed the stairs and rang the doorbell. Anthony answered promptly.

"Detective Lindsey, right?" Anthony extended his hand in greeting.

"This is my partner, Detective Patterson." Lindsey's eyes were steely.

Anthony nodded. "Nice to meet you. So what's up?"

"We'd like to ask you a few questions. Sorry I wasn't at the station when you stopped by."

"No problem. Come on in." He gestured toward the living room.

Lindsey wasted no time. "I have to tell you from the start, that a few things bother me about your statement."

Anthony looked amused. "Oh? Like what?"

"Well, your statement says the assailant held a knife against your neck, but the pictures they took of your throat didn't show any marks."

"I explained that to the officers. He wasn't pressing very hard."

"The knife the killer uses is razor sharp. Even mild pressure would have at least broken the skin."

Anthony shrugged. "I don't know why it didn't. Maybe he forgot to sharpen it."

Lindsey shook his head. "And the report says there wasn't a single bruise on your body."

"He really didn't hurt me."

"But an assailant always makes sure he has a good grip on his victim." He studied Anthony, then continued. "And there's something else. You said you elbowed him and he took off running."

"That's how it happened."

Lindsey scratched the back of his head. "Peculiar. Everything we know about this guy so far is that he's no lightweight. He's built pretty well. Most likely, in excellent condition, in fact. Seems like it would take a lot more than a poke of an elbow to stop him."

Anthony shrugged. "All I can say is, that's what happened. And I'm not exactly a lightweight either, in case you haven't noticed. I'm sure I must have knocked the wind out of him."

"Oh, that's the explanation." He turned to Patterson. "Was that explanation on the report?"

Patterson shook his head. "Nope. Never said anything about knocking the wind out of the guy."

"Well, I'm assuming that's what happened." Anthony's face reddened slightly. "What other explanation could there be?"

"There's only one I can think of." Lindsey pulled out a cigarette and took his time lighting it. "You don't mind do you?" He exhaled a blue stream in Pinto's direction.

Anthony shook his head.

Lindsey drew in more smoke, then exhaled leisurely. "Yes sir, there's only one other explanation I can think of." Lindsey finally took a seat. "What about you?" He asked Patterson.

Patterson nodded. "I'm in agreement. Only one explanation comes to my mind too."

Lindsey stared down at his cigarette. "Got an ash tray?"

"Well, no. Actually I don't smoke. But wait a minute. I'll see what I can find." As Anthony rose to go into the kitchen, they noticed tension along his jaw line.

Patterson grinned and gave Lindsey a thumb's up.

Anthony returned and handed Lindsey a saucer. "Here, I'm sorry, this is all I have."

"No problem." Lindsey flicked the ash onto the plate and set it on a coffee table. "Maybe we better all sit down. This might take awhile."

Anthony frowned as he sat across from Lindsey.

Lindsey leaned forward in his chair. His elbows rested casually on his knees. "The explanation is this, Pinto. You made up the whole story. The question is why?"

"What?" Anthony's brown eyes widened. "That's ludicrous."

"Is it?" Lindsey locked onto his eyes and held them fast. "I don't think so. What about you, Patterson."

"Nope. Doesn't sound ludicrous to me either."

"I resent the hell out of this. I didn't even want to make out a report. Agent Cross talked me into it." His voice grew loud. "How dare you come in here and accuse me of being a liar."

"It's been my experience that people lie about this sort of thing for one of two reasons. One is to get attention. The other is to try to make themselves look like a victim so they aren't considered a suspect themselves."

"What the hell? Now you're saying I'm either a person who starves for attention or a ghoul that kills innocent people?" He extended his hands, palms up. "Look at me. Do I look like a man who could possibly lack attention? And my reputation is flawless. Check me out if you want. I've never broken the law in any way, let alone killed someone." Anthony's face flared with indignation.

Lindsey's eyes squinted. "I'm a pretty good judge of character and I've got a sixth sense when it comes to people lying to me. I'm telling you right now, I don't believe you. Something is wrong. Something is very wrong with you and your story. I don't have the answer yet, but I will. I'm going to be watching you. Understand me?"

Anthony got up and walked to the stairs. "You've obviously got some sort of personal bias against me and I'm not about to put up with you or your sidekick over there for another minute." He yelled. "Now, get out of here. If you ever want to talk to me again, you'd better have a warrant."

Lindsey and Patterson eyeballed him on their way to the stairs. "And if it comes to that, you'd better have a good lawyer," Lindsey said.

Pastor Davis was working at his desk, when John knocked on his office door and walked in.

"John, it's so good to see you." He got out of his chair and shook John's hand. "You look wonderful. We've all been praying for you."

"Thank you. Please keep it up. The enemy thought he had me this time." He sat down in a chair.

"We'll keep you on our prayer list."

"Thank you. Put my brother Allen on the list, too."

"I heard what happened to his wife. I'm so sorry. He must be hurting badly. I can't imagine what it must be like, especially since he doesn't have the Lord to cling to."

John nodded. "I'm doing all I can to help. After all, I am his older brother."

The pastor nodded pensively.

"The police say whoever murdered Debbie also killed Mr. Shield, the man who worked for Allen." John shivered. "This man must be very sick. I've been praying that they catch him. I've also been praying for his salvation."

"That's very generous of you, John. Especially since he's caused your family so much heartbreak."

"He's a human being, regardless of his sin and he's in need of the Lord's forgiveness. Just like all of us." John's eyes did not meet the pastor's. "Please remember him in your prayers as well."

"Absolutely."

He was quiet for a moment. "I'd like to come back to services, but..."

"I understand." His aged eyes were soft and warm. "Your mother still thinks I turned you into a religious fanatic."

He nodded.

Pastor Davis closed his eyes. "I remember a time when she loved the Lord and was proud of it."

A slight smile brightened John's face. "It seems so long ago."

"Don't worry about her, John, she'll come back once the bitterness fades. She's been through a lot. It might take a little time."

John stood, walked to the window, and looked up at his apartment building. "Sometimes, I guess it's a person's time to die. No matter how much you pray for them, if God wants them, there is nothing you can do to prevent it."

"Are you thinking about Debbie?"

"Yes, and Mr. Shield. I was there the night he was killed."

The pastor's forehead furrowed. "At Mr. Shield's? Why were you there?"

"My brother told me Mr. Shield was blackmailing him. He was afraid his job was in jeopardy. I didn't want Allen to get hurt, so I went there to intervene."

Pastor Davis' heart rate increased. "Were you there around the time he was murdered?"

John shrugged his shoulders, still gazing out the window. "I don't know. I might have been. I was there almost the whole night, but it didn't do any good, I failed him. I planned on praying outside his door, but after a few minutes I fell asleep."

"Have you told anyone else that you were there, John?"

"No. Should I?"

"Yes! I think you should tell the police." Pastor studied him carefully. "I have to warn you, though, the police might think you killed him."

John's face appeared distant when he turned to face him. "There's something else, Pastor. I remember hearing the killer talk. Not at Mr. Shield's place, somewhere else. I remember something he said and I believe God is trying to help me remember more."

Pastor Davis' eyes were wide with alarm.

"I love my mother and I know she wants me to stay out of Allen's business. But I also love my brother and I have to live up to my responsibilities. Sometimes a person has to make difficult choices."

"John." Pastor took a deep breath. "You can only do so much for your brother. He has to be responsible for himself now. He's an adult. He must handle his own problems. The only thing he needs from you right now is prayer."

"That's what I do. I pray all the time."

"And that's all you've been doing for him, right?"

John looked back up at his kitchen window. "I better go. My mother will be looking for me." He walked toward the door. "Thank you, I'll be back to see you soon." John smiled briefly, then left.

Pastor Davis watched him walk across the street and into his apartment building. His heart still raced. Could he have been wrong about this young man whom he had loved all these years? Could the boy have two completely different sides to his personality? Was one of those sides a monster? On the other hand, was he innocent and about to be falsely blamed for these horrendous crimes?

He turned around, walked into the church, and headed for the altar. With tears streaming down his cheeks, he stared at the large wooden cross on the wall before him. Quickly, he lay face down on the floor and cried out to God.

CHAPTER 12

Heather sprang to the door. "Get in here before someone sees you." She grabbed Allen's hand and pulled him into her apartment.

Allen searched her face. "You look scared."

"The police know we were having an affair."

"They're bluffing." Allen felt his pulse quicken.

"No way, Paul Shield told his roommate about us. That's how they found out."

Allen threw up his hands. "Great! This is just great! This keeps getting worse by the minute." He paced the floor.

As he stepped halfway across the room, Heather stopped him with a hand on his shoulder. "I want you to look me in the eye and tell me the truth. Did you kill them?"

"No!" Allen answered emphatically. "I know it looks bad, and I can understand why you'd think I could have." Allen's mouth trembled slightly. "But I didn't do it. I swear, Heather! I had nothing to do with it."

"Did anyone else know anything about the problems you were having with Debbie and Paul Shield?"

He thought for a moment. "My brother knew about everything. I don't know if he told anyone else or not."

"You discussed this with a maniac?"

"He's not a maniac! He's got a brain disease. As long as he's on his medicine, he's fine," Allen snapped. "Just like a person with an irregular heart or epilepsy."

"I still don't understand why you ever told him. Seems pretty stupid to me."

"Long story. I was ticked off about something and

I...oh hell, I don't know what I was thinking. But I'm sure John won't say anything to get me in trouble."

"Well, I guess it doesn't matter anyway. The police seem to know everything. She was quiet for a moment. She combed her dark hair back from her eyes with her long manicured nails. "Is he dangerous? The violent type?"

"Who, John? No way, he's passive as hell."

"I thought you told me your brother runs away sometimes and goes off his medication."

"Yeah, but even then, he still isn't the violent type." Allen locked eyes with her. "What are you getting at?"

"I was wondering if John could have killed them."

"Oh please. You're being ridiculous."

"Maybe I'm just more objective." Heather bit down lightly on her forefinger. "It wouldn't hurt to consider it."

"This is crazy! Let's just drop the subject."

"Okay, for the time being. Meanwhile, I just want to let you know that if I have to testify, I'm going to tell the truth about our affair. I'm not about to do time for you."

"Do time? What are you talking about now? They're not suspecting you of anything."

"They said I might have to give a deposition. I'll be included in your trial, if it goes that far. Ever hear of perjury or obstruction of justice? There is no way I'm going to make that mistake."

Allen shut his eyes and tried not to explode. "Look, from what you've told me, all they really know is that Shield walked in on us. It's not like we were naked or anything. It really wasn't that big of a deal. We can tell the cops exactly what I told Shield. We were just doing a little harmless flirting, but we weren't having an affair. There's no way they can prove anything."

"Do you seriously think they won't question my neighbors?"

Allen shrugged his shoulders. "We'll say I occasionally drop off reports at your place."

"At twelve o'clock at night? How stupid do you think they are?"

"Well, we'll think of some explanation."

"And what if they ask about your personality?

Whether you have a violent temper. Or if you like to pretend you're a blood-thirsty killer."

"Don't even go there." Allen's voice grew loud. "You're the one that got me started on that crap."

She ignored his threatening tone. "If it wasn't already a part of your make up, you would have refused. Anyway, the bottom line is, I'm not going to lie under oath, and that's all there is to it."

"I don't believe you!"

Heather narrowed her eyes. "Of course there's one way to eliminate the possibility of me having to testify."

"What's that?"

"A wife doesn't have to testify against her husband." Heather smiled cunningly. "Remember?"

Allen considered this for a moment, then cupped his forehead with the palm of his hand and sighed with relief. "You're right, I never gave that a thought." His eyes were suddenly bright. "This is the answer! You wouldn't have to say a word!" He took her hand and pulled her against him. "You're a genius." He smiled."

She grinned.

"So we'll do it as soon as possible."

"There's just one thing that bothers me." She pushed back and looked into his eyes.

"What?"

"How will I ever know for sure?" She paused. "For all I know, I could be marrying a murderer."

"I guess you'll just have to take your chances. No matter how many times I tell you I didn't do it, you'll probably never be completely certain I'm telling the truth." He ran his finger up and down her throat. "But let's face it, you and I both know, that's just the kind of thing that turns you on."

She opened her mouth as if to protest, then stopped. She looked dreamily into his pale blue eyes. "You know me too well."

Debbie's funeral service and burial was limited to family members only. A priest from Debbie's church gave the eulogy. Afterwards, the family went to Carol's apartment. Linda had been there earlier to prepare the food, then left before they returned.

"Why do people always expect you to eat after funerals?" John stared at the buffet. "It never did make sense to me."

Carol pressed her fingers against her temple. "It's a tradition."

Allen flopped down on the couch next to his brother. "I feel like I'm in another world. Like none of this is really happening."

John smiled slightly. "I can relate to that."

Allen's eyes were uncharacteristically soft as he glanced at John. "I know you can. Are you doing okay?"

"Yes, I'm getting through it."

"That's good. Hang in there."

John looked up at his mother. "Are you getting another migraine?"

Carol sighed. "Yes, I'm afraid so. I'm going to have to go to bed. I'm sorry I can't be with you."

"That's okay. Let me know if I can do anything for you, Mom," John said, in a comforting tone.

"Thanks." Carol walked slowly out of the room.

John shook his head. "I wish I could help her. She suffers so much from those headaches."

Allen didn't comment.

""It's nice to have you around again, even under these circumstances," John said.

Allen looked away from his brother for a moment. "I'm sorry I've stayed away. I got all screwed up somewhere along the line. I don't know what the hell is wrong with me."

"You can change. It's not too late. God can help you. And I'm willing to help in anyway I can, too."

Allen met John's eyes again. "You know the police think I killed Debbie and Paul Shield?"

John nodded. "I know you didn't do it."

"I appreciate your confidence in me."

John continued, "The truth will come out in the end. I'm praying for you."

Allen shook his head. "I've really made a mess of my

life."

"That's because you turned away from the Lord. It's when we think we can handle it alone that we get messed up." John's face glowed. "When we walk with God and accept His will in our lives, we find contentment, even under the worst of situations."

Allen shrugged. "But we still have to take action sometimes. You know, on our own." Allen took a deep breath. "The problem is, once you've made a bunch of mistakes, it's hard to know what to do next." He paused, searching for words. "Remember me telling you about my secretary, Heather Martin?"

John nodded.

"Well, I'm going to have to marry her. She reminded me that a wife doesn't have to testify against her husband. I really don't want to have to do it, but I don't see any other way out."

"Allen!" John shook his head, "If you marry her, you'll look even guiltier. Plus, I'm pretty sure that rule only applies if the crime took place while you were married. Marrying her now would be after the fact. Your best bet is to tell the truth."

Allen flopped back against the sofa and rubbed his forehead. "You're right. I can't marry her. You see how messed up I am? I can't even think straight." He sighed. "But how am I going to get out of it? If I back out, she'll tell the police everything. They'll hang me for sure."

"Everything will turn out right," John promised.

He lay in bed reminiscing about the day his mother left him with his father. He was very young...maybe four or five. She was dressed in a tight red dress. Her hair was long and unkempt and her eyes looked like they'd been circled with black magic marker. His father slapped her around, called her a whore, told her how much the dress suited trash like her.

"You see your mother, boy? His father shouted. "She's leaving you to go whore around in an alley somewhere. She's nothing but trash. She doesn't love you, never did. Trash, that's all she is."

At the time, it was the anger behind those words that disturbed him. He barely knew the meaning of any of them. But they stayed in his mind and a few years later, he learned their meaning and he never forgot.

He remembered the last words she spoke to him as his father pushed her out the door. "Sweetheart, I'm sorry. I've got to go right now, but I'll be back to get you. I promise."

He believed her. He hid the cloth bag of wooden soldiers in the back of his closet so his father wouldn't find them. His father never allowed toys in the house. The soldiers had been his and his mother's secret. He planned to take the soldiers with him when she came back. Although days turned into months and his father's beatings became more frequent and torturous, he still believed she'd keep her promise.

He shook himself from the past. He had to contemplate his next move. Things had been going perfectly, but he had made a grave mistake...underestimated the enemy. He'd become a suspect. He hadn't counted on that.

His biggest concern was that he'd be apprehended before hitting his ultimate mark. He hated her almost as much as he hated his mother. He'd hoped to put if off awhile longer. Because he knew that once he killed her, every other target would be anti-climatic.

Detective Lindsey was closing in on him. Lindsey was definitely a problem. The man was smart, there was no doubt about it. Somehow, he'd have to throw him a curve...get him off the case. Then he could take his time, building to a crescendo.

When John entered the office, Lindsey and Cross sat straighter in their chairs than usual. They'd been surprised when they found out he'd made an appointment to meet with them.

"Thank you for seeing me." John closed the door behind him.

"No problem." Lindsey pointed to a chair. "Have a seat."

John sat down, his hands folded in his lap, his legs

pressed together, his feet flat on the floor. "I talked to my pastor and he said I should tell you something."

"Oh? What is it, John?" Sharon's voice was friendly.

"I was at Mr. Shield's apartment building the night he was murdered."

"Why?" Sharon asked calmly.

"I went there to pray for him. Allen told me Mr. Shield was blackmailing him, so I wanted to pray that Mr. Shield would stop." He looked at his hands. "The problem was, I closed my eyes to pray and before long, I fell asleep."

"What happened next?" Sharon asked.

"When I woke up it was almost daylight, so I ran home. I didn't want my mother to know I'd been out. She wouldn't like that."

"How often do you sneak out at night?"

John's face reddened slightly. "Frequently. You see, I have trouble sleeping. If I take a walk, it relaxes me and I'm able to sleep much better when I get back."

Lindsey eyed John carefully. The detective sat, his elbows resting on the arms of the chair, his hands up, thumbs stationary and fingers tapping rapidly against each other. "John, did you speak to Mr. Shield?"

"Oh, no. Like I told you, I just stayed outside his door."

"Did you hear anything from inside the apartment?"

"Not a thing. I listened for awhile before I started praying. It was very quiet inside."

"No conversations…no television…nothing?"

John shook his head, "No sounds at all. I was a little worried that he wasn't even in there and that he might come home and find me outside his door, but I decided to take my chances."

"Did you see anyone else while you were there?"

"No one."

"Well, we appreciate you coming forward with this information, John. It couldn't have been easy."

John frowned. "What do you mean? The truth is always easy."

Lindsey eyed him carefully. "John, are you aware that your brother is a suspect in Mr. Shield's murder and his wife's?"

He nodded. "Yes sir, I am. And I can see why you think he might be guilty, since he wasn't getting along with the two of them. But I know in my spirit that's he's innocent."

"In your spirit?" Lindsey's eyes squinted. "What does that mean? Does God talk to you?"

"Not audibly. I just sense Him deep inside at times."

"If God told you to go out and kill someone, would you do it?"

"God wouldn't tell me to do that."

Lindsey plopped his hands on his desk. "What if He told you to kill someone really bad...like a prostitute?"

"No matter how bad a person is, He wouldn't tell me to kill anyone. Jesus said we have to love our neighbor as ourselves." He tilted his head slightly to one side. "Besides, God loves a prostitute just as much as He loves you and me."

"If God communicates with you," Lindsey said, "why don't you ask him for the name of the person who is committing these crimes? Then we could clear your brother and get the killer off the streets." Sarcasm rang in his voice.

John hesitated for a moment. "I never thought about asking Him for the name of the murderer. That's an excellent idea. I'll start praying for that right away. And if He tells me, you and Agent Cross will be the first to know." He looked down at his hands again. "I don't know how to explain this yet, because I haven't been able to put it together myself, but there's something else I want to tell you." He looked up. "I heard the killer talk. I'm not sure where. I'm praying that God will help me remember. I believe once He does, we'll all know who the killer is."

Lindsey frowned. "You said you didn't hear any talking at Shield's place. Could you have heard the killer when your sister-in-law was murdered?"

John shook his head. "I don't think so. I believe I heard the killer's voice before those murders. While I was living on the streets in Orlando. Since then, I've heard the voice occasionally...like in my mind."

Lindsey lit a cigarette. "What does the voice say?"

"It says, *You can't point your finger at me!*" John's eyes reflected his pain.

Lindsey extended his hands, palms up. "That's it? What the hell is that supposed to mean?"

Sharon glared at Lindsey.

John shook his head. "I don't know. I probably should have waited to tell you about this until I have all the answers."

As Lindsey glanced at Sharon, his frown lines deepened. "Did the voice sound familiar to you?"

John sighed. "Not at all. It was horrible. Like pure evil."

"Is there anything else you remember? Anything you could think of, that might be helpful?" He asked.

John's eyes traveled from Lindsey to Sharon and back again. "I'm sorry."

Lindsey changed the subject. "John, do you own a computer?"

He nodded.

"Do you know how to gain access to private sites?"

John frowned. "I'm sure I could. But it's against the law, so I've never tried."

"Would you mind if we took a look at your computer?"

"No, but I'm sure your computers are much more sophisticated than mine. I don't know how mine could help you."

"Just the same, we'd like to see it."

He shrugged. "Fine with me. Only I'm taking a pastoral course and exams are coming up soon so I can't afford to do without it for very long."

"You plan on becoming a pastor, John?" Sharon asked.

"I don't know exactly how He's going to use me. I know I must seem like an unlikely person to do God's work because of my illness, but I believe everyone is usable. We can all be His vessels if we just open ourselves to Him and do His will."

"I think that's very commendable," Sharon said. "Now, concerning the amount of time we'll need to have your computer. I'm sure it wouldn't be any longer than one day."

"Oh, well then, okay. That'll be fine," he said.

Lindsey called the main desk and arranged for someone to get Carol's signed permission.

John's eyes exuded warmth. "Is there anything else I can do to help you?"

"Yes." Sharon reached into her attaché case. "I have a medical release form here that I was going to ask you and your mother to sign, so that I can talk with your psychiatrist. Do you have any objection?"

John shrugged. "I don't know how it would help your case. But if you think it's important, I'll do whatever I can."

"Also, before you leave, I'd like you to go to our lab and let them take some hair samples from your head."

"Why would you...?" John hesitated. "Oh, I see. You want to make sure that I'm not the killer. That my hair doesn't match any you might have found at the crime scenes."

"Yes. I hope that doesn't offend you, but we have to check out everyone until we narrow it down to the person who is responsible."

"Then sure. I'll cooperate in anyway possible."

"Wonderful, John. We appreciate that very much." She handed him the release form, along with a pen. "Just sign on the line with the red X."

John set the form on her desk, moved the pen to the line, and then stared at the X. Deep lines burrowed his brow.

"Anything wrong?" Sharon asked.

John shook his head. "I don't know...I'm not sure." He scratched out his name, then dropped the pen. "I'm not feeling very well," he said, then got up, and walked out of the room.

Lindsey and Cross sat quietly for a few minutes before Lindsey turned to her. "Well? What do you make of that?"

"I think the red X knocked him for a loop."

"Sure did." Lindsey grinned. "Pretty clever of you."

"That's why I get paid the big bucks," she said. "But the question is why. Did Allen tell him about the X's on the victims? Did he actually witness one of the killings? Or did he put the X's on the victims himself?"

Lindsey shook his head as he lit up a cigarette. "If John is the killer, he sure acts like he doesn't have anything to hide. After all, he's letting us have access to his computer. If he's a hacker he knows we can get a lot of information off the hard drive even if he's deleted files. And the fact that he freely signed that paper for medical information and DNA testing makes him look innocent too." He dragged on his cigarette. "Plus, admitting he was at the Shield crime scene is pretty up front."

"I agree." Sharon pursed her lips. "But this business about hearing the killer's voice has me concerned. I'm beginning to wonder if we could be dealing with a split personality."

"Meaning, his so-called alter ego is doing the killing and he doesn't remember anything about it." Lindsey blew smoke above her head.

"I've never bought into that diagnosis before. A lot of psychiatrists are skeptical as to whether such a brain disorder even really exists." She thought for a moment.

"So what's your gut feeling?"

"The only feeling I have is an emotional one."

"Come on...don't leave me hanging."

"Okay." Her cheeks quickly colored. "I don't want it to be John."

Lindsey shook his head. "Women!"

"You see? I knew I shouldn't have told you." She poked his arm with her fist.

The phone rang; Lindsey was laughing when he grabbed for it.

"Daddy?"

"Hey Jen. We were going to call you tonight. Sharon wants to ride with you this weekend."

"Daddy, I need to see you."

"Is something wrong, Baby? You don't sound like yourself."

"Could you come over right away?"

"Of course. Is your mom okay?"

"Yes, this has nothing to do with Mom. A man came to the stable today. He acted weird and he scared me."

Lindsey's body grew rigid. "I'll be right there." Lindsey jumped up from his chair and headed for the door.

"Can I come?" Sharon was already out of her seat.

Lindsey turned toward her. "Yes."

Sara and Joe were pacing the living room floor when Lindsey and Cross arrived. When Jen saw her father, she ran up and hugged him tightly.

"Hi, Baby, don't worry, everything will be all right." Lindsey tenderly brushed her hair back from her face with his hand. He led her to the sofa and they sat down. Sharon walked off to the other side of the room.

"Daddy, I hope I'm not making a big deal over nothing. I just thought you should know since...well since that man is still out there killing people." She choked back tears.

"You're doing the right thing, Jen. Now, tell me, what happened."

"I saw him for the first time when I was working Sebastian in the round pen. You know how he gets rank sometimes when he hasn't been ridden for a few days? Well, lunging him gets the goofiness out so he can concentrate under saddle and..." She shook her head. "Oh forget about that, it's not important. The thing is, I looked up and this man was sitting on the fence just about twenty feet away, watching me work the horse." She took a breath, to collect her thoughts. "I'd never seen him before. He didn't say anything at all. He just sat there staring at me. At first I thought he might be a new trainer, but I found out later he wasn't."

"Could he have been someone you know from school?"

"No, Daddy. He was old. Well, not as old as you, but he was probably in his thirties. Sorry, Daddy, I didn't mean to say you were old but...well, you know what I mean."

"Yes, now go on, what happened then?"

"Well, Mrs. Bronson, you know the lady who owns

the stable? Well, I saw her coming up the path and when I turned back around, he was gone. I just assumed Mrs. Bronson had seen him before he left. Since she didn't say anything about him, I thought she knew him and everything was cool." Jennifer took another breath. "Anyway, I took Sebastian back to the stable and cross-tied him in the aisle so I could put on his saddle. Mrs. Bronson went up to wait for me with Mom and Joe at the main ring... so I was alone. Just as I pulled up the cinch, the same guy just seemed to appear out of nowhere, blocking the entrance of the barn. The sun was behind him so I still couldn't get a good look at his face. He walked in a few feet and just stood there. I got scared. I didn't know what to do. Finally, he asked me if I was Jennifer Lindsey. I told him I was and then he said for me to tell you he said hello. Then he walked back out." Jennifer's eyes were desperate and welling.

"Can you tell me anything about his appearance, honey?"

"Well, he was about your height, maybe a little taller, and built a lot like you. Maybe a little narrower through the hips. He looked like he worked out a lot. He was wearing a cowboy hat. When he was on the fence, most of his face was shadowed, but his eyes still stood out. Actually, I could see them pretty well. They were real blue...and weird...piercing. I guess that was what bothered me most about him. His eyes were scary!"

Lindsey glanced back at Sharon who mirrored his alarm.

"What color was his hair?" Tom asked.

"Dark, I think. It was hard to tell because the hat covered it. But his mustache was definitely dark. It was one of those real thin ones."

"Would you be able to recognize him if you ever saw him again?"

"I don't know."

Lindsey turned to Sharon. "Get the crime lab out to the stable right away. Tell them we'll meet them there."

"Daddy, do you think it was him?"

"I don't know, sweetheart, but it's possible. Anything

is possible. We have to check it out and see if we can collect evidence. Do you feel up to going back there with us?"

"Tom!" Sara rushed toward them. "Don't be ridiculous!" Her eyes frosted. "Can't you see how upset she is?"

"I'll be okay, Mom." Jennifer said, then blew her nose.

The rage on Sara's face seared Tom's heart. He wanted to reason with her, but decided against it. He knew that look too well. Her anger would just have to run its course. Instead, he clutched Jennifer's hand and walked out of the house without saying a word.

Several hours later, after no evidence was found, Lindsey and Cross took Jennifer home, then returned to his apartment. Lindsey drank bourbon, stared at the wall and brooded.

Sharon stood quietly by the window, giving Lindsey time to cool down. Finally, she walked up behind him and gave his shoulders a gentle squeeze. "Are you okay?"

He sipped his second drink without answering or looking up.

She stepped around and knelt down on the floor in front of him, her hands on his knees. "Maybe he's just trying to scare you."

"Well, he's got my attention, that's for sure."

"She has a bodyguard with her now. At least you know she'll be okay tonight."

Tom scowled. "Sara should have let her stay with me."

"Come on. You know that wouldn't be practical or safe. Besides, he's probably just playing head games with you. If he gets you to lose control, you'll get kicked off the case and he wins the game."

"The only way he's going to win this game is if he walks," Lindsey said. "I'll tell you one thing, there ain't no way that's gonna happen. When I definitely know who he is, I'm going to make sure his killing days are over."

"Within the law. Whether you like it or not. You know you've got to let the system take care of him."

His eyes narrowed. "Don't you *dare* talk to me about the stinking system. I'm sick of loopholes and technicalities. The system just doesn't work anymore." His voice was harsh. "If he so much as comes near her again, I am going to kill him."

"You don't mean that."

"The hell I don't." He met her eyes soberly. "

"That's the bourbon talking." Her smile quivered.

"You don't know me as well as you think," he said.

"Yes I do."

Lindsey shook his head subtly. "You know the person I was yesterday. Today, everything has changed. It's gotten personal."

"Personal or not, I won't sit back and watch you screw up your life! Do you hear me?" Her voice was sharp-edged. "Besides, it's not just your life anymore. It's ours. Do you want to throw away our relationship, too?"

Lindsey pulled back as if he'd been hit. "What relationship?" He scowled. "We're co-workers...that's all it's ever been and ever will be," he said firmly.

Sharon's eyes scanned his for several seconds, as if hoping to see something that would contradict what he'd just said. They were cold and unyielding. Seconds later, she got up and left.

When the sun peeked over the horizon, Allen sat at the station again, surrounded by Lindsey, Cross and Patterson.

"We're getting pretty frustrated, Allen," Lindsey said. "We've got a homicidal maniac running around and we know it's only a matter of time before he strikes again.

"Well, that's your fault. If you'd stop wasting your time on me, you might find him."

Patterson leaned his head to the right and then the left, but stopped short of completing the routine when he noticed Lindsey's sudden glare. Instead, he begrudgingly pulled out a notepad and leafed through the pages, while Sharon stood back to concentrate on Allen's demeanor.

Lindsey forced a smile that was so phony he could feel facial muscles he'd never used before. He had to be consistent and continue the role of good cop, but it was taking all the discipline he could muster. "Have you called your attorney?"

"No. I've had too much on my mind. I'm still mourning my wife's death, for crying out loud."

"I understand. But the investigation has to go on. I would think you'd be just as anxious to catch this guy as we are." Lindsey's stomach burned.

Allen didn't answer.

"I got to tell ya, when a person refuses to talk, he makes us even more suspicious," Patterson interjected, "If you were innocent, you wouldn't have anything to hide. So what's it gonna be, Randolph? You want to call your lawyer now? Either way, you're going to have to tell the truth."

Allen hesitated, then said, "Okay, we can talk, but if you start playing games like you did the other day, I'm definitely calling an attorney." He raised his chin in defiance. "So, what do you want from me?"

"We have eye witnesses…and solid facts which prove you have been lying to us."

Allen stared straight ahead.

Sharon's eyes focused on Allen's increased breathing rate and a line of perspiration that formed quickly across his brow.

"Okay, this is the deal." Lindsey struggled to keep his temper in check. "Paul Shield's roommate told us that Paul walked in on you and your secretary and saw the two of you fooling around. Since the last time we talked, we sent some of our men to interview Heather Martin's neighbors. They said that for over a year, you've been hanging out at her apartment just about every night." Lindsey held up his forefinger as a warning. "Now don't insult our intelligence by saying you two were conducting business meetings."

Allen shook his head and looked down at the floor. His bottom lip trembled twice. He wiped the sweat from his forehead. "All right. All right. So my marriage wasn't perfect. I didn't tell the whole truth, but that doesn't mean I killed my wife."

"But you are finally admitting you and this Martin woman were having an affair, right?" Patterson stretched out his legs.

"Yes, but I didn't-and don't-love her. If I ever left Debbie, it wouldn't have been for trash like her."

Lindsey glanced at Sharon, then turned back to Allen. "Okay. Let's leave that subject for a minute," he said. "We also found out Shield blackmailed you into giving him a raise." Lindsey crossed his arms over his chest.

"Blackmailed?" Allen's indignant expression was not convincing. "I don't know what you're talking about! All he did was ask for a raise. He told me he really needed it. I have people asking for raises all the time. Shield was my right hand man. I felt like it was the least I could do for him."

"We talked to your brother just yesterday. You told him the man was blackmailing you." Lindsey said.

Allen's face reddened. "John gets things mixed up. You can't believe anything he says."

"Really? He seemed very lucid to us."

"Well, then you don't know anything about mentally ill people."

"We know more than you think," Patterson snapped.

"Look," Allen said, "Paul told me he needed the money right away. He didn't say why, but I figured it must have been important, so I wanted to help him out. That's all there was to it."

Patterson spit out the question. "Where were you the night Paul Shield was murdered?"

"At home...sleeping in bed with my wife."

"Convenient since she isn't here to confirm that." Patterson smirked.

Allen winced.

Lindsey scowled at Patterson. "I apologize for Detective Patterson's insensitivity," Lindsey said. "What about the night Debbie disappeared? Morris' report says you stayed at the Peabody."

Allen hesitated. "That's right." He paused uncomfortably. "I didn't want to stay at the Hoebel for obvious reasons. The truth is, I wasn't happy about Debbie going away. She was upset with me and I didn't want to make things worse. So I left while she was packing and got a room so she could have time to think it through. I hoped she would change her mind. Of course, the next morning when I came home and found her suitcases missing, I realized she was gone."

Patterson's face was hard. "You checked in at the Peabody at one forty-five. Didn't you just tell us you left while she was packing so she'd have time to think things over?"

Allen nodded. "I drove around awhile before going to the hotel."

Patterson leafed through the thick Randolph file. "You told Morris that Debbie left around twelve-thirty or so. How could you have known when she left, if you left before her?"

Allen took a deep breath. "I circled the block several times and saw when she left."

"You just said a minute ago, that it was the next morning when you realized she was gone."

Allen paused. "What I meant was, I knew she left that night, but I was hoping she'd turn around and come back. When I went back in the morning and saw all the suitcases were gone, I realized she was planning on being away for awhile."

Patterson laughed and shook his head. "You got an answer for everything, don't you?"

Allen stared straight ahead.

Lindsey leaned forward. "Tell me something. Why didn't you want your wife going to St. Augustine? And, why did she want to go in the first place."

Allen hesitated. "Our marriage was on the rocks and it was my fault. I cared about her, but I just wasn't attracted to her anymore. Then one night I got drunk, we had sex for the first time in years, and that's how she ended up pregnant. I couldn't believe it. The timing was terrible. I was frustrated. We argued about it. Part of me didn't want her to leave because I still cared about her. The other part of me wanted her to stay for selfish reasons. I knew there would be a lot of talk at work. Everyone knew what a great person Debbie was. I didn't want them to look down on me." He sighed deeply.

"So you made sure she never had an opportunity to bad mouth you," Patterson said matter-of-factly.

"I didn't kill her." Allen looked him in the eye. "But that's why I lied about our relationship."

Patterson shook his head. "If all you are saying is true, why did you go to Missing Persons to begin with? It doesn't make any sense."

Allen frowned. "What do ya' mean?"

"What...do you think? I'm an idiot or something?" Patterson stood up quickly. "If a man knows his wife is leaving him and where she's going, he has no reason to go to Missing Persons?"

"I didn't think she was going to stay away so long. And I thought she'd at least call me."

"But that doesn't explain why you didn't ask Detective Morris to start a search once you got there. I mean, two weeks had gone by. If you were really concerned, you would have done that."

"Like I said, I wasn't sure what was going on and I wanted to try to avoid embarrassment, if it was at all possible. When I went back the second time, I intended to tell him to go ahead and do it. But then I started thinking about things and realized it was possible that she could have been involved with another man and had left me to be with him." Allen lowered his eyes.

"Yeah...yeah...I read the report...missing red coat and all that crap. Funny how there was no sign of that coat when we found her," Patterson spoke with sarcasm. "Oh wait...I know...the killer thought it was so attractive, he decided to take it home for his lovely wife."

Allen shrugged.

"Let me tell you what I think happened." Patterson's eyes narrowed. "I think you went down there to cover your butt...so that when her body was found, it'd be on record that you'd been concerned."

"That's not true. I was just all mixed up. I didn't know what in the world was going on and I really was concerned...it wasn't fake."

Patterson chuckled. "Yeah, right." He glanced at Lindsey. "It doesn't look good for him, does it Detective Lindsey?"

Lindsey shook his head slowly, staring at Allen over the top of his coffee mug. "You don't have an alibi for the nights when the murders took place, you've lied and contradicted your statements, and you had the motivation to commit these crimes. There's no one else who had anything to lose if those two people continued living. We really were hoping to clear you and move on but..."

Allen rubbed his brow with his fist. "I know how this looks, but I didn't kill anyone. I don't know what else I can say or do to prove it to you."

Lindsey and Patterson looked at each other. "There is something you can do," Lindsey said, "How about taking a lie detector test?"

Allen's face turned red as he mulled over the suggestion. "No. I have too many guilt feelings where Debbie is concerned."

"Guilt feelings?" Lindsey asked.

"Of course." He glanced at both of them. "Wouldn't you? I was a lousy husband. She deserved better."

"Okay." Lindsey crushed his cigarette in an ashtray. "We'll just ask questions about Paul Shield? The way you made it sound, you shouldn't have any guilt feelings regarding him."

Allen shook his head. "I'll have to think about it. Right now, I feel guilty about so much that I don't know how to compartmentalize it all. Can you give me a few days?"

"Compartmentalize," Patterson laughed. "Ooooh. Big word. I'm impressed."

"Okay, you're free to go for the time being." Lindsey patted him on the back. "But at least do me one favor. On the way out, I want you to get your picture taken."

Allen paused, then said, "What for?"

"To keep on file," Lindsey answered. "Who knows, it could possibly get you off the hook."

Allen thought for a moment. "All right. Whatever."

The investigators were sitting in Lindsey's office when

Jennifer and her mother arrived. Jen's face was flushed as if she'd been running in the sun.

"Where's the picture, Daddy?" She asked.

Lindsey snatched up a glossy sheet of paper and handed it to her. Lined up, were photographs of eight different men. Four on top, four on the bottom. Jennifer studied them carefully, then shook her head.

"I just don't know." She continued to stare at the pictures. She pointed to Allen. "This one's eyes are like the man I saw, but he looks friendlier here. I guess the cheekbones and mouth are similar, but I'm not sure about the shape of his jaw or his nose. She pointed to the picture above his. "This one has the same mean look and his eyes are pretty scary, too. It's just hard to say, Daddy. I mean, all these guys have blonde hair and they don't have a mustache either." She pointed to Allen's picture again. "If he was wearing a cowboy hat, I might..."

"No problem." Lindsey handed her a drawing. "I had our forensic artist add a cowboy hat and color his hair dark and add a mustache," he said. "What do you think now?"

"Wow." Her eyes widened. "That looks a lot more like him. But since the sun was in my eyes and I couldn't see him well enough to be positive. I don't want to say it's him without being absolutely sure."

"I understand." Lindsey's heart raced. "But, at least we know, out of eight men, he looks the most like the person you saw. That makes Allen Randolph a very strong possibility."

"Possibility?" Patterson spoke up. "Come on, we all know it's him. There's no doubt about it. We got our man. Now all we have to do is prove it."

Lindsey's adrenaline surged, but he caught hold of it before it went too far. "That's the hard part. We don't have anything but circumstantial evidence and we don't have a positive I.D."

"Well, then we got to dig around some more." Patterson headed for the door. "I'm going to have forensics make me a picture like this, minus the hat, then show it to the two girls from the bar."

"Good idea," Lindsey said. "Call me as soon as you talk to them."

Sara walked toward Lindsey, her eyes icy, her face strained. "Could I have a word with you? Alone?"

Lindsey glanced at Sharon and Patterson. As they were leaving, Sara told Jennifer to accompany them.

Lindsey leaned back in his chair. "Okay, let's have it."

Sara's lips moved with the ugliness of resentment. "You and your lousy job! First it broke up our marriage, now it's put our daughter in danger." Her voice was shrill. "I begged and begged you to quit. But no...your job was way too important...much more important than your family." Her hands suddenly clamped on her hips and her eyes looked merciless. "You've never cared about anything but yourself and your ego. Bringing down the criminals, getting your name in the paper. Superman! Fighting for truth, justice and the American way! Well, I never wanted a superman. I wanted a family man. And look at what happened. I had to go somewhere else to find one." Her face was dark with rage. "You're going to pay for this, one way or another. You can count on that. You make me sick!" She stomped her foot. "I hate you! Do you hear me? I hate you."

Lindsey looked down at the floor. "I don't blame you for being upset, but you have to know in your heart that I'm doing everything I possibly can to get this man. We're pretty sure we know who he is now. I promise you, once I know it's definitely him, I'm going to stop him immediately. Whether we have enough evidence to arrest him or not. He'll never be able to scare Jennifer again."

"Yeah? Well, what do we do in the meantime? Tell me that?"

"If I have to personally pay for a bodyguard to stay with her twenty-four, seven, I'll do it."

Sara rushed forward as if she was going to hit him. "Like you could afford to pay for a bodyguard on your lousy salary."

Lindsey threw back his chair, slamming it against the wall and stormed out of the room. Sara walked behind his desk and touched the back of his chair with trembling fingertips, then sat down and buried her face in her hands.

Everyone outside the office heard the argument, including Jennifer.

Jennifer didn't speak to her mother for the rest of the night. She'd never rebelled, never spoke an unkind word to her in the past. Now, however, she felt the need to retaliate. She wanted to make her worry. Punish her for the way she'd treated her daddy.

Just before sunrise, she tiptoed down to the garage, started the engine to Joe's Mercedes, and pressed the button to the garage door opener. Despite the fact that she'd never driven a car before, she easily put it in gear and quietly backed it out. She then switched to drive and passed the police car sitting in the driveway, and the officer whose head was resting against the window as he slept. When she got to the stables, she saddled up her horse in the semi-darkness and took off in a wild gallop.

She and Sebastian charged down the side of a road that she had taken before with other riders and followed the perimeter of a long stretch of wooded acreage. She felt exhilarated because it was the first time she'd ever gone on a trail ride alone. Excitement unleashed her imagination. They jumped fallen branches and chased imaginary foxes. She became a jockey in the Kentucky Derby, standing up in the stirrups of her English saddle and pumping her arms to increase his speed. The thrill of the ride had made the anger inside her subside and the fear of danger fade.

After another eighth of a mile, she glanced down at Sebastian's wet neck and heard his labored breathing. She saw the deserted road stretched out before her, as if for the first time. Reality punched through the insulation of escape. She tried to rein him in. The horse snorted and shook his head and neck in protest. Jennifer started to give and take with the reins and pushed her seat muscles further down into the saddle in an effort to drop him into a slower gait. But, when he shifted into a lower gear, he took hold of the bit and surged with new determination into the fastest trot of his and her life.

"Whoa! Slow down!" she reprimanded him as she posted, her bottom lifting up and down from the saddle, like a piston on a run away steam train. "Cut it out! This is ridiculous," she yelled. "Come on! I've had it," her voice broke slightly. "I've had it with you. Now slow down, you moron! Don't you hear me? I've had it with you. With everything. With everybody. With Mom. With Joe. Even with Daddy." Bitter tears welled up in her eyes. "Why did this all have to happen?" Her bottom lip and jaw trembled as tears spilled down her red cheeks. "I thought they loved each other. Why did they have to get divorced?"

She heard a car approach from the rear. As the tires crunched the gravel behind them, she could feel the horse's tension increase. "Oh great!" She bit her lower lip. "Calm down, blockhead. It's okay. It's just a car, for crying out loud. Relax." She knew he hated cars...always had. But on most days, she was able to talk him through his fear. But today was more difficult. They were alone, she'd gotten him overly excited, and he was razor-sharp...one thousand pounds of jumbled nerves, abraded by her own anxiety.

He shook his neck again, then broke into a half canter, half prance mode. His body bent away from the street, while his head turned to face the car as it sped by. "Calm down, stupid. For crying out loud, act normal." She jerked his head around and pressed her legs against his ribs, which forced him to travel in a straight line. "I just want things to be normal. Just normal. That's all I ask," she cried, biting her lower lip.

She watched the car make a right at the intersection before her, in the direction she planned on going. "Oh man, I sure hope he's out of sight before we turn that corner."

In an effort to tire Sebastian, she steered him into the deep sand against the edge of the tree line where his legs sank several inches below his fetlocks. Just before they got to the intersection, the horse came to an abrupt stop. She could see his bulging eyes scan the woods beside them.

"It's okay. Everything is fine," she forced herself to sound calm. Suddenly he raised his head higher and trumpeted sharply through his wide nostrils, then pranced sideways, out onto the asphalt where his hooves made a clacking, shuffling sound. She pressed her outside leg against his side and forced him off the street.

"You are such an idiot!" She yelled. "I'm going to put you up for sale the second we get back to the barn." Sweat poured off her face and trickled down her neck. Her shirt was wet and her hands slippery.

She wished she hadn't taken Sebastian out alone, especially so far off without even telling anyone where she was going. She thought of turning around, but she was three quarters of the way back now. All she had to do was turn the corner, travel less than a hundred yards, make another right, and take a short cut through the orange groves and she'd be back at the barn in no time. She told herself that she could pull it off, as long as she kept calm.

She took a deep breath and tried to relax her body, but she could feel the tension in the animal below her, building like steam in a pressure cooker. She knew he was ready to do something crazy, but she could think of nothing else to do but continue pushing him forward. As they took the turn, Sebastian immediately spotted a car parked along side of the road. Jennifer's stomach dropped when she saw and recognized it as the same one that had passed them several minutes ago. Was she being followed? Or was it just someone who stopped to steal an orange? That happened all the time in Florida. Sure, that's what it was. It had to be.

She tried to reassure herself, but she couldn't help but wonder if her horse had been trying to tell her something all along. If she could just see the person in the car, she'd feel better. Where was he? Was he lying down? Maybe taking a nap?

She was almost parallel to the car when without warning, Sebastian stopped dead and braced himself, then spun around and landed back on the street. Jennifer tried to keep his body centered between her legs, not allowing him to bend in either direction. She reined him slightly toward the trees and back into the deep sand for control. He cantered in place like a parade horse, his neck arched, his body tight and ready for flight. Suddenly something white flapped and snapped peripherally. Sebastian veered hard to avoid it, and nearly fell as his feet scrambled to right himself. Jennifer lost her balance but was just about to regain it, when a man jumped out. He screamed while waving a white pillowcase above his head. Sebastian twirled sharply, sending Jennifer plummeting toward the ground. Her eyes squeezed shut as her body hit the hard asphalt and a feeling of doom flooded her when she heard the sound of Sebastian's hooves as they faded down the road. When she looked up, the man was standing over her; his blue eyes hard, his mouth, smiling. She recognized him immediately.

CHAPTER 13

Sharon sat across from Dr. Walters as he read the medical release form signed by John and his mother. When he finished, he set the paper aside and clasped his hands. "So what can I do for you?"

"John Randolph. Capable of murder or not?" She asked, bluntly.

"Not." He shifted in his seat. "Of course nothing is impossible. But it would shock me if it were true. I've known him a long time and I don't think he's capable of it."

"What about when he's off medication?" Sharon clicked her pen.

Dr. Walters shrugged. "Mild violence maybe. In self defense perhaps. He had a minor incident once, but nothing to speak of."

"Tell me about it."

"After a couple of months on the streets, he was psychotic. By the time the police caught up with him, he was hallucinating. He was delusional...thought he had seen the devil. Actually punched a couple of the officers, which was unusual behavior for John."

"I never saw that in the police report. May I see your files regarding that event?"

He picked up the phone and called his secretary. He turned back to Sharon. "She'll have it in a few minutes."

"What about Allen Randolph?"

"Allen was never a patient."

"How has John seemed over the last several weeks?"

"Fine. We meet every other week. He seems to be doing great. No more hallucinations or abnormal thinking that I can detect."

"Would you consider Mrs. Randolph to be a good mother?"

"Yes. Maybe a little overprotective."

"Do you know if she ever abandoned him or his brother?"

Dr. Walters frowned. "Not that I know of. Of course, I didn't meet them until John was a teen-ager, but I certainly haven't picked up on anything like that during any of our sessions."

"John has never acted like he resents her?"

"Not really. I think he resents the fact that she has to be his caretaker when he isn't well. When John is functioning properly, he is an intelligent young man and would prefer to be independent. Because of the disease, their lives have become intertwined. I've seen this scenario happen frequently and it isn't always the healthiest situation."

"Has he ever been violent?"

Dr. Walters raised an eyebrow. "The night we brought him in, he grabbed her hand and wouldn't let go. His grip was so hard I thought he might break her bones." He sighed. "He didn't know what he was doing, I'm sure."

His secretary walked in with a file. After thumbing through it, he handed it to Sharon.

She skimmed it, then went back to the middle of the report. "It says John was running around telling people that he had seen the devil making axes...and that the devil turned a girl in an alley into a jack-o-lantern." Her eyes were intense as she waited for a reaction.

"Yes...yes, I remember that gibberish. Like I told you, he was in terrible shape."

"Did you discuss this with him?"

"I tried to reason with him the next day."

"Did you ask him what he meant by axes?"

"No, not really. An axe is an axe. I assumed he thought he'd seen the devil use one to kill the girl he was talking about. I certainly didn't take him seriously."

Sharon thought for a moment. "Are you certain he was saying "axes"?"

"Well, yes, that's how it sounded."

Sharon hesitated. "Could he have possibly been saying, X's?"

Dr. Walters raised an eyebrow. "I guess that's possible. It was hard to understand him at the time and I suppose those two words could be confused. Why? Is that significant?"

Sharon nodded. "Very. I believe John was telling you about a real murder and is now starting to remember some details about it. A young woman was killed the night before John was brought to MHC. The killer carved X's across the girl's eyes." She read another sentence. "He said the devil was dressed in black, including his face." She shook her head. "There's no doubt about it. John was definitely there."

Hoping to find something to convince him of Allen Randolph's guilt, Lindsey reviewed his files. He reread every interview, every piece of information. His frustration was growing.

His office door opened and Sharon and Chief Henry walked in. Sharon looked like she'd just been diagnosed with a brain tumor, and Henry wouldn't even make eye contact. Lindsey immediately prepared himself for the worse.

"Tom, I'm afraid I've got bad news," Henry said." The Chief had never used Tom's first name before. Lindsey could feel his breakfast backing up into his esophagus.

"Your daughter's missing." The corners of Henry's lips jerked downward. "I'm sorry," his voice cracked. "It happened near the Bronson Ranch. Our men are out there now."

Lindsey looked at Sharon as she wiped tears. Suddenly nothing seemed real. A strange calmness took over him, a surprise to everyone, including Lindsey. "How long has she been missing?"

"About two hours," Henry said. "The guys have been searching for over an hour. She'd gone out for a ride on her horse. He came back to the barn without her. Our men were able to follow her trail. They found the spot where the horse threw her."

"Then maybe she's lost. Just couldn't find her way back." Hope glimmered in his eyes for only a second.

Henry shook his head. "There were other tracks at that point. Tennis shoes," his voice broke. "Nike's. And there were car tracks nearby."

Lindsey's eyes glazed over.

"Look," Henry talked faster, "I don't think he's going to hurt her. I think he's just trying to slow things down. He knows this is a way to keep you off his back."

Lindsey turned to his boss. "Meaning, you're going to take me off this case."

Henry nodded. "I'm sorry. You know I don't have any other choice."

Lindsey stood up, his face taut with anguish and then the door swung open. Sara stared at him through horror-struck eyes, then flew into his arms. "Tom, I'm sorry. I'm so sorry," Sara lamented. "Jennifer was mad at me for the way I talked to you yesterday. I'm sure that's why she took off. It's all my fault. If I could take it back I..." She buried her face in his shoulder. Her eyes slammed shut, tears squeezed through, and flooded her face. "I didn't mean anything I said. I was just scared and frustrated. Please forgive me." She pushed away from him slightly, and searched his face. "Tom, I need you. You're the only one that can find her."

Lindsey pulled her against him again. He closed his eyes this time. Sharon walked out, and closed the door gently behind her.

Later, Lindsey went home and found Sharon sitting on the floor in the hallway outside his apartment door. Her brief case and laptop surrounded her. He didn't acknowledge her, but left the door open for her to enter, went right to his computer and got to work. Sharon busied herself in the kitchen and made coffee, then returned with two mugs. She handed him one and sat next to him.

"I just want you to know, I'm going to keep you informed every step of the way...despite what Henry says.

If it was his daughter, he wouldn't leave the case alone, either." She paused. "That is, if you promise me you won't...well you know."

Lindsey kept his eyes on the screen.

Though she didn't receive a response, she continued, "I talked to John Randolph's psychiatrist this morning and found out John did witness one of the prostitute murders."

Lindsey turned his head towards her, his eyes haunted.

"The night John was brought to the psychiatric ward, he was terrified. He tried to tell people about the murder, but everyone assumed he was hallucinating. He referred to it from a witness' standpoint, not the killer's."

"We've got to make him remember everything," Lindsey said, calmly. His lips barely moved.

"I know. I'll use hypnosis."

"Do it. As soon as possible."

She nodded. "I will."

Lindsey turned back to the computer. "Meanwhile, I want to try something." His eyes never strayed from the monitor. "When we did our search in New York, we were mainly looking at murders taking place over the last ten years...taking into account the fact that serial killers continue killing until they are stopped. They don't just quit for years and then pop up again." His face showed no emotion. "But what we weren't considering was the fact that the killer might have been incarcerated and not able to kill for an extended period of time. Since these clothespins are old, maybe we need to go further back, and see what we come up with."

"You're right," Sharon agreed. "Forensics said the clothespins were over fifteen years old, right?"

Lindsey nodded.

"Wait a minute." Sharon ran her tongue along her upper lip. "The description we've had of the suspect has been a man in his early to mid thirties."

Lindsey grunted, "I don't care. Maybe he's had facelifts. Or maybe he was a kid when he started killing." Lindsey pointed to her equipment. "Access your files and see what turns up."

She set up her computer and focused on the New York City police records, via Quantico. They sifted through murders, according to years, starting at 1984 and going backwards, using the keywords, "strangulation and clothespin".

Lindsey's hope faded as each year proved fruitless. By the time they got down to 1975, he was slumped in his chair, his eyes glassy. He grabbed a bottle of Mylanta off his desk and unscrewed the cap. As he chugged down the contents, the search hit 1972 and the screen suddenly filled with information. "What's that?" He moved closer to Sharon's monitor. "On July 15, 1972, Leonard Alberghetti was arrested for the murder of his wife, Lena Alberghetti, missing since 1969. Reports of spousal abuse aroused suspicion of police and neighbors, but no body was found, and there was no arrest.

In 1972, Alberghetti's maid informed the police that he was digging up his wife's remains in the back yard. A rope was around the neck of the victim, secured by a clothespin."

"I don't believe this." Sharon turned to Lindsey.

Lindsey's eyes came to life as he raked his fingers through his hair. "This is it! This is the break we've been waiting for." He continued reading. "Alberghetti's wife had left him. He killed her when she came back in the middle of the night to take their son with her. He said he dug up her remains three years later, because her ghost came out of the ground every night and he was afraid someone else might see her."

"Sick man." Sharon shook her head.

Lindsey continued, "Alberghetti was convicted of first-degree murder and sentenced to life in prison, but died of a heart attack in December of 1975, after serving three years in the state penitentiary." Lindsey pounded his fist on the desk. "Damn!" A scowl furrowed his brow.

Sharon frowned and rubbed her chin.

Lindsey kicked back his chair. His face was red and the veins in his neck bulged.

"Look, there's no reason to be discouraged. There

has to be a correlation here somewhere." She scrolled down the report. "Look, here's the maid's address. If she's still alive, we might be able to get some more information."

His eyes were intense as he looked at Sharon. "I'm flying there first thing in the morning."

He gazed out the window. Wispy strands of clouds floated across the full face of the moon. Nights like these always stirred the urge, even if recently appeased. It didn't matter now, if Lindsey had been thrown off the case or not. The full moon was a green light. The night and the mood were right. The time had come.

He'd waited for over an hour and was growing impatient. He plunged his hand into his pocket and fingered the cold steel of his switchblade. He received the knife from his father. A reward for finally accepting the truth about his mother. He earned his father's respect and on that day, he'd become his father's son. The knife was a treasured monument. And it performed well for him, cutting deep and fast, with little resistance.

His breathing quickened now as he anticipated the job before him. He wished he could perform in an alley, where trash belonged, but he knew she'd never go voluntarily. She was much too smart for that. He'd just have to make do. Maybe improvise a little to make up for it.

He lifted his head and sniffed the air, like a carnivore smelling for prey. Her perfumed scent was everywhere...weakened and stale...but captured and lingering in her furniture, the carpet, and the clothes in her closet.

This would be the kill of a lifetime. She was not a stranger. He knew her intimately. What she had done in her past. What she was doing now. She deserved what she was going to get more than all the others put together.

Suddenly, a taxi pulled up and she stepped out. She bent over in her short skirt and paid the driver. He hated her immodesty.

Just before she turned toward her apartment building, he shut the gap in the venetian blind, then moved quietly into the bedroom. He pulled the ski mask down over his entire face.

As the key turned in the lock, he could barely contain himself. She entered the apartment, and the smell of perfume intensified. She flipped on the lights and headed for the kitchen. He waited breathlessly, behind her bedroom door. Knowing she didn't suspect the danger that lurked within yards from her intrigued him. He always delighted in that perspective. One minute they think they are safe. The next, they're not.

The television came on. She clicked through the channels with her remote, then settled on a movie in progress. He heard her bump into something and cuss loudly. She thinks that hurts? He held his hand over his mouth to suppress his laughter. The anticipation made him giddy.

During a commercial, she mumbled and walked to the bedroom.

This was it. He licked his lips and took a deep breath.

She walked past him, unbuttoning her blouse, and went directly into the bathroom and snapped on the light. He stayed very still. He could hear her fumbling in a closet. He wondered if she was going to take a bath. That would be interesting. But a shower would be even better. With all the noise, he'd be able to sneak up on her and... No, on second thought, a shower would be too cliche. He caught himself about to laugh again.

She slipped into silk pajamas, turned off the bathroom light, and was halfway across the bedroom when he slammed the door shut and barred her exit.

Heather jumped and froze. She stared in his direction. Within seconds, the brightness of the moon enabled her to make out his image. Her head tilted slightly as she squinted her eyes directly at him and then she shook her head and laughed. "A ski mask and surgical gloves? Allen, what are you going to think of next?"

He stood motionless, confused. This wasn't the reaction he'd anticipated. Anger replaced disappointment. He bolted toward her, yanked her long hair, and pulled her down to her knees.

"Hey! Don't hurt me," Heather spoke the words like a novice actress.

Immediately he knew what was in her mind. She thought they were playing *the game*. She'd never learn. But he could use this to his advantage. Without a word, he rolled her over, pulled out a cord from his jacket pocket, and quickly tied her hands behind her back. She made a feeble attempt to get away.

"You're really into this tonight." She turned her head to the side, to look at him. "But loosen that rope, it's too tight."

He shook his head, then flipped her onto her back.

"Hey! Not so hard. You might leave bruises again. With everything that's going on, I don't think that's a very good idea."

He kneeled above her, reached for her shoulders and shook her hard. Her head snapped backwards and banged against the floor.

She cried out. "Allen! That's enough. You're getting carried away." A look of confusion slowly spread across her face. Before she could react, he pinned her to the floor and pulled out a rag from his pocket. He could tell her mind was racing now by the bewildered look in her eyes. He sensed the exact moment when she finally distinguished truth from fantasy.

Before she could scream, he stuffed the rag into her mouth. She tried to bite him twice and he smacked her across the face. When she looked at him, he held his finger up, warning her not to struggle and she obeyed.

He noticed she'd lost the bold, seductive glint that had been there just seconds ago. He felt so alive.

He went about his work diligently. As his hands tightened around her neck, she thrashed from side to side, trying to throw him off, but she was unsuccessful. Her useless attempts of escape delighted him. He also enjoyed the vulnerable feeling of her fragile neck in his grasp...the once strong pulse, now weak and thready.

He watched her eyes flutter as they rolled back into her head, exposing the whites. The next second, they flipped forward again into a fixed stare. Pulling her upward, he wrapped a rope around her neck then removed a clothespin from his pocket, jammed it on the rope, and twisted it. As the ligature wound tighter and tighter, he smiled wider and wider. The smile reached his eyes and an instant before she blacked out, he could tell she had observed it.

He released her limp body, got up and walked casually into the kitchen to get a glass of water. When he returned, he unwound the clothespin and loosened the rope, then splashed the water on her face. Heather's chest rose sharply and her lungs filled, like the primordial instinct of an infant when it is pulled from the depths of his mother and introduced to the air. Dead eyes flickered with recognition. Within seconds, she tried to talk, but the rag and weakness made her speech indistinguishable. But he knew what she was trying to ask. The same thing they all asked. Why are you doing this to me? He shook his head, almost laughing aloud. How could they not know? They knew what they'd done. They all knew they deserved it. How could they question it? Especially her.

He straddled her again. She shook her head. He watched the pink flow of circulation creep up from her chest, to her neck and into her face. He was in no hurry.

She pleaded with her eyes and tried to talk again. He hesitated. He wanted her to think he might reconsider and stop. It worked. She had that unmistakable look of hope. Her eyes softened with promised forgiveness. She was smart, he had to hand it to her. But he was smarter. He pretended to think it over as his hands slowly traveled toward the rope. He knew she thought he was going to remove it. Instead, he gave the rope a quick jerk, stabbed the clothespin on the section where both ends met and twisted until she blacked out again.

After Heather regained consciousness, he removed the knife from his jacket pocket. When he snapped it open, the moon peeked through the window blind, and deposited a dancing stripe on the blade. He paused, a moment to admire it, then showed it to her, as he ran his fingertips up and down its shaft. He placed it between his teeth and dragged her into the kitchen. He pulled a chair out from the table and pushed her down into it. Folding the knife, he put it back in his pocket, then opened her refrigerator. He removed an apple, then casually sat down on a chair in front of her. As he bit the flesh of the fruit, he stared into her eyes. He felt like a cat with a mouse.

He focused on her facial expression. It was blank. This displeased him. The look of fear had to be rekindled.

He considered his options and gave thought to the artwork that would accompany her to the grave. Because this event was so special, he decided to add another dimension to his masterpiece. Carving the dead was easy and redundant; he was ready for a new challenge. He finished his apple, then jammed the core in his pocket, careful to leave nothing behind to incriminate himself.

He stood and moved toward her, then stopped when he realized he'd need additional rope to tie her to the chair and bind her feet and knees for the new procedure. If she moved, it would ruin the affect. Only clean cuts were acceptable.

He glanced around the room, then smiled when he remembered the venetian blinds. The knife cut through each cord like a razor. When he turned to face her, he dangled and swayed them back and forth as if he were a magician building suspense.

Close to her chair, his attention diverted as he separated the longest cord from the others in his hand. Seizing the opportunity, Heather kicked out and delivered an excruciating jolt to his crotch. His eyes bulged with disbelief as he screamed and then his knees buckled and he dropped to the floor. Though writhing helplessly in a fetal position, his eyes stayed fixed on Heather as she struggled to her feet and scrambled out of the kitchen and through the living room. He watched her turn and approach the door backwards, twist the knob with her hands still tied behind her and flee as soon as the door opened. He lay there for several seconds and listened to her feet descend the stairwell. With a loud groan, he gathered himself up, left the apartment, and disappeared into the night.

CHAPTER 14

Lindsey's telephone shook him from the escape of a deep sleep. He fumbled for the receiver, then muttered into the mouthpiece. "Yeah."

"Lindsey!" Patterson's voice was loud. "We've got him, man. I have a live victim sitting right in front of me. Agent Cross is here, too, and she said cancel your flight to New York and get your butt to the station, pronto."

Fifteen minutes later, Lindsey burst into the office, breathless. He nodded to Sharon and Patterson and raised his eyebrows at Heather. "Looks like you've had one hell of a night."

"That's the understatement of the year." Her voice was hoarse.

Her bruised face added to Lindsey's fears. He had to find Jennifer quick. "Henry know I'm here?" Lindsey asked Patterson.

Patterson snorted, "He's sick in bed with that stomach flu. So what the man doesn't know...blah...blah...blah."

Lindsey turned his attention back to Heather. "Have you been to the hospital?"

"No. I jumped into a cab and came right here." She nodded towards Patterson and Cross. "They called an ambulance a few minutes ago."

"So, what's the story?" He glanced at all three of them.

Heather sighed. "I want Allen Randolph arrested for attempted murder."

"He did this to you?"

Heather nodded.

"What happened?" Lindsey's pulse pounded in his neck.

Heather's hand shook as she pushed her hair back to expose her neck.

Lindsey leaned in to observe the red and blue swelling and deeply etched rings.

Patterson sat back. "I told you Allen Randolph was our man."

"Did he use anything beside his hands to strangle you?"

"A rope and a clothespin. I'd black out, then the next thing I knew, I'd be awake with water all over my face." She swallowed with difficulty. "It was horrible! I was so scared. I swear, I think he's the devil himself. At one point I wished he would just let me die and get it over with." Her voice was weaker. "I need a drink of water."

Lindsey walked to the water cooler and gave her a cup. "Thank you." She took a few sips. "I can hardly get this down. My throat hurts so bad," she tried to clear her voice.

"Anyway, after I woke up the second time, he took out this knife and he stared at it like it was trophy. Then he took me out into the kitchen and ate an apple! Can you believe it? After what he had just done to me, he wanted a snack." She shook her head. "When he was finished, he cut the cords off my venetian blinds and came toward me again. As soon as he got close enough, I kicked him in the crotch and took off."

Sharon shook her head. "You're very lucky to have survived an encounter with him. And we're lucky you are able to make a positive identification. Actually, it kind of surprises me that he didn't try to conceal his identity."

"Oh, he did. He was wearing a ski mask," she said, just above a whisper.

Lindsey turned to Patterson. They both frowned. "Wait a minute." Lindsey turned back to Heather. "You did see his face at some point, right?"

"Well, no...he kept the mask on, but I saw his blue eyes. Plus I recognized his build and height."

"Did he talk to you?"

"Come to think of it, he didn't." She tried to drink again and couldn't swallow. She spit the water back into the cup.

"Damn!" Lindsey threw up his arms.

Her swollen eyes darted back and forth between them. "Look, I know it was him."

Lindsey's voice boomed, "In case you haven't noticed, he's not the only guy in town that's six feet tall and has blue eyes. You've got to give us something more than this. Like, was he wearing any rings or a watch. Or familiar clothes? What about his shoes? Or his cologne?" Was there anything else you recognized?"

Sharon clutched Lindsey's arm and warned him with her eyes.

Heather trembled as her eyes filled with tears. "No. I guess not." She touched her neck gingerly. "But look, he had the motive. I lied to you before. Allen and I *were* having an affair, and I was pushing him hard to divorce Debbie and marry me." She strained to make herself heard. "Debbie was giving him problems, too. He told me she was driving him nuts. Paul Shield was blackmailing him and Allen was furious about it. He even told me he was going to stop him one way or another. Even back then, I wondered how far he was going to go. Think about it...he had the motivation to kill me, his wife, and Paul Shield." Her last few words were barely audible.

"Actually, he admitted the affair with you, when we last interviewed him. So he really didn't have a reason to kill you," Sharon said.

Heather tried to clear her throat again. "Oh, yes he did. He wouldn't have wanted me to testify against him." Her shoulders raised as she tried to take a breath. "Believe me, I know too much about the real Allen Randolph."

Sharon regrouped. "Did Allen ever talk about prostitutes?"

She frowned. "Prostitutes? Not that I can recall." Her eyes looked distant, and then her mouth fell open. "Do you think he had something to do with the prostitute murders, too?" She whispered.

"We're not sure of anything yet."

Lindsey massaged the small of his back. "Try real hard. Is there anything else that made you think it was Allen?"

Heather closed her eyes and was about to shake her head, then remembered. "Yes. He acted like Allen."

"How? Give me details."

"Well, this is embarrassing," Heather made another attempt to swallow. "We were into play acting. We called it, *the game*. Kind of a predator/victim thing." She blushed, and looked down at her hands. "I shouldn't have gotten him started on it. It backfired on me once before." Tears ran down her cheeks. "My shrink says it has something to do with my childhood. I don't know. Maybe he's right." She wiped her eyes gingerly. "I guess in some ways I'm just as sick as Allen." She hesitated. "But at least I don't go around killing people." She glanced at all of them. "Anyway, that's why, when I saw him dressed like that, it didn't really freak me out. I just thought he wanted to play *the game* and he'd come up with a new disguise."

"So this isn't the first time he's worn a disguise or restrained you?"

She shook her head.

"And he was already in your apartment when you got home?"

She nodded. "I gave him a key months ago."

Lindsey looked at Patterson. "Anyone check the door yet?"

"No sign of forced entry," Patterson answered smugly.

"So what did he do when you first saw him?" Lindsey asked.

"He just stood there looking menacing, so I pretended to be scared because that's all part of it. Then he went too far, really started hurting me and I couldn't stop him. At that point, I could tell by his eyes that he'd finally snapped," she whispered.

Sharon tapped a pen against her cheek. "Heather, this will sound like a question out of left field, but it's very important. Have you ever been pregnant?"

"Why? What's that got to do with anything?" Her words

were barely coming out.

"It could be crucial to the case." Sharon stepped closer and the men leaned toward Heather. They were all having difficulty hearing her.

She looked at her hand and slid her pinkie ring up and down her finger. "I got pregnant a couple years ago. It was before I moved to Florida and met Allen. I didn't know the man very long, but I was crazy about him. He was the best looking man I'd ever met."

Patterson picked up the tape recorder from the desk and placed it close to Heather's mouth.

"He had great eyes and a dangerous mouth, a lot like Allen. I guess I always go for that type of guy." Her hands touched her throat and stayed there. "Anyway, that's a long story and I'm afraid my voice is going to give out. So I had better get to the bottom line. I had an abortion, left him and moved down here."

Sharon's eyes narrowed in thought.

"You ever tell Allen that you had an abortion?" Lindsey quickly asked.

"Yes, why? What does an abortion have to do with all this?"

"Plenty," Lindsey said. An ambulance pulled up on the street two stories below and its flashing lights reflected on the window. "Looks like your ride is here." He turned to Patterson. "You got her statement?"

Patterson held up the document. "All she has to do is sign it."

Heather's eyes were slits. "Then hurry up. Give me a pen. I want him off the streets as soon as possible."

An hour later, Lindsey sat alone in his office next to an intercom speaker. He listened as Patterson and Cross talked to Allen Randolph in the interrogation room. His hands shook as he lit a cigarette and his eyes looked like a dog ready to lunge.

Patterson was all business. "Have a seat. I know you were read your Miranda rights, but I'm going to repeat them."

When he was finished, Allen asked, "Who filed

charges against me? And what the hell for?" He slurred his words and the alcohol on his breath caused Patterson and Cross to push their chairs back from the table.

"Heather Martin. For attempted murder, as if you didn't know," Patterson replied.

"Attempted murder? You mean someone tried to kill Heather, and she thinks it was me?"

"Thinks? She knows it was you."

"That's crazy," he burped.

Patterson shook his head.

"I still haven't talked to a lawyer."

"We can make a call and get one for you right now. You call the shots." Sharon's voice was as hard-edged as Patterson's.

"Okay." He took a deep breath. "Go ahead, make the call. I'm getting sick and tired of you people."

Sharon made arrangements over the phone. "I left a message on his pager. If you don't want to talk until he arrives, that's fine. It's entirely up to you."

"Well, I'd like to know how Heather is. Is she okay?

"Just got a call from the hospital. By the time Heather arrived, her throat closed up. They had to intubate her and put her on a ventilator."

"Poor Heather. I can't believe it."

"Yeah, yeah. You feel so bad for her. Just the other day, you called her trash." Patterson pressed on. "Where were you at midnight?"

Allen shrugged. "In my car, I guess. I had dinner at the Red Lobster in Kissimmee, hung around the bar for awhile, and got drunk. Then I went out in my car, drove somewhere, parked and slept and then went back to my house. That's when you're people picked me up."

"Unbelievable." Patterson turned to Sharon and chuckled. "Another vague alibi that can't be verified."

"But it's true. You can check it out." He mumbled.

"Oh really? Where did you park? Do you have the name of someone who saw you sleeping in your car?"

Allen's droopy eyes stared straight ahead.

Sharon walked over to the counter, poured a cup of coffee, and handed it to Allen.

"Thank you," he said. When he took a sip, his head jerked back. "Man, that's hot."

Patterson snickered under his breath. "So, Allen, were you with anyone at the bar?"

Allen frowned. "I was alone."

"Of course you were. I don't know why I bothered asking."

"I remember the waitress. She was a short brunette named, Denise," he muttered, with his eyes closed.

"Hey!" He glanced at Sharon. "The man actually came up with a name."

Sharon leaned toward Allen. "Why did you go to the Bronson Ranch a couple days ago?"

Allen's eyes opened. "Bronson Ranch? I never even heard of the place. What in the world are you talking about?"

"Don't play games with us," Patterson barked. "We know it was you. You went there to scare Detective Lindsey's daughter. Then the next day you kidnapped her."

In an attempt to jump to his feet, Allen got tangled in the legs of the chair and fell forward.

Lewis Schwartz, Allen's appointed attorney, burst through the door. "Good evening. I was in the building when I got your page." He looked at Allen, then back at Patterson. "I trust you two haven't been interrogating or harassing my client in my absence." Schwartz was a stocky man with an attitude.

"Your client didn't say anything he didn't volunteer on his own free will."

Schwartz' eyes narrowed. "It appears to me that my client is intoxicated. If this goes to court, anything he's said will be stricken."

"Don't worry, he hasn't said anything worthwhile since he got here," Patterson snorted. "Let us clue you in on the information we've previously accumulated."

After he received their information, Schwartz scratched the side of his fleshy face and stared at them for several minutes. His eyes shifted back and forth between them. He grinned. "This is it? This is all you have?"

Patterson met his eyes. "Heather Martin knew your client intimately for over a year. She recognized his eyes. Everyone knows the eyes are the most easily identifiable part of the human body. In addition, she's familiar with how your client moves and the kind of sick games he likes to play. When you combine that with motive, a pattern of lies, and a lack of alibis, there ain't no way your client is going to go but down."

Schwartz stood and gestured for Allen to follow him. He shook his head at Patterson. "Let's face it man, you ain't got squat." He opened the door. "After my client sobers up, we'll confer and then meet with you sometime in the early afternoon."

In the solitude of his office, Lindsey seethed as he stared at the intercom. In one quick swoop, he knocked the speaker to the floor. "Schwartz is right. We still don't have enough to hang this guy. I'm going to have to take Randolph down myself."

Despite a nasty hang over, Allen was coherent by the time his attorney arrived in the morning. Schwartz set up a folding chair in the aisle outside the holding cell. He always conducted the first interview with a client this way. He believed it gave them greater incentive to cooperate.

Allen gripped the bars. "Has anyone posted bail? If not, I got plenty of money. I can do it myself."

"First things first. You haven't even been arraigned yet."

Allen exhaled loudly. "This whole thing is nuts. I didn't do anything."

Schwartz' beady eyes showed he'd heard that before. "Oh, great. Even my attorney doesn't believe me."

"It's not important whether I believe you or not." Schwartz set a file on his lap. "Let's get something straight from the get go. If you're innocent, I want to know everything. Even if it seems insignificant to you. Also, if something occurred that could make you look even guiltier, I need to know about it right away. I don't want any surprises when we appear before the District Attorney. I

want to be prepared. You get it?"
Allen nodded.
"Okay," he said, opening the file. "Let's get started. I've read most of the information from the police department, including the report from Missing Persons." He shook his head. "What the hell were you thinking?"
Allen didn't answer."
"You've dug yourself a grave. And now, I'm going to have one hell of a time digging you out of it."
Allen sat down on the edge of his cot. "So, what do you want to know first?"
"Tell me about Heather Martin, the so called *eye witness*."
Allen sighed. "We worked together. She was invaluable. We were a great team." He hesitated. "Unfortunately, we were a team after hours too and I know that makes me look bad."
"I assume she knew your personal business pretty well then...the two of you talked freely."
"Yeah, pretty much."
"Tell me something," He cocked his head to one side, "Is she petite or is she an amazon?"
"What the hell difference does that make?"
"Just answer the question."
"She's around five foot six and weighs about one hundred twenty pounds."
He mulled this over. "Sounds like a light weight. Does she lift weights? Know karate?"
Allen frowned. "What the hell are you getting at?"
"She benefited by your wife and Shield dying, correct?"
"Are you saying you think she could have killed them?" Allen's eyes widened. "First of all, that's ridiculous. Second, the way the cops talked, she was in terrible shape. She couldn't have done that to herself."
"Anything is possible." Schwartz caressed his fat jowls with his fingertips. "Did you two have a falling out? Could she have done it to set you up?"
"No. In fact, the last time we were together, I convinced her that we were going to get married. She was

ecstatic." He shook his head. "No, no way. Heather's not the killer."

"All right. Let's leave that angle alone for awhile. Who else knew about your problems?"

Allen thought for a moment. "Only my brother. But I doubt he would have told anyone else."

Schwartz raised an eyebrow. "The report mentions John has schizophrenia. Says from the time you two were kids, he was notorious for getting you out of trouble."

Allen nodded. "That's right. There wasn't anything he wouldn't do for me." Allen scratched the back of his head. His eyes glimmered with moisture.

"And when you got in trouble this time, you repeated the pattern. Went to big brother for help."

"I just needed someone to talk to," Allen snapped. " I didn't expect him to help me."

Schwartz thought for a moment. "Just how far do you think John would go to help you out?"

Allen didn't respond.

Schwartz bit the corner of his lower lip. "Let me swing this one by you. John is mentally ill. He also loves you and is willing to do anything to make you happy, just like the old days. Isn't it conceivable that just maybe he took it a little too far this time? Maybe in his warped mind, he thought he was doing you a favor by wiping out the people that were hassling you."

"That's nonsense. Besides, John loved my wife. He wouldn't have hurt her. There's no way."

Schwartz shrugged indifferently. "What's he look like?"

"John? A little like me. Why?" Allen frowned.

"Same basic build and eyes?"

Allen nodded. "Close, but not exact."

Schwartz placed the tip of his forefinger at one corner of his lip and thumb at the other while he ruminated. His fingers traced his bottom lip until they met in the center. "Think about it. Heather thought it was you because the attacker had your build and blue eyes."

Allen stood up. "No. I don't like where you're going with this."

"That's too bad. It might be your only ticket to freedom."

"Well, I'm not about to let my brother go to jail, just to keep me out."

Schwartz watched Allen pace. "Maybe you'll change your mind when I tell you what I read in the police report." He opened the file. "John's footprint was found outside Paul Shield's apartment the night he was killed." He eyed Allen. "Now you tell me why you think your brother was there that night. Maybe you can enlighten me."

Allen's forehead wrinkled up in confusion. "I have no idea. Are they sure it was his footprint?"

"Absolutely."

"Then they need to ask John. He'll tell them the truth."

"They did ask him." Schwartz chuckled. "He told them he went there to pray for the man."

"Then, I'm sure that's exactly what he was doing. He thought he was helping. Now he's gotten himself involved in this mess."

"Are you dense? Do you understand what I'm trying to tell you? The only tangible evidence they have in this case is that footprint." Schwartz' tongue pushed on the inside of his cheek. "You don't actually believe he went there to pray, do you?"

Allen's eyebrows knit together. "If you knew John, that wouldn't seem unusual." Allen paused. "Besides, what do I have to worry about? Like you said, they don't have any tangible evidence against me."

"They have an eye witness. Now I can tear her character up without problem...discredit her. Or, I can work on convincing her of John's guilt. That would be the best route to take, believe me." He leaned back, his hands clasped on his bulging belly. "Let me ask you this. Can you think of anyone else to blame this on?"

"No."

"Then the way I see it, the guilty person has to be you or your brother. Now you tell me who it's going to be?"

Allen turned and stared at him angrily. "Neither one of us. You're my attorney. You find out who really did it."

"Before I go on a wild goose chase, I'm going to have a long talk with your brother. If I feel there's nothing there, then we'll go in another direction."

"No. You don't know John. He gets stressed out very easily."

"Listen, if you're found guilty, odds are you'll end up meeting "Old Sparky" up close and personal. On the other hand, if it turns out it's your brother, the worse that could happen is he'd be put in a mental hospital, where he most likely belongs anyway. He'd be taken care of for the rest of his life."

Allen turned away, his face pale, and walked over to the small window in his cell and looked down. It was a sunny November day. People on the street walked and jogged like nothing was wrong. Life was going on without him. It seemed surreal.

"So what do you say?" He paused and watched his client.

Allen squeezed his eyes together. He couldn't believe he was about to let this happen. "Okay, bring him in. But go easy on him."

Patterson and Cross were not at the police station when John arrived. He was disappointed. God had answered his prayers and revealed everything to him. He wanted to tell them what he had learned. The officer at the front desk told John that Allen's lawyer wanted to see him as soon as possible. John scratched two words on a piece of paper, handed it to the officer, and asked him to give it to Cross when she arrived.

John immediately took a bus downtown to Schwartz's office. After they shook hands and sat down, the corpulent attorney went into action.

"Your brother is in big trouble. I assume you realize how serious this is?"

"Of course." John nodded.

Schwartz pointed to a tape recorder on his desk. "Mind if I tape our conversation?"

John shook his head.

Schwartz pushed the play button. "If we don't find out who murdered those people and who attacked Heather Martin, your brother is most likely going to fry in the electric chair."

John's face paled. "We can't let that happen. He's innocent."

"How do you know? What makes you so sure?

"I witnessed one of the prostitute murders that they are talking about on the news. I couldn't see the killer's face, but I could tell by the way he moved and talked, it wasn't Allen. I believe he's the same man that killed my brother's wife and employee."

Schwartz put his hand near his mouth, to conceal his smug smile.

"I was looking for food at the entrance of an alley. I heard someone talking. I looked back and saw a man carving X's across a dead girl's eyes. She had long dark hair and was wearing a beige top and shorts. She had a rope around her neck. He'd strangled her. He talked to her as if she could hear him. He told her he was cutting her so she couldn't identify him. He kept saying, 'you can't point your finger at me'. Over and over again, he kept saying it." John rubbed the bridge of his nose with his fingers as he shook his head.

"Then he bent over again and started to cut near her mouth. I got so upset, I lost my balance and knocked into a trash can. He heard the noise, stopped what he was doing, and stared at me. He raised the knife and pointed it toward me. He looked so evil. He wore a dark ski mask and I couldn't see anything but his eyes. I thought I was looking into the face of Satan. I was afraid he was going to kill me next, so I ran away." John's face reddened slightly.

"When all this happened, I wasn't thinking very clearly. I'd been on the streets for a couple of months and had been off my medicine. When the police brought me to the hospital, my doctor filled me full of drugs and I forgot all about what I'd seen until now," John explained.

"But during these last couple months, I kept hearing

the voice of the killer. At first, I thought I was hallucinating again. Then I realized I was being reminded of what happened. I prayed that the Lord would completely restore my memory. A few hours ago, he answered my prayers."

Schwartz fiddled with a pen in his hands. "The prostitute murders all took place in very dark alleys."

"I know this one was dark."

"How far away were you from the killer?"

John shrugged. "At least thirty feet."

Schwartz rubbed his jaw. "Taking into consideration how dark the alley was and how far away you were, it seems odd that you were able to see as much as you did."

"Portions of the alley were less dark because of the street light and the man kept stepping in and out of the shadows."

"It also seems strange that you were at two of the crime scenes. The odds of that happening are slim to none."

"Then I guess God must have had his hand in it. I was meant to be at both places."

"Yeah, right." Schwartz grinned. "I think we have a lot of ground to cover, John. Might as well make yourself comfortable."

Two grueling hours passed before Schwartz finished. He told John to stay seated, and rushed out of the room to call the police. Not wanting to wait, John left quietly.

CHAPTER 15

A detective stopped by Carol's apartment. He told her he needed to bring John in for questioning. The detective left after Carol convinced him that her son wasn't there.

Carol felt like her whole life was suddenly in a downward spiral. The phone rang continuously and reporters gathered outside her apartment building. She'd experienced a series of flashing lights out of the corner of her eye minutes after the officer left and was now in the middle of a full blown migraine.

Her cell phone rang again. Carol stared at it through glazed eyes, then punched the power/off button. She couldn't deal with anything. She walked into her room and lowered herself onto the bed. Nothing else mattered now but sleep. However, the medication she'd taken supplied no relief for the pounding pain and relentless nausea.

She wasn't able to sleep. She reached for the prescription bottles on the bedside table, poured all the tablets into her hand, and stuffed them in her mouth. She washed them down with a glass of water, then laid her head back on the pillow. A feeling of peace followed a sense of resignation.

Minutes later, the nausea worsened, and she reached the bathroom just in time to spew every tablet into the toilet. Each time she vomited, the veins in her head felt as though they would burst. Once her stomach emptied, she fell against the wall, tears streamed down her face, and her body trembled. She stood up slowly, staggered to the medicine closet, and removed a razor. She sat down on the edge of the tub, placed the cold steel against her wrist, closed her eyes, took a deep breath and cut. Before the razor reached the major vein in her wrist, someone called her name from her living room. It was Linda. Carol froze, dropped the razor, and then pressed her fingers across the wound.

"I'm sick, could you come back later?" Her voice was barely audible.

"We heard about Allen and wanted to make sure you're okay." Linda's tone didn't mask her concern.

We? That meant Anthony was with her. "Please, I have a migraine and I've been throwing up. I don't want any company." The blood streamed through her fingers and ran down her wrist and onto the floor.

"You sure?" Linda's voice was now coming from outside the bathroom door.

"Positive." She felt dizzy.

"Could I come in for just a second?" She talked through wood.

Carol remembered she hadn't locked the door. She stood up to turn the latch, then fainted before reaching it. Linda heard her hit the floor.

Linda and Anthony rushed in and found Carol, the blood, and the razor.

"Oh, my God! She slit her wrist," Linda screamed.

"Watch out." Anthony pushed Linda aside and examined the injury. He held his fingers against the wound, then motioned to the medicine closet. "See if there's any cotton and gauze in there."

Linda retrieved the supplies he requested and Anthony wrapped the wound securely.

"Let's give it a few minutes to see if the bleeding slows down," he said. "I want to avoid taking her to the hospital if at all possible. She doesn't need to be there, especially now, when her son needs her so much."

Linda gestured toward the living room. "Let's carry her to the sofa." They lifted her up, took her out of the bathroom, and laid her down gently.

Anthony sat next to Carol on the floor and elevated her arm. He checked her wrist. "The blood doesn't seem to be spreading over the bandages. That's a good sign."

"Thank God." Linda's big eyes dripped with tears.

"I can't believe she did this. Suicide is such a selfish act. It's not like Carol." Anthony looked bewildered.

"Well, you've got to take into consideration what she's been going through. This has been a horrible time for her."

"Nevertheless, her boys need her. She can't run out on them."

Linda frowned at him. "For crying out loud, she was having a migraine. The pain from that alone can drive a person to suicide. Plus, she's having to deal with this mess with Allen. It's no wonder she went off the deep end."

"It's still no excuse."

"Oh, cut her some slack! She's going to need our support when she wakes up."

Anthony shook his head. "I thought she was different."

"She's a human being. Get over it," Linda shouted.

Carol groaned as she regained consciousness.

"It's going to be okay," Linda consoled her.

Carol's face contorted and she pressed the heel of her hand against her temple.

Linda whispered in her ear, "Is there anything I can do for you?"

"Yeah, get me a trash can. Quick!" Linda retrieved it just in time. Carol vomited again. When she stopped, she grabbed Linda's arm. "I just remembered. I've got a shot in my top bureau drawer. Will you get it for me?"

"Sure." Linda rushed out of the room and then hurried back in. "I thought you stopped taking these shots a long time ago."

Carol nodded. "I'd developed a tolerance to it. Since it's been so long, maybe it will work for me again," she groaned. "I'll try anything to get rid of this pain." She held the applicator against the top of her thigh and pressed a button. The needle popped out and delivered the medicine quickly. Carol lay down and curled up into a ball, her eyes closed.

Linda turned to Anthony and motioned him to follow her into the kitchen.

"You see?" She whispered. "The migraine just got the better of her. Haven't you ever been in unbearable pain?" She looked back over her shoulder at Carol. "Pain can make anyone go crazy."

Anthony's eyes drifted.

After thirty minutes, Carol slowly sat up and pushed the hair from her eyes.

"Feeling better?" Linda rushed to her side.

Carol nodded. "Yeah. The pounding has stopped. I wish I'd have thought of trying that shot earlier. I'm sorry I caused you both so much worry."

"That's okay. I'm just glad we stopped by in time." Linda paused. "Hey, it just occurred to me. John's not here. Where is he?"

Carol shook her head slightly. "I'm not sure. The police are looking for him. They want to bring him into the station for questioning. I'm sure they think he is somehow involved in the murders." Her voice was fragile.

"Oh, that's ridiculous." Linda frowned.

"Allen has messed things up for everyone. As usual."

Linda glanced at the telephone. "Have the reporters been bugging you?"

Carol nodded. "I can't take it anymore, Linda." She grabbed her phone and staggered slightly as she walked into the kitchen. She made two calls, then hung up. "I just told the boss I'm not coming into work on Monday. I also made an airline reservation. I'm taking my vacation now. I need time alone. I've got to get away from here."

Linda gasped, "You can't be alone at a time like this. Look what you just tried to do." She pointed to the bandage on Carol's wrist.

"I'm not going to stay here, and that's all there is to it."

"Okay, I understand. You need a break. That's fine, but I won't let you go by yourself, I'm going with you," she said with conviction. "So, where are we headed?"

"Allen's cabin in the Poconos."

"You want to go all the way up to Pennsylvania?"

Carol sighed. "The further away the better."

"Okay. I'll call the airlines, pack and be back as soon as possible." She turned to Anthony. "Will you stay with her while I'm gone?"

He nodded. After Linda left, Carol went in her room to prepare. Anthony stayed in the living room, ruminating. Fifteen minutes passed before Anthony stood in the doorway to her bedroom.

"You're much too weak to be going on a trip." He walked over and checked her wrist again. "I think the bleeding's under control, but you're very pale and you're trembling."

Carol sat down on the edge of her bed. "I am exhausted, but I think I'll be okay. The mountain air will do me good."

Anthony looked at her, his face expressionless. "You can't do this."

"Do what?"

"Leave your sons. It's not right."

Carol stood up, grabbed a sweater from her closet, and threw it on her bed.

"You need to stay here and support them."

She rubbed her head and closed her eyes. "I can't. I don't have anything left to give. I have to think of myself for once. I need time to get away and relax." She removed more clothes from the closet and stuffed them in her suitcase.

"You can't possibly think they're guilty."

"I don't know what to believe anymore. The only thing I'm really sure of, is that I need to get away from both of them."

"I don't believe this." His voice was bitter. "First, you try to kill yourself and now you're walking out. I thought you were different."

Carol snapped, "You shouldn't have put me up on a pedestal. I told you all along that I wasn't special."

"I guess you were right."

"I'm glad you finally realize that." Carol scowled. "I've been trying to get that through your head ever since we met."

"I never dreamed it would turn out like this." The dimples, the charming smile, and the warm glowing eyes were gone.

"Look," she noticed the transformation, "we're both upset and saying things we'll probably regret. I'm only going to be gone for a week or so. Let's stop this bickering before we go too far. I really do value your friendship."

Anthony stepped towards her. "Our friendship is over. I don't want to have anything to do with you."

"Anthony!" Linda slammed the front door and rushed across the living room with her suitcase in hand. "Leave Carol alone."

Anthony glared at both women, then shook his head and left.

Carol and Linda searched each other's faces, as if trying to make sense of everything that was happening.

Carol's cell phone rang. Something told her to answer. "John! Where are you?"

"Orlando. At the entrance to the parking lot of the Science Museum. I don't have enough money to get back home. Can you pick me up?"

Carol hesitated for a moment, and then tears filled her eyes. She cupped the mouthpiece with her hand and whispered to Linda, "Is it okay if we pick up John at the Science Center."

Linda glanced at her watch. "Okay, but we'll be cutting it close.

Carol's words rushed as she talked into the mouthpiece. "We should be there in a half hour or so. Stay put."

"I'll wait for you. Don't worry."

Linda raised her brows as Carol hung up. "Are you planning on taking John with us?"

Carol nodded.

"The police are trying to bring him in for questioning and if you take him away, you might get in trouble."

"I don't care," Carol said over her shoulder, as she headed for John's bedroom. "Anthony's right, John needs me. I'm going to pack a bag for him. Besides, I know he hasn't done anything wrong. I wish I could be as sure of Allen."

Carol made another airline reservation, then they fought through the crowd of reporters on the street. Once they were in Linda's car, Carol shook her head. "I just realized you could get in trouble, too."

"Don't worry about me." Linda winked. "You never told me anything about the police wanting to talk to John."

"You're a wonderful friend. Thanks."

When they arrived, John looked troubled as he slid into the back seat.

"We only have a half hour to get to the airport," Linda reminded Carol.

Carol's eyes darted to the dashboard clock. "Let's hurry."

John sat forward in his seat. "Why are we going to the airport?"

"We're taking a vacation. Going to Allen's cabin."

"But why now, of all times?"

"Don't worry. I've packed our heavy jackets. There'll be plenty of firewood. We might even see some snow. We'll have a good time."

"I wasn't talking about the weather. I was referring to Allen and this whole situation." He frowned. "We can't leave him right now. Not with all that's going on. He needs us."

She took a deep breath. "There's nothing more we can do for him."

"You're wrong. I can do a lot for him, and you should at least be there for moral support, if nothing else. Besides, the police are going to want to see me."

Linda caught his eye in the rear view mirror. "John, your brother's attorney will help him. Your mom is at the end of her rope. She needs to get away."

. "I don't like this." John rubbed his forehead.

Carol turned around and faced him. She noticed for the first time how bad he looked. "Have you been keeping up with your medicine?"

"I might have forgotten to take it this morning," he

said.

She fumbled through her purse. "Oh no, I packed your medicine in the suitcase and it's in the trunk."

"Do you want me to stop?" Linda slowed.

"No, we don't have time. Besides, the reporters could be following us." She looked at the road behind them. "John, remind me to give you your pills when we're on the plane. My suitcase is a carry on."

He shook his head. "When we get to the airport, I'm going to turn around and come back home."

"No, you're going with me, and that's final." Carol eyes demanded submission.

John stared out the window. He felt scrambled.

Another prostitute murdered. The crime lab van and several patrol cars were already at the scene when Patterson and Cross arrived. Two cops walked towards them, their faces pale. Patterson didn't even attempt a joke as he and Sharon passed them on the way to the alley.

The extent of torture was immediately apparent. Rope bound the victim's hands and feet. Her mouth was packed with a rag, then taped shut. Huge portions of hair were missing from her scalp and her face was purple where she'd been beaten. Her nose lay off to one side, broken and swollen. The signature cuts included the ears this time. The center of each X crossed the ear canal and the right lobe dangled, suspended by a thin piece of connective tissue. The jagged X's were off-center and blood was everywhere. It covered the trashcan, the surrounding walls and the ground. The victim's hair was saturated and sticky with coagulated serum. The X's had been carved while the victim was still alive. Sharon and Patterson looked at each other's strained faces, then got to work.

After hours of observation and gathering of information, they stopped to collect their thoughts. Sharon leaned against the brick wall in the alley. Something was eating away at her. She felt like she'd heard a phrase that should have rung a bell. But she just couldn't remember who said it or even what it was about. The answer was so close to entering her conscious mind, that she felt like she could almost touch it and reel it in.

"Hey! Where you at?" Patterson interrupted.

Sharon shook her head.

"Something tells me Allen Randolph wasn't real happy after he left Heather Martin's apartment." Patterson nodded toward the corpse. "But I've got to admit, it's definitely his most memorable work."

Sharon nodded. "Yes, it is. And I finally understand the meaning of his signature. Speak no evil, see no evil, and hear no evil. He performs the ritual to keep his victims from identifying him. Now, with the pressure on, he's escalating. Getting more and more paranoid and psychotic."

"You think he actually believes he's covering his bases by gouging them like that?"

"Well, it's worked pretty well for him so far." She tossed a notepad in her briefcase. As they left the scene, her mind, again, tried to invoke the phrase that kept eluding her.

Sharon received John's note as soon as she arrived at the station. She was about to open it when Schwartz approached her. She absentmindedly stuffed it in her purse and accompanied him and Patterson into the conference room.

"It's about time you all got back," the lawyer said. "I need to give you some information. You mind?" He pointed to a seat and took it.

"So what have you got? Your client's plea bargain?" Patterson asked.

"Very funny." Schwartz wasn't laughing. "Actually, I've solved the case for you."

"Oh, really?"

Schwartz set his briefcase on the desk, opened it, and removed a file. "Let's talk about John Randolph, shall we? Did you know he has a habit of sneaking out of the house at night? Or that he had full knowledge about the problematic relationship between my client and the victims? Did you know he committed a violent act toward several police officers? And do you realize how much he and my client look alike...including their eyes and build? Did you know that John would do anything to help his younger brother? And that John had a pattern of getting his brother out of hot water ever since they were children?"

Sharon placed her hands on her hips. "Where did you get this information?"

"From John himself. This morning as a matter of fact."

"Well, you haven't told us anything we didn't already know."

A leisurely, self-satisfied grin spread across his face. "Then let me tell you something you don't know."

"By all means." Patterson tapped his pencil on the table impatiently.

"John Randolph is the murderer. We talked for two hours and I have it on tape."

Patterson's face darkened. "You better not be jerking us around, Schwartz."

"I'm a professional...I don't play those games." He reached into his suit jacket, then handed him a tape. "Listen to it." He stood up, and returned the file to his briefcase. "Meanwhile, Allen Randolph has been released on bail."

"What? Why weren't we notified? Where's John now?" Patterson shouted.

"You two weren't answering your pagers," he said. "As for John, he left my office before I could get a cop to come get him. He's going to be brought into the station for questioning. And after that, I'm sure he'll be arrested." With a slight nod of the head, he turned and left.

Patterson threw his pencil across the room. "Damn! Of all people, why did Schwartz have to solve this thing?"

Shock coated Sharon's face. She picked up the phone, called Lindsey, and told him the news.

Lindsey shook his head at the cell phone. "I'm at my apartment. Get here right away."

When they finished listening to the tape, they burst

into Schwartz' office together. Lindsey noticed the man's cheek jiggle as he quickly turned to face them.

"What do you think you're doing?" He looked at Lindsey. "I thought you were off this case."

"Just consider me an observer." Lindsey positioned himself against the back wall.

Patterson slammed the tape on the desk. "This is bullcrap."

The lawyer's frown carved deep vertical crevices along the bridge of his nose. "What the hell are you talking about?"

Lindsey pointed to the cassette. "What kind of game are you playing?"

"As I told your colleagues earlier, I don't play games."

"The man said the killer wasn't his brother, and that he witnessed one of the crimes. Any nit-wit would know that's not a confession."

"I never said it was a confession. We're talking about adding two plus two here."

"No, we're talking about creating a scapegoat."

"When I spoke with Chief Henry and the D.A., they didn't see it that way."

"Then they're just as nuts as you."

"I'm sure they'd be interested in hearing your comment."

Lindsey stepped forward. "I'm on my way to meet with them. I'll probably call them worse than that when I get there."

Schwartz blinked rapidly. "What's the matter? Are you upset that I broke this case in less than a day, when you've had several months to investigate it? Maybe you do need to get out of this business. You're coming unglued."

Sharon touched Lindsey's hand and nodded toward the door. Lindsey took a deep breath, then said, "Let's go."

The District Attorney, Roger Smith, stood at his office window looking down at the mob of reporters on the street when the investigators arrived. Chief Henry sat in a chair across from his desk. The furrows on his brow were deeper than ever.

Smith's eyes fixed on Lindsey. "I hear you're a little upset."

Lindsey's face was steely.

"Why don't we all take a seat." He pointed to the chairs adjacent to his desk.

Carol sat. Lindsey and Patterson remained standing.

"Under the circumstances, Tom, we can understand why you're here. So we're willing to work with you, but we hope you will give us the courtesy of behaving like a gentleman."

Henry looked away, disgruntled. Lindsey wasn't sure of the source of his agitation.

Lindsey held the tape and pointed it toward the District Attorney. "This is an eyewitness account."

"It's an accurate description of one of the murders. The man admits he was mentally incompetent at the time it took place and his medical records show he was also psychotic and violent. I know he comes off as a witness, but with all the details he gave, his guilt is obvious."

Lindsey shook his head. "Doesn't it seem strange to you that he could only describe one of the murders? He depicts what went down during the Amy Rockwell case. He saw X's over the eyes and tells in detail how the killer was about to cut her mouth when he disturbed him. John was the man who interrupted the killer, not the man who killed the victim."

Henry turned to Lindsey, his eyes heavy in thought. "Look, I'm not convinced about anything yet. But I will say this. The evidence points to John Randolph. The man is crackers. This is an established fact. Then, we have an incriminating time line that can't be ignored. And the footprint at the Sheild's apartment. You also have to consider this: John freely admits he was at two of the murder scenes. How the hell can we believe that was a coincidence?" Henry shook his head. "And then to top it off, the man hears voices." His eyes traveled to Sharon. "Reminds me of a profile I heard early on in this case."

Lindsey rubbed the back of his neck. "I admit you have a good argument, Chief, but the footprint bothers me. It was outside the apartment. It was not consistent with the others. The consistent prints were inside, which lends credence to John's explanation that he stayed outside the door praying." Lindsey rubbed his forehead. "I want a chance to interview John again."

The DA laughed. "Is this how they do it in New York City? Give suspects a chance to worm their way out? Maybe you should be a defense lawyer, buddy, cause you sure aren't on our side."

"I think Schwartz is framing him just to save his own client."

"Why are you so protective of John Randolph?"

The veins in Lindsey's neck pulsated. "You have three damn good investigators standing here, and none of us think John did the killing."

"Why?"

"Experience and gut instinct," Lindsey said.

Smith gave them a dead pan stare. "Look, after three long months of investigation, John's footprint is the only tangible evidence we have. We don't have anything on Allen, except motive and a statement from a woman who didn't see anything but blue eyes and a physique. Schwartz could easily discredit her testimony before a jury. One thing is certain. John Randolph was involved in some capacity." Smith closed his eyes and shook his head. "Hear that?"

Lindsey frowned. "What?"

"Those reporters." He pointed to his window. "They've been harassing me day and night. Once John is locked behind bars, they'll be satisfied and I'll have something I haven't had in a long time. Silence. Do you realize I haven't had a moment's peace since this case began?"

"And you think I have?" Lindsey took a step toward him.

Henry stood up, his face hard as he eyed Smith. "As far as I'm concerned, they are still both suspects. And frankly, I think the judge who let Allen Randolph out on bail has a screw loose. No judgments should be made about John Randolph until we personally question him."

Smith shrugged. "So, where is he? Why haven't your men found him? This town is in a panic."

Henry gave him a stare that would have brought most men to their knees. "We'll bring him in. Don't you worry about that." Henry turned to Lindsey and nodded toward the door. Lindsey followed him. "Listen," he spoke quietly, "I promise you, Allen Randolph will get what he deserves. I want you to keep your head. Let the guys bring him in. Stay out of it, for your sake and your daughter's." He locked eyes with him.

Lindsey shook his head slightly. "I can't. I'm sorry, Chief."

Henry sighed, then walked out the door.

Smith tossed his pen on his desk. "Lindsey, you've got to step back and let this thing alone."

Lindsey's jaw muscles bunched. "My daughter is out there somewhere and the killer is the only one who knows where she is." He moved another step closer. His eyes looked ready for conflict. "Seven people have been murdered! Seven! I won't sit back and let her become the eighth. As long as Allen Randolph is roaming the streets, I can't leave it alone."

"He's not off the hook yet. As soon as we get more evidence, Allen will be locked up again. Now, for your own sake, don't do anything to jeopardize your future."

"I don't give a damn about my future. My daughter's future is all that matters to me."

The investigators walked out the door together. When they hit the street, Lindsey took off in another direction.

"Tom!" Sharon called after him. "We'll let you know as soon as we have something."

"I've already got everything I need. Now all I have to do is find him."

Sharon watched as he got in his car and pulled way. Tears flooded her cheeks.

"Come on." Patterson spoke in an unusually quiet

tone.

"He's going to kill Allen Randolph. You know that."

"Not if we find Allen first." They got in the car and took off.

Sharon reached for her purse to retrieve a tissue and spotted the note from John. After wiping her eyes, she picked up the paper and opened it. Her mouth fell open. "Oh my God!"

Patterson nearly went off the road. "What?"

"John left me this note. It says, *Roberto Alberghetti!*"

"And that's significant because?"

"There was a case in New York where a man used a clothespin to secure a ligature. It dated back to the early seventies. His name was Leonard Alberghetti. Lindsey was going to fly to New York and follow up on the story, but he got sidetracked when Heather was attacked. Somehow, John has come up with this same unusual last name! It's got to be significant." She picked up the telephone to call Lindsey.

CHAPTER 16

The Alberghetti's former maid, Mrs. Williams, sat with Lindsey in her den. The room was dark, shades tightly drawn as if daylight was an allergen. She had gray hair and permanent vertical creases on each side of her mouth. Her eyes drooped as if sadness had once visited and decided to take up residency. He guessed she was in her eighties.

An air of despondency consumed her as she answered his questions. "Roberto was Leonard and Nina's son." She shook her head ever so slightly. "The poor child. God forgive me." Old eyes moistened with tears.

"Tell me everything. I need to know the whole story."

She lowered her eyes and concentrated on her lap. "I came to work for Mr. Alberghetti in nineteen-sixty. My husband had died and I was desperate for a job. Mr. Alberghetti went to visit his family in Italy a few years later and came home with a child bride. He told everyone Nina was eighteen, but I found out later that she was only thirteen years old. No one even knows where she came from, exactly. I think he kidnapped her from some poor family in Italy. She got pregnant right off and when the baby was born, Mr. Alberghetti was jealous of him. Wouldn't let the misses attend him properly. When he was home, I took care of the child. But as soon as Mr. Alberghetti would go to work, Nina would take over. She was a wonderful mother."

"As much money as that man had, he wouldn't let the child have anything but the basics. Food, shelter and clothing. That was it. The child never even owned a single toy...except for the soldiers."

"Soldiers?"

She nodded, and finally looked up. "His mother taught

him how to use his imagination. When the mister was out, Nina and Roberto would go out in the back yard and play. They'd take the clothespin bag from the laundry basket and sit in the shade of a big tree and march those pins around in the dirt like they were little wooden soldiers. And the child loved it. I can still remember his laughter and his precious face. He just lit up every time they were together. He loved his mother so much." She wiped tears from her eyes with a shaking hand.

"But the life they were forced to live was just awful. It seemed like Mr. Alberghetti got meaner every day. He kept accusing poor Nina of cheating on him, which was nonsense. The girl was so sweet and innocent. She rarely went anywhere. He started hitting her." She sighed. "Each week it seemed to get worse. It got so I never saw her without a bruise on her face. Neighbors started talking. They could hear Leonard ranting and raving and saw Nina's' face when she took Roberto out in the yard to play.

"I wanted to call the police so many times, but I was afraid. Mr. Alberghetti was in the mob. I thought if I said anything, they'd come after me. I even tried to quit my job, but he gave me a look that made me think better of it. He was a frightening man."

"I understand. Go on," Lindsey said, quickly.

"Finally, he got it in his head that Nina was a prostitute. I think he was insane, I really do. The beatings got worse and he did it right in front of the child. He called her the most horrible names." Mrs. Williams covered her eyes with her hand. "If only I'd done something then. I was a coward."

"You were in a difficult position. Now, please continue. This is very important." Lindsey sat on the edge of his seat.

"One day he came home from work at noon. Nina and the boy were in the back yard. He caught them playing with the clothespins. It was terrible. He was outraged. Can you imagine? Getting angry over clothespins?" Her chin trembled. "He put the pins in the bag and threw them in the trash. The next morning I started to throw away some trash in the can and noticed the clothespin bag was gone. Later, I found it in the back of Roberto's closet.

"That night, he beat her so badly. She screamed and screamed, and little Roberto did, too. Then he made her put on a terrible dress. It made her look like a hooker. He dragged her into the kitchen and called the boy and me into the room to see her. Her eyes were so black and swollen, I could hardly recognize her. He mocked her, kept calling her names. It was all because she told him she was going to leave him. He pushed her out the door. Roberto clung to her leg, and begged her not to go. I'll never forget the look of fear and desperation on that child's face. Mr. Alberghetti wouldn't let her take Roberto just to be spiteful. She told me earlier in the day that she was going to sneak back and get the boy when her husband was asleep. I heard her come back later that night, but Mr. Alberghetti caught her. There was a terrible struggle and then it got very quiet. I know that's when he killed her." Her eyes glazed.

Lindsey nodded.

"After that, Mr. Alberghetti started taking his anger out on Roberto. He was merciless. This went on for two more years." Her cloudy eyes turned red. "He justified the beatings. He told Roberto that he had to beat out the parts of him that were like his mother. It was so sick.

"Then the strangest thing happened. The boy's attitude toward his mother changed. He started talking badly about her. He called her the same degrading names as his father. Then, like overnight, the beatings stopped and the two of them got very close. It just didn't make sense." She looked at Lindsey briefly, then turned away.

"The third year after Nina's disappearance, I overheard a conversation between them. Mr. Alberghetti told Roberto that he'd gone to the Lower East Side the night before and found Nina working as a prostitute. He told Roberto that he had to stop her, so he strangled her, then brought her body back to the house, and buried it.

Of course I knew he was lying. She'd already been dead for years. I remember standing outside the door waiting for Roberto to explode. Instead, he sounded happy about it, as if it was a reason to celebrate. It sickened me. Roberto blindly believed everything that terrible man told him.

"A few months after that, the boy started waking up in the middle of the night screaming. He'd be at his window looking out at the back yard. He claimed he saw his mother's ghost pointing at his father's bedroom window. That's when I knew for sure he'd gone over the edge. He'd yell for Leonard and the two of them would stare out the window together. Towards the end, Leonard thought he was seeing her, too. All this talk really gave me the creeps. I looked out the window every time they did to make sure I didn't see her. I had to reassure myself that I wasn't going batty like them.

"Then he got afraid one of the neighbors might see her and figure out he'd buried her there. I heard him tell the boy how he was going to stop her from pointing at him from the grave. He was going to dig up her body and blind her eyes and cut out her mouth and ears. I guess in his messed up mind, he thought that would put an end to it.

"Well, in a way, I guess he was right, because that was when I finally reached my limit. When I saw the two of them out there in that hole where Nina was buried, I put an end to it. I didn't care what happened to me anymore. I called the police...something I should have done years before."

Lindsey stared at her for a long time. Finally, he asked. "What happened to the boy?"

"HRS took him. I heard he'd been adopted."

"Do you know the name of the adoptive parents."

She shook her head.

"How old was he when he left and what did he look like?"

"By then he was about seven or eight. He was the most beautiful child I'd ever seen. He had blonde hair, unusual since both his parents had dark brown. His eyes were pale blue and they could look right through you. He was ashamed that his eyes were the same color as his mother's." She shook her head. "I'm sure Roberto must have turned out to be a very handsome man."

"He turned out to be a monster," Lindsey said.

The landlady heard Patterson and Cross banging on Carol's door. She came upstairs to investigate.

"Can I help you?" Her impatience showed in her tone, but disappeared quickly when they flashed their badges.

"Oh, I was afraid you were some more of those nosey reporters."

"We're looking for Mrs. Randolph and her son, John."

"I don't know where John is. Carol told me she and her friend, Linda were going to the Poconos for a vacation. Her son Allen has a cabin up there. She asked me to keep her mail until she got back."

"Have you seen Allen recently?"

"Oh yeah. Allen was here a couple of hours ago. Boy was he mad when he found out she left town." She shook her head. "I never did care for that young man. He was really upset...like a little kid. Couldn't understand why his mother would leave at a time like this. Can you imagine that? A grown man! All she wanted to do was get away from all the tension. Tension he caused. The only thing he cared about was himself. He's no good. I hate to say it, but it's true." She leaned toward them and whispered, "He scared me. I thought he was in jail. Then, all of a sudden, there he was at my door. Why in the world did you people let him out?"

"Trust me, it wasn't our idea," Patterson said.

"Anyway, Allen's on his way up there. He told me he was gonna book the next flight to Pennsylvania."

Sharon and Patterson looked at each other.

Patterson spoke quickly. "I'll call the airlines and book us a flight and arrange to have a police helicopter ready to take us to our location."

They got in their car. They were quiet, deep in their

own thoughts. Sharon's frustration was settling in the pit of her stomach. The elusive phrase kept nagging her. What was it? She tried to clear her mind. Who said what and when did they say it? She believed two separate people described someone recently using the same terminology. It was haunting her. She had to bring it to the forefront. She took a deep breath and tried to relax. She'd heard one account on tape. She was sure of it. She wished she had time to go back to the office and collect all the taped interviews. But that was out of the question. The other time she'd heard it was in person. She glanced at Patterson and was about to talk to him about it when she looked at his lips. Elvis Presley popped into her mind. At first, this confused her. Then she remembered Patterson had mimicked Elvis when they looked at Allen's picture at Hoebel's Corporate Offices. "That's it! Great eyes, dangerous mouth."

Patterson glanced at her. "Huh?"

Her eyes squinted in thought, as she remembered. "One of the girls at the bar described the suspect in that way. And last night, Heather had said the same thing about someone. Was she referring to Allen?"

Patterson frowned. "Yeah, who else could she have been talking about?"

Sharon dialed the hospital. When Heather answered, she put her on speakerphone. "Well, obviously they removed the tube, or you wouldn't have been able to say hello. How are you feeling?"

"I'm miserable as hell. Most of the swelling went down over night, so they removed the tube an hour ago. My throat still hurts though," she whispered. "I just heard on the news that Allen was released. How is that possible?"

"The judge let him out on bail. Now they're looking for his brother. They think he might have been involved."

"His brother? I suspected him for awhile, too. But I don't buy it now. I've been thinking a lot while I've been lying here. I remember all the times Allen threatened me and pushed me around over this last month. He's been out of control. This was just the culmination of it all. He has a real hatred for women. He reminds me so much of the guy I knew from New York. The one that got me pregnant."

Sharon snapped her finger. "Oh yes, the one you described as having great eyes and a dangerous mouth."

"Yeah, that's the one."

"You said you knew him in New York? Tell me about him."

"I only knew him for a few months. He was in New York on business. Anyway, he and I used to play *the game*. One day he got carried away with it just like Allen did. After that, I decided I didn't want to have a baby with him, so that's when I terminated the pregnancy. When he found out about the abortion, he went totally nuts! He beat me up so bad I thought I'd die. I think he would have killed me if it hadn't been for his next door neighbor responding to my screams. I was almost in as bad a shape then as I am right now. I'm telling you, he and Allen are like evil twins."

Sharon and Patterson exchanged glances. "What was his name?"

"Robert. Robert Alberghetti. I was too afraid of him to go to the police. He mentioned once that he had links with the Mafia, so I figured the best thing I could do was take off. That's when I came down here. Now I wish I'd have had him arrested. Men like him and Allen need to suffer the consequences."

"Heather, did you ever mention his name to Allen or his brother?"

"No. Never."

"What did he look like?" Sharon's face flushed as she glanced at Patterson.

"Robert? Gorgeous...only way to describe him. Tall, dark, big brown eyes, built."

"Heather. I want you to think very hard. Could the man that attacked you last night have been Robert?"

"No way, not the same eyes. Not at all."

"Forget about the eyes, what about the rest of him?"

She was quiet for a moment. "Well, he and Allen are built similarly. Actually, except for coloring, they could be twins. But like I told you, it was Allen's eyes. Robert's are brown."

When she hung up, Sharon called Lindsey and they exchanged information.

When they finished, Lindsey said, "Looks like we have all the pieces. Now, it's just a matter of putting them together."

"I agree."

"So Robert is our killer and he was wearing brown colored contacts when he knew Heather a few years ago," Lindsey said.

"Exactly." She paused. "Could Allen actually be Robert? Could changing the color of his hair and eyes be enough to fool Heather?"

"Anything is possible. We have to find out if Allen or John were adopted."

"They both look so much alike. They have to be related."

Lindsey gave that some thought. "Maybe Leonard Alberghetti was the father of both boys, just different mothers. Carol and her husband could very well have adopted John first, and then when Allen became available, adopted him." Lindsey bit the corner of his lips. "We have to trace through the adoption process to find out. Use your resources to cut through the red tape."

"I'll get right on it."

"Have they caught up with John yet?"

"No one knows where he is. The landlady said he wasn't with Carol and her friend when they left."

"But you're sure Allen's headed up to the mountains?" Lindsey asked.

"Yes, but..."

"I'm on my way to Leonard Alberghetti's house. The maid said it's been abandoned for years. I'm hoping something will turn up there. Then I'm headed for the mountains."

"No! Lindsey, it's not a good idea."

Lindsey hung up.

Patterson did the shrug like his life depended on it. "If it turns out that neither one of the Randolph brothers were adopted, how could John have come up with Robert Alberghetti's name?"

"Lindsey told John to ask God to give him the name of the killer." Sharon picked up the telephone to dial Quantico. "And John said he would pray for the name and promised to tell us as soon as he got the answer."

Patterson chuckled.

Sharon's expression was introspective.

Wrapped in a layer of fog, overgrown trees and tangled bushes, the ramshackle house stood like a ghostly apparition. Lindsey removed a flashlight from the glove compartment of the car and made his way through the underbrush, which was once a walkway, to the front door. The windows were broken and the door tenuously clung to bent hinges.

Lindsey stepped in quietly, his gun drawn. His flashlight prodded the first room. Vandals had obviously had a heyday in this place. Furniture lay torn and flipped, graffiti marred the walls. He could imagine the mystical lure the house must have had on the curious minded. Especially teen-agers or young college students earning their initiation rites. Each room he entered displayed more damage, but no signs of recent visitors. Ceiling to floor cobwebs were left undisturbed, and the dusty floor was free of footprints.

On the second floor, he checked each room thoroughly, then noticed a door at the end of the hall. He went through it, climbed the stairs, and entered a large attic. A board squeaked and his heart rate accelerated. Something scrambled near his feet and he looked down just in time to see a long skinny tail slip between two old footlockers. Scattered throughout the attic were file cabinets and boxes of all sizes. He knew there had to be a wealth of information stored in this area, but realized it would take days to sort through it all. There was no sign of human life...or death, so he walked back down the stairs and out to his car.

As he reached for the door handle, he heard a muffled sound. He froze and listened. He heard it again. It sounded like a cry. Almost like a kitten. He turned and walked in the direction he thought it was coming from. Again, the cry sounded. It was coming from the back yard. He skirted the side of the house. When he reached the back, his flashlight illuminated a stretch of sun-bleached tape with faded printed letters. It was attached to a stake in the ground, half-torn, and blowing in the breeze. He realized immediately that it was crime scene tape. Several sheets of plywood lay on the ground and as he got closer, he could see they partially covered a large hole. This had to be the spot where Nina Alberghetti's body had been buried.

Lindsey's hands shook as he inched forward, his gun pointing toward the abandoned grave. He heard it again. A frantic whimper.

He whispered aloud, "God let it be, let it be." His eyes grew bright with tears and his bottom lip trembled. When the cry resounded, he ran toward it. He stuck the gun in his holster, then pulled the plywood back and flashed his light to the bottom of the pit. Jennifer lay on her back, her mouth gagged, her face and clothes thick with mud, her limbs tightly bound.

John stared at the fire he'd started. Carol made the beds, while Linda busied herself in the kitchen. A cold front had passed through. But with the help of the small heater and fireplace, the cabin was cozy. Carol sat down when she was finished and rubbed the back of her neck. "You've been so quiet, John. Are you okay?"

He didn't answer.

"Don't worry about Allen. He'll be all right." She tried to sound cheerful. "Let's talk about what we're going to do tomorrow."

John turned to look at her.

"Let's walk down to the meadow in the morning. We can bring the binoculars and check out the wildlife. If we leave early enough, we might see deer."

"I guess that will be okay, but after we're finished, I really think we need to head back home."

"Please, John, not yet."

Linda walked in from the kitchen, carrying three cups of hot chocolate. "This ought to do the trick."

"It smells great." Carol took a cup and sipped carefully.

John did the same.

"I heard you talking about looking for wildlife in the morning. Can I come, too?" Linda asked.

"Absolutely," Carol said. "I was also thinking about hiking the mountain trail later in the day."

"Sounds like fun." Linda stared at Carol over her steaming mug. "I think you were right about getting away. You're looking and sounding better already."

"Well, I got some rest on the plane, and there's just something about being in the mountains that relaxes me. I'm glad we came. Maybe we should turn in early tonight, since we plan on getting up early."

John stood up. "Mind if I take my shower first?"

"No, go ahead," Carol said.

John carried his cup into the bathroom.

While John showered, they sipped their hot chocolate and watched the fire as it snapped and lapped three large logs on the hearth. Carol was grateful for a place of refuge. She felt like nothing could upset her here. They were isolated from the rest of the world. This was just what she needed.

Her cell phone rang and she shook her head. "These reporters just won't give up."

"What if it's something important? Why don't you pick it up and not say anything. Wait to see if someone talks and if you recognize the voice."

"All right. I guess it won't hurt." She pressed the button and listened.

"Mom? Is that you?"

Carol covered the mouthpiece with her hand. "It's Allen. What should I do?"

Linda shrugged. "I don't know. It's up to you."

"Yes, Allen, what is it?" She rubbed the bridge of her nose.

"I've been trying to reach you all day! Why weren't you answering the phone?"

"Reporters."

"Oh." His voice sounded strange.

"Are you calling from the prison?"

"No. They let me out. They found out who really killed all those people."

"Oh, what a relief." Carol closed her eyes.

"Did you just get to the cabin?" The line crackled.

"No, we've been here for a couple of hours. How did you know we were coming here?"

"Talked to your landlady," Allen said. "Is anyone with you?"

"Yes, John and Linda." There was more interference.

"John's with you?" He hesitated. "I know this is going to come as a shock, but I've got to tell you. John was at my lawyer's office earlier. The police believe John is the murderer. I'm afraid he might hurt you next."

"Oh, don't be ridiculous." Carol turned to Linda and shook her head.

"Mom, it's true. Where is he now?"

Carol glanced toward the bathroom. "He's in the shower," she whispered. "Look, I don't believe this for one minute. John wouldn't hurt anyone. You must be making this up."

His anger nearly reached through the phone. He contained it. "Look, I'm telling you the truth." He paused for more control. "My lawyer has his statement on tape. John knows things about the murders that no one but the killer himself could know. You've got to get away from him. Listen, I rented a car from the airport and I'm only about three miles away. While he's in the shower, just hop in your car and head north on 402. I'll have my headlights flashing. That's how you'll know it's me. You just stop and we'll go to town and get help."

"Allen, this is silly. I'm not going anywhere. Just come to the cabin and we'll talk this whole thing out."

"No. Who knows how John would react if I confronted him with this. He might kill all of us. You can't waste another minute. You've got to do what I'm telling you."

"Allen, you know your brother. You know he's not capable of..."

"Mom! I never thought he'd do anything like this either, but it's true. John's sick. You've got to face it. With a disease like his, anything is possible. Look, I've never asked this of you before, but I'm going to now. Please trust me. Please believe me. Get out of there!"

When Carol heard the sincerity in his voice, a chill surged through her.

"Mom? Are you still there?" Allen shouted. Then there was more interference and the line went dead. Carol stared at the receiver for a few seconds, then set it down.

"What's wrong? What did he say?" Linda's voice was high-pitched.

"Allen was released from jail. He says John talked to his lawyer today. The police believe John is the murderer," she kept her voice low.

"Oh my God!" Linda's eyes darted to the bathroom door.

Carol retrieved their coats from the closet. "I think we better get out of here just to be on the safe side. Look, you start the car while I write John a note."

Linda threw on her coat. "Okay, but hurry up!" She snatched up the keys from the table, then flew out the door.

Carol removed a piece of paper from the desk and stared at it. What could she say? What explanation could she give for leaving him? Decided to go shopping? Be back soon? She bit her lower lip, then scribbled a few lines on the paper. The water continued running in the bathroom. She reluctantly folded the note, wrote his name on the top, then left it on the desk. She began to step away, then turned back, and looked down at it for a moment, torn between loyalty and fear. How could she doubt him? How could she believe he'd do such a thing? If he were innocent, would he ever forgive her for doubting him?

She slowly slipped her arms into her coat and pondered her options. Maybe she should just call the police and wait for them to arrive. He was too smart to believe her note. Knowing she doubted him would be devastating. As if she had all the time in the world, she sorted through her emotions. The clock didn't wait for her. Several precious minutes were wasted. Outside, a rustling sound shook her from inaction. She glanced in the direction of the bathroom again. "I'm sorry," she said, softly.

She tiptoed across the room, closed the door quietly, and ran toward the car. She stopped, halfway there. The engine was not running. The door to the car was slightly ajar, but the dome light was not lit, and she couldn't see Linda behind the wheel. Her heart hammered. She strained her eyes in the dark and glanced around at her surroundings. "Linda? Where are you?"

Linda didn't answer. Carol looked back at the cabin and noticed the light in the bathroom. The shower was located at the window and she saw no signs of movement through the frosted glass.

She turned back to the car and took a few steps forward, then stopped. "Linda?" Her voice cracked with tension. "Please say something." Tears welled in her eyes as an ominous feeling began swallowing her whole. The full moon, the night, the silence, and the cold screamed danger. Her heart beckoned her to return to the cabin, but her mind told her to flee.

Carol took small steps. "There's got to be a rational explanation," she said, as if logic could erase all frightening possibilities. She peered, wide-eyed, straining to see inside the car. Suddenly, a twig snapped and she spun around. "Linda?" She saw and heard no one. Desire to escape finally overrode her fear of the unknown. She bolted for the car and swung open the door. Linda tumbled halfway out, her upper torso hung toward the ground. Blood from her mouth and eyes dripped on Carol's white tennis shoes. Carol screamed and jumped back. "Oh God! Oh God!" Her eyes stayed morbidly glued on Linda's face. She shook her head frantically to break the hold.

"No...no!" She stepped backwards again. There was another noise. This time, without turning around, she ran toward the mountain trail.

CHAPTER 17

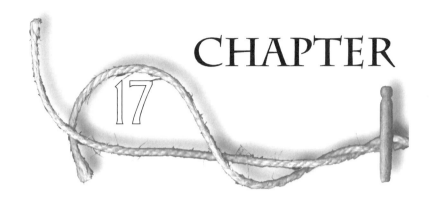

Frigid air turned John's breath into puffs of fog as he called out for his mother. She ignored him and he called again, but she continued to run. He stormed back into the cabin to get his coat and knit hat. He knew he would have no trouble catching up to her. He felt a familiar feeling. Energy, originating from the depths of his soul, surged upward and activated a section of his mind reserved for special occasions. Renewed and invigorated, strong and bold with a purpose, he was in total control now, his mind clear and focused on just one thing. His mother.

Carol glanced over her shoulder and saw a form fade in and out at the bottom of the trail. He was definitely in pursuit of her. Despite her weakened state, adrenaline enabled her to run like a person half her age.

Her thoughts ran just as quickly. Images singed her mind like brands on hide. Her dearest friend! She could still see her face. John killed her. How could he have done such a thing? Her wonderful son. The one she adored. When had he changed? How could she have been so blind? She asked herself that question repeatedly.

In case he was following her footprints, she ventured off the path. She hoped he'd think she'd abandoned the trail. As minutes flew by, the initial burst of energy dissipated, and she had to push harder. Finally, the clay ground gave way to jagged rocks and she slipped often, banged her knees, and lost precious seconds. Pain and exhaustion hit her straight on. She realized her determination was much stronger than her body.

She returned to the trail, but it grew steeper; she lost her footing more frequently, and her legs felt like they were about to buckle. A severe spasm ravaged her calf muscle. She stopped quickly and leaned against a tree trunk. She gulped air, then bent over and massaged the afflicted leg. Steam faintly formed a shimmering halo around her wet silhouette as a debilitating wave of weakness struck her like a train. Her legs collapsed and she landed hard on the ground.

She turned her head nervously toward the path. She knew it was only a matter of minutes before he'd be there. Struggling to get up on her knees, she dropped again. She rolled on her side and rubbed the knotted muscle in her leg, but the spasm didn't let up. Her teeth chattered and her gasps for breath were so loud, she feared he would hear her long before he'd see her. Efforts to be quiet were in vain. It seemed impossible.

If she could control nothing else, at least she could master her thoughts. She closed her eyes and concentrated. She had to think of a place to hide. Where could she go? She could barely move. What could she do? She glanced around again, then had an idea. She rolled under a nearby canopy of low hanging branches and tried to convince herself that it would be a sufficient hiding spot. Then she looked up at the full moon and reality hit home. Blonde hair and a light colored jacket would stand out like a cardinal in the snow.

As hopelessness ate away at determination, dampness from the deep bed of wet leaves beneath her sparked a childhood memory. Each fall, her father raked leaves into piles in their back yard. When he wasn't looking, she'd burrow inside one of them and he'd search for her. That was the solution. She raked the leaves toward her, scooped, then mounded them over her body. The process was noisy but not as bad as it could have been. At least the leaves were damp, from a recent rain and not dry, and crispy, like after a dry spell. She continued until she was completely covered. Her breathing slowed slightly. However, her teeth still chattered and body shivered. The wet leaves were not helping matters. However, she had no other choice but to stay put, wait, and try to be quiet.

Only minutes passed when footsteps pounded on the rocky path. A few seconds later, his labored breathing joined her on the mountainside. For the first time in many years, she prayed.

Carol could almost feel his frustration. She wondered if he would see marks on the ground where she'd gathered the leaves. Her heart beat rapidly. She could not resist the urge to peek out and see what he was doing. She carefully poked her finger between a layer of leaves, and then slowly positioned her eye to see out of the hole she had just made. At first, he was not in view, but then he moved to the right and stepped into her line of vision. His back was facing her. With his hands locked on his hips, he surveyed. Her teeth chattered out of control. She stuck her finger between them to stop the noise. She knew any sound at this point would give her away. She had never known fear like this before. She wondered if he would kill her as he had the others.

Linda's face flashed before Carol's eyes. She shuddered and the leaves rustled. He quickly turned in her direction. A breeze blew tall pines above them and a sliver of moonlight flashed across his face. She strained her eyes to make sure what she was seeing was real. When she was certain, she threw off the leaves, and struggled up to a sitting position and cried out, "Allen! Thank God, it's you! I thought you were John."

Allen stared darkly. "Why didn't you get in your car, like I told you? It was stupid to come up here."

"I didn't have any other choice! When I got out to the car, Linda was in the driver's seat. She's dead. Murdered! Oh God, Allen, it was horrible." Carol's eyes looked haunted. "John must have killed her." She held the palm of her hand against her cheek. "I'm so glad you're here. I'm so scared, I don't know what I'm doing." She reached out her hand. "Here, help me up so we can get going."

He yanked her hand. She stood on one foot and

leaned on him for support.

"How did you know I came up here?" She asked, still breathing hard.

"I saw you when I got out of my car. Didn't you hear me calling for you?"

She shook her head, then lowered her foot to the ground. She winced slightly. "No. I wish I had. I felt so alone. I'm so glad you found me and that we're together now."

"Oh really? You didn't care about being together earlier today when I was in jail."

"I couldn't help it." She brushed the leaves off her clothes. "My nerves were shot, the reporters wouldn't leave me alone. It was terrible. I just wanted to get away from everyone."

"Everyone except John, of course, and that friend of yours."

"Linda insisted on coming along. And you know I couldn't leave John behind. You know he needs me." The knotted muscle in her leg finally relaxed.

"What about me? Did it ever occur to you that I might need you?"

"Why are we talking about this now?" Carol's frowned. "We're wasting time. We've got to get out of here."

"No, I've got to get this off my chest, once and for all." He held onto her arm. "Your whole life revolved around John and I meant nothing to you."

"That's not true." Carol's eyes looked frantic. "It might have seemed that way, but you have to understand..."

"Oh I understand. John is all that ever mattered to you. I was the bad son. The stupid one. I wasn't special. I didn't need your attention."

"Allen, let's talk about this later." She was wringing her hands. "John's going to be here any minute."

Allen snarled, "You just don't get it, do you."

"Look, that's enough. I've been through the worst ordeal of my life. I just found out my son is a murderer and my best friend has been killed. I've been to hell and back."

"Yeah? Well, so have I."

"Stop it! Just stop it, Allen!"

Allen squeezed both of her arms. "No mother, I'm not finished with you yet."

Carol looked at his face and no longer recognized it. Wildness invaded his eyes. He looked crazed. He sounded concerned for her welfare earlier on the phone. Why was he treating her with such obvious contempt now? Had he been lying about John? Had she come out of her safe hiding place into the hands of the real killer? She pulled away and stumbled as she tried to run from him.

Exploding from the thicket to their right, a dark mass grabbed Carol from behind and pressed a knife firmly against her throat.

Allen saw pale eyes through a dark ski mask and raised both palms toward him. "Listen, John. We need to talk this over."

"I heard what you said to her. You were right. She shouldn't have left you by yourself when you needed her most. I tried to tell her, but she wouldn't listen." His voice was unusually raspy.

"Hey, John, I was just pissed off. Mom made a few mistakes, but we've all made mistakes. Especially me. You know how much she loves you." He took a step toward them.

"That's not true. She was just putting on an act." He increased the pressure of the knife and tiny droplets of blood appeared just below the blade. "Don't try to get any closer, Allen. If you do, I'll kill her."

"You don't mean that. You love her."

"That's because I didn't really know her. I thought she was a wonderful mother. And, I thought if you were ruined, she'd be devastated. That's why I eliminated your problems one by one. Of course now I realize she didn't even care about you. I shouldn't have bothered."

"Look, if you want to kill someone, kill me...not Mom. She's innocent."

"Oh yeah, right! She's just as bad as the rest of them. Plus, she made me go off track. When I was just killing whores, no one had a clue it was me. Helping her made me a suspect. Now they're on to me. It's all her fault.

And now she's going to have to pay." He pulled her to the edge of the wooded trail. "Stay right there!"

"No!" Allen ran toward him. "Let her go."

"One more step and she's going to start spurting blood all over you. I don't think you have the stomach for that."

Allen froze.

Carol screamed. "Oh God! Help me!"

The sound of a deep rumble caught their attention. It increased and filled the air with the rhythmic thumping of a helicopter that finally emerged and roared over their heads. A beam of light scanned the ground. When the light fell upon them, the helicopter leaned sideways and descended somewhere close in the ridge below.

The killer pulled her backward down the slope. Allen didn't move until they were out of sight. Slowly inching their way down the hill, the dark figure pulled her off the path. They thrashed through deep underbrush and overhanging tree limbs. Despite scratches and lacerations, they continued downward. Carol was far too weak to struggle. She was limp in his arms as he dragged her along. She resigned herself to imminent death.

Not looking where he was going, the madman continued tugging her backwards until his foot slipped into air. Before he could catch his balance, they plummeted off the rocky side of the mountain. Their screams seemed to echo forever. Tree branches bruised and battered them but also helped break their fall as they ricocheted off into different directions. His knife fell out of his hand moments before they hit the ground, and bounced somewhere out of sight. They lay beaten and stunned, separated from each other in the darkness.

Allen heard the screams but was unable to ascertain their point of origin. He continued to run in the same direction he'd been traveling, hoping he would find their tracks.

Just as Allen came to a bend in the path, John suddenly blocked his way. "John!" Allen's eyes went from shock to curiosity. John wasn't wearing the same clothes he'd had on minutes ago. "How did you change your clothes so fast?"

John frowned, then looked down at himself. "What are you talking about? And where's Mom?"

"I was just going to ask you the same question. What have you done with her? If you killed her, I'll..."

"Killed her? I came up here to help Mom, not kill her. How could you even think such a thing?"

"But my lawyer said he talked to you and that you were involved in those murders."

"I saw the killer and the girl he murdered. I didn't kill anyone."

Allen took a deep breath in an effort to clear his mind. "Are you sure? I mean...God, John, I'm so sorry. I should have known better. This is all my fault." He started down the path, and yelled over his shoulders, "A man in a ski mask just took off with Mom. We've got to find them." Allen pointed ahead. "This way. Come on."

John caught up with him and grabbed his arm. "Be quiet. Listen."

"I don't hear anything," Allen whispered. "Come on. We can't waste time. He might be getting ready to kill her right now."

"No," John said firmly. "They separated somehow. She's safe for the moment. We still have time, but we've got to go this way." He pointed in a different direction.

"How do you know?"

"Never mind. You wouldn't believe me if I told you." He pulled Allen off to the left. After dodging their way through several hundred feet of thick forest, John stopped again. "Come here Allen." John pointed to a rocky ledge before them.

Allen still wrestled with a residual sense of distrust where John was concerned. Half-afraid his brother might throw him off the ledge, he approached cautiously. "What am I suppose to be looking at?"

"Look! They fell off. Right here." He nodded toward footprints and the broken tree branches. John ran parallel to the edge of the mountain, with Allen at his heels. When the cliff became less steep, they zigzagged their way down. The ever-increasing rumble of the helicopter caught their attention as they ran. It was low in the sky again and hovered right above them. The treetops surrounding them swirled in the turbulence.

John spied a log and attempted to jump it. In midair, his ankle hooked onto a jagged branch. He lost his balance, and fell sideways, twisting his entire leg.

"What's wrong?" Allen shouted, above the roar of the chopper.

"I think I broke my leg. You'll have to do this on your own, Allen. It's all up to you, now." He gestured ahead. "Keep going that way. That's where they are."

Allen hesitated for only a second, then set off to rescue his mother.

The rumble of the chopper added to the killer's frustration. Not only couldn't he see his victim, he was unable to hear her as well. The area in which they landed was thick with pine trees, which diminished the light from the moon. He stayed low and used his arms to pull himself across the ground in the direction in which he thought she'd fallen. Briar patches and ancient glacial rock were in his path, and the threat of the helicopter was ever present. However, his obsession surpassed his pain and fear of capture. He slithered forward. He needed to kill. Pure and simple. Nothing else mattered.

Carol was unconscious after the fall, but now awakened gradually. Her eyes opened and she idly watched the moon shine between the treetops. The breeze blowing through sprays of pine needles sounded like rain. Lulled by the restful drone, she closed her eyes again and nearly fell asleep.

Finally the pain in her body registered and she remembered why she was lying in the middle of nowhere. She carefully got up to her knees and crawled. She had no idea where John was. If she stayed in one place too long, he'd eventually find her. A beam of light flickered and lit the web of underbrush several feet in front of her. When the light disappeared, her eyes struggled to readjust to the dark. Her breath came in ragged gasps. She couldn't hear anything but the roar above. She didn't know which way to go...which way was safe. She just knew she had to keep moving. Her knees could not withstand the rocky surface, so she struggled to her feet. Tree limbs helped support her as she felt her way through nature's obstacle course.

Whenever the chopper came near, she waved her arms above her head, hoping she'd be spotted. However, the beam of light seemed to flash everywhere but on her. She entered a small clearing and increased her pace. Just as she thought she was making progress, something clamped around her ankle and pulled her legs out from under her.

She landed on her back and screamed, "Oh Jesus! Help me!"

"Shut up." The killer covered her mouth with his hand. "He doesn't want anything to do with you. You ran away from Him, just like you ran away from your kids. Remember?" With his other hand, he reached into his pocket, pulled out a rag, and quickly stuffed it into her mouth. Carol's fingers reached toward her face in an effort to remove it. He grabbed her hand and squeezed it hard. She froze.

Lights flickered and filtered through the area near where they lay. She realized immediately that they were coming from flashlights this time and not the helicopter. A search party was out there on the ground now...somewhere near by. She prayed that they would find her in time.

Patterson and Cross held their guns in one hand and flashlights in the other. They picked their way through the rocks and tangled tree roots around their feet. The helicopter circled about one hundred feet from their location. They listened to the pilot on his earphones.

"Reinforcements are on their way. I spotted two people east of you. There's a blonde female and a man dressed in black. He's very hard to see. The injured Randolph brother is still down on the ground and the other one is closing in on the blonde and the man. He's going to get to them before you."

The killer placed his mouth near Carol's ear. "You lucked out. The police are too close. I'm going to have to kill you quickly." Just as he reached for the rope in his pocket, he heard a crunching sound. Before he could even look up, Allen slammed into him. The force behind Allen's weight caused them both to roll away from Carol. She scrambled off to the side as Allen punched the assailant repeatedly on the face.

Carol pulled the rag from her mouth and screamed. The two men struggled; their evenly matched bodies made it difficult for one to overpower the other. The killer saw the lights coming closer. He spotted a rock, which lay within his reach. He stretched his arm, snatched it up, and smashed it against Allen's head. Allen went limp and the killer jumped to his feet and ran off in the dark.

"Allen!" Carol shrieked. "Are you all right?" She crawled over to where he lay and cradled his head. "You saved my life! Do you hear me? You saved me. You have to be okay. Oh God, please let him be all right." She leaned down and kissed his forehead. "Allen, I love you. Please don't die."

Allen moaned, then reached up, and gently touched the side of his mother's face. As blood streamed from his temple, Carol clasped his hand and held it against her cheek.

Patterson and Cross rushed out of the thicket and dropped down next to Carol. "Oh thank God it's you." She gasped. "Allen needs help. Please! He needs to be taken to a hospital."

"They'll take him." Patterson pointed to the chopper overhead. He bent over Allen to check the wound, then removed a handkerchief from his pocket, and held it against Allen's head. A long rope ladder dropped down from the helicopter and two paramedics rapidly descended. "Hold this on the wound, Mrs. Randolph. We have to go after the killer. Did you see which way he went?"

"Will you promise not to hurt John?" Her eyes pleaded.

"Mrs. Randolph, John isn't the killer," Sharon said. "John's over there in the woods." She pointed left. "He broke his leg while he and Allen were trying to find you."

"It wasn't John?" Carol trembled. "Oh thank God," she sobbed. "But if it wasn't John, who was it?"

With Lindsey behind the wheel, the rental car flew south on State Road 402. He'd been in contact with Sharon and received the results of the adoption search. He'd also been listening to his police radio and knew the chopper was flushing the killer out of the woods. He also knew the direction he was running. If the killer stayed true to course, he'd end up on this road and Lindsey wanted to be there when he did. Lindsey's loaded Glock sat next to him on the seat. His other revolver, warm from his body heat, set in his shoulder holster, also ready for action. He slowed when he saw the chopper hover inside the woods, about one mile directly to his left.

His headlights reflected on something further down the road. He first thought it might have been a road marker or the eyes of an animal. As he traveled closer, he realized it was a taillight of a car, parked off the road and semi-concealed under the trees. Lindsey came to a stop, got on his radio, and called the local dispatcher for a license check. In a few minutes he found out it was a rental car.

"Bingo." He said, aloud. "I've got you now, you sorry bastard." Lindsey drove past the car. Fifty feet down the road, he pulled off onto a narrow hunting path and parked. He ran back to the killer's rental, crouched down behind it, and waited.

His thoughts returned to Jennifer. When he left her at the hospital, she'd been sedated and was receiving treatment for shock and hypothermia. Her doctor assured him she'd be okay and that she'd probably sleep until morning, so he wasted no time. He called Sara, who immediately arranged to fly to New York. Then he took off to finish his job.

Lindsey thought about how the case would go if it went to trial. He was certain the killer would be found guilty, but he wasn't sure he'd be given the death sentence. As far as he was concerned, time in jail or a mental institution was not acceptable. This man had to die.

However, death in the electric chair was not sufficient either. Lindsey talked to people who had attended the execution of Pedro Medina several years back. "Old Sparky's accessories malfunctioned and caused twelve-inch long flames to shoot out from Medina's face and head for up to ten seconds. The smoke filled the execution room and the smell of burning flesh was evident even in the witness room. Many people thought he suffered before he died.

That execution was probably the worst case scenario but, in Lindsey's opinion, still inadequate retribution. Lindsey shook his head. Death by electrocution was way too easy and impersonal. Plus, it looked like lethal injection was on its way to Florida. Rumor was, inmates would have a choice between it and the chair. The muscles in Lindsey's jaw knotted. There was no way he'd let him simply be put to sleep.

Across the street, the woods suddenly came alive with sound. Frost-bitten underbrush crunched and dry branches snapped under the weight and force of the enemy's arrival. The killer was coming. Lindsey was ready.

Gun in hand, Lindsey kept his head low as the killer leaped out of the woods. Moonlight bathed the monster like a spotlight. Frightful as a nightmare, he bolted toward the car. Lindsey sprang out before he could reach it and stopped him short. He held him captive with the threat of his gun.

"Down! Lay down, damn it!" Lindsey bellowed.

The killer dropped to his knees. Breathing heavily, he still wore the black ski mask. Lindsey rushed him and shouted close to his ear. "Take that thing off your head. Take it off now!"

The psychopath didn't move. "No, just get it over with," he gasped. "Shoot me. You know that's what you're going to do anyway. So, why wait? Do it."

"Not until I see the fear on your face. You're not going to deprive me of that." Lindsey glanced up at the chopper stationary inside the woods about six hundred feet. "Hurry up! Take it off!"

He shrugged, and removed the ski mask. He smiled, dimples and all. "There, is that better?"

Lindsey was stunned. Anthony's eyes looked like blue glass and they drastically contradicted his smile. The contrast between his dark hair and skin made his eyes even more eerie. His daughter had seen these eyes and been at their mercy.

Lindsey moved in closer and jammed the gun against his head. "You better wipe that smile off your face, or I'll torture you first...put you through the same thing you put your victims through."

"Torture doesn't phase me. I've been through worse than you're capable of inflicting."

"Don't bet on it. I can be real creative."

Anthony's eyes zeroed in on his. "Before you do anything rash, don't you want to know where your little girl is hiding?"

Lindsey whipped the butt of his gun across Anthony's ear. "I'm one up on you. I found her without your help."

Anthony held his ear, but refused to show his pain. He kept his eyes locked on Lindsey. "Then kill me, Detective Lindsey. Do it now. I know how you feel. Hatred is eating you up. You have to release it. You can't hold it back. I know exactly what you're going through. We're very much alike.

Lindsey crashed his knee into Anthony's nose, and flipped him backward. "Don't you ever say that again. There ain't no way we're alike. You killed innocent people. They never did anything to hurt you. You used them to try to get back at your mother."

"Don't mention her." He gasped and rolled to his side. "I don't want to think about her."

"Oh! So I found something that bothers you." Lindsey smirked. "Then I've just got to tell you the rest of the story." Lindsey's forehead beaded with sweat. "You did all this for nothing. You think your mother abandoned you, but she didn't. She came back to get you the same night she left, but your old man caught her and killed her." Lindsey kicked him in his ribs and he heard them crack. "And you know what else? Your mother wasn't a whore, either. Your father lied about that, too."

Anthony rolled onto his back, his knees drawn up to his abdomen, his face smeared with blood and contorted with pain. "Stop it. You don't know what you're talking about." His voice broke as he spoke.

"Remember Mrs. Williams, the maid? She was there. She told me everything. She said your mother loved you. Your father twisted your mind into thinking she was the enemy."

Anthony shook his head. His face became a kaleidoscope of emotion.

"She told me all about it. All this time you should have been going around killing men who beat up on innocent women and children. At least there would have been some respect in that." Lindsey brought his free hand up to help steady the gun in his other hand. He tightened his finger on the trigger and was almost past the decisive point when a forlorn expression seemed to overtake Anthony's eyes.

Lindsey frowned, puzzled. "Come on! Stop it! Get up and face me like a man."

Anthony's face puckered like a child whose feelings had been hurt.

Lindsey licked his dry lips. "The past doesn't matter now, anyway. So get up. Come on, get up on your feet."

Anthony let out a mournful cry, than wailed hysterically.

Lindsey's eyes darted from Anthony to the chopper, now almost over head, and back again. "Come on man, get hold of yourself." His voice was less forceful and his hands shook nearly out of control. "Come on! Snap out of it."

Anthony covered his ears with his hands and didn't move.

Lindsey shook his head slowly. This wasn't turning out the way he planned. He wished he hadn't told Anthony the truth about his mother. He couldn't even figure out why he did it in the first place. What purpose did it serve? None! It just made Anthony seem pathetic.

Lindsey didn't want to think about what he'd learned from Mrs. Williams. He wanted to block it out of his mind, but the more he tried, the more he remembered. He thought about children, and how vulnerable they are; helpless against abuse, so easily damaged and totally at the mercy of their guardians.

Lindsey thought about John. He wondered how he came up with Roberto Alberghetti's name? Was it a miracle? Was there a God? Had God answered John's prayers? Lindsey shook his head. What other explanation could there be? One thing he knew for sure. If John hadn't given Carol that message, he'd have killed the wrong man. And his daughter would have died.

He looked at the blood on Anthony's face. He realized that he'd just subjected him to one more beating. A beating, similar to those Anthony repeatedly experienced as a child.

Lindsey was nauseous. He felt like he'd just kicked the leg of a crippled man. What had he become? A monster blinded by hatred, unwilling to accept the law of cause and effect as it pertains to the psyche of human beings. Anthony was right. They were alike.

Lindsey pictured the little boy and his mother sitting in the shade, playing with the only toys the child ever knew. Those wooden soldiers eventually became instruments of death, as did a once innocent child. The killer was a victim, too.

Sweat poured from Lindsey's face as he looked down at the hopeless creature on the ground. Lindsey's mouth trembled. He squeezed his eyes shut for a second, then lowered the gun, and sighed. He backed up to the car, leaned against it, and waited for the chopper to land.

The helicopter's beam of light slid across Anthony and Lindsey then set down on the road one hundred feet away. Sharon and Patterson jumped out and ran toward them. In the dark, it was difficult to tell if Anthony was dead or alive. As Sharon approached, she saw the blood on Anthony's face. Patterson quickly bent down and placed his fingers against the side of Anthony's neck to check for a pulse.

When Sharon got close enough, she looked at Lindsey. His mouth was relaxed and for the first time since she met him, his eyes looked peaceful. Patterson mumbled something about Anthony's status, but Sharon didn't bother to listen. She knew now that Anthony was alive. She threw her arms around Lindsey and after a few seconds, he drew her closer and nestled his cheek on the top of her head.